SKIN MEDICINE

By
Tim Curran

Copyright © 2004 by Tim Curran
Copyright © 2009 by Severed Press
www.severedpress.com
Cover art Copyright © 2009 by Jesse Cutler
dypsomaniart.deviantart.com
All rights reserved. No part of this book may be reproduced or transmitted in any form or by any electronic or mechanical means, including photocopying, recording or by any information and retrieval system, without the written permission of the publisher and author, except where permitted by law.
This novel is a work of fiction. Names, characters, places and incidents are the product of the author's imagination, or are used fictitiously. Any resemblance to actual events, locales or persons,
living or dead, is purely coincidental.

Second Edition
First Published 2004 by Hellbound Books

ISBN: 978-0-9806065-1-5
All rights reserved.

PART ONE: THE OBLONG BOX

1

Utah Territory, 1882

The moon came up.

It slid from a satiny, wind-blown grave.

It came up over the mountains like some huge, luminous eye staring down from the misty sky above. Its pallid light sought and touched serrated horns of exposed rock, winked off drifts of snow, and imbued spruce and pine with a ghostly ambience. The wind blew and the trees bent, shadows dripping from them in writhing loops, finding craggy ground and slithering across the landscape like greasy black worms, filling hollows and glens and dark, secret places with night.

And high above, that bloated moon kept watch.

Not daring to blink.

If this was an omen, then it was a bad one.

2

The wagon came pounding down the hard-packed, frozen road that cut through the silver mining camps of the San Francisco Mountains. Like a jagged knife blade, it slit open the underbelly of night, probing, slicing. It bounced over deep-cut ruts laid down by ore wagons and was drawn by a team of black geldings blowing steam from their nostrils. Their iron-shod hoofs rang out like gunshots. A whip cracked and the team vaulted forward and the wagon thumped and bumped and careened.

"Christ almighty," Tom Hyden said, clutching the plank seat for dear life. "You're gonna get us killed, old man. You're gonna pitch us straight down into one of them ravines. See if you don't."

Jack Goode grinned, a cigar stub protruding from his weathered lips. "Man pays me to do a job, sonny, and that job I do," he said, cracking the whip again, his long white beard blowing up over his face like a loose neckerchief. "I do what he asks and I do it quick as I can on account I got better ways to spend my time."

Hyden felt the wagon thrashing beneath him, wood groaning and iron creaking. His ass bones were getting jarred right up into his throat. He clung to the seat with one hand and his shotgun with the other. The box in the back rattled in its berth like dice in a cup.

"Dammit," he cried, "all we got in the back is a body. A dead one at that. It don't care if we're early or late."

Goode just laughed.

The road dipped, climbed, then cut through a shadowy cedar brake and leveled out as it meandered across a rocky plain. The moon washed everything down with ethereal, uneven light.

"There," Goode said. "Whisper Lake ain't but a cunt-hair down through that gorge. We can slow up some. Here, kid. Take these ribbons." He passed the reins to Hyden and struck a stick match off his boot, cupping it in his hands, firing up his cigar again. He blew smoke and coughed. "We're making good time. Luck holds, I'll be in town just in time for a swallow and a tickle."

Hyden could see sweat glistening on the horses' flanks like dew. And maybe some of it was blood. Way the old bastard was working that bullwhip, he'd probably laid their flanks clear open. Hyden sighed, kept his eye on the countryside, kept imagining he saw dark shapes flitting about—shapes like little men. But he was tired, his eyes caked with sleep. If he didn't put his head down and pretty goddamn soon, he was going to fall right out of the wagon. Squinting his eyes, he thought he saw something running across the twisting road ahead...something that ran upright.

"You see that?" he said to Goode.

Smoke barreled from Goode's nostrils like fumes from a foundry stack. "Nope. Didn't see a thing," he said. "And I didn't, because I ain't looking. If there something out there, mayhap I don't wanna see it."

"It looked like…" Hyden sighed. "Nothing, I guess."

"Sure, it was nothing. These goddamn mountains are full of nothing. That's why I rode us so hard back there—if there was something back there, I didn't want to see it. Particularly if it looked like little men that weren't men."

"You seen 'em, then?"

"Nope. Ain't seen nothing I wasn't supposed to see." Goode stretched, his back popping. "Listen to me, boy. Just keep yer eyes on Whisper Lake. We'll be there in an hour or so. Just think of the women and the strong drink and the sins of the father."

Hyden just shook his head. Sometimes he just couldn't figure Goode out. Sumbitch had a way of talking about something while he was talking about something else entirely. Hyden watched and saw no more shapes. Imagination, that's what. Fatigue. He didn't believe in the tales of little men. It was some kind of Shoshone legend. Hyden's grandpappy Joe, when he wasn't pulling off a bottle of rye and reminiscing about all the gold strikes he'd been on, talked about 'em. Said they were real. Said he'd seen 'em in the mountains. Said he knew a trapper up in the Needle Range had shot one and stuffed it, sold the mummy to some sideshow fellow from Illinois for a case of Kentucky bourbon and a Sharps rifle.

But grandpappy Joe, he did go on.

Hyden had a packet of home-rolled cigarettes and lit one up. They'd been on the trail since the afternoon before. Were bringing a pine box and its occupant from the Goshute tribal lands of Skull Valley down to Whisper Lake in Beaver County. Fifty a piece some injun was paying 'em. Just to bring a body home.

Shit, but it was a living.

"Hey, boy, how old you now?" Goode asked.

"Twenty-three come spring."

"Twenty-three." Goode laughed. "When I was twenty-goddamn-three I had me a Sioux wife and three young-uns up in Dakota Territory. Had me a strike of the yellow stuff worth near hundred thousand."

"Then what the hell you doing hauling stiffs for a hundred bucks in this godforsaken land?"

"I spent it." Goode went silent, thought about it. "Twenty-three, twenty-three. You ever get yer lily pressed, boy? By a white woman, I'm saying. Why, I know this one down Flagstaff way—runs herself a crib of meat-eating felines with more curves than a loose rope. This one, though, Madame Lorraine, she dunks you in a hot bath, rubs you down with oil and Louisiana perfume, then sucks yer Uncle Henry so goddamn hard, yer eyes get pulled back into yer head—"

"Quiet," Hyden said. "I heard something."

"Just my bowels blowing off steam, son."

"No, damn you, not that."

Goode listened. Couldn't hear a thing but the wind skirting the trees and whipping through empty spaces. The sound of the horses hoofs. Not a damn thing else.

"Boy," he said, "you quit worrying about them little folk. Got yerself spooked. You might be better looking than a bluetick, but you ain't much smarter."

"It ain't that. It's something else." Hyden looked back in the hold, at that narrow pine box. Could see moonlight reflecting off the brass bands and square nail heads. "Something moved in there."

"Stop with that. Dead 'uns don't move, take my word for it."

Hyden just sat there, the countryside too dark and shadow-riven for his liking. He tried to think about Whisper Lake. A soft bed. Some hot food. But then he heard it again...a thumping sound. He was sure it came from inside that casket.

Goode would not look back there. He took the reins back and piloted them through the frosty night. A few snowflakes lit in the air like flies. With any luck, it wouldn't build into anything before they reached Whisper Lake.

"What's worrying you, son?" he finally said.

"What's in that box, I guess."

"It's just a dead body."

"I know it's a dead body," he said. "But I thought..."

"You better quit thinking, then," Goode said. "We're a long way from nowhere to be thinking such things. Dead 'uns are dead 'uns. They can't hurt you no more than a rocking chair can. Keep that in mind."

Hyden chewed his lip, clutched his shotgun tightly. "I guess I'm wondering what's in there, what's in that box. I don't like it."

"Dammit, boy, I don't like what's in yer head, but you don't hear me complaining."

They rode on and the moon slid behind a cloud and the night grew darker, went black to its roots, seemed to gather around them in clutching, sinister shadows.

"Boy, light that lantern."

Hyden reached over the seat...froze-up tight when he thought he heard a shifting sound from inside the box...then quickly grabbed the oil lamp and lit it up with a cupped match. The shadows retreated, but the night seemed bunched around them like a fist anxious to grasp something. It hung to either side of the wagon in sheets and blankets of murk. The hold was creeping with stygian forms.

Goode said, "Yer hearing things back there and that ain't so strange. Not really. This road is bad and that body is knocking around same as us. Don't pay it no attention, son."

But Hyden kept hearing those sounds and something was stirring his guts with a willow twig. "I just been thinking is all," he said, his breath frosting from his lips. "Been thinking on Skull Valley where we got the box from. Kind of creepy up there. Kind of lonesome and desolate...it puts your mind to things."

"What sort of things?"

"Skull Valley...that's Spirit Moon's grounds."

The old man licked his lips slowly, deliberately. "I hear tell Spirit Moon's dead."

"Some say he don't die same as others."

Goode laughed. "Bullshit. Besides, Spirit Moon is from the Snake Nation, boy. Skull Valley is Goshute land. What would Spirit Moon be doing there?"

"The Snake is just Shoshone, anyhow. Goshutes are tight with 'em. I heard his tribe is up there in the hills, doing what they do."

"Maybe, son, but what you heard about Spirit Moon...those is just witch-tales, is all. Injuns think he's some big bad medicine doctor, but a white man should know better. Just some Snake witch doctor. A damn injun and he don't scare me none."

But Hyden didn't believe that. Goode even pronounced Spirit Moon's name kind of low in a whisper...like he was afraid the old injun would hear him from his grave. And maybe he would at that.

"You ever hear of Walking Mist, boy?"

Hyden said he had. Another Snake medicine man, but from years back.

"Well, let me tell you about him. Walking Mist was a Snake hoodoo man, too, like Spirit Moon. In fact, he was his ancestral granddaddy. Well, back in the '30's, so I was told, up in the Wasatch, Walking Mist got on the wrong side of a couple beaver trappers from Fort Crockett. The three of 'em were boozed-up and looking for a fight and happened upon Walking Mist who, it was claimed, refused their offers of marriage to his sisters. They shot Walking Mist down, chopped off his head and buried it in a box. They buried his body somewheres else." Goode's face was set and stern in the lamplight. "Well, now old Walking Mist he had himself a high yeller girl for a wife, some nigger out of a Baton Rouge plantation. She was said to be one of them conjure-folk. Said she used to make up love potions and cures for the sick. Made little dolls out of clay and burlap, sprinkled the hair and fingernails from someone she didn't like in 'em and put the hex on 'em. Folks used to pay her to do so...horses, skins, rifles, what not.

"Well, this high yeller girl goes into one of her voo-doo trances and, sure enough, she locates old Walking Mist's head with a rod cut from an ash tree. She opens that box and old

Walking Mist's head, powerful crazy medicine man that he was, is still alive. Eyes open. He tells her where his body is buried. Not long after, Walking Mist is seen ambling around, head stitched back on, a funny light in his eyes."

"And what about them trappers?"

Goode grinned like a bear skull. "They found 'em one day. They had twenty-foot stakes shoved right up their asses. Up their asses and right into their throats. Just bobbing in the wind up atop them stakes that were driven into the ground. Thing was, nobody never did find their heads." Goode spit his cigar butt into the night. "I heard that from an old Ute I used to do some drinking with."

"I thought you didn't like Indians?"

"This 'un was different."

Hyden was nodding his head up and down. "That story, I believe it. My grandpappy Joe said that Spirit Moon was part demon and part human, could do anything he set his mind to. Grandpappy said a copper miner lost his hand in a cave-in and Spirit Moon rubbed something on it and called names into the sky and a month later, that hand grew back. Grandpappy Joe said it was true. Said Spirit Moon had eyes like coals. When them eyes looked at you, you were never the same again."

"Country's ripe with bullshit, son."

"Some of it's true."

"Maybe."

"There was a Paiute from the Cedar Band that had two heads," Hyden said. "I saw him once. It was true enough."

Goode laughed. "Next you'll be telling me you can rope a bronco with yer pecker and still have enough left to make a dance hall gal whistle Dixie in the dark."

Hyden felt his ears burn like they'd been branded. "If you don't believe in nothing, then why you tell me that story of Walking Mist?"

"To pass the time, boy, strictly to pass the time and to see how gullible you are. And dammit, yer gullible. That Ute believed what he told me, but I expected better from you being a white man. If I'd known you were afraid of spooks, I woulda got me another boy to ride shotgun."

"My grandpappy Joe—"

"Yer grandpappy Joe was full of more shit that a privy pit," Goode said. "And don't take that the wrong way, son. But he liked to talk is all. Now, enough with this fool yarning, I say."

And it *was* enough.

Hyden was thinking about Skull Valley. The day before, they'd pulled into a little Goshute camp situated at the base of a rise punched through with caves. Some young buck in an army shirt and bowler hat was waiting for them with the pine box at the side of the dirt trail. A couple old men in trade blankets were standing in a loose circle muttering some nonsense. The buck—didn't look like no medicine man—paid Goode without so much as a word, seemed relieved almost. The body was that of some white man who had kin in Whisper Lake. They never learned what the Goshute were doing with it and they didn't ask. But now, thinking on it, Hyden was wondering what those old men were up to and if that young buck was some kind of shirt-tail relation to Spirit Moon.

Hard to say.

Hyden didn't know if they were Goshute or Snake. He'd only seen Spirit Moon once. Over at the store in Ophir, Toole County. Spirit Moon had been there with his sons, who were loading his wagon. The old man was wrapped up in a buffalo robe and there were beads and feathers braided into his hair. His face was a maze of tiny scars that seemed to move like writhing maggots. Hyden had turned away then, before the old man looked upon him. Before—

There was a shifting in the box and both of them heard it this time.

They looked at each other in the eerie, flickering lantern light, something like fear cut into their faces. They quickly looked away. Hyden licked his lips, but he didn't have any saliva left.

Something was happening.

He could pretend otherwise, but something was building around them like heat lightning and they could both feel it. But they were men. Grown men with a job to do and it had to be done.

From the box there was a thump, then a rustling.

"Boy," Goode said, his breath not coming real easy, "take a look back there for the love of Christ...what the hell am I hearing?"

Hyden felt a white-hot terror in his belly, felt it feeding up into his chest. He leaned over the seat, shotgun in one hand, lantern in the other. His skin was crawling in undulating waves. He was cold to the bone...but it was not from the clammy April night. He looked at the box, the lantern casting tongues of light over its lid. The brass hasps were still fitted into place. All them those—Jesus, had to be a hundred of them—still pounded into the lid. Only...only, didn't it almost look like five or six of them were sticking up now? Like maybe something inside was pushing them through? Hyden felt a grim weight settle over him, crushing him down like a granite graveyard slab. He felt weak, paralyzed even. The atmosphere around him was blanched, soured, thick with something that just ripped the heart straight out of his chest.

As he watched, two of the nails slid out of the lid with a groaning sound. They popped free and clattered into the hold.

"What in the Christ?" Goode said, his voice sounding choked and dry. The moon came back out and his face was discolored and sickly. "Mind me, boy! *What was that?*"

"Nails..." Hyden tried to say, but there was no air in his lungs. Just something blowing and drifting like desert sand. "Them nails...they're starting to pop free..."

"Yer imagining shit!" Goode said. "Or...or maybe that body's bloating. Known 'em to burst a box right open...happens sometimes."

But Hyden just shook his head. Things like that didn't happen in cold weather.

Then they both heard it. A noise from inside that box—a scraping, scratching sound like fingernails on wood. There was horror in both men's eyes. A huge, relentless horror that spilled out like tears and into the night, surrounding them, enclosing them, wrapping them tight in a shroud. The darkness slithered and whispered.

Then: thump, thump, thump. Pounding fists.

Goode drew in a sharp breath: "Get up! Get up!" he cried to the horses, his whip cracking like thunder. *"Get-up you sonsofbitches! Get-up!"*

Hyden just kept watching the box, wondering maybe if his scattergun would be of any use against what tried to climb out of it. Whatever was happening in there, it wasn't good. Wasn't natural. There were arcane mysteries fermenting in there, dark alchemies brewing, spectral truths rattling their teeth. In the black, noisome darkness, something was breathing and aware. And that something was worse than anything Hyden could imagine.

The wagon was really rolling then, down a bend that cut through the hills and over a creaking wooden bridge that spanned a rushing, icy creek.

"Only a few miles now!" Goode cried out, the wagon thundering towards its destination, the horses pounding forward like the devil himself was chasing them...and maybe he was. Goode kept looking over at Hyden apprehensively, then back at the box. "Just hang tight! I can...yeah, I can see the lights below!"

Hyden took his word for it.

He did not turn and look.

He could not turn and look.

His eyes were wide and staring, that frosty wind buffeting him mercilessly. But he did not feel it. Did not feel his numb fingers on that wooden stock. Did not feel that icy mortuary chill that crept through his bones and locked them tight and hard as iron in a deep freeze. All he knew was the box. It was the center of his universe. It was a dark star and he was a speck of dust caught in its malefic orbit. All he could do was watch those nails twist up and pop free, one after the other.

And in the box, a flurry of scratching and pawing and thudding.

Something in Hyden suddenly snapped. A wild, shrieking terror ripped through him and he began to shout: *"I'm getting out of here! I'm jumping out of here! This is crazy—"*

But Goode forced him back down and told him to shut up, shut up, goddamn it, it was all in his head, all in his head. But the idea of being alone in that wagon with that box in the back and what it contained...Goode knew he couldn't do it by himself. Just couldn't. And Whisper Lake was right before him now. To either side were the derricks and mainframes and hunched shacks of the outlying mining camps.

Something back there made a loud, snapping sound and Goode didn't need to turn to see that one of the brass bands had broken open and the other wouldn't be far behind and then...and then...

Hyden's breath was coming in sharp, hurtful gasps. He was shaking so badly he could not hold the shotgun. It clattered uselessly to his feet.

And then they were in town and whatever was in the box seemed to sense that, for it settled back down into its cold berth and waited things out. Goode and Hyden let out a collective sigh, but did not relax until they found the undertaker's and got rid of the damnable thing.

3

Hiram Callister was who they found.

Rotund, greasy Hiram Callister, undertaker and cabinetmaker. He prepared the bodies and fashioned the boxes they were tucked carefully into. Cheap pine affairs or sometimes imported black mahogany shipped in by rail for rich miners or railroad men. Hiram preferred to work by lamplight just as his younger brother Caleb—and co-owner of Callister Brothers Mortuary—preferred the light of day. And when Hiram was not handling wood and deadwood, he secreted himself into his chambers above and poured over his collection of pornographic pictures, most of which were sent to him by a friend in New Orleans where such things were readily available to the connoisseur...for a price.

Hiram had never been very good with women.

With people in general.

At least, not living ones. He had been a plump, bookish child and had become a heavy, unsightly man with a bevy of quivering chins that herded about his lower jaw and neckline like pink hogs at a trough. He was fond of cakes and candies. Had an abnormal condition of the sebaceous glands which caused him to sweat profusely. His hands were oddly cold and he was given to stuttering in civilized company. Children often pointed to him on the streets. He could be found by night, chewing taffy and chocolates and French crèmes amongst the sheeted forms in the mortuary, dabbing continually at his moist face and brow with a handkerchief. For this was his world, a world of caskets and chemicals, corpses and silver gleaming instruments. A world that was close and dim and smelled of iodine and alcohol and less pleasant things.

But it was Hiram's world and he coveted it.

Let Caleb have the daylight. For Caleb was something that belonged in the daylight—handsome and charming and sure. He spent his days consoling widows and his evenings in gambling dens and brothels telling off-color stories of the dead. People called him friend and lover just as they called Hiram ghoul and deviant, telling nasty stories about him.

Hiram did not care.

In the end—man, woman and child—they were always his.

He fancied the women. Particularly the young ones. Not the upstanding wives and sisters—if there were such things in a seething mining town like Whisper Lake—but the prostitutes. They had been touched and fondled in life, so Hiram figured it was no sin to do the same with them in death. But only the prostitutes. Never anyone else. Regardless of what people whispered about him, he did have standards, professional ethics.

When the two men with the casket showed up, Hiram had the body of a young whore stretched out before him like a cedar plank. She'd slit her wrists. Hiram was touching her, sweating and breathing heavily...then those two banged on the door. One was some old grizzled desert rat, the other a kid with freckles on his cheeks. But both had wide, unblinking eyes and hands that shook. They looked like they'd seen their own ghosts threading at them in the darkness.

Hiram had never seen two men so...*afraid.*

They brought in the box, set it on an empty table and got out just as fast as fast could be, practically fighting to be the first out the door. But some people, Hiram knew, were apprehensive around the dead. No matter.

He had been wired about the casket.

It contained the body of James Lee Cobb. Cobb had been something of a hired gun and outlaw, a notoriously sadistic, evil man and the world was better without him. His only kin was a Mormon squatter over in near-by Deliverance—one of the Mormon villages. A half-brother name of Eustice Harmony who was willing to plant him...long as Cobb's injun friends footed the bill. And they had.

As Hiram looked over the box, he saw that many of the nails fastening it shut were missing. One of the brass hasps had broken free. Rough handling. But the sort of thing Cobb deserved.

Hiram left the box where it sat.

He had more pressing matters than dead outlaws.

4

Long after midnight, a sense of dread settled into him.

He could not explain it. Did not try to.

After he'd finished with the painted lady, had locked her down in a cheap cedar box paid for by her madam, Hiram started on the Byrd brothers, Thomas and Heck. He pulled back the sheets and studied their graying faces. A shame. Both had been business owners—Thomas owned a livery stable and Heck a meat market. And now, of course, they were only so much meat themselves. It was no secret they'd both been romancing the same woman...Heck's wife...and it was only a matter of time before such wanton fornicating would lead them here.

Hiram knew only a few details.

They'd gotten into a drunken brawl at the Cider House Saloon and Heck had pulled his old Army Colt and shot Thomas and Thomas, before his blood had run out, had slid a skinning knife into his brother's throat. They had died in a communal pool of their own blood, locked in a fighting embrace. They had been brought in that way. It had taken both Hiram and his brother to pull their stiffened limbs from one another. Heck's wife Clarissa was paying for the funeral, wanted them in nice boxes and wanted them presentable so they could be photographed side-by-side, cheek-to-jowl for kin back in Missouri. She could afford it—

as the only living relative, she owned a livery stable and meat market now.

With gray, watery eyes like wet tin, Hiram got down to work.

His fingers were nimble and busy, forever searching and prodding, slitting and plucking. He stitched and sewed, gummed and pasted. Knives flashed and saws bit, wax pooled into hollows and catgut sealed cadaveric mysteries intact. He embalmed the brothers with a solution of arsenic and covered them with sheets until the caskets arrived.

Pumping water into the basin, Hiram pulled off his rubber gloves and washed his hands thoroughly.

The wind picked-up outside and a tree limb scratched at the roof. For a reason Hiram could not understand, a chill swept up his spine. That sense of dread again. It had been gnawing at him for hours now...but why? He found himself thinking of the two men that had brought the casket.

They'd been scared white.

But why? Why? Fatigue, maybe. They'd been on the trail for two days from Toole County to Whisper Lake. And cold, inhospitable days they had been. Such deprivation and exposure could do strange things to men. Hiram cleaned up his instruments, decided against working on Cobb tonight. The oil stove in the corner was chugging away, yet he felt cold. Worse, his skin actually seemed to be crawling in turgid waves. He wanted out of the mortuary in a bad way and was not sure why.

He paused, a droplet of sweat coursing down the hill of his cheek.

There was something, something.

He could not hear anything, but...he turned around, staring at the casket. He stood there, watching it, his brain filled with cryptic thoughts. It was ridiculous...but he had the unnerving sensation that he was being watched, studied, stared at.

Children peeking in?

No, it was too late and the shades were drawn. Carefully, slowly, he went to the windows, peered around the shades. The dirt street outside was empty. He could see the town stretching out in the distance—clustered roofs climbing the hills and dipping into hollows. He could hear the wind skirting the lonesome spaces. Hear a wagon somewhere in the distance. The sound of voices over towards saloon-row. The ever-present rumble of mine machinery.

But no one looking in, watching him.

The shadows seemed to be growing longer in the mortuary, spilling out from crevices and cracks and crannies, tangling like mating snakes across the floor. The lanterns still burned bright, yet everything seemed oddly murky.

Eyes watching me.

Imagination?

Hiram had no use for superstition. He would have no truck with it. Yet, something in him was alive and electric and concerned, afraid maybe. He walked across the room to the casket. Licking his lips, he ran his hands over the roughhewn cedar, fingering nail holes and splintered knots.

Eyes staring at me.

That body in there...James Lee Cobb...Hiram began to wonder about it as something inexplicable began to take hold of him, but so gently he was not even aware of it. All he could think about was the body in the box, body in the box. Cobb had died up in Skull Valley, they said. His injun friends had bought him a casket, paid for him to be shipped back to Whisper Lake.

Now why would injuns do that for a white man?

Hiram wiped sweat from his brow. He knew there was a reason, but he couldn't seem to remember what it was. Cobb had come home to the only kin he had. Sure. Had a half-brother over in Deliverance, the Mormon settlement just west of Whisper Lake. That's why Cobb was sent. The half-brother was going to pick up the box day after next, he said.

Hiram's hands were trembling now.

He mopped more sweat from his brow, thought: *What the hell is wrong with me?*

He couldn't seem to think straight. His brain was filled with wild, leaping thoughts that could not be strung to together into anything reasonable. There was a tenseness behind his eyes. Perspiration was beading his face, pooling under his eyes, streaming down his jowls. A few droplets struck the surface of the box. *Plop, plop.*

For one irrational moment, Hiram thought it was blood.

Yes, like a sacrifice. A blood sacrifice offered up to some malefic pagan god. Blood. Burnt offerings. A tribute of blood and flesh and burned entrails. Atonement. Expiation. Some gods demanded these things, they—

Hiram began to whimper, tears mixing with sweat.

Eyes that won't shut, won't die, won't stop staring.

He stumbled over to the tool bench, found a small crowbar.

Standing over the casket, he looked upwards, seeing only the stained tiles of the ceiling, but maybe hoping for some divine intervention from God. From the Lord Jesus Christ even though Hiram did not believe in him or anything else. Regardless, something had hold of Hiram now and his thoughts were a jumble and his brain a buzzing hive of wasps. His eyes were wide and unblinking, tears bled away, taking his sanity with them. His lips moved, but no sounds came out.

Blood offering.

Watching me.

Frantically, he began pulling the nails from the box, ripping them from the cheap plank coffin. One after the other until he was panting and wheezing and his heart was pounding and his temples throbbing. He broke the remaining brass band and it clattered to the floor along with the crowbar.

The eyes are watching me.

He tore the lid from the box and let it drop away. Then he was looking inside the box and seeing he did not know what. A body in a black burial suit, yes, but wrong, all wrong. Too many shadows crawling and slinking and shifting and maybe not shadows but the body itself.

Hiram's heart thudded dully, his breath was locked in his lungs.

Something in him shattered like white ice and he saw the eye. A single green eye, wide open and staring. Like a silver coin, it shined and glimmered, reflecting a burning light that got inside Hiram's head.

Then there was a scalpel in his hand and he held his left wrist out.

Blood offering. Expiation.

He slit his wrist, dark arterial blood streaming into the box in loops and spirals. Something in there moved and rustled.

"God help me..." Hiram's voice echoed from another room.

And a single rawboned, fleshless hand snaked from that pit of conspiring shadows and took him by throat.

It was like the hand of God.

5

Early the next morning, Caleb Callister found his brother's body.

It had been stuffed in the casket, white and bloodless and shrunken. Caleb did not cry out or go into theatrics. He summoned the coroner quite calmly for he was a man used to death in all its unpleasant forms.

The coroner came and gave his verdict of suicide.

An odd suicide at that. Hiram, for reasons unknown, had slit first his left wrist, then his right. Then he had climbed into the box. The scalpel was still locked in his fist. The box had contained the body of James Lee Cobb. But as to where that body had gotten to, no one could guess.

Suicide, then.

The only thing that concerned the coroner were the bruises at the throat, the crushed windpipe. But he was willing to overlook this on account he had no viable explanation and Caleb was not interested in pursuing it.

Let the dead rest, Caleb told him.

Forever Amen.

PART TWO: GONE TO HELL

I

Seven Months Later...
    The black sky unbuttoned itself like a corset, spilling cold, freezing rain by buckets that found the wind, joined with it, becoming a raging, angry thing that pounded the landscape, lashing and whipping and driving anything with blood in its veins to cover. Dusty, sun-cracked soil became mud. Mud became swamp. Swamp became rivers and creeks that overflowed their banks and sank the world.
    Two hours after sunset, the water began to freeze and the rain became snow and the San Francisco Mountains were sculpted in ice. Through the maelstrom came a lone rider trotting through muck and snow and freezing rain.
    His name was Tyler Cabe and he was a bounty hunter.
    A yellow slicker wrapped around him like a wet, flapping skin, Cabe rode into Whisper Lake. He couldn't see much of the town through the snow that became pelting rain and then snow again, but was simply glad to be anywhere. Anywhere he could find warmth and hot food.
    He brought his strawberry roan to a gallop and stabled it at the first livery he found. Stowed his saddlebags and guns. Then he crossed the muddy, sucking streets and fell through the door of a tent-roofed saloon called the Oasis. Inside, the floor was covered in sawdust. There was a bar and tables with pine benches pulled up to them. A woodstove in the corner belched greasy fumes that mixed with tobacco smoke, cheap cologne, and body odor. A dozen worn, beaten-looking men slouched over beers and whiskey. A lone gambler played solitaire in the corner.

Whisper Lake was a company town, Cabe knew. These men and everything around them would either belong to the company or exist through its permission.

Cabe shook the rain off his flat-brimmed Stetson with the rattlesnake skin band, pulled off his slicker and hung them both from a hook near the woodstove. Dressed in striped pants, high-shafted boots, and a black frock coat, he found himself a stool at the bar, studying the oil painting above the bar which showed some fleshy jezebel displaying her charms. He saw himself in the mirror—the scars across his bony face, the sharp green eyes peering from narrow draws.

"Thirsty, friend?"

Cabe looked over at the bartender, a heavy-set man with a neck thick as an old cottonwood stump. His nose was flattened, eyes peering out from puffy pads of flesh. He had the look of a barefisted fighter about him.

"Yeah," Cabe said. "Damn if I ain't."

"Beer? Whiskey? Got some rye if it's to your taste."

Cabe shook his head. "No, nothing like that. Need something that'll warm me up. I'm not sure if that's a dick between my legs or an icicle."

The bartender laughed. "Frank Carny," he said.

Cabe introduced himself. "You fight?" he asked.

"Once," Carny said. "Years back."

"Do any good?"

"Held my own. Can't see outta my left eye no more, too many hits. A wise man does something other with his head than use it for a punching bag."

Cabe nodded at that, made good sense.

One of the miners at the bar laughed. "Where you from?"

"Been riding all day," Cabe said. "From Nevada. Was starting to think I just wouldn't make it."

"Helluva day for a ride," the miner said. He turned to the bartender. "Make him something special, Frank."

Carny grinned. "Ever had a Brigham Young?"

Cabe just looked at him. "A what?"

"Brigham Young," the miner said. "After one of those, you'll become a confirmed polygamist."

Cabe smiled.

"Or maybe a Wild Bill Hickok? Two swallows and you're a crack shot gunman. You'll pull iron on anyone."

Cabe allowed himself a laugh.

The bartender shook his head. "Nope. I think our friend here needs a Crazy Horse. You put one back and you're ready to take on the U.S. Seventh Cavalry."

Carny started pouring and mixing and the smell of alcohol in the air was enough to curl the hairs at the back of Cabe's neck. A glass was set before him. He didn't even ask what was in it. As he brought it to his lips, he felt the fumes burn up through his nostrils and right into his brain. He put it to his lips and threw it back in one swallow.

Jesus.

It landed in his belly like liquid metal, melting ice and setting dry tinder ablaze in the mother of all firestorms. Cabe started coughing and gagging and sputtering and for one divine moment, he saw the face of Jesus...and then fingers of warmth were threading through him, igniting him in places he didn't know could burn.

"Damn," he said. "Goddamn."

A couple miners were laughing. Carny was smiling.

Cabe found his seat again, ordered another. He rolled himself a cigarette and lit it up. Everything in him was blazing away nicely now and he honestly didn't have a care in the world. He'd been following a man for near six weeks now, a killer, but right then he would've traded shots of whiskey with him. The Crazy Horse was one damn fine drink.

He sipped carefully on the second. "I don't think my ass has been burned so thoroughly since the war, gentlemen."

Carny nodded, wiped out some glasses. "What side you fight on?"

"Confederate," Cabe said, offering no more. The war was in his mind every day, but he did not speak of it. Not unless he was with another veteran. Some things were better left in the past. "You?"

Carney shook his head. "Not me. Had me a brother died at Shiloh fighting for the Union, Eighth Illinois."

"Sorry to hear that," Cabe said and meant it. "I truly am. Lot of good boys died on both sides and the older I get, the more I start to wonder what the hell it was all about."

"Amen," said the miner.

Someone coughed, then gagged, then began to mumble something. Down at the end of the bar, a man in a filthy sheepskin coat raised his head. He pulled off what was left of his whiskey, gagged and spit most of it on the floor. He had a shaggy black beard that reached to his chest and eyes like setting suns.

"*War, you say?*" he managed, a tangle of drool hanging from his lips like a dirty ribbon. He wiped it away with one grubby fist. "War betwixt the States. No...*War of Northern Aggression.* Yes sir. I fought. I sure did. Goddamn blue bellies, goddamned Yankees. Sonsofbitches."

The miner winced as he saw the bearded man begin to stagger over. Maybe it was that he knew trouble when he saw it or maybe it was the man's smell...he stunk like a heap of rancid steer hides.

Cabe eyed him up, didn't like what he saw. That long stringy hair, that heavy beard all knotted-up and filthy like he used it to wipe out spittoons. His rheumy eyes were red-rimmed, but beneath that haze of alcohol...just as dusky as open graves. Some drunken, ignorant hellbilly, that's what.

Carny stopped wiping the bar. "Sit your ass down, Orv. Just sit it right down. The house'll buy you another whiskey. Otherwise, you can get the hell out."

"Fuck you," the hellbilly said, scratching at that rug of beard. He came on with a stink of urine. The stains at his crotch said he'd pissed himself and it wasn't the first time. "Goddamn war, yes sir. I was in that war. Yessum. Lost two brothers in that goddamn war." He stared at Cabe, not liking what he saw. "Yankee, ain't you?"

Cabe sighed. "No, Confederate. Second Arkansas. Popped my cherry at Wilson's Creek and lost my soul at Pea Ridge."

The hellbilly didn't seem to hear or want to. "You was on our side? Hell you were. Probably some goddamn guerilla out killing babies and robbing farmers. Probably rode with Bloody

Bill and his murdering, raping cowards, didn't you? Not like me. No sir, not like me. Not a real soldier."

The miner tapped a finger to his skull, indicating that the hellbilly was crazier than dancing cats. But Cabe had already deduced as much. Didn't take a tree full of owls to figure that.

"Now, Orv," Carny said and said very calmly like he was talking to his pet beagle that had just shit on the carpet. "This fellow's just having himself a drink. He don't want no trouble. He ain't a Yankee like me or Bob here. He's a Southern boy like you and he was a real soldier. So just let him be, hear?"

The hellbilly hawked up a gob of phlegm and spit it at his feet. "Fuck you know, you sumbitch."

Cabe figured old Orv was making a mistake. By the looks of Carny, he could hammer cold steel into tent pegs with those fists of his. And you just didn't want to think about how many faces he'd disfigured or skulls he'd fractured. You didn't get on the bad side of a man like that. It was damn dangerous. That's what Cabe was thinking...until the hellbilly's sheepskin coat drifted open and he saw that big, mean-looking 1851 Colt Navy .44 hanging at his side.

Cabe stopped worrying about old Orv's face and started wondering how quick the blood would run from a .44 hole in his own belly. He figured it would run pretty damn fast.

Licking his lips with a tongue drier than desert canvas, he let the fingers of his right hand casually drift down towards the butt of his Starr double-action .44 conversion. It was a smaller weapon than Orv's Colt. He had no doubt he could pull it faster...but, hell, last thing he wanted was any killing. That's not why he was here.

The hellbilly was still advancing, but coming on slow like a mad dog deciding where to sink its foamy teeth.

Cabe said, "Let me buy you a drink, friend. We'll drink to the old CSA and all the good boys we lost. What say?"

Orv's hand slid down to his belt, brushed the butt of the mankiller waiting in the holster...and proceeded to his crotch where it began to do some scratching.

Cabe relaxed slightly.

A couple of miners sitting at tables quietly excused themselves, slipping out the door in a blast of wet, black night. Those that remained kept their distance, staying well away. Cabe didn't like any of that. Way he was figuring things, if people were getting out, then this wasn't just some crazy drunk. He was a crazy drunk that liked to kill.

Carny made a move for something behind the bar and the hellbilly, maybe not quite as drunk as he looked, pivoted and brought out his Colt smooth and easy.

But Cabe was already on his feet, Starr in hand.

There was a moment of pained, tormented silence, the tension so thick you could've speared it with a stick.

The hellbilly was laughing, but there were tears in his eyes. "Got yerself a Starr, boy? I seen 'em in the war. Cap and ball pistol, ain't it?"

"Converted," Cabe heard himself say, struck by the absurdity of two men about to kill each other discussing weapons. "Had it converted to metal cartridge. Easier that way."

The hellbilly laughed, giggled really. Saliva ran from the corners of his trembling lips. "I like my 1851, yes sir. Cap and ball, roll yer own, eh? I killed me a score of Yankees with it at Fort Donelson, didn't I? Bluebellies begged fer their lives and I scattered their brains, didn't I?" He cackled madly now, that gun just shaking in his fist, hungry for flesh. "Tenth Tennessee, yes sir. Bloody Tenth, they called us. Know why? Because we killed so many and took so many casualties. Blood...hee, hee...all that blood. Just a-running everywhere. You couldn't get away from all that blood, could you? Still can't get it off m'hands. Yankees captured us, that it? M'brothers were all dead, all dead, you say? Yes sir, I believe they was. They sent me to Camp Douglas, the POW camp up near Chee-cago. Oh m'Lord, but them Yankees had fun with us! At night they'd shoot through the barracks walls, make bets on how many Johnny Rebs they could kill with a single ball? Hee, you remember that?"

Cabe cleared his throat of dust. "I was captured, too, Orv. After Pea Ridge. I was at Douglas. Later they exchanged us...we mustered back in, went to the fighting again—"

"*Liar! Liar! Liar!* Goddamn bluebelly liar!" the hellbilly stammered, drool flying from his mouth, his brown and yellow teeth snapping open and shut like a beartrap. "Yer a Yankee! I can smell yer stink! Dirty murdering bastards killing Roy and Jesse! Fucking bluebellies! I kill 'em on sight, I kill 'em on sight!"

He brought the gun up.

Cabe began to apply pressure to the trigger of the Starr.

"If you kill 'em on sight," Carny said. "Then you better ready yourself, because here comes one now."

The door had swung open and a tall man had stepped in.

He wore a knee-length overcoat, the cuffs and collar trimmed in fur. Atop his head was a round buffalo fur cap. His face was narrow, angular, the mustache riding beneath the sharp nose trimmed immaculately. He was a handsome man and his pale blue eyes simmered with authority and bearing. There was a badge pinned to his breast. It read: SHERIFF BEAVER COUNTY UTAH.

The hellbilly was staring at him, but so was Cabe.

Cabe was speechless. Something hot and wet had spilled inside of him and it made him shake, made him angry, made him boil inside. But he said nothing, not yet.

"Orv," the sheriff said in a flat tone. "Give me your gun. You don't and I swear to God I'll kill you where you stand."

The sheriff hadn't even opened his coat to show his guns...if he even had any. But those eyes...Cabe remembered those eyes...they were merciless. And when they looked at you and into you, your insides melted like butter on a stove lid.

The hellbilly looked to Cabe almost desperately. His head shook slightly from side to side.

The sheriff walked over. "The gun," he said. "Right now."

Old Orv looked fit to shit himself, except by the stink, he probably already had. His fingers tightened on that big life-eating 1851 Colt. His knuckles were strained white as pearl buttons. He looked from Cabe to Carny, cast a glance at the miners. He looked oddly helpless.

The sheriff unbuttoned his coat, made damn sure the hellbilly saw how slowly and calmly he did it. And made sure he got a good look at the butt of the short-barreled .45 Peacemaker waiting in the hip scabbard.

He held his left hand out. "The gun," he said and those words were sharp enough to cut steel.

Old Orv made to hand the gun over...then maybe the tension of the moment or just plain machismo got to him, because he started to bring it back, his eyes gone ebon and savage. But the sheriff was too quick, too sure. He took hold of the hellbilly's wrist with his right hand, gave it a nasty twist, and that big revolver dropped into his left. He took it by the barrel and, with no more thought than swatting a fly, smashed old Orv across the face five, six times with the butt until he sank to his knees. Orv clasped his bleeding face with those soiled fingers, moaning and gobbling.

A big man wearing a tin star on his Fish slicker came through the door, looked at the 'billy, then at the sheriff.

"Lock this trash up," the sheriff said. Then he turned to Cabe. "Sir, if you would please, leather that pistol."

Cabe found himself doing so without even thinking. That voice, those eyes...they were almost hypnotic somehow. But then he came to himself as the deputy hauled the hellbilly non-too gently out the door. That cocky, crooked grin opened up in his face. "Well, well, well, Jackson Dirker," he said. "As I live and breathe."

The sheriff raised an eyebrow, showed no sign of recognition. "Do I know you, sir?"

Cabe smiled and that smile burned with hate. "You should." He touched the old scars running from one cheek, across the bridge of his nose, and to the next cheek. "These marks I bear..."

"What about them?"

"You gave 'em to me," Cabe said.

2

The Beaver County Sheriff's Office.

A dirty single-story brick edifice stuck in-between the county courthouse and a mine broker's office, looking straight out at the town square and the taverns lined-up beyond like prostitutes offering an easy time.

Cabe stood outside in the blowing, wet wind, his boots caked with mud like wet cement.

He wasn't sure what he was feeling just then, but it wasn't good. Part of him wanted to kick though the door and gun down that arrogant sonofabitch of a county sheriff. But that wouldn't do and he knew it. That was not how things were done in real life. He had thought of Jackson Dirker for years, playing out revenge fantasies in his mind for the time when they met up again—if ever—and now it all fell to his feet. Like the shed skin of a snake, these fantasies were simply dead.

He came through the door and saw the big deputy sipping from a tin cup of coffee. He was a large man, heavy in the middle, but broad in the shoulders and powerful-looking. He wore no gun. He hadn't at the saloon either. Cabe figured he was like old "Bear River" Tom Smith down in Abilene years back, enforcing law and order with his bare fists.

"What can I do for you?" he asked. "I'm Henry Wilcox, deputy."

"Tyler Cabe. I have business with Sheriff Dirker. He about?"

"In the back," Wilcox said. "I'll get him."

Cabe found a straight-backed chair and pulled it up to what he assumed was Dirker's desk—a big oaken antique outfit, papers and the like organized very neatly. Yeah, that would be Dirker. Officious, stern, militaristic.

Sure as shit.

Cabe had been in lawmen's offices in dozens and dozens of towns, if not hundreds. Some were nothing more than tumbledown shacks with shackles bolted to concrete blocks to hold prisoners. Planks set over barrels for desks. But not here. Not in a rich mining county. The job of county sheriff would be a very lucrative one.

You could expect nothing less of Jackson Dirker.

Cabe waited there, lighting a cigarette and studying the wanted dodgers on the walls, town ordinances, a rack of repeating rifles chained into a hardwood case.

The door to the back—the holding cells, Cabe figured—opened and Dirker stepped out and Cabe felt butterflies take wing in his belly. Dirker wore a striped suit with a gold watch chain and a string tie. The sort of duds a banker might wear. But Dirker had impressive bearing and he would've looked like the man in charge had he worn a corset and dress.

He sat down across from Cabe. "You have business here, Cabe?"

Cabe felt his voice catch in his throat, snag there like denim on a nail head. For a moment he wondered if maybe he had the wrong man here…but no, there was only *one* Jackson Dirker. Cabe had known it was him the moment he'd come into the Oasis. The face was older, lined impeccably by experience. There was a touch of gray at the temples. But those eyes, you couldn't forget them. Twenty years had not tempered their ferocity. They could still burn holes in cinderblock.

"You remember me, Dirker?"

The sheriff nodded. "I do."

"Didn't seem like you did back at the saloon…"

"It took a moment."

"The scars refreshed your memory?"

Dirker arched an eyebrow. "Scars are hardly a novelty in this country, Cabe. Now what is it you want?" he said. "What're you doing here?"

"I came to see the ocean, feel the spray."

"The ocean is hundreds of miles from here."

Cabe slapped his hat against his knee. "Damn…I must've taken a wrong turn."

Dirker was not amused. "Is this business or personal?"

Now there was a question. Good old Crazy Jack Dirker. You just couldn't rattle the man. He could talk about dismembering a baby same way he talked about trimming his toenails. That chiseled face was incapable of emotion. It knew not hate or anger, love nor happiness. Only the eyes were alive in that mask. Course, last time Cabe had seen him, he was wearing the dark blue sack coat and Jeff Davis hat of a Union Army lieutenant.

Cabe drew off his cigarette. "I tell you, Crazy Jack...folks still call you that?"

"They do not. During the war, only Johnny Rebs referred to me as that, I understand." He said this indifferently. Names meant nothing to him. You could call his mother a whore and if he didn't want to kill you, you couldn't make him do it. But if he was in the mood, look out.

"I can't tell you how long I've thought about you, what I'd do to you when I finally caught up with you."

"The war's over," Dirker said. "Act like a man and move on. That's what has to be done. The South underestimated the will and strength of the North. Such assumptions lose wars. Everyone did what they felt they had to do. Now it's over. We're united and have been for many years. We have to look to the future and learn from the past."

Cabe's teeth were clenched. "Sure enough, sure enough. I'd like to forget the whole sorry mess...but every time I look in damn mirror, Dirker, I remember. These scars don't let me forget." Cabe let himself simmer down. Dirker was in control, like always. He would not let the man win this discussion, make him into some hot-headed fool Southerner. Not this time. "We lost, Dirker. When you lose, it ain't so easy to forgive and forget. You think of how it could have been different. It's tough on a man."

Dirker arched that eyebrow again. "Sometimes it's tough on the victor as well. You think of what was done and how you could have treated your foes more civil, excused them for their transgressions."

Goddammit. The sonofabitch was acting like a poet and preacher and statesman now. Trying to make Cabe think he actually had some sort of heart beating in that empty chest of his. But Cabe did not believe it. "Pea Ridge. You remember it? I do. We got our asses cut to threads there. You bluebellies scattered us to the four winds. Me and my boys...we weren't even sure where we were. No shoes. No food. No ammunition. You rounded us up, Dirker. That bastard sergeant of yours shot down Little Willy Gibson! Then you took that whip of yours to the rest of us. When

I begged you...begged you to stop, you did this to my face. I was down and you were still whipping me..."

Dirker's lips had formed into a tight line now like a saber slash. "You *boys*...yes, I remember you *boys*. I remember what you did to those soldiers we found. Their corpses were mutilated, Cabe. It was disgusting. I should've killed you and the rest of that gutless Southern trash then and there. But I didn't."

Cabe was on his feet now. "You bastard! You goddamn fucking Yankee bastard! I told you then and I tell you know, we didn't touch them bluebellies! When we came upon them, they were already like that...guts hanging out and faces hacked-off...we just wanted their guns, their food! We were starving for the love of Christ!"

Dirker listened to Cabe's dramatics, did not believe a word of it. "We can discuss this until we're blue in the face, Cabe, but it won't bear flower. I don't believe you. I never have." He folded his hands on the desktop. "Now, did you come here to debate the war or was there something else on your mind?"

Cabe shrank down into his chair, very much feeling the weight of the gun at his hip. But once a man had made up his mind, you couldn't change it. You had to let it lay, like it or not. "All right, Dirker. All right. I been tracking a fellow. Hunted him through Nevada and he went to ground, I think, around here somewhere. I don't know his name and I have only the vaguest description of this animal. But I know what he did—"

"You're a bounty hunter?"

"A man's got to make a living."

"I wasn't judging you, merely establishing the fact. Go on."

Cabe found it easier if he didn't look at Dirker, so he looked at the wall, pretended he couldn't hear the sound of that whip in his ears. "This fellow, newspapers call him the Sin City Strangler. He jumps from one mining town to the next, losing himself in the influx of strangers."

Dirker nodded. "I've heard of this one."

"Be hard not to. This sumbitch likes himself prostitutes, Dirker. Has what you might call a special taste for them," Cabe said grimly. "He likes to get 'em off somewheres alone where he can get a scarf around their throats, you know? Likes to fuck 'em whilst they's dying. And then he takes a big knife—skinning knife maybe—and cuts 'em open, spreads their goodies all over the place."

Dirker was unmoved. "Disgusting," he said, but it was hard to tell if he really meant it or not.

Cabe agreed with him on that. It *was* disgusting. The Sin City Strangler had murdered six prostitutes in the past five months. First one was at the Barbary Hotel out in San Fran, followed by two more at hell-for-leather mining camps in Churchill County, Nevada. Then Eureka, Osceola, and finally Pinoche—all sprawling mining towns, all veritable "dens of iniquity", as the preachers and reformers said. For once money started coming out of the ground, it attracted the parasites and bottom-feeders like blowflies to a carcass.

A pissed-off miner had first put the bounty on the Strangler.

A thousand dollars…even though no one had truly ever seen him or had any real idea what he looked like. Eyewitness descriptions ranged from tall and fair to short and swarthy and everywhere in-between. Some said the Strangler was a Mexican who'd slipped from some insane asylum and others were certain it was some European immigrant. Regardless, sickened by the severity of the crimes—and it took a lot to sicken folks in mining towns—more money was thrown at the Strangler and now the bounty was up near five-thousand. The governor of the Utah Territory had thrown another thousand on top of it for information leading to the identity and/or whereabouts of the Sin City Strangler.

"I been tracking this bastard since Eureka," Cabe said. "That's where I started after him. In Osceola I got a good long look at his handiwork…it was bad, Dirker. You and me…we both seen things in the war…but this, Jesus, I ain't never seen nothing like this."

"And you think this animal is here?" Dirker said.

"I think he's in Beaver County. Whisper Lake is exactly the sort of place he'd come to hunt…I just have to wait and see. Sooner or later, he's gonna fall into my lap."

Dirker sighed, shook his head. "Cabe, ten years ago Whisper Lake was a placer camp with one store, a saloon, and a scattering of shacks. Then they struck a large silver ore deposit and pretty soon we had mining companies in here buying up everything—the Arcadian, Southview, Horn Silver. We have nearly five-thousand people in and around this town, another eight-thousand over in Frisco. Point being, we got hundreds of people tramping through here in a month...to find one man in that human stew, it'll be a hell of a job."

Cabe said, "I'll get him, dead or alive."

"Just make sure you get the right one."

Cabe stood up, stretched, pulled on his slicker. "One of these days, Crazy Jack, we gotta have ourselves a chat about the war. Just you and me."

"Get out of here, Cabe," Dirker told him. "And don't make any trouble. I already have my hands full."

Cabe went out into the storm, grinning. Maybe if things worked out right, Dirker's hands would be even fuller.

3

The hellbilly's name was Orville DuChien.

His cell in the Whisper Lake lock-up was eight feet long and four wide. The walls were brick and the floor was covered with straw. It was cold and damp and water dripped from the ceiling. In the summer the cells were filled with bugs; in the winter, just as cold as an icehouse. The cot Orv sat on was barely wide enough to hold a man and the single army blanket issued was little protection against the frosty night.

So Orv sat there in his own commingled stench, scratching at his beard, thinking and remembering and becoming generally confused as always. For he was certain there was something he was supposed to remember, but for the life of him, he just drew a blank. But sometimes his mind was like that. Like some blackboard scribbled full of interesting and pertinent information, but if you didn't run up there quick and read it, all those words and ideas just sort of faded away.

So Orv sat there and was glad it was cold because when it was cold it killed off the nits in his beard and hair. And those damn things, why, they could just about drive a sane man crazy with all the itching.

Orv thought: *Quit thinking about yer livestock, you damn idiot, you ain't here on account of that. Yer her because...because...*

Dammit, there went the old memory again. Like a chip of lake ice caught in July sunshine, it just plumb melted away. Made Orv wonder sometimes if he was crazy and maybe he was, but just because his brain had gone to grass, didn't mean he was raving. Though, sometimes, sure, he raved and maybe got a little out of control. And when that happened, Dirker had Henry Wilcox or Pete Slade or one of them other deputies lock him up like a pea in a poke and that was okay.

Beaver County jail?

Hell, it was damn comfortable compared to that Yankee military prison at Camp Douglas. Food was better, too. You didn't get beaten or used for target practice. You didn't have to drink out of the cesspool or watch all them good boys with empty bellies wander about like living, breathing skeletons just this side of the grave. And that had been just pitiful, when you thought about it, because the bluebellies *had* food. Had plenty of it, but they liked to watch their enemies starve.

Starvation.

Now that was a hell of a plot to hoe. Used to be a sergeant at Douglas from Alabama had just gone mad. Was so thin you could've slipped him in an envelope. Orv only heard him say one sane thing whole time he was there. *Boy,* he said, *way I'm a-figuring it, I'm about six-hundred miles from home and six-inches from hell."* Orv never forgot that. Most of the time that sergeant was trying to dig bugs up from the dirt or hiding rat corpses under the shacks for a sweet midnight snack or telling the guards he wanted to speak with President Lincoln and that Andrew Davis could kiss his white Alabammy ass for leaving him rot in that hole. And if old Andy Davis wanted to bang his sister Nell, why just go right on ahead, because she'd laid with everything from injuns to wild boars and a lying politician ought to slide in just about right.

Orv tried to pull his head back out of the war and it was no easy feat.

Sometimes all he could see were Yankees. Dead ones and living ones. Dirker was a Yankee, so was Henry Wilcox. Peter Slade, too...no, that wasn't right. Slade was from Mississippi. But he smelled like one. Orv hated that Northerner smell they had about 'em. Like that one time over in the Oasis, that Yankee sumbitch said he was with the 2nd Arkansas. Said he was at Pea Ridge, but it was a lie. Sumbitch carried a Starr revolver and had that red-blonde hair to his shoulders and them scars on his face. Probably some Kansas redleg out murdering honest folk. Yeah, goddamn Yankee, lying like that. Who'd he think he was?

Orv told himself to pay it no mind for that was years back.

No, no, that wasn't right either. Yesterday or maybe today. Sure, because Dirker had taken away his 1851 Colt Navy, same gun he'd carried since the Bloody Tenth where he'd taken it off an officer. Taken if off him when he hid under them bodies...and, damn, where were Roy and Jesse?

Oh, dead and dead. Sure, for years now. Died in the war.

Orv clasped his head in his hands and tried to make his brain work, but it just didn't want to and how was that for a bag of beans?

Listen.

Sure, Orv's mind was clearing some now.

He could hear things up in the hills, bad things. Things riding horseback that looked like men maybe, but weren't really men. Oh, it was bad, bad, bad. His people were from the Smokey Mountains in Tennessee. His mother's kin were all conjure folk and they had the second sight and sometimes Orv did, too. Sometimes he'd see things in his head before they happened...only it didn't do him much good because he always forgot by the time they came around. Mother's people were like that. Grandpappy Jeremiah Hill was like that, too. Time them farmers from up in Hawkins County had cheated him out of his prize hogs, but did it legal-like so Jeremiah couldn't do much about it but curse and dance a jig. Only, Jeremiah went into a black mood and hexed them boys and crows came in the dead of night and pecked their eyes out which wasn't a bad thing really, because Jeremiah's witching had shown 'em things they didn't want to look on no more.

Orv went to the tiny barred window.

Damp wind blew in his face and it felt good and he looked up into the shadowy hills climbing above the town, knowing that was where the evil was, where the bad things roosted. He could see faces and forms in his mind, but they were indistinct and the voices were only a little clearer. And it all made something black and toxic twist in Orv's belly because he could smell death, death circling the town. Just like he'd smelled it in Camp Douglas and heard it there at nights, picking through the piles of bones and rags and unburied corpses. Now death was here and his mind showed him that and he knew, as always, that death was always hungry and its belly always empty.

Knowing this, Orville DuChien slid down the wall like a teardrop and began to whimper, praying for dawn.

4

Tyler Cabe came into the St. James Hostelry out of the storm, rain dripping from the brim of his Stetson. He wiped the mud from his boots, crossed to the fire in the hearth and warmed himself. A slim woman in a blue denim bustle dress was polishing the banister with a rag.

"Good evening," she said.

"Ma'am," Cabe said. "I need me a room. Maybe for a week, maybe more. Possibly less."

The woman walked over to the desk, opened the ledger. "I'm sure we can set you up, Mister—"

"Cabe. Tyler Cabe."

He got a good look at her and saw she was quite pretty. Her hair was just this side of midnight, her cheekbones high, her eyes like melting chocolates. And her voice was nice, too. Velvety, sweet. It had a fine Southern twang to it...but one softened by an upper class upbringing. Cabe figured she was from a fine family.

"And your business?" she asked.

Cabe just looked at her. Most hotels and rooming houses did not ask such questions. But Whisper Lake was a wild town by all appearances, so you couldn't blame the lady for being particular.

"I'm a bounty hunter, ma'am," he said, neither proud nor ashamed. "I hunt down folks for a living. Sometimes animals. That bothers some people. Does it bother you, ma'am?"

"Not in the least." She wrote these things in the ledger. "Just let's understand ourselves right off, Mr. Cabe. What you do is your own business, just don't drag it back here. This is a respectable place for respectable people. You want to drink, whore, and gamble, that's your affair, but keep it out there. I won't have it under my roof. Is that understood, Mister Cabe?"

He walked over from the fire, rubbing his hands together. "Yes, ma'am. It is. I'm not here to hell around, I'm here on business."

"Very good. The rooms are five dollars a day. Breakfast is at eight and supper at five, promptly. Lunch is your own affair."

"Five dollars...that's pretty steep, ma'am."

She nodded. "Yes, it is. But this is a mining town, Mr. Cabe. There are other hotels that charge fifty dollars a night. But if you prefer something more economical, there are many bunkhouses you can get a bed at. A straw-filled mattress for two bits a day, still warm from its previous occupant. But here, the rooms are clean. There are no bugs. And the food is good."

Cabe paid her for two days. "Guess you talked me into it."

Grabbing his bag, he followed her up the stairs. His room was small, but comfortable. Bed, bureau, wash basin, tiny closet. A window looked out over the rainy/snowy streets.

She lit an oil lamp with a stick match. "So you're a bounty hunter. Hmm. Never met a bounty hunter before. You hunt down men and collect the bounties. How does that make you feel, Mr. Cabe? Does it make you feel important? Like a big man?"

"No, ma'am. More like a small man with a full belly."

She smiled at that. "An impertinent answer to an impertinent question."

Cabe sat on the bed. "I could use a bath, ma'am, if you could arrange it. By the way...I didn't catch your name?"

"Oh...yes, how rude of me. Janice Dirker," she said.

5

Well, this was really gonna be something, wasn't it?

Cabe soaked in the hot water and thought about the war and Jackson Dirker—his wife and the hotel he owned. More he thought about it, more he started thinking how funny it all was. How everything comes back to a man sooner or later. His past was like some ghost he'd stuck away in a box, trying to forget about it, and now it had gotten loose, was coming right back at him.

And Dirker? Jackson Dirker?

How did he honestly feel about him? That was a good question. He did not like the man, not really...*yet*, he didn't exactly hate him anymore. Time had dulled his anger. He felt neutral, if anything. It would have been much easier to hate him if Dirker was more offensive, was inclined to brag about what he'd done. But that's not the sort of man he was. Sure, Dirker was still a dirty son of a whore, but he was hardly the demon that had plagued Cabe's memories all these years.

And that only made things tougher.

Cabe thought: *You ain't here to address past wrongs. Keep that in mind. Giving Dirker trouble won't fill your poke. You're here to find that Strangler, to run that mad bastard to ground. That's it. You start trying to crowd Dirker, there's gonna be trouble. He's the county sheriff. He could make life real unpleasant for you.*

But...Sammy, Pete, Little Willy Gibson. What of them?

Gibson had died in the woods that day, Sammy at Camp Douglas. Pete had been exchanged with Cabe, mustered out to another unit. Was it justifiable to hate twenty years after the fact? The bible preached forgiveness, but Cabe had never been a real forgiving sort and wasn't much on scripture. But on the other hand, he was not a hateful nor violent man, despite his occupation. Whenever possible he tried to get by on his wits, to outsmart his adversaries.

But Jackson Dirker...dammit, the man knew how to yank his chain. Cabe had gone into his office, planning on staying in control and that sonofabitch had worked him into a lather without never once raising his voice.

The South had lost the war. It was a fact. Like any good son of the Confederacy, that still hurt some, still burned in a secret place. But Cabe couldn't sit around stewing that the

Yankees had trampled the family holdings like others. His people were dirt poor sharecroppers from Yell County, Arkansas...they never had shit to begin with. If the Yankees had burned the farm, it would have been a distinct improvement.

So he couldn't cling to that.

Sometimes, he wondered just what there was to cling to.

Running callused fingers over the scars threading his face, he decided to hell with Dirker. He'd sort that out later, if and when the time came. Now there was business and money to be made.

6

Sometimes Caleb Callister thought about his life and the building blocks that it was erected from. But not often. Now that Hiram was dead and buried some seven months, Caleb was the sole owner of the Callister Brothers Mortuary which would soon be renamed Callister Funeral Parlor. Occasionally, Caleb missed his brother, but not too often. They'd always had a pretty good arrangement—Caleb made the coffins and Hiram embalmed the bodies. Handling corpses was nothing Caleb cared for. After Hiram died, he'd tried his hand at it for a time, but it made him sick touching that cold clay so he'd hired an embalmer named Moss out from Stockton, California.

Moss was capable and he minded his own business, which was a plus. Caleb didn't have that much to hide—not since Hiram's passing that was—but last thing he needed was some young snip fresh out of mortuary school nosing into his affairs. Caleb was a gambler and a womanizer and most knew it, but he liked to keep such things quiet. For by day he was a respectable business owner. And he didn't need Moss spreading stories about the teenage girls Caleb had brought to the mortuary or what he did with them in the rooms above.

Some things had to be kept secret.

Like the history of the Callister brothers, for instance.

Nobody in town knew much about them. Like everyone else they had just drifted in like leaves before a harsh Autumn wind. They blew in and set up a cabinetry shop and then the local undertaker had died, so Hiram decided they should get into that end of things, too, since most cabinetmakers were undertakers as well.

So they did and in a town with a very high mortality rate like Whisper Lake, it proved very lucrative. Extremely so. Eventually (and with the population boom) the Callisters gave up making cabinets and concentrated on coffins and undertaking. And this is all people really knew about the Callister brothers, aside from whispers and gossip.

They didn't know that they were from Logansport in western Louisiana or that their father had been a cabinetmaker and his father before him. They didn't know what it was like growing up with a man who was hardened by life and physically powerful from uncounted years of harsh manual labor. A man that liked to drink and use his fists on his family. Caleb himself had tasted the fury of those fists on numerous occasions as had Hiram. And that time the old man had caught Hiram out in the barn with that other boy doing those disgusting things, he'd nearly beaten him to death.

Only Caleb's intervention had saved his life.

And sometimes Caleb wondered why he'd bothered because as the old man said, Hiram was "touched and not by the hand of the Lord." Hiram was a strange boy, plump and bookish. He didn't run and play with the other children. He collected beetles and toads and anything dead he happened upon. Liked to sun-dry dead things and sit around and look at them. Caleb thought it was sick, but Hiram was blood and what could he do but protect him? Except, the older they got, the more peculiar Hiram became. And it was Caleb himself, just shy of his twentieth birthday, that had to pay that boy off after what Hiram had done to him. And it wasn't the first time. For Hiram was a pervert and he had fondness for children, especially boys. But Caleb protected him and kept his secret, though sometimes he'd wake in the middle of the night, his skin crawling at the memory of things he'd seen.

But that was a secret.

The Callisters had been good at secrets. The old man had a few of his own. By the time he was fifteen, Caleb had been to the local brothel more than once, striking up friendships with some of

Like the Callisters, these secrets were tended in the lonely tracts of the town's sordid soul.

7

Despite being warm from his bath and just as relaxed and easy as a kitty curled up in a drawer, Tyler Cabe threw on a deerskin jacket and a pair of gray woolen pants and went back out into the elements. The rain had stopped and the wind had died down, but it was still cold and his boots sank four inches into the mud sea of the road.

At the Oasis, Frank Carny was still on duty. A swamper was mopping bloody sawdust from the plank floor. There had been a knife fight, Cabe learned. No one had died, but it had been a messy affair as such things often were. A few men were playing poker and a few others were huddled at tables, telling stories of strikes in the Montana goldfields.

Cabe drank beer and told Carny why he was there and the two got down to some serious talking.

"Well, I'm sorry to hear that you and the sheriff don't get on so well. All I can say is that he's a good man, far as I can tell," Carny said. "Like him or not, you gotta admit that boy's got a real set on him. Shit, I'll wade in on anybody with my bare fists...but they got a gun? Forget it. I become a coward then. Dirker? Hell, he goes right after anybody, he figures they're causing trouble in his county."

Cabe sipped off his beer. "I ain't saying he's a bad sort, Frank. Ain't saying that at all. We just have a history is what. So much water under that fucking bridge, it'd drown a bull elephant."

He hadn't told Frank Carny everything. Just enough so he'd understand the lay of the land, so to speak. Understand who and what Tyler Cabe was and who and what Jackson Dirker was to him. Cabe figured that was important, because he needed a friend in this town, someone he could trust and was plugged into the local grapevine. Sometimes a little confession softened a person. Sometimes you had to expose your flanks to win the battle.

Carny put his elbows on the bar, looked Cabe dead in the eye. "Listen, Tyler. You seem like a right sort to me, so I'll tell you something. Dirker's got a lot friends in this town...and he's got a lot of enemies. I tell you this, just so as you don't speak out of school to the wrong person. I like Dirker...but I've been around, I understand how it must be for you. I've got enough lumps and bumps and scars...but, we'll say they were self-inflicted. Your scars are of a different stripe, aren't they?"

Cabe swallowed his beer. "I would say so."

Carny drew himself a beer from a wooden keg. "Can I be bold here, Tyler?"

"I wish you would be."

Carny poured half the mug down his throat in a single swallow, wiped foam from his wiry mustache. "Wars are bad business. Never been in one, but you don't have to be to figure that. You and Dirker...you were twenty years younger back then. Full of piss and vinegar. Both fighting your asses off for a cause you firmly believed in. But you were kids, neither of you had the common sense and tolerance that comes with age and experience. Keep that in mind."

Cabe licked his lips. "Young and randy?"

Carny laughed. "Exactly. Hot-headed, pissed and pumped with the sort of craziness only youth knows and which wars—and the bastards who start 'em—like to exploit. Just keep that in mind, friend. I'm of a mind that neither of you are the same men you were."

Part of Cabe didn't like Carny telling him his business and how he should feel about the shit he'd waded through...but, damn if he hadn't asked for it. It was food for thought. So Cabe took a bite, swallowed, found it didn't lay so bad in his belly after all. He didn't hate Yankees like some. Maybe the rich easterners pulling the strings, but not your common man or soldier. Just cogs was what they were, he figured. Hell, up in Dakota Territory he'd struck up a friendship with a Union vet who'd lost a leg at Gettysburg. And the bottom line there was that, old enemies or not, sometimes only vets could understand other vets and what they'd been through.

"I'll keep that in mind," Cabe told the bartender in all sincerity.

Carny served a few beers, poured a few shots, came back. He clipped the end off a cigar and fired it up, lighting Cabe's cigarette for him. Watching each other, maybe understanding each other, they did not speak for a time.

"Tell me about Whisper Lake," Cabe finally said.

"It's a mining town, Tyler. Not a company town per se, more of a three-company town—the Southview, the Arcadian, Horn Silver. They don't own everything here, but most of it. They're always trying to buy one another out and steal away each other's workers and the like. The strings they pull are big ones. Caught in-between are the miners and prospectors and some of 'em are pretty tough types. They come from back east or across the sea, just about everywhere. Then you got the usual assortment of prostitutes, gamblers, shootists, outlaws, petty criminals, you name it. Stuck in the mess are the business owners. Just one big human soup simmering away and, as you might figure, the worst possible things can and do happen here."

"Sounds like every mining town I've ever known."

"Sure. World's full of places like Whisper Lake, Tyler. Once they strike ore, it's all over but the dying and the scheming. Once the paint's dry, the people show and the garbage starts piling up and said garbage collects flies."

Cabe listened and didn't hear anything he hadn't heard before...yet, he had the oddest feeling that Carny was trying to say something without saying it. He finished his beer. "And?" he said.

"And what?"

Cabe studied him long and hard, his green eyes refusing to blink. "There's something else. I can hear it in your voice."

Carny set his cigar in the ashtray, put his elbows on the bar again. "This place is a cauldron like I was saying. Only it's about to boil over. See, there's trouble here. We've got hardrock miners vanishing out in the hills and people saying it's Mormon militias that are responsible."

"You believe that?"

Carny shook his head. "No, I don't. I mean, hell Utah Territory is mostly Mormons. But mining towns like this one or Frisco are mostly gentile. Mormons don't care for places like this—bastions of sin, they call 'em—but I can't see them murdering folks on account of it. They have some blood on their hands after that Mountain Meadow Massacre and the rest, but I found them to be generally peaceful folk. Clannish, but always willing to help a stranger in need. You can understand how they might not like places like this, places that might corrupt their sons and daughters."

Cabe understood that. Mormons were no different from ordinary Christians in that respect. Places like Whisper Lake had a way of expanding their boundaries, drawing in the worst sort of people and practices. He said, "But you don't think they had anything to do with these disappearances?"

"No, sir, I do not." Carny re-lit his cigar. "But get folks around here to believe it. Shit. I've heard there's vigilantes that have formed, are planning revenge against the Mormon camps."

"Sounds like Dirker's got his hands full."

"In more ways than you can guess, friend." Carny's voice dropped down to a whisper and he continued. "See...there's been not just disappearances, but *murders*. And I'm not talking shootings or knifings because people here don't pay them any more mind than the brothels or gamblers. These murders I'm talking about...goddamn, folks have been *slaughtered*, Tyler. Mutilated in the worse ways. Heads torn off, bellies opened up, limbs ripped free. I've heard rumors that these bodies, *they were eaten*."

A long gray ash fell from Cabe's cigarette. "*Eaten*? Well, shit, sounds more like wolves or a wild dog pack. I've heard stories about Mormons, but never that they ate folks."

"I agree. But, again, get people here to believe that. They've formed vigilance committees and are shooting at shadows. Things are getting crazy."

But Cabe could understand it. The Mormons. They were different, they made good targets. Good ones to vent your frustrations on. Because when people got scared, they formed into gangs and these gangs needed a common enemy. If they couldn't find one, they created one.

"I guess all I'm saying to you," Carny began, "is that this Sin City Strangler of yours, he couldn't have found a better place to squat. He'll fit into this madhouse like a needle into a button hole."

Cabe didn't doubt that at all.

8

Later, in his room, Cabe did some thinking.

A mining town. Dance houses, gambling halls, saloons, brothels. There was nothing money could not buy in such a place. The riches coming out of the ground would attract killers and thieves and scoundrels of every conceivable stripe. Immigrants would flood in, bringing trash from every corner of the country with them. The mining companies would pay men three-dollars a day for ten and twelve-hours workdays, six days a week if not seven. Drillers and muckers and jackers. Powermen would gouge out drifts and slopes, gut the mountains to extract ore. And the mines would hum around the clock and timber would be stripped from hillsides for bunkhouses and shacks and offices. Run-off from the smelters would kill the vegetation and foul the creeks and rivers and the lake with waste. The fish would all die and those that remained would be fouled with toxins. The town itself would be just as filthy and stinking as a boring cob. The company—or three of them, in this case—would own just about everything and everyone. It would have stores that sold everything from beef to Bibles to bed sheets and the miners would pay in company script, keeping the workers nicely in debt. There would be company doctors and company housing and company stables. And, if all else failed, a company coffin in six-feet of rank company earth.

Men would come by the hundreds to sell their souls to the malefic company god. Lots of men would die in the shafts—from cave-ins, from gas, from explosions, from dangerous equipment—but that wouldn't bother the company none because they had ten men lined-up and ready to take the company oath...soon as they pushed your corpse out of the way.

Yeah, that was Whisper Lake.

Like some huge human hive where flesh and blood were as cheap as desert dirt and the rich owners and their lily-white board of directors sat up in the high offices, pressed and starched and spotless. Never caring how much blood was on their hands because it always washed off and if there was enough green, it canceled out oceans of red.

Whisper Lake. A human cesspool where humanity was a commodity like hides or whores.

Then you add to that heady mix these murders and the Mormons and the vigilantes and too many hot-hands and not enough cool heads and you had real trouble.

And that, Cabe knew, was Whisper Lake laid bare. The town stripped of skin—raw quilts of muscle, yellow fat, and greasy rank blood that stank of mordant corruption.

The perfect stalking ground for the Sin City Strangler.

Looking out his window at the muddy streets below, Cabe waited. Maybe for the Strangler. Maybe for something else. Because whatever it was, it was coming. And it was going to be bad.

9

The prostitute's name was Katherine Modine, but folks in Whisper Lake just knew her as Mizzy Modine, Dirty Mizzy, or "Old-Squirm-and-Kick". Behind her back she was called "The Crab Queen of Beaver County"...and more than one scratching miner could attest to that one. But to her face she was never called anything but Mizzy. And mainly because she had a vile temper and packed a Smith & Wesson pocket .38 and was not afraid to use it. She had killed one man and shot up three others.

Mizzy was freelance, operated out of a crib over on Piney Hill, which sat in the brooding, gray shadow of the Arcadian mine...or one of them, at any rate. Her crib was a glorified shack that stunk of cheap whiskey and cheaper perfume, body odor and twenty-dollar sex. When the wind blew, the shack rattled and swayed and quite often it rattled and swayed when no wind blew.

While townspeople might have said old Dirty Mizzy was "horizontally employed", Mizzy didn't look upon herself as a whore. She'd been selling what God gave her since she was fifteen and had worked dozens of mining camps, cow towns, and military depots from West Texas to the Wyoming Territory and had missed very little real estate in-between.

Mizzy considered herself something of an entrepreneur.

And maybe she was. In Whisper Lake, she serviced a steady stream of customers who weren't real particular as to where they stuck their business…just grateful there was such a place. For those with more respect for what dangled between their legs, there were always the painted ladies who operated out of the sporting houses or high-dollar brothels where ten minutes with an imported French or Portuguese delight could cost you $400 or more.

Mizzy was an equal opportunity nightworker and was willing to spread her legs for any who could pay the price, regardless of race or cultural affiliation. And at twenty bucks a pop, what she offered was a bargain. And particularly in a mining town where prices tended to get inflated. And if you didn't have twenty dollars, Mizzy was always willing to take what you did have in trade. Be that horses or cattle, buffalo furs or customized Winchester rifles, injun ceremonial daggers or a fancy pair of lizard boots. Because when she wasn't whoring, she was selling goods out of her little shop…and she always had an eye on the inventory.

Some nights were busy, some nights were slow.

And tonight was just plain dead. So when there was a knock at the door of her crib, Mizzy grinned and the cash register in her mind rang up a sale. She quick lighted up the red tapers and turned down the oil lamp and prepared to receive a gentleman caller.

He came in out of the wind, his face just as pallid as spilled milk, offset by a sharp black mustache and eyes just as dark as chipped coal. He was tall and thin, dressed in a ankle-length frock coat and matching bowler hat.

"Well, come in, kind sir," Mizzy told him, "and just make yourself comfortable. Name's Mizzy. Can I get you a drink Mister—"

"No thank you, madam. That's not why I'm here."

Music to Mizzy's ears. She sat back on the bed, a large fleshy woman with breasts the size of bunk pillows and a face painted-up brighter than carnival glass. Her visitor dropped a twenty-dollar gold piece in Mizzy's glass compote tray and set his hat on the chiffonier, laid his coat across it. Mizzy loved the sound of that money ringing out against the glass. Maybe she didn't like this fellow with those dark eyes and that graveyard marble skin and that hard slash of pink mouth...but she liked his money just fine, thank you very much.

He was not the romantic type.

He ordered her to strip and she did and he pushed himself into her almost immediately, an odd passionless look on his face as if he found the very act tedious and banal.

"Oh yes, baby, oh yes," Mizzy said, going through her spiel, pretending to be beside herself with his masculine talents, moaning and groaning and making the sharp little squeaking sounds that always got them going.

But it wasn't getting this one going.

His thrusts had not become more frantic; they were even and slow, impartial really, possibly disinterested. His face betrayed no emotion...it was white and smooth set with those opaque, unblinking eyes and was for all the world like the face of a manikin or a bust cut from granite.

Mizzy was a businesswoman. She liked to bring things to a close quick as could be. Hated to keep other customers waiting in line...even though there probably weren't any more on a stormy, bleak night like this.

She laid it on thick, just totally beside herself at the sight of his greased member sliding into her, cooing and muttering filthy words and throwing down the whore-talk spicy and hot like Mexican peppers.

"Close your eyes," the man suddenly said, his voice just as dead and flat as a crushed possum.

Mizzy did so, hoping he was getting close now. He was squeezing her breasts roughly, but if that's what he liked, that's what he liked...so be it. Her eyes pressed shut and her pelvis meeting his every thrust, Mizzy heard a swish of something satiny and before she could do more than gasp, he'd looped a silken scarf around her throat, pulling it tight and tighter like a jungle python trying to squeeze her life away.

She fought and thrashed and tried all the tricks she knew to throw off an unwelcome rider...but he persisted, slamming into her now as black dots danced before her eyes. Her lungs began to ache and she felt that scarf shutting down the flow of blood to her head until her face was hot and felt like it would explode from the pressure.

And he was panting.

He was drooling.

His eyes were huge and black and glistening.

"You love me...don't you?" his voice was saying. "You love me...you love me...don't you...don't you...*don't you*..."

Mizzy's fingers kept trying to find that little .38, but it was gone, just gone.

And then the scarf was so tight that she sank into a darkness that just kept getting darker and more complete and from some far-off place she could feel him slamming into her and she was dying, but didn't seem to mind so much because what was it all worth? All the struggling and swindling and whoring? Who needed that when you could slip down into ocean depths and fields of black velvet...

"...don't you...don't you...don't you..."

Some five minutes after Mizzy was clinically dead, the tall man stopped thrusting, spending his seed in the cooling lower regions of Mizzy Modine, shooting life where there was now only death. When he was finished and had calmed, he took a skinning knife and slit Mizzy from navel to throat, pulling out the dripping jewels and loops of meat he found within, scattering them happily about the room. Then he slit her breasts off, cut her eyes out and replaced them with silver coins.

Then he sat and smoked a cigar and marveled at his handiwork.

Before he left, he violated Mizzy's corpse one last time. Then he donned his coat and bowler hat and slipped out into the blowing, frigid night, became a shadow that was swallowed by others and then did not exist.

And it was a strange, ominous night in Whisper Lake. The wind blew and dogs barked and a raw malicious evil twisted thickly in the air.

10

Tyler Cabe did not like to think of the war, but sometimes it reared up in his head, big and hungry and dark, chewing right through him like a cancer. And often in the dead of night when he was alone and all the little worries and fragments of guilt a man has hidden away in his soul started coming back to him, nipping at the edge of reason and resolve. The war, then, would return as he tried to sleep...or it would jerk him awake at four a.m. with cold sweats and shakes. It would not be a memory, but a physical, palpable thing that he could feel and see, taste and smell as it oozed from his pores like diseased blood, drowning him in horror.

Cabe had been a member of the 2nd Arkansas Mounted Rifles.

His first engagement was at the battle of Wilson's Creek where all his wide-eyed naivete had been purged from him in the worst possible way. He often thought that it was here that he truly lost his virginity. And if that was true, it was no sweet lovemaking in the dark, but a brutal violation. A rape of all he had known and believed in up to that point. Twelve miles southwest of Springfield, Missouri, on Wilson's Creek, General Nathaniel Lyon's Union forces struck at the Confederate lines at five in the morning. The fighting that ensued was savage and horrible. Cabe saw men—men he'd known and trained with—blown to ground meat all around him. He was splattered with their blood and entrails. A grisly baptismal. He crawled through their remains, ducked under their anatomies that dangled from tree limbs like garland, tasted their hot, salty blood on his lips.

In the billowing smoke and confusion, half out of his mind, all he could hear was the thundering cannonade and the screams of the dying. The 2nd pulled back from what was known as Bloody Hill, but then through sheer zeal and fortitude, were able to stabilize their positions. The Confederate forces attacked Union positions no less than three times, inflicting and *taking* horrendous casualties. After the third charge, the Yankee columns fell back to Springfield, but the 2nd Arkansas and others were just too beaten-up and threadbare to pursue them. The Confederate victory—if you wanted to call it that with some 1200 dead—bolstered Southern sympathy in Missouri, but the cost was staggering.

Cabe came out of that shocked, distraught, burned and bruised and damaged.

That was his first taste, his induction into man's oldest preoccupation.

After that, the 2nd was sent to Indian Territory to quell an uprising by the Creeks and Seminoles. By then, Cabe was desensitized by combat and, instead of wanting to run and hide as he had at Wilson's Creek, he dove into battle viciously. The Indian fighting was often close-in and barbaric and he found that he liked it that way. There was something far too impersonal about putting a ball through a man from a distance or shelling him indiscriminately…when you came at him with pistol and knife, were splashed with his blood and saw his agony, it woke up some primal beast that lusted for more.

And there was always more.

Pea Ridge came next.

The 2nd Arkansas, mustered into the CS Army of the West and, thrown together under the command of Generals Price and McCulloch, began the bloody affair on the southern tip of the Ozark Mountains. The combined force stood at over 20,000 including 5,000 Indians from the Five Civilized Tribes. With a near-two-to-one superiority in numbers, the Confederates, sensing a sure victory, split their army into two columns and attacked from front and rear. But Curtis, the wily Union general, flanked both Confederate armies and mercilessly pounded them with artillery fire until the Southerners were forced to retreat.

For Cabe and the 2nd, it was a living hell.

There'd been a blizzard a few days before and the weather was bitterly cold. Everyone was tired and hungry and near-frozen when Confederate General Van Dorn forced them into the fight. They deployed just east of Leetown in Morgan's Woods. Confederate generals McCulloch and McIntosh were killed just two hours into the fighting and the 2nd was left leaderless, pounded and harassed by the 36th and 44th Illinois relentlessly. The Confederate army was now in full retreat, pursed by the 1st and 2nd Union Divisions. Cabe's company, cut off now, took shelter in an abandoned farmhouse.

Shoes worn to threads, uniforms hanging in ragged strips, Cabe and the others shivered in the cold. Starving, scratched, torn and bleeding, they waited for relief that never came. There was no food to forage and scarcely any blankets or overcoats to keep warm with. Ammunition was long used-up. Many of the men were wounded, some severely. Just a tattered band strung together with bloody bandages and pride that was quickly eroding.

Within an hour, the shelling began.

The walls collapsed, the roof caved-in. The wounded and weak were buried alive in the rubble. Johnny Miller, Cabe's best friend in the world, was decapitated by shrapnel. The survivors tried in haste to dig the others out—their screams and pathetic whimpers echoing through the frosty air—but it was hopeless. As the Yankees pressed in, shrieking and blood-hungry, Cabe slipped off into the woods with three others—Sammy Morrow, Pete Oland, and little Willy Gibson. They trudged through swamps and crawled through bramble thickets until they were caked with cold mud, their faces scratched to the bone and uniforms cut to ribbons.

Little Willy was out of his mind, alternately giggling and sobbing and Sammy Morrow kept yelling at him, calling him a mama's boy and telling him it was time to get weaned off that fucking tit already. But Little Willy ignored him, carrying on conversations with men long dead.

"He's crazy, Tyler," Sammy told Cabe. "We can't make a run with this bastard at our heels. He'll give us away."

"We can't leave him."

"Why the hell not?" Sammy wanted to know.

But Cabe figured if he didn't know the answer to that one, what was the point of explaining it to him?

Just around sunset, fatigued and shivering, having had no food in well over twenty-four hours, they were ready to lay down and die. Pete Oland, reconnoitering ahead, discovered a tangle of dead Yankees in a little clearing flanked by a dark, denuded thicket. Cabe counted ten men. Ten men in blue rags that had been obscenely mutilated. They had been scalped and dismembered. Faces had been gouged from the skulls beneath. Their bellies had been opened, internals yanked out and strewn in every which direction like bailing wire.

"Goddamn," Pete said. "Ye ever seen anything like it?"

"Injuns," Sammy told them. "All them Injuns under Pike."

And maybe he was right, Cabe had thought. The Cherokee and Creek, Chocktaw and Chickasaw. Wouldn't have been the first time that Indian troops had gotten a little excited in the carnage and reverted to their old ways.

"I don't like them Yankee bastards," Sammy said and kept saying. "But this...Christ in Heaven, there ain't no reason for this! Ye hear me? Ain't no reason! Goddamn injuns! Civilized tribes, my ass!"

Cabe told them to get control of themselves. The men were dead and they had died horribly and savagely, but they were dead. There was nothing to be done for them. He had his boys dig through the corpses and viscera, stripping off greatcoats, blankets, knapsacks, and cap boxes. Any food they could find and especially weapons. Whoever had slaughtered these men had left their Enfield rifles. Cabe figured that well-supplied and well-armed, his group could make it back to the retreating Confederate lines.

It was a plan...only it didn't happen.

As they looted through the dead, disgusted to a man, a platoon of Yankee cavalry came bounding out of the thickets, ringing in the Confederate soldiers like a noose. There was no escape. No quarter. No nothing. Cabe had been through a lot up to that point...but robbing the enemy dead and then being caught at it like a bunch of ghouls...well, that was pretty much the end of the sad, old road.

The bluebellies dismounted.

Although a lot of them looked a little worse for wear with their dirty, ripped uniforms and gaunt faces drawn hard by war and atrocity, they were looking pretty good compared to Cabe and his men.

The Yankee soldiers got real excited when they saw the condition of their fallen comrades. They had to be physically restrained by their sergeants. As it was, they were like a bunch of slavering mad dogs surrounding the Southerners.

Then an officer walked through their ranks.

A tall, wiry lieutenant in a flapping blue frock coat and a Hardy hat, campaign sword at his side catching the dying sunlight. His face was set hard as marble, those blue eyes just as electric as ball lightening. He walked around the litter pile of the dead Yankees. Flipped one over with his shiny black boot. He showed no emotion, but his eyebrows kept arching, the corners of his lips pulled into a skullish frown.

Cabe knew he had to defuse an ugly situation. "Corporal Tyler Cabe, Second Arkansas Mounted Rifles, sir."

The lieutenant announced he was Jackson Dirker of the 59th Illinois.

Something about his bearing and steely silence made Cabe's blood run cold. Here was a man who obviously garnered instant respect from his troops and was no doubt a good soldier...but here also was a man who, despite his reserve and indifferent manner, seemed to have an almost violent, savage aura about him that bubbled just beneath those crystal blue eyes like acid waiting to devour flesh and bone.

"Sir...we, we came upon these bodies in this condition. Our unit was chopped up at Pea Ridge, we've been on the dodge since yesterday. My men haven't had a decent meal in days," Cabe explained, his voice shrill and cracking, because, God, he knew how bad it looked. "We were only going to gather some weapons and food off these...these dead...just enough to survive with."

The Union soldiers were all shaking and filled with a blank, mindless rage. Little Willy started babbling nonsense that no one could understand and a burly sergeant told him in an Irish brogue to shut his peckerwood Johnny Reb mouth and shut it right fucking now. But Little Willy was crazy and lost in some dream world and he kept right on, choosing the worst possible moment to begin bragging about how many Yankees the 2nd had killed. The sergeant made a pained, choking sound and pulled an Army Colt and shot him in the head. Little Willy's skull came apart like a shattered glass vase and his brains vomited into the grass and he fell straight over like a dead tree.

Cabe and the others started shouting and yelling and the Yankees quickly overpowered them. Cabe was knocked to the ground with a rifle butt to the temple and Sammy and Pete were roped to ash trees, then stripped to the waist.

Dirker came walking back from his mount with a bullwhip, something about him just as dark and venomous as rattlesnakes coiled in a ditch. "Graverobbers, ghouls," he said in a weird, whispering voice. "Killing a man is one thing...but to mutilate him, to *do...something...like...this...*"

The whip began to snap in the air, its braided length curling and unfurling, waking and stretching...and then Dirker began venting himself. The whip lashed against the bare flesh of Pete and Sammy's backs, laying them both open in bloody gashes. Dirker kept snapping that whip until both men quit screaming and went limp, their backs like bleeding meat. Cabe came to his senses about then and threw two Yankees out of the way, making for Dirker and then that whip licked him across the face with an explosion of biting agony that dropped him to his knees. It lashed out again and ripped into his cheeks, opened his nose in a ragged laceration. Then he was down and near senseless and that whip clawed at his face again and again and again.

The next thing Cabe knew, he was in a field with maybe a hundred other Confederate soldiers. They were force-marched to the Mississippi River where they were loaded onto the rotting hulks of old steamboats. They were packed into the lower decks and the next week or so was spent down there in the filthy, cold blackness, eating and sleeping and living on stone coal that was two-feet deep. The boat took them up the Mississippi via St. Louis to Alton, Illinois where they were loaded into cattle cars for the trip to Chicago. By the time they reached port, there were dozens of staring corpses packed down there with them...men who had succumbed to the cold, starvation, disease.

In Chicago, the Confederate soldiers were marched some two miles to Camp Douglas through icy mud and stagnant water. Their wet uniforms frozen stiff as steerhide. People came out to gawk and stare and jeer the columns of beaten Southerners...though many did seem sympathetic and some looked almost ashamed at it all. Children sometimes threw things. Other times they waved and smiled. At least...until their parents told them better.

Cabe spent six months at Camp Douglas.

Originally erected as a training base for the Union Army, it had been converted into a POW camp after the Confederate surrender at Fort Donelson. There were over 7,000 prisoners and a single surgeon to see to their needs which were many. The camp was a cesspool of standing water, unburied corpses, rotting bones, rampant disease, and vermin. Rats roamed the grounds freely, feeding off the dead and sometimes the living who were simply too weak and sick to move. Men froze death. Men were beaten to death. Men were executed and tortured for the most minor offenses. Famine killed hundreds. Outbreaks of smallpox and dysentery killed hundreds more. The water was polluted with run-off from the latrines to the point that wounds cleansed with the foul stuff quickly became infected with gangrene. In the summer, the camp became a hive of buzzing flies and biting mosquitoes which filled the air in dense clouds. The unburied dead and heaped refuse became breeding grounds for maggots and rats.

The guards were called "The Hospital Rats" and were sadistic beyond reason, often preferring to toss food into the garbage rather than see the prisoners eat it. They beat men mercilessly, made them stand naked in the snow, and often held lotteries as to which prisoner could survive the longest without food or medical care. An average of eighteen prisoners died each day. Death wagons were pulled through the camp on an irregular basis, cadavers stacked upon them like cordwood in tangles of broomstick-thin limbs and hollowed faces. Often those near-death were thrown on as well. The wagons were often left to broil in the sun for days at a time until the heaped corpses literally shuddered and writhed from the action of feasting worms and rats, expanding gases.

Cabe had not been fed very well while in the CSA.

By the time of Pea Ridge, he was down from his trim 170 pounds to a gaunt 140...but by the time he left Camp Douglas as part of a prisoner exchange, he weighed barely over a hundred pounds. A stick figure scrawled hurriedly by a child's hand, one dressed in rags and sewn-together bits of uniform and filth-caked blankets.

After a short stay in a Confederate hospital, Cabe was mustered back into the 2nd Arkansas which was merged with Bragg's Army of Tennessee. Cabe saw action at Murfreesboro, was under General Joe Johnston's ill-fated attempt to relieve the Union siege of Vicksburg. And, afterwards...Chickamauga, Chattanooga, the Atlanta Campaign. He was badly wounded by shrapnel during the Carolinas Campaign, but survived to stand with his brothers when the Army of Tennessee surrendered in North Carolina in April, 1865.

After the war he drove steers from Texas up to Kansas, worked as a nightherder, a railroad detective, and rode shotgun on a bullion stage into California. He took up bounty hunting not long after.

But for all he had seen, all he had done, the horrors of war and the living nightmares of Camp Douglas, one event still overshadowed all else...his capture in Morgan's Woods following the Battle of Pea Ridge.

And his first meeting with Jackson Dirker.

The man who would become his own personal bogeyman and haunt his dreams for years and, very often, his waking moments.

II

The job of county sheriff was not an easy one.

Jackson Dirker kept busy seven days a week, very often putting in fifteen-hour days. Besides enforcing law and order in the county—no easy feat with wild boomtowns like Whisper Lake and Frisco under his jurisdiction—Dirker was also charged with the upkeep of the county jail, serving court orders, and maintaining order in police court. He spent several days a week giving evidence at trials, arranging prisoner transfers, overseeing his deputies, and charging through the mountain of paperwork all this entailed. He was also something of a fire inspector, health inspector, and sanitation commissioner. He was called in to settle disputes between the mining companies and the local army of independent prospectors, townsfolk and immigrants populations, Indians and Mormon enclaves. He was part soldier and part diplomat, part clerk and part regulator.

He was everything and all to the folks of Beaver County.

When good things happened, he was the last one to know. But when the shit rained down, he was expected to be the first on the scene with the biggest shovel.

But for all its trouble, the position was also quite lucrative.

As a high-ranking county official appointed by the territorial governor himself, Dirker was also the county's chief tax collector. And he kept 10% of everything he brought in, which was quite a bit. He also collected licensing fees from saloons, brothels, and gambling houses. This, along, with dispensing county contracts for new roads and bridges, brought Dirker upwards of $30,000 a year.

He also owned the St. James Hostelry, which in itself was a fairly profitable venture. But he had nothing to do with that. His wife, Janice, ran the entire enterprise. From the purchase of the hotel some four years before to its renovation and operation, Janice was completely in charge.

For Jackson Dirker was a busy man.

He spent more time these days pouring over arrest records and selling the property of tax delinquents than running down fugitives—these tasks he dispensed to his deputies more often than not—but there were still things he liked to keep his hand in. Things the people expected of him.

Things that were simply too dirty to pass down to his deputies.

And these were the things that haunted Dirker.

Because when he threw it all together in his mind, mixed it up like some foul stew, the stink of it all made him wince. So he slid it to the back burner where the smell wasn't so bad and simply brooded over it.

Because, in his thinking, Whisper Lake was a cauldron that was getting ready to boil over. And when that happened, a lot of people were going to get burned.

There was the vigilante problem. Dirker didn't know who they were—though he had certain suspicions—but he had no doubt they existed. Some vigilance committee that had formed to harass the local Mormons. The townsfolk blamed the Mormons anytime anything went wrong. And with all the disappearances out in the hills and the savage slaughter of no less than a dozen miners so far, people were scared. Dirker understood that. But to put the blame on the Mormons when those murders were clearly the work of a marauding dog or wolf pack was ridiculous. Dirker had put bounties on the animals and as far as the missing people went, shit, this was mining country. People came and went by the hundreds each month.

The real criminals here were the vigilantes.

And what they were doing was stirring up a mess of trouble. For already there was talk of Mormon militias out seeking revenge. The Mormons were building themselves a town up on the Beaver River and people seemed to see this as evidence that the Mormons were up to no good. Again, ridiculous. As county sheriff, Dirker found them by far to be the easiest group to manage. He had much more trouble with the gentiles. The mines had brought in squatters and immigrants and outlaws. Shootings and knifings were commonplace and not a one of those incidents had ever involved the Mormons.

They were insular, isolationist, but God-fearing and law-abiding from what Dirker had seen in these past five years as county sheriff.

But, for some reason, people just couldn't swallow that.

Maybe it was because they hated anything they didn't understand or maybe it was because of Deliverance, another Mormon town about four miles outside of Whisper Lake. Something had happened there, something had gone bad, it was said, and the town had gone bad with it. There were crazy rumors of devil-worship and witchcraft and even the Mormons themselves shunned the place. Dirker figured Deliverance had merely splintered from the teachings of Joseph Smith and become perhaps more puritanical and offbeat, but all those stories were nonsense.

He himself hadn't been over to Deliverance in months and months.

Last time was when he'd provided an escort for a federal prisoner wagon passing through Beaver County. They'd stopped in Deliverance to water their horses. The place was very clannish, very odd, but the people were peaceable enough, if not exactly friendly.

No, the Mormons and Deliverance were just another symptom of the cancer that was eating away the heart of Whisper Lake. Vigilantes. Mormon militias. Outlaws. Immigrants. Crazy miners. Weird animal attacks. Yes, it was all building and it was going to blow.

And into this steaming stew had come Tyler Cabe hunting his deranged maniac.

That gave Dirker another headache.

He didn't need another killer stirring up the population. And he sure as hell didn't need Cabe constantly baiting him and rubbing the war in his face. If it kept on, there was going to be trouble. And although Dirker was a fair man and an honest one, he fully realized he could only be pushed so far.

And if Cabe kept pushing, there could only be one outcome.

God help him, if he made a nuisance of himself.

With all this bubbling away in his brain and making his temples throb, Dirker poured himself a cup of coffee. As he brought the tin cup to his lips, the door opened and the wind blew in, scattering papers from his desk.

Pete Slade stood there in the doorway, water dripping from the brim of his pinch-crowned hat.

"Shut that damn door," Dirker told him, maybe a little more harshly than intended.

Slade did.

He was Dirker's undersheriff. Whereas Henry Wilcox was big and fleshy, Slade was long and lank, a mustache just as thick as a grooming brush sprouting from beneath his nose. It completely covered his mouth. Slade was a dependable man and a tough one. He regularly hunted down horse thieves and gunmen single-handedly in the mountains.

And right then he looked scared, looked weary...looked *something*.

"Sheriff," he managed and that voice was filled with dread. "Sheriff...we got us a murder."

Dirker stared at him, wondering why a simple killing had him so spooked to the point of being physically ill. But, deep down, he knew it would be nothing simple.

"Bad?" he said.

Slade nodded. "Dear Christ...I...I never seen nothing like it..."

12

Once upon a time, Sunrise had been a booming gold town, but the ore had all but played out within a year or two and now it was nothing more than a little placer camp. A collection of hollow-eyed buildings and skeletal cabins, it sat on a little gravel butte between two towering rises of shale that sheltered it from the elements. The town was maybe two miles as the crow flies from Whisper Lake, but in reality more than a dozen along treacherous roads that climbed steep hills and plunged into rugged canyons.

It was isolated, hard to reach, and pretty much forgotten in its remote location. Except by the placer miners that worked the mountain streams and the prospectors who came there but two, three times a year to provision up at the remaining general store. A place that was a combination store, brothel, assayer's office, and saloon.

It had whiskey. It had women. It had gambling.

And for the hard luck miners that refused to move on when the real deposits dried up, it was home. If you broke your ass panning for gold from sunup to sundown, you might get a few nuggets...enough, at least, to keep you in whiskey and gambling until it was time to crawl off to one of the dozens of abandoned homes and buildings to sleep it off. Most of these places were little better than shacks. Many had been torn down for firewood. But if you weren't too choosy and didn't mind the wind howling through the walls or the rain dripping through the roof, you had yourself a bunk.

That was life in a failed mining town.

***

It was night and Sunrise was dark.

The red-earth that showed through clumps of witchgrass and broomweed had turned to mud with the passing of the storm. Everywhere, it seemed, water dripped and pooled and ran.

Jack Turner, pissed to the high seventh on Taos Lightening, was leaning up against a shack across the road from the store. He was shaking the dew off his lily—and pissing most of it right down his leg—when he saw the riders coming in down the high trail. Though his vision wasn't much after all the juice he'd swallowed and the night was just blacker than a mineshaft, he could see that there were maybe six or seven of them.

Quiet forms on quiet mounts.

No talking, no laughing, no griping. No nothing. Just the sound of hooves sinking into that muck and being pulled out again. The rustle of cloth and the muted jingle of spurs and equipment. They rode down into the remains of Sunrise single-file in that busy flurry of silence.

Turner stood there, swaying, his business in his hand, thinking for one crazy moment that the riders' eyes...all of them...shined a luminous yellow-green in the darkness. Like the eyes of wolves reflected by firelight. But then it was gone and he blinked, figured it was just the hooch kicking up hell in his brain.

Sometimes, you got a belly full of that stuff, you saw all sorts of things that weren't there.

The riders came on, just as silent as tombstone marble. Turner was going to call out to them, but he was just too damn drunk.

He slipped into the shack, threw the bolt on the door so someone else wouldn't fall on top of him, found his bedroll on the floor and it was enough for him, enough for one night. As he drifted off, the riders passed by his shack, then paused outside the store, their horses snorting. For one moment, Turner smelled something, something sharp and musky like the stench from a snakepit...but he did not acquaint it with the riders.

Maybe it was just his britches.

He passed out.

***

Inside the store, Hiley was telling a tall tale of a gigantic gold nugget he'd pulled out of a streambed in California during the big rush of '49. How the damn thing was so heavy he near threw out his back dragging it up the hillside. Said it took two mules and three stout men to get it up into the assayer's office there. "But I made it, all right," he told them. "Shit if I didn't. It kept me in booze, cards, and hot women for near two months. Maybe if I'd been smart, I'd have banked it, but, damn, nobody ever said I was smart."

"Amen to that," a scraggly miner said, tearing off a strip of jerky with his remaining teeth.

There was laughter at that.

Hiley laughed, too. He could afford to laugh. Of all the men in the room, Hiley was the only one really making it. He owned the store. He owned the rooms above. He took a juicy cut from what his whores took in. The booze was his. The barrels and sacks of dry goods. The sides of ham and salted beef. Anything worth having in Sunrise belonged to Hiley. He'd long ago given up hardrock mining, deciding and deciding wisely that there was more money to be made selling than digging and panning.

While most of the men in the room were a slat-thin, desperate-looking bunch whose worldly possessions consisted of a pick, a sluice box, and the ratty, stained clothes on their backs, Hiley was ruddy-cheeked with a belly just as round and full as a medicine ball. That gut was a source of endless barbs, but Hiley took them all, smiled, and proudly said it was merely a trapping of success. As he was often wont to point out: "When you got a tool like mine, boys, you gotta build a shed over it."

There was a plank bar down one side and maybe a dozen grubby men pushed up to it. There were a few tables where the whores were working their prospects, trying to part the ragged, leather-faced men from the gold dust they'd collected in their buckskin pokes. Under the glare of hurricane lamps a half dozen others were playing a hand of poker with greasy cards and well-thumbed chips.

The whores were laughing, the men were drinking, the gamblers were losing…and all and all it was an average night in Sunrise and by dawn the only one richer would be Hiley.

The double-doors opened and two men in gray dusters stepped in. They wore wide-brimmed hats that thrust their faces into pools of shadow. Their eyes seemed to glisten like wet copper.

Everyone stopped what they were doing, watched the strangers.

The two of them stood there a moment, looking around, drinking it all in. Behind them, out in the darkness, a horse snorted…or something did. The strangers closed the doors. They looked on all and everyone with flat, dead eyes, hungry eyes. The eyes of wolves taking in a tasty herd of steer, wondering which one they would take down first.

The men looked at each other, nodded, then came into that crowded room just as smooth and oily as serpents sliding up out of a crevice. Their spurs rang out on the plank flooring, their dusters swished. They took their time, admiring the racks of picks and shovels, the barrels of salt pork and beans, the soiled doves working the miners. They seemed to like what they saw, grinning with smiles of narrow yellow teeth. One was bearded, the other clean-shaven with pitted scars along his jawline.

Together, they leaned against the bar, set identical sawed-off Remington pumps on its surface.

They did not speak and all eyes were on them.

Maybe everyone was smelling something bad coming off these two, some inexplicable, savage odor that turned their insides to sauce. Because it was definitely there. A strange and heady odor of slaughterhouses and bone pits. The smell, say, wild dogs might carry with them from hunting and scavenging, chewing on dead things.

Hiley managed to clear his throat of whatever was lodged in it. "You gents thirsty?" he asked.

The bearded one laughed and it was a hollow, barking sound. "You hear that, Hood? Man wants to know if we're thirsty." He laughed again. "You thirsty, son?"

Hood stroked that scarred jaw. "Reckon I am. But I don't see my favorite drink distilled anywheres. Figure I'll have to tap my own keg in my own way. You understand my meaning, Cook?"

"Suspect I do."

A miner at the bar with a Remington model 1858 .44 hanging at his hip, said, "What the hell's that supposed to mean?"

"Here that, Hood? This one wants to know what that means."

That made Hood laugh. A staccato, metallic laugh like a hammer banging at a forge. It was not a human sound. "I heard him. Figure this feller just don't understand what we're about is all."

"Maybe you should show him," Cook said.

"Maybe I'll have to."

Hiley, behind the bar, his hand resting on the stock of an Army carbine just out of view, licked his lips carefully. "We don't want no trouble here, gents. All of us are just drinking and playing cards and minding our own. I suggest you do the same."

Hood was grinning again and it was the sort of grin a corpse might have...two months in the ground. "That some sort of threat?"

The miner with the .44 nodded. "Damn straight it is, boy. You can either be sociable and peaceful...or things can happen the hard way. There's only two of you and there's about two dozen of us, give or take. You might want to weigh that out."

"I suspect I will," Hood said, "being outgunned and all."

Cook wiped the back of his hand over his beard, said, "You'll have to excuse us. Hungry is what we are. Bellies are just plain empty, growling something fierce."

It was Hiley's turn to laugh now, only it was more of a nervous tittering. "Shit, boys, all you had to do was say so."

"Believe we just did," Cook reminded him.

Hiley didn't seem to catch that or want to. He could feel every set of eyes in the place watching him now, seeing how he was going to handle these hardcases. He knew the situation had not been pacified yet, that just about everyone in the room was armed and lead could begin flying at any moment. He did not want this. This was his place and bullets caused damage. That cost money. Bodies he could sweep out with the trash...but stock, now that wasn't easily replaceable up here on the far left side of the Devil's asshole.

"What you boys need," he said, "is a some meat in your bellies. That'll fix you up."

Hood and Cook looked at each other and laughed. Then they looked around the room, taking in all they saw. Their faces were drawn and sallow, their eyes wide, unblinking, just as dark as open graves.

"Meat," Cook said. "You hear that? Feller here's offering us meat."

"I heard it and I figure that's right neighborly of 'em," Hood said, wiping drool from his lips. "Because meat's what we came for. Fresh meat. I like my meat raw. That's what. Nice and raw. Like that taste of blood, hear? Puts iron in my pants."

Some eyes widened at that. Others narrowed. Bodies shifted in chairs. Fingers slid down towards holstered pistols. One whore made a face, another smiled...finding these men *interesting*.

The miner with the .44, said, "What is it you boys do?"

Cook drummed his fingers on the bar. Hiley saw that a pelt of reddish hair covered the man's wrist, that it flowed over the back of his hand like wild grass and furred his fingers...which were oddly long, thin enough to pick locks.

"We're what you call Hide-Hunters," Cook told him. "Thing is we don't hunt animal hides. We hunt the other sort."

The miner was about to say something about that and maybe Hiley was, too—or any number of others—but there was a pounding at the door. A thudding sound and not like a fist would make, but maybe the butt of a rifle. Whatever it was, it kept banging away.

"You gonna answer that, Hiley?" one of the poker players said, but in such a voice like maybe he thought it wouldn't be a good idea.

Hiley looked at the strangers, then at the others. He swallowed hard. "I suppose I'll have to."

"It would be neighborly," Hood said. "Wouldn't want them out there bursting in uninvited and all."

All eyes on him again, Hiley went to the doors, taking the carbine with him. He stopped a few feet away, seemed to smell something or hear something that just laid on him wrong. He looked back into the bar, maybe for help, maybe for divine guidance, but got none.

"See who it is," someone said, a strange edge to their voice.

Swallowing again, Hiley threw open the doors.

In the barroom, people saw that darkness out there just as black as bubbling pitch. Saw it shifting and swirling and oozing. Then there was motion. A blur. A wild, rending activity. Hiley shouted, maybe he screamed. But it all happened so fast no one could do anything but jump to their feet, reach for their guns.

And by then, it was over.

Hiley was gone.

The doors swung shut and there was a spattering of blood on one of them.

In a wild, shrieking voice, a miner said, "Something grabbed him! Something took him! *Something dragged him out into the night...*"

Those words echoed and died in the silence.

No one moved.

No one spoke.

No one did a damn thing. Maybe they were all waiting for someone else to do something. Herd instinct. They would all move...but not until they were led. That's how things worked in tense situations and this one was so tense, apprehension hung in the air thick as fog.

Silence.

Blood glistening on the grubby plank door.

Outside, there rose a shrill howling sound that went through everyone like a sharp knife.

The miner with the .44 started moving, then stopped. The hairs were standing up on the back of his neck and his balls had gone small and hard and cold. He turned to the strangers, unleathered his pistol. "You two! Goddammit, you two brought this!" The pistol shook in his hand. "What's out there? What the hell sort of game you playing?"

Cook just smiled...and it was funny, but his teeth had gone just as long and shiny as leather punches, his lips shriveling away from them. His eyes were huge, glassy, just as green as emeralds. The pupils were horribly dilated.

"Ain't no game, friend," Hood said and it seemed that shaggy beard of his had crawled up his jaw, was encroaching on his cheekbones. The bones of his face were thrusting out, stretching the skin taut as a drumhead, the nose flattening and going canine. His jaws pushed out, teeth flashing now like knifeblades.

Somebody started screaming.

The miner backed away. "Dear Jesus," he uttered.

"Ain't got nothing to do with him," Cook said, his face a skullish, wolflike expanse of jutting bone and deep hollows. His teeth were long and sharp and his voice dropped two, three octaves to the growl of a rabid dog. *"Nothing to do with him whatsoever..."*

Hood advanced on the miner, his eyes gone yellow as swamp gas, the pupils just pinpricks of black. The miner saw those long teeth like hooked needles...and then Hood leaped and those needles were in the miner's face, shearing the flesh from the bone.

And the barroom came alive with shooting and shouting and screaming. People tried to run and they ran into each other, knocked each other out of the way, went right over the top of one another. Upstairs there was the shattering of glass and thumping and thudding sounds. More screams. Guns going off. People shouting.

Hell had come calling...and some fool had let it in.

Just as a gang of miners made it to the doors, they exploded in and five or six men thundered in on horses just as black as midnight. Like Cook and Hood, they wore wide-brimmed hats and dusters. And like them they had wolf faces and sharp teeth. Tables went over, cards and chips raining in the air. The horses plowed bodies to the floor and their hooves crushed and stomped bone and flesh. The riders...the Hide-Hunters...dove from their mounts into the mass of screeching, fighting people. Their hands were furry, the long fingers ending in claws like the talons of hunting hawks.

The carnage began.

**

Upstairs, a whore named Milly Short was trying to push her white, heaving bulk under a bed. A miner had been on top of her, pumping away like a derrick, and then the door blew in, coming apart like kindling and something like a man...but, God, *not* a man...had pulled him off her and dragged him out into the corridor. She heard a tearing, ripping sound and the miner tried to make it back into the room, maybe to his gun. But something had hold of him and dragged him back out there.

His fingernails clawed ruts into the floor as he was pulled away.

His face had been pinched gray and bloody and Milly had never in her born years seen such a grimace of absolute horror.

And Milly, caught in some gray netherworld between shock and terror, tried to make it under the bed. But she was a large woman, fleshy and full and wide, and it was like trying to force a barrel through a bullet hole. There was a deafening roar and then the sound of spurred boots coming into the room.

Milly looked over her shoulder, sweat beading her face.

She saw a set of worn cavalry boots. Saw drops of blood falling onto them, splattering.

Something grabbed her by the ankle, flipped her over...and she was staring up at a lewd face that belonged to a demonic wolf, but whose owner walked upright like a man. Lips shivered back from teeth like icicles and a low, snarling sound came from the tunnel of that dark throat.

Milly screamed and thrashed and the thing pulled her to her feet as if she were weightless. She fought and kicked and hit, crying, screaming, saying: *"Dear Christ...dear Christ in Heaven...what is this? What is this?"*

The beast pressed her to him like a long lost lover and she could smell the spicy, raw tang of its bloody pelt, felt herself being swallowed by those huge yellow-green eyes full and leering like sacrificial moons. Loops of bloody drool dangled from the gnashing teeth...and a voice...not human nor animal, but somewhere in-between said, *"It's the skin medicine, ma'am, it does things to a man..."*

And the voice became a growling and she was crushed in the beast's arms, her bones snapping, her insides pressed to jelly and foaming from her mouth. Then the teeth sank in her throat, nearly severing her head in a single bite

***

Downstairs, it was certainly no better.

The beasts were clawing and chomping, severing limbs and opening bellies. Bones were splintering beneath powerful jaws and flesh was divorced from quivering meat. And the screams of the dying were only eclipsed by the howling of their tormentors and the firing of guns. The air was thick with smoke and mists of red.

Everywhere there was blood and wreckage and bodies and things that could have been men but were not men, devouring and eating and tearing. It looked like some grisly scene from a medieval hell.

A whore trying to leap away over the dead and dying was bowled over as a decapitated head struck her in the back.

A man crying out for Jesus and Mary was battered senseless with his own dismembered limbs.

Two of the Hide-Hunters, laughing with hideous mirth, gored a gambler to death one bite at a time.

A miner named Danny Smith crawled on his hands and knees through a sea of blood, half out of his mind. His Colt was in his hand and he saw the beasts and saw people shooting at them and often just hitting one another. He saw a window explode inward in a shower of glass and the darkness poured in, became a clutch of clawed hands that dragged two miners out into the night. What seemed seconds later, one of them was tossed back into the barroom, tumbling across the floor in a heap. He was bloody and scratched, his clothes hanging in strips...but he was alive.

Alive and screaming, begging for help.

But there was a noose around his throat and a length of rope leading out into the night. Suddenly, as he tried to crab-crawl in Smith's direction, the rope snapped tight as wire and he was yanked across the floor. Pulled by the throat up and out the window again.

Smith saw the door standing open, the night stygian and flowing like black silk. He could make it, knew he could make it. On hands and knees, he made a wild charge for it, his mouth babbling nonsense even he could not understand.

He got to his feet and one of the beasts stepped through the doorway, its duster crimson with blood. It held the severed hand of a man in one paw, slapped it against its leg. Smith could smell its rancid yellow breath, see graveyards and gallows reflected in those green sucking pits it had for eyes. Its wolfish face grinned with all those teeth. *"Going somewhere, friend?"*

Smith let out a wild cry and pumped two bullets into the Hide-Hunter's belly and it laughed with a cruel, mocking sound. The eyes blazed with triumph and one of its hands swiped at Smith's belly.

Smith felt the impact...but figured he was okay, okay, but then he saw that his abdomen was open in a bleeding gash and that his viscera was hanging out in glistening clocksprings.

He stood there, shocked and amazed by it.

He wasn't standing long.

***

And upstairs, there was one survivor.

Up to three minutes before, there had been two others. One was slaughtered by the Hide-Hunters...another took his life before the claws fell on him.

And now there was just one.

A man. His name was Provo and he hid in a closet. He was just another hard luck miner with a bad liver and lungs crystallizing from silicosis, the much-dreaded miner's disease. When the bloodbath began...when the beasts came leaping through windows and hammering down doors...he had been waiting for an overweight prostitute called Abilene Sue. Waiting alone in her room.

Quickly then, he darted into a closet.

In the cramped, close darkness he heard the sound of boots and the jingle of spurs as the beasts looked into the room, departed. He had not heard a sound of them upstairs in over ten minutes now. Even downstairs, it had gone to a grim silence. There was a finality to that sound. A cessation, he thought, of hostilities.

His heart pounding and his breath wheezing in his lungs, Provo opened the door a sliver.

The room appeared to be empty.

His ears listened and heard nothing but a distant dripping, a loose board on the roof rattling in the wind.

Quietly, he slipped out of his hole. His chest was tight and pained, he could barely draw a breath. He stepped out into the corridor...and promptly went on his ass in a pool of blood.

And in the light of a single oil lamp, what he saw...dear Christ.

Blood was sprayed and spilled everywhere. It was pooled on the floor and painted on the walls and even sprinkled on the ceiling. There was a smeared handprint in it just a few feet from him. There were bodies in the corridor with him, parts of them. He saw heads, limbs, a single gutted torso like something hanging in a butcher's shop. There was tissue and flesh and the raw, metallic stink of it got down into his belly and pulled everything back up with it.

Provo vomited and sobbed and coughed.

It could get no worse than this, it could surely get no worse.

But then it did.

He heard something like a low, rasping/snarling sound and one of the beasts stepped from a doorway. It looked very much like an animal, like some wolf right down to the jutting snout and luminous green eyes and feral teeth. But it was dressed like a man, leaning there against the doorway and looking…amused. Yes, *amused*. It had the appetites of a blood-maddened beast, but the brain and overall form of a man. A single claw scratched at a pointed ear.

Another beast came up the steps, walking hunched over slightly, its nostrils flaring, tasting, smelling and then…*yes*, finding prey. Finding Provo. A ribbon of drool fell from its lips. Its brow was exaggerated, furry and jutting, shading those jade eyes in bony hollows.

Provo pissed himself.

But he could not speak, not even think of begging for his life…he was simply awed by these things, these demons what had burst the gates of hell. A stench came off them, an ugly odor of blood and meat. The beasts seemed to nod to one another, thick lips pulling back from those anxious teeth.

A third one came up the steps, elbowed past the others.

The beasts grunted and snapped at one another.

This latest one wore a duster, a wide-brimmed hat like the others. Its shirt was open to the waist, the hairy and oddly muscular chest heaving with each breath it sucked through that blood-dripping maw. It carried a Colt pistol in each clawed hand. And they were hands, Provo saw, not pads or paws, but hands. Human hands. But grotesquely long and narrow, the fingers incredibly thin and taloned.

It spit a gob of blood on the floor. Its teeth unclenched like a spiked mantrap and it made a gargling, guttural sound in its throat that became a voice of all things." *You make it past us, you little fuck, we let you live…*"

The others laughed…a strangled, wet laughter.

Maybe it was instinct or terror or God-knows-what, but Provo sprang to his feet and decided to run the gauntlet. He charged right at the Hide-Hunters and such was his ferocity, they actually stepped back. And maybe he would have made it. Maybe.

But something tripped him up.

Something sent him crashing into that greasy stew of human remains and as he squirmed and fought on the floor to be free...he saw it was entrails. Human entrails spread over the floor like wet ropes and he had stepped into them in his mad dash and snared his foot.

Shrieking, he tried to untangle himself. But they were oily and rubbery and moist. He only tangled himself worse. The first two beasts stepped over to him, almost nonchalantly. Taking hold of him and heaving, they pulled his limbs free, one after the other like a child pulling the wings from a fly.

Provo tried to wriggle away, but his life's blood pissed in an ocean around him. He gagged and coughed and his mind went with a warm wet sound that only he could hear.

The Hide-Hunter with the Colts came over to him.

It pulled his head up off the floor, staring at those glazed, shocked eyes. It stuck the barrel of one pistol into his mouth.

"*I dearly hate to see these things suffer,*" it said in a gravelly voice.

And blew the back of Provo's head out. It kept pulling the trigger until there was nothing but a smoking hole at the rear of the man's head and the slugs chewed into the wall.

It dropped him, leaving the pistol in his mouth.

Then the three of them went downstairs before the best meat was gone.

***

In his shack across the road, Jack Turner—the last human being in Sunrise—came out of a drunken slumber to the sound of scratching, of clawing, of something like nails being drawn over the outside of his door.

An animal. Something.

Maybe a wolf, he thought.

Damn things. Probably hungry, probably forced down out of the high country for food. But it wouldn't get any tonight.

Turner could hear it panting and sniffing and scratching like a dog at a rabbit hole.

Turner threw his bedroll aside and took up his .36 Patterson.

Carefully, silently, he pulled the bolt and kicked open the door.

It wasn't a wolf that he saw...not really. The moon was out, riding a lattice of clouds, and it was bright enough that Turner could see it was a man he was looking at.

A man with the face of a beast.

Whoever or whatever it was, wore a hide poncho that flapped in the wind like a campaign flag. A boiling, hot, nauseous odor blew off him. Turner felt his insides run like wax.

That face.

That godawful devil's face.

To the right it was the monstrous face of a wolf, furry and green-eyed and yellow-toothed...but to the left, just the skinless skull of a beast covered in ligament and muscle, a scarified black cavity where the eye should have been. The skin was perfectly bisected as if some invisible line were drawn down the center of that awful face...half flesh, half bone.

A discolored tongue licked over the spiked teeth.

A horrible, wizened voice seem to come from some great distance, leagues away, echoing through the mountains and riding that black November wind like coveted sin. *"Welcome to hell,"* it said.

And Turner expected those claws, those teeth.

But the beast brought up a sawed-off shotgun and gave him both barrels at point-blank range. The impact blew his chest to fragments and threw him back inside the shack.

Then whatever it was, stalked off.

It made an odd, droning sound that could only have been humming. Amused, satisfied humming.

13

While Hell paid a little visit to Sunrise and Sheriff Dirker got his first look at the remains of Katherine Modine...Tyler Cabe, unable to sleep, was over at the Cider House Saloon pulling back beers and slugging shots of Kentucky bourbon. He told himself he wasn't going to make a habit of it. He was here to work, to hunt down the Sin City Strangler (if he was indeed squatting hereabouts)…but, sometimes, a man needed a taste. And particularly when that man was Tyler Cabe and the war was all over him, engulfing him in a bleak and horrible smell of death and burnt powder. When it got so the memories were so vivid, so very real that you could taste the blood and steel and despair on your tongue, only alcohol would chase them away.

The Cider House was essentially a log house with timber walls and a rough-hewn floor of green wood that had split and cracked in wide gashes. The roof was thrown together out of planks and scraps and leaked like a sprinkling can. A set of dusty windows overlooked the muddy street, ore samples lining the sill. There was a carved mahogany bar against one wall, a real fancy outfit, and it looked as out of place at the Cider House as lace ribbon on slopped hog. It was similar to a dozen other taverns in Whisper Lake…a place tossed-up while there was still money to be had, but surely not built to last.

Men of every stripe were gathered over steel mugs and shot glasses—drifters, tramps, miners, company men, trappers down from the high elevations for a few days of drinking and fucking—and the atmosphere was thick and close and cramped. It stunk of unwashed bodies and wet saddle leather, dirty wool and soiled buckskin, booze, smoke, and dirty dreams.

Cabe was listening to a tall, lean fellow named Henry Freeman who claimed to be a Texas Ranger and had the tin star to prove it. He wore a duck-canvas duster and a stiff-brimmed Stetson. Both spotless and gleaming. His face was gaunt, his eyes just as dead and flat as shoe buttons. Despite being a Texas Ranger, as he claimed, he did not have a Texas accent. Though, of course, the Rangers probably had folks from everywhere in their ranks by that point. But the way he talked…wasn't like a Southerner or a Yankee. An odd, even tone without inflection.

Cabe drank him in along with the whiskey and warm beer, didn't particularly care for his flavor, but what he had to say…that was something else.

"Way I got it figured, Cabe, is this," Freeman said, studying his own dour reflection in the cracked bar mirror. "Our friend...this Sin City Strangler, as they like to call him...he's smart. He's not your average criminal. I'm of a mind that he's of superior intelligence. That this is all some sort of game with him, you know, sort of catch-me-if-you-can. There's a lot of money riding on his head and he gets a kick out of that."

Cabe took a swallow of beer. "What makes you think he's so damn smart?"

Freeman, who made a habit of never looking at who he was talking to, said, "It's obvious, isn't it?"

"Well, maybe you ought to spell it out for a dumb Arkansas farm boy like me."

Freeman smiled thinly. "He jumps from mining town to mining town, a fish...no, a *shark*...that swims in the sea of the population. Mysterious, unknown, unstoppable, just another face in an ocean of them. And mining towns, I don't need to remind you, are not like the small towns you and I sewed our oats in—people come and people go. By the hundreds. Now how can you hope to track a fellow like that?"

Cabe thought it over, arched an eyebrow. "Same way you bring a mountain cat down what's been eating your stock...you lay low, you wait, you take your time. Sooner or later, this sumbitch will show his hand. His ego's too big and his head's too full of shit not to. And when he shows, then you bag the cocksucker."

Freeman looked offended somehow. "You simplify things, friend. Simplify and over-simplify, I think."

"I'm a simple sort," Cabe told him. "I'm hungry, I eat. I'm tired, I sleep. I'm thirsty, I drink. I see some sadistic ass-knocker out killing women, I piss lead into him and collect my money."

Freeman claimed to be on the Strangler's trail, too. But unlike Cabe who'd picked up the scent in Nevada, Freeman said he'd been scouting the killer since West Texas. Said the Strangler started his killings down in Mexico, continued through Texas and then made his next stop in California, then onto Nevada...and, just possibly, Whisper Lake.

It all bothered Cabe somewhat.

When he hunted a man—and he'd hunted dozens and dozens, everything from cattle rustlers to bank robbers—he made it a religion to find out everything and anything he could about his target. He listened to facts, rumors, suppositions. Read anything that was printed. Corresponded with lawmen and jailers and common folk alike. He followed every thread. He believed in being prepared. Yet…Freeman claimed the Strangler had been busy down Mexico way and carved-up a few in Texas before California. Cabe, in all his researches, had never heard a spot about the killer before San Francisco.

Now how could that be?

Cabe pulled out his Bull Durham and rolled himself a cigarette, thought it over. Kept thinking it over as he stared at the huge rattlesnake skin draped above the bar mirror. In the morning, he was going to wire a few lawmen he knew in Texas, see what fruit it bore.

The air in the saloon was smoky, dirty and oily as the bodies that breathed it. The walls were decorated with the pelts of black bear, fox, and mule deer, stretched and tacked. Jutting in-between were the mounted heads of elk, bighorn sheep, and wolf. A stuffed Gila Monster, mouth open, was squeezed amongst bottles of liquor.

Two burly men were arm-wrestling at a table ringed by men. Money exchanged hands and bets were called and oaths sworn and it got so loud over there, you couldn't even hear the two wrestlers straining and grunting and puffing.

Ten feet away, a group of trappers and hunters were passing a whore back and forth, spinning her around and kissing her. She was drunk and each time she whirled, they tore another article of clothing off of her. Her breasts were free and bouncing and a little trapper in a marten cap kept trying to nip them. As Cabe watched—not really surprised, but certainly amused—she finally fell onto a stack of smelly, salted antelope hides. Then the men took their turns with her.

No one seemed to notice the fornicating.

You spent enough time in places like this, Cabe knew, you stopped paying attention to such things.

"You know what, Texas?" he said to Freeman. "I almost get the impression that you respect the Strangler, that you think he's some slick, upstanding sumbitch playing his gentlemen's game and not some sick, twisted-up crazy."

Freeman had thrown open the flap of his duster now, so that his guns—two fine ivory-handled Remington .44s—were plainly visible, butts forward. Cabe wasn't sure if it was for his benefit or not.

Freeman sipped from his whiskey. "Didn't mean to give you that impression at all, Cabe. I'm just saying our man is like no one else."

"Shit, he's crazy."

"There's no evidence of that."

"No evidence..." Cabe felt the bourbon starting to light a fire in him, sparking dry tinder. "For the love of Jesus and Mary and the Sioux Nation, Texas, he strangles women, rapes 'em, and slits 'em open like prize Arkansas hogs...you don't think that's the work of a crazy man?"

"First off, Cabe, quit calling me Texas," Freeman said calmly, but more than a little irritated. "And secondly, these women he's killed, they're *whores*. I'm not saying that makes it right, all I'm saying is that you don't have to rape that kind. They're only too happy to give it for free. To any man, any time, for a price. They have no respect for their womanhood. They are merchandise, are they not?"

Cabe's eyes were narrowed now. "They're turning coin on what God gave 'em, is all. And why the hell not? I don't see a goddamned thing wrong with it, long as it's of their own free will. Hell, why sit on a goldmine when you can work it?"

Freeman looked offended by that and Cabe supposed it came out the wrong way. Maybe the Texas Ranger was some sort of revivalist, had Jesus on the brain. Maybe that was it.

Freeman cleared his throat. "We're not talking a useful, productive segment of society here, Cabe. We're talking prostitutes, we're talking whores, we're talking trash here, are we not?"

"Don't know about you, Texas, but I find those ladies very productive. And not just for the obvious...some of 'em are damn fine people."

"Like hell they are."

"You got some kind of grudge against 'em, Texas?"

Freeman set his glass down and finally looked Cabe square in the eye with a dark, penetrating stare. "I told you to quit calling me that."

Cabe, feeling the alcohol now and liking it, gave him an exaggerated courtly bow. "Excuse me...*Texas.*"

Freeman was about to address that—you could see it in his eyes, something bubbling away in there like hot tar—but a pair of men down the bar caught his attention. One of them was clean-shaven, oddly regal with an arrogant lilt to his mouth, wore a gray linen suit and an English flat-top cap. The other was unshaven, dressed in a fringed buckskin jacket and Southwestern sombrero.

The fellow in the sombrero was eyeing up Cabe and Freeman. He pulled out a hunting knife, cut himself a chew from a plug of tobacco and worked it carefully in his jaw. Then he spit a stream of brown juice on the floor. Had a look about him that said he dared anyone to mention the fact.

No one did.

Cabe was watching him, too. He didn't know who he was, but he figured his partner was Sir Tom Ian, a legendary pistolman. Ian had come across the pond back in the '70's with some British duke, part of a group that came west to do some hunting. The duke and his people had left, but Ian stayed. Had made himself a name as a shootist and, depending on who you listened to, had put down anywhere between ten to twenty men. Had backed down none other than hotheaded John Wesley Hardin when Hardin made to kill a black soldier in Tulsa. And was something of a hired gun.

As far as Cabe knew, he wasn't wanted for anything. Just another fast gun that danced on the periphery of the law and, probably, on the wrong side of it from time to time.

Freeman turned to him. "You know who that is, Cabe?"

"Sir Tom Ian, I'm thinking."

"Then you're thinking is right," Freeman said. "That gruffy-looking saddletramp with him is Virgil Clay. He's a maniac."

Cabe had heard of him, too.

He was no Sir Tom, but what he lacked in skill and professionalism, he more than made up for in pure rage. He was a blooded killer and not exactly picky about whether he gave it to you in the belly or the back.

Sir Tom raised his shot of rye, nodded to Cabe and Freeman. "To your health, gentlemen."

They reciprocated.

Clay swallowed down two shots of whiskey in rapid succession, burped, and wiped his mouth. That mean stray-cat look in his eyes, he sauntered over, a Navy .36 in a cross-draw scabbard at his left hip. He spat tobacco juice about an inch from the tip of Cabe's boot.

"What's all this talk about whores I'm hearing?" he said. His words were slightly slurred, but sharp as tacks.

Before Cabe could open his mouth, Freeman said, "Name's Freeman, from Texas. My friend here is Tyler Cabe out of Arkansas. He's a bounty hunter. He's hunting the Sin City Strangler."

Brown juice ran down Clay's chin. "What the fuck is a Sin City Stranger?"

"*Strangler*," Cabe corrected him, wondering maybe if that was such a good idea.

"I know what I said. Don't you think I know what I said?"

Freeman stepped in-between them. "The Sin City Strangler is the fellow who's been murdering those prostitutes, carving 'em up."

Clay nodded. "I heard about that." He laughed. "Fucking whores anyhow...who gives a fuck?"

Freeman grinned at that. A compatriot. "Well, Mr. Cabe is inclined to disagree with you. Thinks this fellow out to be run to ground, strung up."

Clay pushed past Freeman now. "That so? Well, Mr. Fucking-Bounty-Hunter-From-Arkansas...what if I was that fellow? What you gonna do about it? Take me in? You'd die trying. Maybe I like carving me whores and you ain't got nothing to say about it. Maybe I wish you'd try."

Cabe made a show of looking him up and down. "Son," he said. "I shit bigger than you."

"Never did see a man so anxious to die," Clay told him.

Freeman said, "Our Mr. Cabe...he don't back down from no one."

Cabe just leaned there against the bar. He could hear all the men in the bar shouting and arguing and telling off-color stories and wild tales—it was a steady, monotonous hum in his ears. A constant like the stink in his nose. But all that faded into the background and he saw only Virgil Clay looking for a fight and Henry Freeman egging it on. Because that's what it was really about here. Freeman didn't like him much, didn't like how he dressed or talked or that he called him "Texas" even when he was told not to...so, he was going to make trouble for him.

That's the sort of bastard he was.

Clay's eyes were like ball bearings. They did not blink, they did not emote...they glared. "Oh, you don't fucking back down from no one, eh? Is that the fact of the matter, you goddamn motherfucking shit-worthless scab? Is that the truth?"

Cabe stood up now. "Yeah, you heard right, you fucking moron. Wipe the drool off your lips and clean the dogshit out of your ears."

Clay was breathing real hard. "You got some kind of sand, Cabe. I'll give you that." He nodded, seemed to relax...but not much. Intimidation wasn't working on this Arkansas boy and reputation didn't seem to count for a squirt of pig shit. This was indeed a quandary. Question was...how to work Cabe into a situation where Clay himself was sure to be victorious? Because, truth be told, most of his victims had been killed with the odds very much on Clay's side. A shot in the back. A bullet from a hidden location. Pistols pulled and fired before his adversary had a chance to even think of such a thing.

Surprise was always Clay's element. He liked it that way. An even fight like this...man to man...he didn't care for it so much. Time to try a little verbal humiliation.

"What happened to yer face, boy?" he said. "Supposed to ride that horse, not get drug behind it on yer nose."

There were a few laughs over that.

Cabe smiled. "It was your mama...she done scratched me up while I was putting the meat to her."

Clay looked like hot iron had been shoved up his ass. He came forward, stopped, turned around, danced a crazy little jig. Sir Tom smiled at him and more than one man stepped away from the bar.

Clay looked Cabe up and down, licked his lips, knew there was a fight brewing here, but couldn't make up his mind how to start it. How to start it and be sure he'd win it, that was. His hand drifted towards his gun.

"You pull down on me," Cabe told him, "and they'll be burying your ass come morning. Think about it, peckerwood."

"Oh, I done thought about it, shithole," Clay said, bits of foamy spit collected up in the corners of his lips like a mad dog. "Done thought about it and decided I'm gonna have to kill your ass dead." He stood there, ready to pull iron, knowing there was no other way to save his reputation. He didn't kill this sonofabitch, every wanna-be in the Territory would ride his ass hard on a daily basis. "Slap leather, Cabe. I'm ready anytime you are."

Cabe chuckled. "C'mon, now. What your *really* saying is could I kindly turn my back so you can drill me from behind like you did all those others. Ain't that so? Well, Clay, I'm afraid I can't oblige."

It was all driving Clay nuts. He was shaking and trembling and sputtering. "Maybe you don't know who the fuck I am. Maybe that's it, Cabe. Maybe I'll give you one chance to get down on your knees and beg for fucking life. And if you don't...boy, time I'm done with you, you'll be sucking my willy and calling me daddy."

"Won't happen, Clay. Just won't happen. I don't back down from no man what squats to piss..."

That sort of insult couldn't go unanswered and Cabe knew it. Something in him was telling him he was falling into his old habits here, getting into drunken fights. Was telling him that this was probably a big mistake, but—what with the whiskey filling his veins—he didn't honestly give a shit.

Clay stood there, visibly shaking.

Somebody told them to take it outside.

Miners and drifters fell out of the way.

Freeman looked smug; Sir Tom grinned.

Cabe felt a tenseness at his groin, felt his guts tighten into coils tight as bedsprings. He was tight and hard and ready to pounce.

Clay said, "Ah, fuck you..." He turned away, made it maybe two, three feet, then came around fast and lethal, the Navy .36 filling his hand. He got off a shot as Cabe brought out his Starr double-action .44 in a smooth, practiced motion. The round just missed Cabe, ripping into the bar. Cabe threw himself to the side as Clay fired again and, falling to the floor, he got off a single shot. The bullet punched a hole in Clay's chest, deflected off a rib, and bounced through his torso, macerating organ and tissue before erupting from a hole just beneath his left armpit.

Clay made a weird gagging/wheezing sound and hit the floor, vomiting out a tangle of blood. He shuddered and went still. The blood that bubbled from his mouth was very dark.

"Dead," someone said. "That sonofabitch is dead."

Hands pulled Cabe to his feet and he shook them off, surprised as he always was at moments like this that he had survived yet again. Some were patting him on the back and saying what a crack shot he was and what a set of balls to get into it with someone like Virgil Clay. Others were calling him a killer and still others were saying something about Clay's father, how he was the real nasty one.

Cabe found he could barely stand. It always got like that. Going into a fight he was all balls and hot blood, coming out of it...just shaky and disoriented. Felt like his legs had no bones, were packed with wet straw.

Sir Tom nudged Clay's body with the tip of his boot. His right thumb hooked into his gunbelt, just above the .44 Bisley hanging there.

Cabe was thinking, *Oh, boy, here it comes...me and Sir Tom...I hope they bury me under a nice tree so I get some shade...*

Sir Tom just smiled. His face was pleasant and easy. "That's one fine piece of shooting, Mr. Cabe. My hat's off to you."

Crazy thing was, he seemed to mean it. Like maybe Clay had been no friend, but just some stray dog that had been following him around and sometimes dogs get run down by horses. Life goes on.

Cabe was going to say something, but then Henry Wilcox—Dirker's massive deputy sheriff—was plowing his way through, men falling out of his way like cut trees.

Everyone seemed to be talking at once and Wilcox listened, understanding perfectly that Virgil Clay wasn't nothing but trash and that this was bound to happen. He told Cabe as much, told him it would go down as self-defense...but, there was such a thing as due process. And until a coroner's inquest, he'd have to be held.

"So, give me your gun," he said, "and we'll take a walk."

Cabe took a step backwards...but knew he really had no choice. So, sighing, handed his weapon to Wilcox. "I want that back," he said. "I carried it since the war, had it converted to cartridge at no little expense—"

"You'll get it back," Wilcox promised him. "Let's go."

"To the jail?"

Wilcox nodded.

As he led him away, Cabe said, "Tell me one thing...does Dirker still have that whip?"

14

So, two cells down from Orville DuChien, Cabe was deposited like so much refuse. He was given an army blanket, a piss pot, a jug of water, and told not to dirty the straw if he could help it. He said he'd do his best.

Wilcox told him he was honestly sorry about having to lock him up, but the sheriff had set down specific rules concerning such things. A man was gunned down or knifed, his assailant had to be locked up until the facts were sorted out. No exceptions.

So Cabe was a prisoner.

He was not truly angry about it, knew and knew damn well it was his own fault, dancing with that inbred shithound Clay...least he was the one locked-up and not toes-up in the mortuary. That was something. His cell was big enough for a cot and a little slip of floor upon which to pace. To either side were the bars separating his from the other holding cells. He tried pacing for a bit, but his head was pounding from the cheap whiskey and excitement. He sat down then, massaging his temples.

He remembered then the farm back in Yell County, up in the foothills of the Ouachitas. It wasn't much of a place—just a plot of land with some hogs and chicken, corn and barley. Cabe's old man rented it from some rich bastard name of Connelly from Little Rock who owned just about everything and everyone in the county. It was but one miserable step up from being a sharecropper. Connelly's monthly rent was so high, that even when things went good—which was seldom—the elder Cabe barely had enough to feed his family.

Tyler lost two sisters to a diphtheria outbreak. His old man had a fatal heart attack in the fields one afternoon. And his mother had a stroke and died while Tyler was off fighting the War Between the States. The land and Connelly's greed had wiped out his kin. The Yankees had burned and looted Connelly into the poorhouse during the war. And that was the only time Tyler Cabe ever cheered for the North.

But thinking of the farm...he could see his old man sitting on a willow stump one morning, dirty and sweaty and beaten from trying to wring a living from the thin soil. "Tyler," he said. "Yer my only boy. Ye ain't the smartest I've ever done seen, but damn if ye ain't the most determined. I figure ye'll do okay. At least, I shore hope so. But whatever ye do...don't ever let another man own ye..."

And Tyler Cabe never had and never would.

He figured if he had nothing else, he always had his self-respect.

Wilcox let him keep his Bull Durham, papers, and matches, so he rolled himself a cigarette and felt sorry for himself.

Damn, he thought, old Crazy Jack was going to love this one.

Locked-up, eh, Cabe? Killed a man, did you? Still the same hotheaded old Southern boy you was back when, ain't you? Figured it would come to this, boy. You ain't got the brains God gave a piss-drunk rooster.

Damn.

Water was dripping down on him, just a few droplets, but he figured he'd be soaked by morning. Soaked and freezing and didn't he just have that coming?

"Cot's not bolted down," a voice from the next cell said. "Slide it over to the other wall or your blanket'll be frozen stiff come morning."

Cabe struck another match, held it up to the bars off to his left. He saw an old Indian sitting cross-legged on his own cot. He was dressed in a blanket coat and campaign hat, his hair long and steel-gray. His eyes were black dots set in a worn face with more wrinkles in it than an unmade bed.

"Just a suggestion," the Indian said. "I'm good with suggestions, but not much with following them."

Cabe smiled despite the pounding in his head. "Name's Tyler Cabe...you?"

In the gray darkness, Cabe saw that the old man just stared dead forward like he was seeing something no one else could. "You want my injun name or my white name?"

"Injun name would be fine."

The old man adjusted his hat. "No, you couldn't pronounce it and I can't remember it. In white tongue it meant "One Who Waits". Something like that, I recall."

"And what is it you're waiting for?"

"Don't know rightly. Figure I'll stay around until it comes to me."

"Just keep waiting, eh?" Cabe said.

The Indian shrugged. "Surely. I'm always waiting for something. When I was a free-running injun, I suppose I was waiting for the U.S. Government to take my land away. When they did that I used to wait on the reservation for my beef ration, my flour and corn. Never came too much, but I always waited for it. Now I wait here in Whisper Lake. But if I wait in any one place too long...some white-eye feels the need to kick me around. But that's life as an injun: You wait long enough, something always happens."

Cabe didn't know what to make of all that. The old man seemed to be joking and to be dead serious at the same time. But Cabe knew from the Cherokees back home that they were not like white men and you could not read them as such.

"What's your white name?"

"Charles Graybrow," he said. "Graybrow...that's injun, too. Means man with gray brow."

"Really? I'd have never figured it."

"Learn something every day, Tyler Cabe."

Cabe rubbed his temples again. Christ, it was a doozy, that headache. Older he got, harder the liquor was on him. And Graybrow wasn't helping none...Cabe got the impression that he was being insulted and befriended at the same time.

"Here," Graybrow said. "This'll help your head."

Cabe lifted his hand and a small leather pouch was passed to him. The Indian's fingers felt very rough like untreated hide.

"What is it?"

"Injun head-magic," Graybrow said. "Though some whites just call it headache powder."

Cabe washed it down with water, splashed some more water in his face. He passed the pouch back through the bars.

"Why were you locked-up, Tyler Cabe?"

Cabe grunted. "For being a damn fool, I suppose. I stopped by the Cider House for a drink. Next thing I know, I killed a man. Shot him. Virgil Clay was his name, they tell me. Hell, one less speck of trash in the world."

"Virgil Clay?" Graybrow clucked his tongue. "That's bad medicine there, I tell you. Oh...when an injun says 'bad medicine' it means the shit's about to fly and you're gonna catch some."

"Don't say?"

"Yep."

Graybrow told him that the Clay's were an ornery mountain clan from back east in West Virginia. Something happened to them during the Civil War and they pretty much had to leave their beloved hill country or face prosecution. Graybrow couldn't be sure, but he thought he'd heard something to the effect that the clan had been doing more than a little murdering and horse-thieving and most of the county had hounded them out. They'd ended up in Utah Territory, attracted maybe by the mountains. Most of the clan was gone now. As far as Graybrow knew, only a few of 'em lived up in the high country and they didn't cotton to strangers poking about...as more than one miner or trapper had learned the hard way.

Cabe asked about Virgil.

Trash, Graybrow told him, just like you said. A speck of trash in a big smelly heap called Whisper Lake. He thought of himself as the fastest gun since Wild Bill, but to call him a shootist would be giving him far too much credit. Shit, Graybrow said, calling him a *man* was giving that animal too much credit. Virgil was strictly a bottom-feeder, a product of a demented backwoods clan that bottle-fed their young on violence, hate, and intolerance. You wanted to call Virgil Clay something, "murderer" was always a good tag. Maybe sidewinder or weasel was applicable. Bottom line here, Graybrow pointed out, was that Virgil Clay was an ornery, dirt-mean life-taker with all the morals and sense of fair play as a leg-chomping river gator.

"Man like that? I tell you what, Tyler Cabe, you don't hang him; you hang his mother for pumping out that filth and his father for grooming him into the reptile he became."

Cabe listened and listened, finally couldn't help himself. He asked Graybrow if maybe, just maybe now, he had an ax to grind against old Virgil. That made the old man sigh. "Ax to grind?" he said. "I'm an injun, Tyler Cabe. We grind stone knives and tomahawks, didn't you know that?" Graybrow told him one day, well over a year before, he and his brother-in-law Robert Sun-Bird—finest, kindest injun that ever lived, had to feel sorry for him marrying my foul-mouthed, snake-mean sister—were on the road outside Frisco. They were bringing a wagon of lumber back to the reservation to throw up a couple lean-tos. They'd paid real money for it, too. He said the ore wagons came and went and no one paid the Indians much attention until a lone rider showed.

Virgil Clay.

He seemed pleasant enough when he stopped Graybrow's wagon, inquired about the weather, saying only injuns could truly predict the weather. Sun-Bird told him this was true, looked to the sky and forecasted a dry spell for the next week. Clay thanked him, asked for a match to light his cheroot with and was promptly given one. And, yep, he was a pleasant sort, Graybrow said, but his eyes were just plain crazy, beady and close-set. A scorpion wearing a man's flesh. After Clay got his light, he pulled a pistol and shot Sun-Bird dead. Before Graybrow could do much more than wipe the blood from his eyes, Clay yanked him from the wagon and pistol-whipped him there on the road until his eyes were swelled-up and he couldn't see.

"So, maybe you're right, Tyler Cabe...maybe my ax needed some grinding. Maybe in my heart I still sharpen it from time to time."

Graybrow told him that that was Virgil Clay, what he knew of him. Though it was rumored he'd run roughshod over Indian Territory, running whiskey in the Nations and robbing and looting redskins and whites alike up and down the Arkansas and Canadian Rivers. Was put on trial once at Fort Smith...but was acquitted of something involving rustled cattle and changing brands with a running iron. In Whisper Lake, he hung tight to Sir Tom Ian ever since Ian showed in town a month back.

Cabe said, "I suppose the rest of that brood is just as bad?"

"Worse," Graybrow said. "Damn worse."

Only person Graybrow ever knew that rode up to the Clay family spread and rode back down again was Jackson Dirker. Dirker made himself pretty clear on the subject of the Clay's: Long as they obeyed the law, he couldn't run 'em out of town, but they so much as spit on the sidewalk, he would ride a posse up into the hills and burn the lot of 'em out.

No, there wasn't many of them left...but one of them happened to be Virgil Clay's old man, Elijah, and he was plenty. Graybrow told him to imagine Virgil, but bigger, meaner, just as crude and coarse as a rutting hog...a hog that ate raw meat and shit razor blades, thought that roasting babies on a spit was how you whiled away a slow Sunday afternoon.

"That bad, eh?"

"Bad Medicine," Graybrow told him. "When an injun says that—"

"Yeah, I know."

Cabe figured none of this was good news. If he got out of this mess, the Clay clan might come gunning for him. He'd better watch his back. Course, Dirker might find it amusing—one crazy Southerner hunting down another.

"But, you know, Tyler Cabe, I'm an injun and sometimes we do go on. I got a good imagination," he said. "I can read, you know that? I like reading them dime novels and I know everything they say is true. All those stories of redskins attacking wagon trains and kidnapping white women and children...just a shame. I know whites would never kill and burn like that. It's a good thing the white man came out here and sorted out all us heathen red devils. I'm truly thankful for it."

Cabe ignored that, lighting another cigarette. "Well, tomorrow, the next day," he said, "you see that sumbitch Elijah Clay riding in after me, you let me know."

"I will...if I'm sober."

Cabe asked him what he was locked up for.

Graybrow took his time in answering. "Not sure. I was drunk at the time. But I figure I musta done something. Maybe I scalped some innocent, God-fearing whites or peed on 'em. Something like that. I been known to do both and sometimes at the same time." He was silent for a time. Finally, he clucked his tongue, sighed. "Whatever I did, must've been bad, you think? To be thrown in here? You don't suppose I got locked-up just because I'm an injun, do you?"

"No, white folk wouldn't do that. We got too much respect for you people."

Graybrow slapped his knee. "You're right. But for a minute there...boy, I was scared."

Cabe told him he didn't strike him as a man who scared easy and Graybrow launched into a tirade about how he was just a simple savage and the white world was so fast and complicated...it frightened him. All he wanted from life was a tipi and a fire to dance naked around. And maybe a buffalo robe and a chew of tobacco. Maybe a woman...or two of them. And some horses and cattle. Maybe his own bank and livery, now that you mention it...

"All right already," Cabe said.

"Sure, I go on. I know that. It's because I got a taste for the firewater, makes my head funny. Can't think right."

The talk drifted to what Cabe was doing in Whisper Lake and he told the old man all there was to tell. The old man agreed with Dirker that the Sin City Strangler had finally found a place he could call home. He recounted much of what Carny the bartender had told him earlier that night at the Oasis—vigilantes, animal attacks, tensions brewing.

"There are two Mormon villages heresabouts, Tyler Cabe," Graybrow said, now dead serious. "One of 'em is called Redemption and was once a mining town. The Mormons have taken it over and are fixing it to right. People around here, they blame them from Redemption. But they're wrong. Redemption is just an ordinary town."

"What about Deliverance?"

"That," Graybrow said, "is another matter. I'm tired now. Maybe another day I'll tell you about that place, but not tonight. Maybe tomorrow. That is, if I'm—"

"Sober?"

"Yep."

15

Cabe figured he slept maybe two, three hours and then came awake to the sound of keys jingling at his cell lock. The door swung open and there was a figure standing there. His head still throbbing from the booze, his eyes glued to slits, and his mouth carpeted in fuzz, he wasn't sure if he was awake or not.

Regardless, he knew the dim figure was Jackson Dirker.

"Sorry to disturb your beauty rest, Cabe," he said. "God knows you need it, but you don't belong in here. C'mon, we need to talk."

Cabe, after some effort, got his boots down on the floor and managed to sit up. His head pounded and his guts tried to climb up the back of his throat. "Shit," he said. "I feel pretty much like shit."

In the cell next to him, Graybrow was snoring away louder than a crosscut saw biting into hardwood. Cabe once heard that Indians were real quiet, that they didn't even snore. So much for that one.

He splashed water in his face, gulped some down, and pissed into the pot, getting some on his boot. Making moaning sounds, he followed Dirker out into the front office. Dirker shoved a cup of hot coffee into his hand.

"Drink it," he said. "I need you fresh...or as fresh as you can be."

Cabe drank the coffee and it tasted like maybe they had made it with water dredged from a privy, but it went down, all right. Dirker poured him another cup, leaning up against the wall, looking very dire. Cabe had to wonder when the hell it was that Jackson Dirker slept.

He set his cup down. "Now, listen to me, Crazy Jack or Sheriff or whatever the fuck they call you here...it was self-defense. Before you go off on some wild tangent on how I'm shooting up the town...that boy there...goddamn Virgil Clay...he pulled on me, got off the first shot. I put one in him because I didn't have much of a choice."

Dirker just nodded. "I know that. I heard all about it."

"Then you ain't charging me with nothing?"

"No, not this time around, anyhow," he said. "But hear me on this and hear me good. I won't have you going around shooting people whenever the need strikes you. After awhile folks are going to start tripping over the bodies and they're not going to like it."

Cabe told him it couldn't be helped. And Dirker said maybe and maybe not. He had no love for Virgil Clay or the clan that hatched him. They were trash and everyone knew it. If it hadn't been Cabe, it would have been someone else. *But*...and he emphasized this pretty sternly...the witnesses, a lot of 'em anyway, were saying that Cabe had been drunk and running his mouth. That he could have walked away from it at anytime, no harm done.

"Oh, but there would have been harm done, Dirker," Cabe said. "I would have lost all credibility with them people there. They would have thought I was some sort of coward."

Dirker licked his lips. "Those people you talk about, Cabe, they're not exactly high-stepping gentry. Most of 'em would slit your throat for a ten-dollar gold piece. You got nothing to prove to that bunch."

Cabe knew he was right, but wasn't about to admit as much. He finished his coffee. "Can I go now?"

"No." Dirker unlocked the property cabinet and gave him back his Starr, knife, and cartridge belt. "You're gonna take a little walk with me. There's something I want you to see."

"Unless it looks like a bed, I don't want to see it."

"You will, I think."

"Why?"

Dirker swallowed down something. "Because your boy is in town. He's finally struck."

16

Figuring that he was hungover, trail-weary, and hadn't had much sleep, Cabe didn't need to be looking at this. Didn't need to be seeing the slashed and hacked remains of a whore named Mizzy Modine in all their ghoulish splendor.

He stood there in the doorway, his guts percolating away, bile kicking up the back of his throat. His jaws were locked tight.

Dirker was standing there with him. "Well?" he said. "Any question in your mind that this is your boy?"

Cabe did not answer him, could not answer him. His jaws were still locked-up and his voice had sunk down into some dark, muddy pit. All the rooting around he did down there did not produce it. What he was looking at...Christ, it was the worse yet. The very worst.

"Excuse me," he finally said, stepping out into the chill air.

Cabe had seen a lot of death over the years. A lot of blood and flesh mangled up in the worse possible ways. He'd come to the conclusion long ago, that the human being...though possibly

God's finest creation...was also the most disgusting when you opened it up and saw the slimy, drippy things that made it operate.

Cabe had not been physically ill in years looking at a body, but, damn if he wasn't real close right now. That bile in his throat tasted of cheap whiskey, flat beer, and things far worse. He tried to roll a cigarette, but his fingers were thick and clumsy and maybe the light from the lantern hanging outside Mizzy Modine's crib just wasn't enough.

Dirker rolled one for him. Rolled it, stuck it between his lips, struck a match and cupped it against the wind while Cabe puffed it into life.

Dirker said, "It hits you hard the first time you look on it. I been looking on it for hours now...but the shock just won't go away."

Cabe nodded, pulling off his cigarette.

Okay, he thought, enough. You went on a good one tonight and you put a man down, but pull yourself together because you have to look at what's in there. You have to take a good, long look. Dirker wants to know if it's the Strangler and he expects you to tell him.

Can you do it? *Can you?*

But Cabe knew he could. Somehow. Some way. Still dragging from his cigarette, he thought about when he took up the trail of the Sin City Strangler. It was in Eureka, Nevada. The fourth victim. The fifth was in Osceola and the sixth in Pinoche. In Pinoche, Cabe got his first good look at the handiwork of the Strangler. The sheriff there was a hardcase named Cyrus Long who carried a sawed-off double barrel shotgun in a sheath at his hip. The stock was plated in iron and it was dented from Long smashing it over the heads of miscreants...or anyone that pissed him off. Long was rumored to have been a Kansas redleg during the war whose obsession, it was said, was hunting down Confederate guerrillas in Missouri and skinning them alive. He was a cruel, evil sort and that look in his eyes...like simmering death...even made Cabe bristle. Cabe had been asking questions about the victim and finally Long himself took him to view the body.

Working a plug of chew in his cheek, Long said: *Now I'm only gonna do you this favor once, Johnny Reb, hear? You bounty hunters...you come stomping about my town, kicking things up, leaving your bootprints all over my ass...and not a one of you ever had the decency to let me know he's even here or what for. But you have, Reb, so I'll do you a good turn back...'cept, you ain't gonna think it's so good once we're done. One thing, though, Reb...yeah, I don't give a good fucking shit what your name is, Reb...you just listen and shut that cracker mouth for two minutes or I'll goddamn well do it for you. I had my fill of your peckerwood Southern asses during the War of Rebellion, so shut it and shut it quick, boy. Okay. Now, I don't mind you bounty hunters coming here and all, just as long as you let me know straight away what you're dirtying up my town about. Don't matter if you're hunting wolves or injuns or men...I wanna know.*

He was a real sweetheart, that Long. You just had to love him. Reconstruction had never touched this boy. He was as mean and ornery and intolerant as he'd been during the war. He took Cabe upstairs of a brothel and into a room at the end of the hall. A white sheet was thrown over a form on the bed. There were great red stains on it. Long pulled it off the body and it came away with a sticky sound like tape pulled from a board.

Long took out a knife and began. *See here, Reb? See how she's been opened from belly to crotch? That's a sure sign of the Sin City Strangler. Trust me...I saw the other one in Osceola. Slit right open, see? Ain't that something?* Long followed the incision with the blade of his knife, using it like a pointer. Like he was an anatomy instructor. *See, this crazy bastard, he stuck the knife right in her business there, dragged it up to her throat. Then he cut her widthwise just below her tits here and then again right at her bellybutton. Opened this bitch like a Christmas present. See? She's all hollow inside on account this bastard scooped out all her goodies, spread 'em around like birthday streamers...you see that? One thing missing, though, is her heart. Yep. He always takes that part with him. Now, out in San Fran they had themselves some hotshot surgeon what looked at the body and said the woman there died about the same time she was strangled. I wouldn't know about that. But see those purple marks at her throat...yeah, them ones...them are from fingers. You can see 'em fine, thumbs and fingers. Now, she died from strangulation and was opened afterward, Reb. I know that on account of what I'm seeing. No, don't turn away. This is the important part. Her eyes are full of blood and her color is blue...oxygen starvation causes that they tell me. She was strangled, all right. Now, Reb, what you're looking for here is a dirt-mean, deranged cocksucker who fancies whores and likes to fuck 'em and choke 'em and gut 'em. Got another secret for you, too, Reb...he fucks 'em after they's dead, too. So you find this character, he'll have a long, sharp knife and maybe a heart and a few other things boiling in a pot...where you going, boy?*

But Cabe had had enough. Only a ghoul could linger in such a place. There was something definitely wrong with Cyrus Long. He was too clinical, too detached. It almost seemed he'd been enjoying it. Sick redleg sumbitch.

"You ready now?" Dirker said.

Cabe crushed out his cigarette. "You?"

"Nope. Not in the least."

They went back in, Cabe leading. They went in and stood at the foot of the bed. The air was redolent with the stink of voided bowels, fresh blood, and salty meat. It was a heady, nauseating odor that crawled down inside both men and made something shiver in their bellies. Cabe looked at everything but what he was supposed to be looking at. He took in the velvet tapestries, the oak chiffonier, the red tapers melted down now. Everything was red and warm and selected to induce passion, he supposed. But what was on the bed induced anything but.

Like the whore in Pinoche...Mizzy Modine had been eviscerated.

But it was worse this time. All her internals had been cut out, arranged next to the body in some unguessable sequence. Her bowels had been draped over the headboard and coiled around her head in a halo. Her eyes had been plucked out and replaced with coins. Her breasts hacked off and set on the nightstand along with her eyeballs and privates.

"Yeah...it's him," Cabe breathed. "I got a firsthand tour in Pinoche. It looked like this. Only this time it's even worse."

Dirker just nodded. "All right, then."

Together they went outside, stood together, let the wind blast them clean. A light mist hung in the air...but even if it had been pouring, it couldn't have hoped to wash the stink off of them. A stink that was mostly in their head by that point.

"You can go, Cabe," Dirker said. "Get some rest. There's no more you can do here."

Cabe looked at him, started to say something...then just shook his head and started down Piney Hill through the muddy, damp streets.

17

At the St. James Hostelry, Janice Dirker said, "My, my, Mister Tyler Cabe, but you smell like the Devil's own brewery. For a man who didn't come to Whisper Lake to 'hell around', you certainly managed to dip in the waters of our taverns quite thoroughly."

Cabe just stood there. "Yeah...it was a hard night."

"You look like hell, Mr. Cabe. If you don't mind me saying so."

"I don't, ma'am."

He wanted very badly to get into bed, to sleep away the day, but she insisted he join her for breakfast. He didn't figure it would be polite to resist. So he followed her into the dining room, thinking it was going to give old Crazy Jack a heart attack if he came in and none other than Tyler Cabe was breaking bread with his woman. Maybe yesterday that would have given Cabe pleasure...but after what he'd been through this day or night or whatever in hell it was, he just didn't have the strength to feel any animosity for Dirker.

It just wasn't there.

The cook brought out eggs and hotcakes, maple syrup and coffee.

Cabe stared at the food, his belly growling, but he kept seeing Mizzy Modine laying in that slaughterhouse. He picked up his fork and set it down again.

"Please, Mr. Cabe, eat," Janice Dirker said. "The other guests are not up yet. I usually dine alone, but I'm grateful for company. I can remember the days when my husband would share breakfast with me. But he's simply too busy these days."

"I think I need sleep, ma'am," Cabe said.

"Of course you do. But sit with me for a moment or two."

She cut a small bite of cakes and chewed it quite delicately. Cabe could see she had fine breeding. Womenfolk he knew back in Yell County shoveled it in before somebody snatched it off their plates.

"So where do you hail from, Mr. Cabe?" she asked.

"Arkansas. Yell County. Yourself?"

"Georgia. Daddy owned a plantation there. He owned lots of things." Her eyes misted for a moment, but something wouldn't let the pain come, maybe breeding. "Daddy's gone now…everything's gone."

She went on to tell him of her life in Georgia, the sort of life she'd had that he could only dream of. The privileges. The fine schools. The genteel upbringing. It was all in great contrast to the South Cabe had known…which had always been hard and unforgiving. She was a lady and the Yankees had destroyed her family's holdings and yet she had gone and married one of them. She was an enigma to say the least. But the war, he knew, had created a great many of those.

"Were you in the war, Mr. Cabe?"

"Yes, ma'am."

"But you don't like to talk about it?"

"No, ma'am."

She seemed to understand. "My husband was in the war, also. He, too, does not like to discuss it."

"It was a bad time, ma'am. A real bad time for all concerned."

She smiled conspiratorially. "But, perhaps, worse for us Southerners…wouldn't you agree?"

He nodded. "I would. The Yankees what stayed behind, stayed home…they probably had it all right. But the ones that did the fighting? No, I can't say they had a good time of it. No one who went through that *hell* could possibly have fond memories. The Yankees were better equipped than us without a doubt. But they bled and died all the same."

Janice admitted that her husband was a Yankee. "I remember him…this was a few years after the war. How tall and proud he was on his horse, how handsome. He wooed me and won me. I am not ashamed of the fact."

"No reason you should be. North and South, men are men and women are women."

Janice told him she appreciated his understanding for there were many Southerners who did not feel that way. Regardless, many girls married Yankee soldiers. She wasn't sure what it was…maybe there was a certain attraction in that they were the victors. Maybe it was a matter of power. Powerful men were…enticing. And maybe it had something to do with wanting badly to get out of the South, the ruin it had become. To escape memories and demons and melancholy things that were buried along with the antebellum South and wouldn't rest quietly in their graves.

"I knew many dashing men that went off to war, Mister Cabe. Those that returned, well, they were broken, beaten men. Their eyes were vacant and they were bitter, angry. At the Yankees, maybe at themselves, their commanders, the politicians that had put them in such a situation to begin with," Janice explained. "Many of them did nothing but drink and fight amongst themselves. Some were touched in the head, didn't believe the war was over. It was all very sad. Maybe I had to escape all that."

Cabe understood. He knew nothing of the life she had led. Privilege and money were alien things to him. When he left for war he had nothing. When he came back, he still had nothing. He got out of Arkansas soon as possible, wanting desperately to be anything but what his father was—just a rich man's belonging. He would not be a tenant farmer, a sharecropper. So he rode west with all the others, looking, looking for something he still had not found.

Cabe cleared his throat. "Your husband…he is a good man?"

"Yes, I think so," Janice said. "He always tries his best, always tries to do right by people…sometimes he fails as we all do, but he never stops trying. In his job, well, let's just say he is unappreciated when things go smoothly and vilified if they do not."

Cabe listened and heard, but was not sure if any of it registered. His thought processes were garbled and he wasn't sure what day it was. He kept seeing the hacked prostitute, Virgil Clay, the old Indian at the jail, Henry Freeman, Jackson Dirker...a parade of faces and incidents that flowed together and lost solidity.

Sipping his coffee, but not tasting it, he thought: Everyone but me seems to think Dirker is a good man...maybe I'm wrong and maybe they don't know him and maybe he's changed and I have, too.

"Do you know my husband?" Janice asked of him.

"The sheriff," Cabe said, nodding. "I've met him."

"Do you know him well?"

Cabe swallowed. "No, ma'am, I guess I don't know him well at all."

18

The next morning, Henry Wilcox released Charles Graybrow from his cell, told him to keep away from the booze and he'd keep out of trouble. Graybrow told him that he had a powerful taste for the whiteman's devil-brew and that him keeping away from it was like a cloud trying to stay away from the sky.

Wilcox just shook his head. "On your way, Charlie."

At the door, Graybrow stopped. "What did I do, anyway?"

Wilcox sighed. "You don't remember? You honestly don't remember? Or are you playing me again? No, I guess you don't recall. Well, Charlie, you gotta take a shit, we'd appreciate it you don't do it on someone's porch. People are touchy about things like that."

Graybrow scratched his head. "I'm just an ignorant savage, what do I know of your ways?"

"Oh, get the hell out of here."

Although outwardly somber, inside Graybrow was grinning like a kid that had written dirty words on the blackboard. Maybe whites didn't find him amusing, but he enjoyed himself immensely at their expense.

He stepped out and although the sun was shining and drying up the mud, there was a chill in the air.

Another deputy, Pete Slade, tied his horse to the hitch post and nodded to Graybrow. "She's a cold one today, eh, Charlie?"

Graybrow shrugged. "I'm an injun...we don't feel the cold."

Slade just shook his head and went inside.

Graybrow pulled his blanket coat tighter to him, shivering. He was about to start down the street when another man came out behind him. He nearly stumbled off the plank sidewalk, then gathered himself. He was thin, lanky, face bruised-up, his dirty sheepskin jacket smelling like he'd just pulled it off the sheep itself. He scratched at his shaggy, knotted beard.

"They got m'gun in there," he said, not seeming to address Graybrow, but someone standing behind him. "1851 Colt Navy. Big .44, that's what. Killed them bluebelly sumbitches with it in the war, didn't I? They got it, say I can't have it back. Not until, until...what did they say? Y'all remember?"

Graybrow told him that he had forgotten.

He knew who the man was: Orville DuChien. Some mixed-up white-eye thought he was still in the war. He talked crazy and people crossed the street when they saw him coming. He was not only disturbed, but dangerous if pushed. A couple miners had decided to have fun once by knocking him around and DuChien had sliced them up pretty with a deer knife.

Like a rabid dog, it was wise to keep your distance from the man.

Graybrow had only seen DuChien from a distance, had never been this close to him before. And now that he was...he was struck by something. He could not put a name to it. Not the smell or the uneasiness he inspired, but something deeper, something *peculiar*.

Orv started to shake and his eyes seemed to lose focus. "Yessum, Daddy, I remember all about that, yessum. Grandpappy say I got to go down into the holler tonight, yessum tonight. Them roots and what...only show by moonlight, he say. Yes sir. I dig 'em and Grandpappy brew 'em up, make them warts just fade right away. Like that time...remember, daddy? Old Wiley, he had that tumor. Grandpappy...he calls them names from the hilltop, them ones Preacher Evrin say is bad, bad, bad, make the stars shake and the dead a-tremble in their graves. Them ones? Yessum. Then he...Grandpappy, yes sir...he say them words and push his hands into the innards of that slaughtered hog...lays 'em on Wiley's tumor. That old tumor, Mister Tumor, he pack his bags and be gone. Yessum. Grandpappy say I got the gift, too...but daddy, I don't like it. Scairt me bad..."

Graybrow knew and did not know. He stepped back from Orv, something in him finding revelation in that crazy, moonstruck hillbilly.

Orv said, "Yessum, ain't nothin' good gonna come of this here town. Not what with them...them other ones all touched by *his* hand."

"Whose hand?"

That made Orv laugh. "The old hand...the old hand from the mountain..."

Graybrow told him to relax, that everything would be fine, fine, but he knew and knew damn well that whatever had Orville DuChien was not something that would ever let go. It was bone deep. It was special.

Orv broke into a coughing fit, then seemed to find himself. "I...I was talkin' to that what ain't there, weren't I? I keep doin' that, don't I?" One filthy paw was clasped on Graybrow's shoulder, squeezing, squeezing. "I talk to them no one else sees and hear them voices. They tell me...tell me what's gonna happen and to who. Tell me things, secret things, about other folks. Things I shouldn't know."

"How long you had it?" Graybrow inquired.

"Always. Told Jesse and Roy they was gonna die, gonna die, gonna die! Didn't believe me, but they died! Yankees killed 'em like I say! Hear? Like I say..."

Graybrow knew what it was. Sure, he was crazy. Crazy because of what was inside of him. Whites would have said he was just plain touched or maybe bewitched and they would be right on both counts...but there was more to it than that. Much more. For Orville DuChien had the talent, he was "sighted". He had the gift. Just like that grandfather he spoke of. It ran in families sometimes. The tribal shaman had it...ability to see sprits and know what would happen before it did. Yes, this hillbilly was a prophet. Undirected, but a prophet no less.

Orv pointed at something, something Graybrow could not see, started jabbering, then shook his head. "You tell yer daddy, you tell him it ain't right takin' the strop to you. Weren't yer fault that pony ran off...weren't yer fault..."

Graybrow was shaking himself now. That pony. He remembered. He had forgotten, but now he remembered. The pony that ran off into the hills and how very angry his father was. The hillbilly had plucked it from his mind.

Orv walked out into the street, stopped, nearly got run down by a lumber wagon. He stumbled back, fell against the hitching post. "Injun...you hear me...you...you tell him the bad man, the bad man is real close...the bad man will kill a fine lady what ain't no whore!"

"Yes, I'll tell him, I—"

But Orv was already gone, running away down the street, clutching his head in both hands, as if trying not to hear something. And people fell out of his way like dominoes, because everyone in Whisper Lake knew Orville DuChien was just plain touched.

Everyone except an old Ute Indian.

19

And each in his or her own way, greeted the new day.

At the Union Hotel, Sir Tom Ian strapped on a customized leather cartridge belt and slid a British .44 Bisley pistol into the holster. As he did so, he thought of what he had witnessed at the Cider House Saloon the night before. He was impressed that Tyler Cabe, though well into his cups, had managed to survive an encounter with Virgil Clay. It was sheer luck that Clay had missed his target at such close range...but there was no luck involved with a man who could dive out of the way and shoot with such accuracy as he fell. Impressive. Sir Tom had no love for Virgil Clay. He had put up with the man following him around like a stray, amused by his lack of social graces. That he was dead now, meant little to Sir Tom. He had a job waiting for him down in Sedona, Arizona Territory...a wild town in need of a crack pistolman with a reputation. But he was in no hurry. And particularly now that Tyler Cabe would have to deal with the likes of Elijah Clay…

And high above Whisper Lake in a sheltered arroyo surrounded by stands of juniper and pinon, Elijah Clay was loading his pistols and sharpening up his knives. Word had reached him about Virgil's murder…and, to Elijah, it *was* murder. Chewing a strip of jerky, he ran the blade of a bowie knife over a wetstone, thinking hard and thinking long about a Arkansas bounty hunter named Tyler Cabe. For Elijah was from hill people. He was part of a hill country clan back in West Virginia. And there were certain codes that were invariably followed. Wrongs were always righted. When kin was killed, blood called that you settled matters. Flesh for flesh. That Cabe was a Southerner meant very little to Elijah. He had taken up no side in the War Between the States, knowing that one government was equally as corrupt as the next. He was a free-liver and a free-thinker as all hill people were. And when it came to vengeance, hill people meted it out accordingly. Thinking these things and knowing them to be true, Elijah found himself thinking of that fancy pistol fighter from Texas that had gunned-down his brother Arvin. It had taken that cowardly sumbitch near eight hours to die when Elijah had worked him with the knife…

At the Callister Brother's Mortuary, Caleb Callister found himself looking at a horror. His new embalmer, Leo Moss, though every bit the ardent professional, was equally as morbid as Caleb's deceased brother Hiram. As Caleb had been going through the books after a heady night of sex and gambling, Moss had called him into the undertaking parlor at the back of the building. You've got to see this, Moss told him. On the slab was some transient found dead in an alley. Thin, wasted, he couldn't have weighed more than a hundred pounds. Moss had been sorting through his innards since before first light and now proudly revealed his prize. A tapeworm. He had it in a five-gallon glass jar of alcohol. It floated in the brine, coiled like some obscene snake. A parasitic flatworm, cut free in sections. Thirty-two feet, Moss told Caleb. Now ain't that just something? Caleb had to agree it certainly was. Life was just full of odd surprises.

In his rooms at the St. James Hostelry, Jackson Dirker bolted awake from a nightmare which he could not remember. But as he lay there...the war was on his mind and he could just guess what he'd been dreaming of. Dirker had been with the 59th Illinois Infantry under Post. His first real taste of war had been at Pea Ridge. He could remember riding up on Tyler Cabe and his ragtag crew of Johnny Rebs. Remember them looting through the heaps of mutilated Union boys. Jesus...those, boys, they'd been scalped. Disemboweled. Faces carved from the bone so that their own mothers wouldn't have recognized them. Dirker's soldiers wanted to kill the graybellies there and then...but Dirker meted out a different punishment. He could remember the feel of that bullwhip in his fist, snapping, snapping, eating into flesh. Looking down on those dead boys, he'd lost control. Lost all sense of propriety. What he'd done was wrong. He knew that now...just as he knew now—and maybe had that day—that Cabe and his men had not desecrated those bodies. But knowing it and admitting it were two different things. For pride was a harsh mistress.

Like Dirker, Tyler Cabe also dreamed of the war. Faces of fallen comrades floated through the mists. He saw all the blood and death, wandered from one battlefield to the next, clawing through heaped Confederate and Union dead, trying to escape, escape. Dirker passed by, shaking his head, asking him how he could allow his men to mutilate those bodies. Cabe told him, no, no, no, we didn't, I would never allow that, *never*. And Cabe came awake, eyes fixed and glassy...he could smell the powder, the filth, the blood. And then it faded and he closed his eyes again.

In a seedy hotel rooming house, the man who called himself Henry Freeman and claimed to be a Texas Ranger sat on his bed, naked and cross-legged. On the bed before him was a Green River knife with a six-inch blade sharper than a straight razor. At one time, the Green River was pretty much the official knife of fur trappers and mountain men. A practical weapon for fighting, hunting, and butchering. It was also favored by buffalo skinners, who could skin off a hide in record time with the versatile tool. And, as Henry Freeman knew and knew well, it had other uses...such as eviscerating women and cutting out their hearts. He had one such trophy before him, carefully wrapped in deerhide. Freeman rocked back and forth, listening to the voices in head. Whores were fine, they told him. They needed to be purged. But there was other game...like maybe the gentile Southern lady who ran the St. James Hostelry...

Over in Redemption, the Mormons rushed about like busy ants, throwing the old mining town into shape. All you could hear were the sounds of saws and hammers, of lumber being stacked and wagons plying the dirt roads. Old shacks and houses were stripped to the frames and sometimes pulled down altogether, rebuilt from the ground up. The air was chill, but there was no lack of spirit or ambition as the abandoned town was rediscovered. Everywhere then, hammering and pounding, cutting and gutting. Sweat and hard labor and aching muscles. For Redemption had to be resurrected, body and soul...it was God's will. And it had to be fortified, for one of these nights, the vigilantes would ride again.

And in Deliverance, the Mormon hamlet that—it was rumored—had given itself bodily to the Devil, there was a haunted stillness of graveyards and gallows. It hung in the air like some secret, noxious pall. Hunched buildings and high, leaning houses pressed together in tombstone hordes, coveting darkness within their walls. Wind blew down from the hills and up the streets, membranes of ice forming over puddles. Weathered signs creaked above bolted doors and empty boardwalks. Sunlight seemed to shun this cramped and deserted village and the shadows, here gray and here black, lay like webs over narrow alleyways and sheltered cul-de-sacs. Now and again there could be heard a moaning or a scraping from some damp cellar or an eerie, childish giggling from behind a shuttered attic window. But nothing more. For whatever lived in Deliverance, lived in secret.

PART THREE: JAMES LEE COBB: A DISTURBING AND MORBID HISTORY

I

James Lee Cobb was born into a repressive New England community in rural southeastern Connecticut called Procton. A tight, restrictive world of puritanical dogma and religious fervor worlds away from Utah Territory. Set in a remote forested valley, it was a place where the moonlight was thick and the shadows long, where isolationism and rabid xenophobia led to inbreeding, fanaticism, and dementia.

First and foremost, Procton and its environs were agricultural, farm country, and had been since the English first hewed it from the encroaching forests and wrestled it from the hands of Pequot Indians. The people there were simple, ignorant, and backward even by the standards of the early nineteenth century. They shivered by October fires when the wind clawed coldly at doors and windows and dead tree limbs scratched at rooftops. They clutched their dog-eared bibles and books of prayer, begging for divine protection from lost souls, haunts, revenants, and numerous pagan nightmares.

In everything there was omen and portent.

Folk still read tea leaves and examined the placentas of newborn calves searching for prophecy. Blood sacrifice in the form of sheep were given to ensure the harvest. But these things, of course, were done purely in secret...for the churches frowned upon them.

At night, entrances were sensibly bolted, livestock locked-down in barns, windows carefully shuttered. Horseshoes were nailed over thresholds to turn back demons, salt sprinkled in cribs and at doorways to keep witches at bay. No sane man ventured out into the midnight fields where frosted pumpkins were shrouded by ropes of fog and nebulous shapes danced in dark glades and oceans of groundmist.

Squatting in their moldering 17th century brick houses, the people of Procton mumbled White Paternoster, hung out clumps of Vervain and St. John's Wort, and prayed to Christ on the Cross.

For evil was always afoot.

And for once, they were right...James Lee Cobb was about to come into the world.

2

In Procton, it began with the missing children.

In six weeks, five children had gone missing. They disappeared in the fields, on woodland trails, the far pastures...always just out of sight. The evidence was scarce—a dropped wicker of apples here, a few threads of cloth there. High Sheriff Bolton made what he considered a thorough and exhaustive inquiry into the matters, but came up with a nary a thing. Unless you wanted to count witch tales and chimney-corner whispers of dark forces at work. And Bolton, a very practical man in all manners, did not.

For the next three weeks...nothing, then in the first week of October, three infants were snatched from their cradles on the same grim night. Bolton made a flurry of arrests—more to allay wild suspicion and mob mentality than anything else—but in each case, the arrested were released for lack of evidence. Regardless, the tally was up to eight children by then. No longer could suppositions concerning marauding Indians or outlaw brigands suffice...there had to be a more concrete explanation. From the pulpits of Procton's three churches, ministers were descrying with a passion that what was happening in the village was not mere human evil, but grave evidence of diabolic intervention. Despite the arguments to the contrary by Sheriff Bolton and Magistrate Corey, the clergy fanned the flames of public indignation.

Witchcraft, they said. And demanded action.

So Elizabeth Hagen was arrested, charged with the practice of witchcraft, sorcery, and murder.

***

Elizabeth Hagen.

She was known as the Widow Hagen and most did not know her Christian name. When someone in or around Procton mentioned "The Widow", there was surely no doubt as to whom they were speaking of. Widow Hagen then, it was known, had lived in the vicinity at least sixty years, and possibly as many as eighty, depending on which account was listened to. She had outlived no less than four husbands…and, in all those years, had not appeared to age beyond a few years. She was not some spindly, wizened hag…but a stout and robust woman with silver hair and a remarkably unlined face.

This, of course, spawned suspicion…but the people of Procton admitted freely that she "had her uses". And she did. Despite their puritanical God-fearing ways, those were hard, uncertain times. And the Widow Hagen was expert in folk remedy and herb medicine. She could and had cured the sick, lame, and terminal. And although the village preachers condemned her from their pulpits through the years, more than a few of them had been her customers when they suffered maladies ranging from arthritis to constipation, heart troubles to skin disease. She was considered to be "second-sighted" and could divine your future (and past) through divination: examining entrails and bones, melted wax and dead animals. There was little that she could not do…for a price. And that was rarely coin, but more commonly by barter…livestock, grain, vegetables. That sort of thing. And payment was rarely a problem, for the Widow Hagen, it was said, could visit tragedy and disease down upon you and your kin in the wink of an eye…and had more than once.

Although equally feared and respected, she was not generally considered evil. She could be found digging roots and tubers in the fields, sifting through graveyard dirt and mumbling prayers to the full moon. She had a shack out by the edge of the salt marshes that was reached via a winding trail that cut through a loathsome stand of woods, where—it was said—that high grasses rustled and the tree limbs shook even when there was no wind.

The shack was dim and smoky, lit by hearth and whale oil lamp. It was strewn with hides and bones, feathers and baskets of dried insects. Shelving was crowded with a dusty array of jugs and retorts, flasks and alembics. There were corked bottles of vile liquids, vessels of unknown powder. And jars of brine which contained preserved dead things, things that had never been born, and others which could not have lived in the first place. So the Widow Hagen amused herself with her old and profane books, the skulls of murderers and suicides, Hand of Glory and exotic medicinals. Folk came to her for remedy and prophecy, for a needed blessing over child and harvest field.

She was never part of the community as such, but her power was unmistakable.

Then things changed.

New ministers replaced the old. They were not tolerant of paganism, regardless of its promise. These young upstarts not only attacked Hagen from the pulpit, but threw together town meetings which they vehemently banned any interaction with the old witch. Saying in no uncertain terms, that to have commerce with her was to have commerce with Satan incarnate. The ministers fed on Procton's puritanism and repressive worldviews, turning them once and for all against what they considered the enemy of Christianity—Widow Hagen and her curious ways.

Year by year, then, less and less sought out the Widow's wisdom and expertise. No more charms and talismans, love potions and cure-alls. Her shack became a shunned place and she became ostracized to the point where she could not even buy her goods in the village.

A month before the first child disappeared, a group of men tried to burn down her shack. When that failed—the wood refused to catch fire—she was publicly stoned in the market square. Raising her hands to the sky, the bloodied and broken

Widow Hagen said loud enough for all to hear: "*A curse then, breathern...on ye and yer ways!*"

Then the children began to disappear.

Village livestock were plagued with nameless afflictions.

Weird storms raked the countryside.

Crops withered in the fields...practically overnight.

And no less than four village women gave birth to stillborn infants.

So when the children turned up missing on top of everything else, there could only be one possible miscreant: Elizabeth Hagen.

Witch.

***

She was duly arrested by High Sheriff Bolton and a posse of deputized men and placed in the Procton stockade: a windowless, insect-infested sweatbox with dirty straw on the floor where the accused lived in his or her own waste and was fed perhaps every second day. The crude walls were scratched with supplications to God above.

And the investigation, as it were, began.

Sheriff Bolton was in complete agreement with Magistrate Corey and the learned members of the village General Assembly—it was all superstitious rubbish.

Then, Widow Hagen's shack was searched.

Upon entering, the posse smelled a vulgar, nauseous stench as of spoiled meat. And no man who went in there that windy, misting October afternoon would soon forget what was uncovered. There were soiled canvas sacks of human bones—children's bones, still stained with blood and plastered with stringy bits of sinew. The skulls were soon uncovered buried beneath the dirt floor. As were the maggoty and headless bodies of the infants. All of which bore the marks of ritual hacking and slashing. And at the hearth in a greasy black pot, some pustulant and ghastly stew made of human remains.

But in the root cellar below was found the most gruesome and unspeakable of horrors, something swimming in a cask of human blood and entrails. Sheriff Bolton later described it as "something like a fetus...a hissing, mewling mass of flesh...a blubbery human fungus with more limbs than it had any right to possess". It was shot and brought into town wrapped in a tarp. The village physician, Dr. Lewyn, a man of some scientific background and possessed of a microscope and other modern equipment, dissected it. Bolton's observations were proven correct, for Lewyn's inspection revealed the creature to be human in form only. It's anatomy was terribly rudimentary, reversed from that of a normal human child and was entirely boneless, unless one wished to count the "rubbery, fungus structure within". The cadaver gave off a hideous, fishy odor and was immediately burned, the ashes buried in unconsecrated ground.

It was said the Widow Hagen screamed from her cell when that particular blasphemy was given to the flames.

The preceding evidence was more than sufficient for Magistrate Corey to form a Court of Oyer and Terminer, much like others that had governed over many another witch trial. Elizabeth Hagen was first examined by Dr. Lewyn. Though a man possessed of scientific reasoning, it did not take him long to give the court the very thing it wanted...physical evidence that the Widow Hagen was indeed a witch. For three inches below her left armpit was found an extra nipple...the so-called "Witches Teat", the seal of a pact with the Devil. Through this nipple, a witch supposedly fed her familiars.

No one was more shocked than Lewyn.

He told the court that supernumerary nipples weren't unknown in medical annals, but his argument was flaccid at best. Even he didn't seem to believe it. And nothing he could say could allay what came next—Elizabeth Hagen was tortured to elicit a confession or, as it was popularly known, "put to the question". During the next week she underwent the ordeal of the ducking stool and the strappado, the heretic's fork and the witch's cradle. She was burned with hot coals, cut, beaten, hung by her feet and thumbs. The needed confession came within a few days...a might too quick for the court's henchmen.

But come, it did.

She admitted freely to the practice of witchcraft, of hexing the village, of conjuring storms and blights. It was enough. The morning of the trial she was dragged from her cell, wrists bound and tied to the rear of a farm wagon. She was pulled by oxen through the streets in this way, her jailer lashing her with a whip the entire way through those muddy streets to the courthouse. The locals lined up to pelt her with rotten fruit and stones. On her belly then, she was dragged up the steps and before Magistrate Corey and his associates, Magistrates Bowen and Hay.

She was bloody and broken, sack dress hanging in strips, her back raw from the whip, her face slashed open from "the blooding", her scalp missing patches of hair from "the knotting". A metal cage known as a Scold's Bridle encircled her head. The jailer removed it, tearing the bit from her mouth that pressed her tongue flat.

She begged for water and was given none.

She begged for food and was ignored.

She begged for mercy and the assembled crowd laughed.

Then the questioning began. The court had already assembled a lengthy list of evidence, not all of which was found in the Widow's shack. People, certain now that she had been emasculated by the law, came forward with tales of horror and wonder. A young woman named Claire Dogan admitted that Widow Hagen had tried to seduce her into the "cult of witchery", promising her riches and power. Dogan claimed that she had witnessed Hagen mixing up "flying ointment" which was applied to a length of oak, upon which, Hagen flew through the air, dipping over treetops and harassing livestock in the fields, laughing all the while.

A farmer named William Constant claimed that, in order to gain control of his neighbor's holdings, he contracted Widow Hagen to "witch" the man. He said he watched her tie the series of knots in rope known as the "witch's ladder"...and soon after, his neighbor was taken ill, dying shortly thereafter. Another farmer, Charles Goode, said that he—"while bewitched by the old hag"—had asked her to kill his shrewish wife. Hagen had taken a bone covered with decaying meat, sprinkled it with unknown powders, said words over it "which withered my soul upon hearing them". The bone was buried beneath his wife's window and as the meat rotted from it, so did the flesh melt from his wife's skeleton. She died soon after of an unknown wasting disease.

A group of village children admitted that the Widow had taught them how to avenge their enemies: another group of children who had teased and tormented them. She showed them how to gather hairs from the other children and press them into dolls made of mud and sticks. The words to say over them. And whatever they then did with the dolls happened to the children in question. When one doll was thrown in the river, one of the offending children drowned. When a doll was thrown into a fire, its namesake's cabin burned to the ground. The court recognized this as sympathetic magic. The children also said that when Mr. Garrity chased them bodily from his apple orchards, they said "strange words" taught to them by Widow Hagen and Garrity's prize milking cow keeled over dead on the spot.

And more than one farmer came forward to say that there was always trouble during midsummer. That it was the time of the Wild Hunt—the legendary flight of the witches. That Elizabeth Hagen and her fellow witches would take to the air with a coven of demons and evil dead and by morning the unwary had been carried off and livestock went unaccounted for. That on nights of the Wild Hunt, wise men stayed indoors for it could be heard coming—a barking and hissing, screaming and churning.

So the evidence, as such, was not lacking.

High Sheriff Bolton told his wife in secret that if the Widow were to be "put to flame", the entire village should burn with her. For there were precious few that had not encouraged her wild talents, had not called upon her in times of need. If she had gotten out of control, then who was to blame for empowering her? When there was trouble, her council was always the first sought. And that she had cured more ills and delivered more babies than any thirty doctors, there was no doubt.

But, even Bolton, after what he had seen at Hagen's shack, had no sympathy for her.

***

On the first day of the trial, the horrors were heard.

Magistrate Bowen: *Elizabeth Hagen...do you admit, then to being a witch?*

Hagen: *I admit, yer lordship, into being that which is called as such.*

Magistrate Bowen: *You admit to bewitching this community then?*

Hagen: *I admit I have my ways. I admit I use them against those what have done me wrong, yer lordship. I was stoned, was I not? My cabin was near-burned, was it not? I have been driven away by those who I have helped numerous times. And now...look upon me! Beaten and bloodied...have I not a right to avenge meself?*

Magistrate Bowen: *Yours is a crime against, God, lady. Yours is a crime punishable by death. Do you admit then to the worship of Satan?*

Hagen: *Satan? Satan? A Christian devil, yer lordship. I have no truck with him.*

Magistrate Bowen: *Then who have you struck your filthy bargain with?*

Hagen (laughing uncontrollably): *Bargain? Bargain, do ye say? Why with him, is it not? With him that crawls and him that slithers. Him that lords over the dark wood and the empty glen, him that commands from a throne of human bone.*

Magistrate Bowen: *How do you call this devil, this despoiler?*

Hagen: *Call him? Him that is She and She that is Him? Him That Cannot Bear Name? The Black Goat of the Dark Wood? She with a thousand squirming, screaming young? Him that calls yer name from the dead and lonely places? Aye! He and She that are It cannot be named! Cannot be held nor bound by such.*

Magistrate Bowen: *Say the name, witch, in the name of Christ Jesus!*

Hagen (laughing): *Jesus do ye say? A Christian charlatan! My doings, right and proper, are with Her, with Him, with It, the ancient Writher in Blackness!*

Magistrate Bowen: *Then you admit to entering into a pact with this nameless other?*

Hagen: *I do, if it please your honor. This I then do.*

Magistrate Bowen: *Do you admit, also, of that abomination in your root cellar? That you were growing it? Bringing it to term, as it were, a horror that would torment the community?*

Hagen: *You ruined me simple fun! What a lark that thing would have been, sucking out the bones of the good and proper!*

Magistrate Bowen: *I command you, lady, to name this devil who you have had commerce with. That which gave you power over man and nature.*

Hagen: *Ah, ye wish I hang meself, do ye? Ye wish I speak of commerce with them from the hollow places? Them that hop and jump and crawl?*

Magistrate Bowen: *You already have, lady, you already have. Tell us, then, of the children. Confess in the name of Jesus Christ.*

Hagen: *I will confess not in the name of a false god, yer lordship. The children? The children? Aye, I took their lives and laughed as I did so! I drank their blood and stewed their meat, didn't I? Just as I loosed him what stole them babes, him that devoured their soft heads and picked his teeth with their tiny bones...it is only the beginning, the beginning! Do ye hear? Do ye hear me, you fat stuffed piggies of Procton? Only the beginning...*

Magistrate Bowen: *Your days of evil are at an end.*

Hagen: *Are they, yer lordship? Are they indeed? I think not! Stoned, I was. Tortured, I was. Eye for an eye, they say, and eye for an eye I shall have in His name! At an end? What I have called up, brought to me side, will be known for ages! The legacy will not end, this I swear by me mother's soul which burns in the dark, cold place. Even now, yes, even now I have sewed the seeds. Even now there are three who bring hell into this world...*

***

And so it came to pass.

While Elizabeth Hagen languished in her prison cell, the most peculiar thing happened: three village maidens became pregnant. And each were the daughters of town ministers—Hope from the Congregational Church, Rice from Christ Church, and Ebers from the Presbyterian Church. The girls declared themselves virgins and examinations by Dr. Lewyn proved their hymens to be intact. Virgin births, then. The village was joyous...yet horrified, considering who and what was currently being held in the stockade.

And in her cell, Elizabeth Hagen chanted and sang songs and spoke in unearthly voices throughout the night.

A week into the trial, for more and more witnesses kept coming forward, the three girls—Clarice Ebers, Marilynn Hope, and Sarah Rice—all in their sixteenth years, began to exhibit the physical characteristics of women in their fourth months. Their bellies were oddly swollen and this, seemingly overnight. Dr. Lewyn admitted it was impossible, that even one such case stretched the fabric of credibility...but that three surely canceled out the possibility of coincidence.

And it grew worse.

On the same night, all three girls underwent violent seizures. They fell into violent fits in which they attacked anyone nearby, screaming and cursing and destroying anything at hand. They scratched madly at their skins, as if trying to free themselves of something that burrowed within. Sarah Rice actually peeled a great deal of flesh from her arms and thighs. All three had to be restrained so as not to harm themselves or others...*and* to keep them from running off in the woods, to someone, they claimed, that beckoned to them and filled their heads with "horrible noises".

Of course, it just got worse day by day.

They would not eat, claiming they could only consume blood and raw meat. They profaned their mothers, fathers, and anyone within earshot. Objects moved about their rooms, things were ripped from walls, timbers groaned and splintered, furniture toppled over. The girls spoke in tongues, in the voices of the dead. They told of hidden secrets that they could not possibly know of. Black, reeking fluids were discharged from all orifices. Profane melodies were heard emanating from their swollen bellies. Polluted, noxious smells seeped from them. And more than one person fled in terror when they heard voices whispering from the girls' vaginas.

There was no doubt: the girls were possessed of demons.

Demons, no doubt, loosed by the hag herself, Widow Hagen.

Exorcisms were attempted by the ministers and all were glaring, horrendous failures. Minister John Rice of Christ Church battled with Marilynn Hope for hours upon hours, trying to wrest her soul from the malignancy that had consumed it. He read scripture over her and demanded she...or whatever lived in her...submit to the will of Jesus Christ. But the girl would only laugh and bark and writhe, speaking in various tongues and languages. She demanded meat and blood be brought her. She demanded the flesh of children. Minister Rice underwent physical attacks from objects flying about the room and from "a malefic force as of a cold wind that threw me about."

The demon in Marilynn spoke in the voice of Minister Rice's long-dead first wife, telling him in graphic detail how she was being sodomized in Hell. How his father and mother were there, fornicators and child-eaters, and to prove this she spoke in their voices...very often at the same time.

After some twelve hours of psychic, physical, and spiritual attacks, Minster Rice was led away...a beaten, broken man, his soul laid raw like a festering wound. Ebers tried next, for Marilynn's father had not the strength to look upon his own daughter in such an obscene condition. Things went well at first and it seemed that whatever dwelled in the Hope girl was relenting. Marilynn began to cry and pour out her wracked soul over the macabre torments she had undergone. When Ebers bent forward to listen to her whispered confession...she licked his ear, said something only he could hear. Something which sucked the color from his face. Something which made him run from that room in that cursed house until he reached his own and was able to press a pistol against his temple. And end it.

It was hopeless.

The three girls were locked in the grip of a seemingly omnipotent evil that owned them body and soul. Whatever it was, it was malicious, perverse, and toxic to any who dared toy with it.

***

The trial of Elizabeth Hagen ended and she remained locked in the stockade. The Magistrates were unable to decide on her fate. If she were executed would the evil in Procton only get stronger? Or would it be purged? These were dangerous matters and ones, they decided, not to be considered lightly.

But public opinion ran high and strongly, so there was little choice in the matter. Elizabeth Hagen was dragged from her cell, lashed to a wagon wheel and rolled through the streets before a jeering, hateful crowd. In a clearing known to locals as Heretic's Field for it served as a makeshift graveyard for "suicides, heathens, and those kin folks were ashamed of", Elizabeth Hagen was burned. The wheel she was lashed upon was tied to the trunk of a blasted, dead oak and set afire.

But even this was no easy matter.

Though heaped with kindling and engulfed with flame, she would not die. She burned for hours...burned, blackened, crisped and curled, but refusing to die. She called out curses upon all present. The wagon wheel finally collapsed under her and the roasted, charred thing she became continued to shriek and wail and scream.

It was dragged from the coals with billhooks and twined tight with rope and chains. The Magistrates had it placed back in the stockade where it continued to howl and screech and profane all things holy. The cremated cadaver lived for days...until enraged locals dragged it out into the light and hacked it to bits with axes. Then it finally died. The pieces were buried in separate locations and the evil was at an end...or not quite.

For the demons that possessed the three girls did not vacate; they clung all that much tighter. They would not leave until their spawn was birthed.

**

Three months into their pregnancies...and scarce days since the destruction of the witch...the girls seemed to be ready to deliver...their bellies huge and round, their birth canals dilated. They had become wasted, skeletal things that gave off a pungent stink of carrion.

And so, they gave birth.

Clarice Ebers and Sarah Rice were first.

The labor pains were so intense, each fell unconscious. Copious amounts of blood and black bile drained from Sarah Rice's vagina and she—a staring, sightless creature whose greasy flesh barely contained the skeleton beneath—ruptured. Or at least, it seemed that way. Dr. Lewyn used every trick he knew, but both child and mother perished in a sea of red. Later, he would—with the family's consent—investigate matters more fully and discover that Sarah had ruptured because her child had teeth. A full set of teeth oddly sharp and long. And with these teeth, the child—a white, limbless horror with huge, lidless black eyes—had bitten its mother to death from inside, severing arteries in the process.

Dr. Lewyn decided wisely to keep this from the family...this and the fact that the child had not only bitten its mother, but had cannibalized her. Digesting no small amount of tissue in the process. He also kept secret the fact that Sarah's child *was not dead* when he opened her up with a scalpel. That the grotesque little monster was living on inside its dead mother, feeding on her like some hellish prenatal ghoul. That when he pulled it from her cleaved open abdomen...an armless, squirming grub that had more in common with a maggot than a human being...he had to tear it free, for it hung tenaciously to its mother's tissues by its teeth.

Lewyn dumped it in a bucket and poured acid on it, upon which, it dissolved like a salted slug.

Long before her child came into the world, Clarice Ebers lost her mind with the agony, if there was any mind left by that point. She cried out in the voice of Elizabeth Hagen, thrashed and fought and finally passed out. What she birthed into the world was a crawling thing, blistered and scorched. Like something that had been burned alive. Wisps of smoke wafted from its incinerated flesh and it, as it died, scratched a black, inverted cross into the stained bedsheets with one withered finger.

Clarice died moments later, her insides scalded.

The child was buried in Heretic's Field, Clarice and Sarah entombed side by side in a Christian grave.

Marilynn Hope, however, lasted another month. Her child, when born in the winter of 1824, was healthy and normal in every possible way. A boy. The only irregularity was a birthmark on his back in the form of a tiny, four-fingered hand. But he was considered by townsfolk to be cursed, the progeny of unholy union. So Minister Hope sent his deranged daughter and her son to live with kin in Missouri where they could be sheltered from the world.

He named his grandson James Lee.

In Missouri he would take the family name of relations: Cobb.

3

Until James Lee's third year up in the Ozarks in Taney County, Missouri, the same ritual was repeated on a weekly basis. When Uncle Arlen returned from the lumber camps or the lead mine he sometimes found regular work at, he would take Marilynn Hope from the attic loft she was sequestered in and drag her bodily down to Bryant Creek. Along with James Lee's Auntie Maretta, they would read from the Book of Common Prayer as Marilynn alternately whimpered and growled like an animal.

Though James Lee grew strong in the simple ways of hill folk, the taint on his mother never lessened. She was a filthy, mad thing dressed in rags with wild, glistening marbles for eyes. Uncle Arlen kept her tied up in the loft where she ate insects and shit herself, whispering to those no one else could see and scratching odd symbols and words into the roughhewn walls with her long yellow nails.

But once a week…purification.

James Lee would sit in the dirt, scratching around with a stick, watching with disinterest what they did with the crazy woman. Uncle Arlen and Auntie Maretta would drag her out with a rope looped around her throat. They'd strip her and toss her into the creek, jumping in with her. Taking turns, one would read from the prayer book and the other would dunk Marilynn into the water, holding her under until she quit thrashing. Uncle Arlen said it would drive the demons from her through baptismal in "Christ's very waters".

James Lee had seen it done many, many times, but it had not helped. Though at three years of age he could not understand nor fathom what it was all about, he knew whatever it was they were doing didn't work. Dunk her, preach to her, dunk her some more, preach some more. He decided it was probably a game...but one only the adults could play. Because whenever he tried to edge closer, wanting badly to splash in the water, too, Uncle Arlen told him to keep away, keep away, hear?

But after three years of proper baptizing and the Lord's word, Marilynn was no better. So Uncle Arlen imprisoned her in a shack in the hills above the cabin so they wouldn't have to listen to "that heathen madness no more". James Lee wasn't allowed to go up there. Uncle Arlen and Auntie Maretta took care of the crazy woman's needs—feeding and watering her like any of the stock on that hardscrabble farm.

It was a hard life up in the Ozarks, miles and miles from anywhere that might have been considered even remotely civilized. James Lee attended a ramshackle school over in the next hollow yonder, learned to read and write. The other children kept their distance, for they knew he was the son of the woman up in the shack, the woman everyone knew was "teched in the head". The kids said—but only behind James Lee's back for even as a schoolboy he had a virulent, raging temper—that the crazy woman ate rats and snakes and toads. That she had two heads, one she gibbered with and one she ate with. But maybe, too, they kept away from James Lee because they could smell something on him, something bad.

So he clung to the Cobb farm, slopping hogs and cleaning pens and picking rocks and chopping wood. He took great, unsavory relish in watching Uncle Arlen put chickens to the hatchet. Liked how their blood spurted from their necks and how, even when dead, they seemed to live on.

"Can folks do that, Uncle?" he asked one day. "Even if they's all dead?"

Uncle Arlen made to swat at him as he often did, but held his hand back, fixed him with those fierce, unforgiving eyes. "Boy...that is, folks is dead they's jus' dead is all, they cain't walk about and such and if'n they do..." He stopped himself there, scratched at his beard. "Well, they cain't boy. They jus' cain't."

"But—"

"Ain't no buts, boy! No back to work with ye! Mind me, boy!"

And the years passed and James Lee got bigger and the children gave him a wider birth except for Rawley Cummings who took it upon himself to tell James Lee that he was no better than the crazy woman in the shack yonder. That, given time, he would drink piss and rut with hogs, too. It was a given. James Lee...though three years younger...jumped the boy like a mountain cat with a thorn digging into its ass. He kicked and punched, bit and clawed. It took four boys to pull him free. Schoolmaster Parnes gave him a good thrashing for that one and Uncle Arlen beat him so hard he closed both his eyes.

To which Auntie Maretta said, "Not m' boy, not m' sweet little angel Jimmy Lee...don't ye lay a hand on him! Don't ye dare lay a hand on him!"

So Uncle Arlen ceased beating him and took the hickory switch to his wife instead. But that got it out of him. Like other times when he got heavy with his fists, he went up into the hills to do some drinking. When he came back, he was better.

The Devil was purged.

***

One night, when they thought he was sleeping, James Lee heard them talking by the stove in hushed voices.

"Don't never wan' that boy finding out, hear?" Uncle Arlen said in his gravelly voice. "Don't need to know that woman's his mother."

"Never ever," Auntie Maretta told him. "Why, Jimmy Lee...he's m' boy, m' big and proud boy. He ain't like her, cain't ye see? He's like m' own flesh."

"He ain't though, woman," Uncle Arlen pointed out. "Place he comes from...well things jus' ain't right there. Ain't proper."

Auntie Maretta chewed on that for a time, decided she didn't like the taste and spit it right back out. "He's more mine than he is hers. Don't ye see? Lord above, sometimes I wish she'd up and expire."

"Woman, now she's kin."

"Y'all wish it, too, Arlen Cobb."

"In a weaker moment, yessum. But, hell, ain't happenin'…she's up in the shack doin' what she does and livin' on…how can that be, woman? How can that be? Don't even freeze to death proper in the winter…now how is that?"

But Auntie Maretta didn't know. "Hexed, is all."

"I jus' worry about that boy…he carries the taint on him and ye know it. What's in her is in him. Blood'll tell and it'll tell every time. Cousin Marilynn ain't scarcely human, I figure. That whole brood is cursed…Jesus, lookit her old man, kilt himself and what! And him a preacher."

"Easterners," Auntie Maretta said. "They ain't right in the head."

"Neither is that boy…he likes blood and killin' too much. Like his mama, he carries the taint on his soul…"

James Lee was thirteen when he heard that.

But it hadn't been the first time.

He didn't know all the story, but he knew enough by then to put some of it together. That crazy woman was his mother and they had come from back east, from some awful place of witches and tainted heredity and things too awful to put into words. At night, he'd lay there and think on it and think on it some more. One way or another, come hell or high water, he was going to learn what it was all about. He figured his first step was to climb up into the hills and get a look at…*at his mother*. He was banned from going up there, but maybe knowledge was worth a good beating.

The very next winter he got his chance.

A bad blizzard had set its teeth into the Ozarks and snow was drifted up near the windows which were locked tight with patterns of frost. Rags had been stuffed in the cracks to keep the wind out, but there was still a chill in the cabin. A chill that set upon you like something hungry if you strayed too far from the fire. James Lee was sitting before it, working out some arithmetic problems by candlelight. His Uncle and Auntie sat at the hardwood table, him with his pipe and her with her knitting.

Whenever Auntie Maretta caught his eyes, she'd give him a sly, secretive smile that spoke of love and trust and faith. A look that said, yer a good boy and I knows it.

Whenever Uncle Arlen caught his eyes, he gave him a hard, withering look that simply said, mind yer schoolwork, boy, and quiet yer damn daydreaming.

So James Lee sat there on the floor, scribbling.

The cabin was a log affair with a plank floor and smoke-blackened beams crisscrossing above. There was a sheltered loft, but it wasn't used now that Marilynn was up in the old shack. A cast iron stove sat in the corner, fire in its belly. Two cauldrons filled with boiling water bubbled on its surface. The air smelled of wood smoke, burned fat, and maple syrup. While Auntie Maretta busied herself washing up the dinner dishes—blue speckled plates and tin cups—Uncle Arlen cleared his throat. Cleared it the way he did when he was about to finally speak what was on his mind.

"Boy," he said. "Ye up to an errand? Ye up to bravin' the snow and night?"

James Lee slapped his book shut, never so ready. "Yessum, Uncle."

"Aw right, listen here now. Want ye to go out to the smokehouse. Them hams in there is cured and ready. Take one of 'em and not the big one, mind, wrap it up tight in a po-tater sack, bring it up to Miss Leevy up yonder on the high road." He packed his clay pipe with rough-cut tobacco. "Now, she been good t' us and we gonna be good t' her. She's up in years. Ye think ye can handle that?"

"Yessum."

"Off wit ye then."

It was bitter cold out there, the snow whipping and whistling around the cabin, but James Lee knew he could do it, all right. Out past the sap-house, he dug snow away from the smokehouse door and packaged up the ham. Then he marched straight through the drifts and shrieking wind up onto the road and fought his way up to Miss Leevy's. She took the ham and made James Lee drink some chamomile tea brightened with 'shine.

On his way back, he cut through the woods.

He knew where he was going.

He knew what he had to see.

Sheets of snow fell from the pines overhead and the air was kissed with ice. His breath frosted from his lips and the night created crazy, jumping shadows that ringed him tight. But the 'shine had lit a fire in his belly and he felt the equal of anything. He carried an oil lamp with him, lighting it only when he made out the dim hulk of the shack.

The forbidden shack.

Sucking cold air into his lungs and filling his guts with iron, he made his way over there. He stood outside in the snow, thinking how it wasn't too late to turn back, wasn't too late at all. But then his hand was out of its mitten and his fingers were throwing the bolt, just throwing it aside fancy as you please.

First thing he heard was a rattling, dragging sound...as of chains.

Then something like a harsh breathing...but so very harsh it was like fireplace bellows sucking up ash.

It stayed his hand, but not for long. *Good and goddammit, James Lee Cobb,* a voice echoed in his skull, *this is what ye wanted, weren't it? To know? To see? To look the worse possible thing right in the face and not dare look away? Weren't it? Well, weren't it?*

It was.

Those chains...or whatever they were...rattled again and there was a rustling sound. James Lee pulled the door open, but slowly, slowly, figuring his mind needed time to adjust. Like slipping into a chill spring lake, you had to do it by degrees. The door swung open and a hot, reeking blast of fetid air hit him full in the face. It stank like wormy meat simmering on a stove lid. His knees went to rubber and something in him—maybe courage—just shriveled right up.

In the flickering lantern light he saw.

He saw his mother quite plainly.

She was chained to the floor, pulling herself away from the light like some gigantic worm. Her flesh had gone marble-white and was damp and glistening like the flesh of a mushroom. Great sores and ulcers were set into her and some had eaten right to the bone beneath. It was hard to say if she was wearing rags or that was just her skin hanging in loops and ragged folds. Her hair was steel-gray and stringy, those eyes just fathomless holes torn into the vellum of her face.

But what struck James Lee the hardest was not the eyes or the stink or even the feces and filthy straw and tiny animal bones scattered about...it was that she seemed to have *tentacles*. Just like one of them sea monsters in a picture book that ate ships raw. Long, yellow things all curled and coiled like clocksprings.

But then...he realized they were her *fingernails*.

And they had to be well over two feet in length...hard, bony growths that came out of her fingertips and laid over her like corkscrewed snakes.

James Lee made a sound...he wasn't sure what...and she opened those flaking lips, revealing gray decayed teeth that sprouted from pitted gums like grayed fence posts. She made a grunting, squealing sound like a hog. And then she reached out to him, seemed to know him, and those fingernails clattered together like castanets.

That's when he slammed the door shut.

That's when he threw the bolt.

And that's when he ran down through the snow and brambles, ducking past dead oaks and vaulting fallen logs. He ran all the way to the cabin and stumbled and fell into the door. Then Uncle Arlen threw it open, yanking him inside, into that mouth of warmth and security, demanding to know what it was, what it was.

But James Lee could not tell.

***

The Ozarks back then had a fine story-telling tradition. Sometimes a man's worth was judged on how hard he worked *and* how good of a yarn he could spin. So James Lee was no stranger to tales of ghosts and haunts, child-eating ogres that lived in the depths of the forests or blood-sucking devil clans that peopled secret hollows. For everything scarcely understood or completely misunderstood, there was a story to explain it. It was a region where folktale and myth were an inseparable part of everyday life. There were faith healers and power doctors, water witches and yarb grannies...you name it, it showed sooner or later.

And one thing the Ozarks never had a shortage of were witches.

Some good, some evil, some real and some storied, regardless, they were there. Ask just about anyone in any locality of the hills and they could tell you where to find one...or point you to someone who could.

The kids at school told of an old man named Heller the Witch-Man who lived up in some misty hollow that few dared venture to. He could cast out devils and call them up, cure disease and make hair grow.

James Lee figured it was just another story...then one day he was down in town. Uncle Arlen was picking up some feed. James Lee was standing out on the boardwalk, kicking pebbles into the street. Suddenly...he got the damnedest feeling. He felt dizzy and the birthmark on his back started to burn something awful.

He turned and some grizzled old man was standing there, staring at him.

He looked like some hillbilly from the high ridges, dirty and smelling in an old hide coat. He had a single gold tooth in his lower jaw and it sparkled in the sunlight.

"Boy...ye got the mark on ye," he said. "Ye got it on ye and ye cain't rid yerself of it..."

Then Uncle Arlen came out and dragged James Lee bodily away. And even after he threw him in the wagon and they made their way out of town, James Lee could feel those eyes on him, feel that mark on his back burning like a coal.

Uncle Arlen shouted and raged and warned James Lee about talking to strangers, because one day you meet the wrong one and soon enough, he sneaks up to the farm and slits all our throats.

James Lee just said: "It's him, ain't it? The Witch-Man."

"Ain't no such thing, damn ye! Ain't no such thing!"

But James Lee couldn't stop. "They say...they say how he can do things. Things no one else can. Maybe, maybe if we brought the...the crazy woman to him, he could cure her—"

James Lee caught the back of Uncle Arlen's fist in the mouth for that. And when he got home, he got a better taste of it. When Uncle Arlen was done, James Lee was folded up on the ground bleeding.

"Ye never, ever, never mention that one 'round me again, hear?" Uncle Arlen told him. "That heathen devil witch-man is nothin' but pain and trouble! He cain't cure nothin' and no one, all he'll bring ye is seven yards of hell!"

After that, James Lee didn't mention Heller the Witch-Man again.

Even Auntie Maretta looked on him differently. She wasn't exactly cold, but gone was the warmth and love he'd once known. Sometimes he got the feeling she was scared of him. And one night he heard Uncle Arlen say:

"What'd I tell ye, woman? Like calls to like."

Although he didn't mention the strange old man, James Lee never stopped thinking about him or what lived in the shack up yonder. Days became weeks that wrapped themselves around months and years. And it was from an old moonshiner named Crazy Martin that James Lee got the answers he wanted. Crazy Martin knew the old man, lived way up in a hollow known as Hell's Half-Acre and with good reason.

So one summer afternoon, James Lee made the pilgrimage.

It took him hours to navigate the mud roads and pig trails that snaked through the deep forest. But finally, in a hollow where no birds sang and no insects buzzed and the vegetation had a gray, dead look about it, he located the Witch-Man's shack.

Heller was sitting before a fire. "Come sit yeself down, boy," he said, without once looking in James Lee's direction. "I knewed ye'd come, sooner or later, I knewed ye had to. So sit down. Folks say I bite people, but don't ye believe it none."

James Lee sat before the fire, refusing to meet the old man's eyes.

Heller had a fiddle on his lap and he played a slow, melancholy tune while his mouth rambled on and on about his crops and how they were taking and it would be a good year, save fire and frost.

"Ye said I was marked," James Lee managed after he realized the old man was no flesh-eating booger like they said. He was just an old man who lived in a weird hollow who worried over his crops.

"I recall, boy, I recall." He set the fiddle on his lap. "Yer pa...no sir, yer *uncle*, I think, yes...yer uncle didn't cotton ye talking to me, did he?"

James Lee was astounded. Here, all these years later, the old man remembered a chance encounter like it was yesterday. And he seemed to know things without being told them. Maybe he wasn't just some old dirt-farmer after all.

"I think...I think he's afraid of ye," James Lee said honestly. "I think lots of folks are."

"Yessum, they is. They certainly is." The old man thought about it. "Yer uncle...I figure he's a wise sort. For commerce with me can come at a terrible price. Boy like you...he cain't afford what I got. Less'n, he don't value his soul. Ye value yer soul, boy?"

"Yes...yes, I do."

"Good boy. Now state yer business, will ye? I cain't pull everything outta yer head."

So James Lee told him. About his mother, the mysteries surrounding their coming to Missouri. He went on and on, telling him the same things and asking him the same questions for these were things he'd never spoken aloud to anyone before, but had always itched to.

"First off, boy, yer mama...she's beyond m' help. M' power does not extend far enough to fight what holds her. She was cursed, boy, cursed by...yes, by that evil old bitch. Yessum, I see her in my head, that hag. She packs a heap of power, boy...even dead, her medicine is strong."

"I was hoping..."

"No, boy. But what has yer mama...yes, it's weakened some. If'n ye wait...surely, there will be peace for yer mama." The old man leaned forward, his eyes burning. "But hear me, boy, ye carry the mark...yer life'll be a dark matter. Ain't no sunshine comin' yer way...jus' darkness."

James Lee couldn't fathom any of that business. Heller waxed on about the "Devil's Mark" and how those who wore it were cursed. But finally, the shadows growing long, Heller let him leave, telling him to follow the trail straight up and out of the hollow. Not to stop, not even to pee. To keep walking, looking straight ahead. That if he saw someone on the trail, to not look upon them, not to listen to what they said. And if he heard voices from the woods…to just ignore them, no matter what they said or what they promised.

"This holler, boy…it's full of them what don't rest easy."

James Lee ran out of there and up into the sunshine and greenery again. When he got back to the cabin, no one would speak to him as if he carried a stain upon him. A stink of crazy old men and witches. The next day, he packed what he had and left the hills, figuring he was seventeen and a man. That it was time to make his way in the world.

West was where he was going.

And on the way he fell in with the wrong type. He seemed to naturally gravitate to them. And as the weeks and months past, whatever had been waiting in him all these years began to sprout, to take root and bloom. But it was no flower, but a mordant and eating cancer that devoured him an inch at a time.

By the time he fought in the Mexican-American War, James Lee had already killed six men…with his hands, his pistols, knife and hatchet.

4

The dry winds were born of blast furnaces and ovens. They scoured the desolate countryside, howling through dry ravines and whistling along the peaks of rocky precipices. Dense stands of chaparral and wiry brush trembled. Sand blew and snakes hid amongst the crags. Buzzards circled in the yellow hazy sky above. Flies lit on the faces of the living and the dead and the wind tasted of salt, heat, and misery.

All in all, Northern Mexico was a parched, godless country just this side of hell.

James Lee Cobb, a Missouri Volunteer, watched as two buckskin-clad irregulars dragged another Mexican corpse from the dirty scrub.

"That's six now, boss," one of them named Jones said, spitting a stream of tobacco juice into the Spanish face of a corpse that had taken a load of grapeshot in the belly. He was just one big, wide opening between sternum and crotch now…you could've passed a medicine ball through him without brushing meat. "Six of them stinking, mother-raping sonsofbitches."

"Every time I see a dead greaser," Cobb said, "I think this land is one inch closer to civilization."

Jones nodded, kicking at a spider in the dirt. "Yep, I would agree with that, James. I surely would." He spit at the corpses again. "You know? Some of this country down here…it ain't too bad. If it weren't were for the Mesicans dirtying it up, might be fit for a white man. You think?"

Cobb narrowed his eyes, watching for trouble, always watching for trouble. "Could be. Hotter than the Devil's own asshole, but maybe."

"Worth thinking on."

Cobb listened to the wind talk and it spoke in the voices of demons, telling him there would be a lot more killing, a lot more ugly dying before this little party was wound up. Licking his leathery lips, this made Cobb smile.

***

Whatever Cobb had been as a boy, he was not as a man. He could never honestly mark the point when he had gone from being wide-eyed and naïve…to what he was now, a blooded killer.

Maybe it had been his first killing.

That drifter he'd knifed in Kansas after his run from Missouri, the one that seemed eager to teach him the ways of sodomy. Maybe when he'd pulled that hunting knife and sank it clear into the stinking pervert's belly and felt all that hot blood come bubbling out like lava through a sharp slit in the earth…maybe that had done it. For once he got that first killing over and done with, it all came real easy and natural-like. A predestined thing.

Just like Heller the Witch-Man told him, his life had become "a dark matter."

Cobb didn't think much of Missouri or Heller or Uncle Arlen and Auntie Maretta much after he left. Not even the horror that was his mother. Staying alive, staying whole, keeping his belly full and his scalp intact—these things tended to occupy his thoughts. He stole horses and rustled cattle. Trapped beaver in the Rockies and Wyoming's Green River country. He bootlegged whiskey to injuns and supplied them with U.S. issue carbines for their fights against squatters and the Army. All in all, there was a lot of murdering and violence involved and this on a daily basis. All the good things in him withered like green vines in a drought and something else, something shadowed and nameless rose up to fill the void.

Something that had been there from the start...just waiting.

Waiting its turn.

When Texas decided to annex to the United States, he'd joined a group of hellraising Missouri volunteers to fight for its independence from Mexico.

War, any war, was a hard business, but something in Cobb liked it.

His first taste of it was at the steaming holding camps at Matamoros where everyone was anxious to fight and there was nothing to do but take it out on each other. The Missouri volunteers went at it tooth-and-nail with volunteers from Georgia and Indiana and particularly with the regular army, which looked down on all volunteers as trash. At best, they decided, they were mercenaries, at worst, just cut-throats and freebooters. So the volunteers gave them hell at every quarter. And when they weren't using their fists, they were popping off their muskets at passing game, shadows, anything that moved and some things that didn't.

Matamoros was one unruly hive of confusion and insubordination. The regular army was incensed over these brigands, these hell-for-leather volunteers.

And the volunteers themselves were amused to no earthly end.

But then Cobb and the others were jammed aboard a riverboat and taken down the Rio Grande. The river had burst its banks, then burst them again. Maybe once after that, too. Point being, the pilots were having a hell of a time with it. They couldn't be sure what was river and what was flood plain. The boats kept getting snagged in mud flats and bottoms. And in that sparse country, the troops had to dismount every so often to gather wood for the boilers...and such a thing required scavenging for miles sometimes.

Finally, the boats arrived at Camargo...a lick of spit that was neither here nor there nor anywhere you truly wanted to be. Just a little Mexican town on the San Juan River maybe three miles from its junction with the Rio Grande. It had once been sizeable, but was now in ruins from the flooding. The troops unloaded, an irritable and ornery lot, into a camp that was plagued by swarms of insects, snakes, and blistering heat. Men washed their laundry and horses in the same water camp kettles were filled. It was a filthy, desolate place where yellow fever and dysentery raged unchecked. The hospital tents were crowded with the diseased and dying.

Cobb and the other volunteers spent most of their time arguing, swatting flies, and burying the dead.

It was that kind of place.

Death everywhere...and the fighting hadn't even begun.

***

Cobb's volunteers slowly threaded out of the rocks, dumping more cadavers on the stinking heap before them. Twelve of them now. Twelve Mexican guerrillas. The sort that preyed on small bands of U.S. soldiers. Cutting them off, gunning them down. Taking them alive if they could and torturing them. Whipping them until they lost consciousness or cutting off their flesh in small chunks until they bled to death, screaming all the while.

Maybe the regular Army didn't know how to deal with these pigs, but the volunteer forces surely did.

When you took them alive, you made a game out of it. You buried them up to their necks in the sand and spread honey over their faces and let the fire ants do their thing. You dragged them behind horses over the rocks until they broke apart. You hung them by their feet and swung 'em through bonfires. You dropped them into pits of diamondback rattlesnakes. You staked them out and let the wildlife have their way. And, if you felt real creative, you took a skinning knife to 'em...it could last for hours and hours that way.

But, best, when you found their villages, you burned them. You shot down their children and raped their women.

One of the volunteers was pissing on the bodies and Cobb had to yell at him. "Is that how ye show respect for the dead, ye sumbitch?" he said, backing the man against a wall of stone. "Is that how ye treat these chilis? Shows that ye don't know shit, my friend. Let me show ye how it's done."

Cobb pulled out his bowie knife, pressed the blade against his thumb until it bled...just to make sure it was real sharp. Then, carefully and expertly, taking one of the dead ones by the hair, he ran the blade of his knife under the jaw line and around the cheekbone and just under the scalp and then traced it back down again until he had made a bloody circle. Then, sawing and pulling, he peeled the face from the bone beneath.

He held up the dripping mask. "All set to scare the kiddies with."

The other volunteers were laughing and clapping each other on the backs. Why, it was the damn funniest thing they'd ever seen. Leave it to Cobb to come up with something like that. Just when you thought he'd exhausted his grisly creativity by using the scrotum of a Mex for a tobacco pouch or making a necklace of fingers...he came up with something new.

Pulling their knives, the others began doing it, too.

Cobb walked amongst them, motioning with his bloody knife like a schoolteacher instructing on the finer points of conjugating verbs. Except, Cobb's classroom was a hot, wind-blown place and his subject was butchering. He made quite a figure standing there in his filthy, threadbare buckskins, forage cap tilted at a rakish angle atop his head. His beard was long and shaggy, his hair hanging to his shoulders in greasy knots. An assortment of Colt pistols, revolvers, knifes, and hatchets hung from his belts. Along with the newly-acquired Mexican death mask and the mummified hand of a priest he'd hacked off in Monterrey and sun-dried on a flat rock.

There weren't enough bodies to go around and there was some argument as to who was going to get what. Cobb settled that by telling the men it was strictly first come, first served. Those of you who got here first, why ye just carve yerself a face, that's what ye want, he told them. Ye others, well ye have to make do with what ye can beg, borrow, or steal. Cobb told them—and they believed him—that there would be plenty of trophies to be had down the road a piece. Maybe tomorrow, maybe today.

"One thing ye can count on, boys," he said to them, "is that there's always gonna be more. Mexico's just full of 'em."

He watched them going to work, hacking and sawing and cutting, singing little ditties they'd learned from the Mexican folk, but didn't understand a word of.

Yes, Cobb watched them, knowing they'd patterned themselves after him. He'd joined up as an enlisted man, but soon enough—maybe through ferocity in battle or sheer savagery—he'd become an officer and their leader. They looked up to him. They fancied all the badges and military decorations he'd taken off dead Mexican officers and pinned to his hide shirt. The necklaces of fingers and blackened ears, the skull of the that Mexican colonel he'd mounted from his saddlehorn.

They wanted to be like him.

They wanted to be a bloodthirsty hard-charger like James Lee Cobb. They wanted to leap into battle as he had at Buena Vista, shooting and stabbing and pounding his way through the Mexican ranks.

It made them fight real hard in battle so they could collect up trophies as he had.

And, yes, they could fight hard and die hard and loot and mutilate the dead all they wanted...but none of them would ever be like James Lee Cobb. They would never have his peculiar appetite for inflicting suffering and death. An appetite born in nameless places where human bones were piled in pyramids and human souls were boiled in cauldrons. They would never have that and they surely would never have the birthmark he had.

The one that looked like a red four-fingered handprint.
A handprint that positively burned when death was near.

***

What happened at the Battle of Buena Vista was this: Some 14,000 Mexican troops commanded by General Santa Anna charged Zachary Taylor's U.S. forces which numbered less than 5,000. Through determination, audacity, and sheer luck, the American's pushed the Mexican's back.

Easy enough to tell; not so easy to experience.

On a dismal morning in February 1847, the troopers under Taylor received orders to strike their tents and march on Buena Vista. Sixteen miles later, they arrived...lacking provisions, wood for fires. Early the next morning picket guards arrived, saying that a large Mexican force was approaching and approaching fast. James Lee Cobb and the Missouri volunteers stationed themselves in a narrow ridge, just beyond an artillery battery and waited for their enemies.

Along with them, were elements of the Kentucky and Arkansas cavalry. Each man waited amongst the rocks, eyes wide, flintlock muskets and carbines primed and at the ready, knives sharpened and hatchets in hand. There was a stink in the air—sour, high, heady.

The smell of fear.

For down below, the enemy were massing and everyone spread out on that ridge could see them, really see them for the first time. The sheer numbers. For once, intelligence had neither over-inflated or under-inflated enemy strength. The Mexicans moved and marched, formed-up into ranks and scattered out in skirmish lines. From where Cobb sat...they were mulling, busy things in perpetual motion.

"Don't look out there and see yer death, boys," Cobb told his volunteers. "Look down there and know, know that if they take ye, yer gonna take ten of them motherfuckers with ye."

Cannonade exploded along the face of the mountain as the Mexican guns—eight-pounders and sixteen-pounders--sought them out. By nightfall, they picked up the pace, raining hell down upon two Indiana rifle companies. Bugles sounded and men died and gouts of smoke filled the air...but the real fighting had yet to begin.

The volunteers and regular army forces waited and waited. Hungry, cold, but not daring to close their eyes as discharges of grapeshot tore up the landscape around them.

At dawn the next day, the Mexican cannons started singing again and things really started moving. Heavy fire erupted in and around the volunteers and was answered by American batteries. The entire mountainside was crawling with the enemy like hordes of Hun filled with blood-rage and steel, preparing to sack a town.

Cobb moved his troops out and charged a hidden Mexican emplacement that had been harassing the Indiana rifles, killing the soldiers and hacking on them until they lay scattered in pieces amongst their damaged guns.

But for every ten killed, twenty more came shouting up the hill at them. And behind them, Jesus, half the Mexican army. Infantry in their green tunics, cavalry in scarlet coats. They carried British East India rifles and long lances, wore brass helmets with large black plumes like raven's feathers.

All hell broke loose.

Cannon balls whistled over the heads of the volunteers, exploding with gouts of shattered rock and flying dirt. Grapeshot ripped into men, spraying their anatomies in every which direction. Smoke hung like a ground fog over everything and the cavalry looked like ghost riders pounding through it. Men were screaming and shrieking, blood covered the ground in viscous, steaming pools. Soldiers—both American and Mexican—dropped and died, piling up like corded lumber. Some rose only to fall again and be crushed under the thundering hooves of horses. Bugles sounded out. Men crawled through the carnage, missing limbs and/or pressing their viscera back into ruptured abdomens. Some wanted to escape...but others, piecemeal, wanted to fight on.

Cobb bayoneted a soldier and slashed the face off another. He saw volunteers fall...but each time he advanced to their aid, bodies fell at his feet, blood and brains spattered into his face, enemy soldiers rushing out at him.

So he busied himself shooting and knifing, taking them as they came.

And around him, the volunteers scrambled over heaped bodies as mounted troopers of the Mississippi Rifles charged into the fray. They wore bright red shirts and broad-brimmed straw hats. The Mexican cavalry met them on deadly ground and muskets sounded and sabers slashed, horses were ripped apart by cannon balls and men fell by the hundreds, the landscape becoming a bleeding, blasted sea of bodies and limbs and glistening internals.

Behind the Mexican cavalry, a body of lancers came shouting and running, infantry with fixed bayonets backing them up.

The Missouri volunteers, many of them burnt black with powder, fought on, ready to take anything that came. Cobb emptied his pistols until they were smoking and hot. He fired his musket, loaded, rammed, fired again with swift expertise. But the Mexicans poured forward in a surging, shrieking tide, severing the American lines, and Cobb found himself crushing skulls with the butt of his rifle, opening bellies and throats with his knives, and taking weapons off dead men, fighting and fighting.

The Mexicans charged not only from the front, but from both sides and behind now. It was sheer pandemonium. Men were falling and writhing. Horses stampeding and throwing their riders, mad now with gaping wounds and terror from the pounding and shooting and screaming. Shells were bursting and rifle balls whizzing like mad hornets, smoke billowing and dust rising up in blinding whirlwinds. Musketry was crashing and big guns thundering. Wagons and their loads were shattered to kindling and everywhere the dead and the dying, blood and smoke and wreckage.

And still more fresh Mexican troops charged in.

Cobb, filled now with a tearing, raging hunger, dashed in amongst their numbers, cutting men down with musket-fire and blazing pistols. He split open the head of a lancer with his hatchet, slit the throat of another, took up his lance and speared a Mexican officer from his horse. He sank the shaft through the man's chest and impaled him into the ground. Killing two or three others, he mounted the Mex's horse—a fine white stallion—and charged in, hacking and cutting, shooting and stabbing.

The horse was blown out from under him, a volley of grapeshot blowing the animal's legs into shrapnel.

From above, the landscape was ragged and gutted, a chasm filled with smoke and fire, swarming with men and riderless horses. It was a slaughter of the first degree and in the confusion, it was hard to tell who was winning and who was losing.

But Cobb didn't know and didn't care.

He fought on, killing more men, stealing horses, slicing through the Mexican lines like a red-hot blade. The fighting continued for some time, but eventually, the dead heaped across the ground in great flesh-and-blood ramparts, the Mexicans broke off their advance. Pounded continually by artillery, their cavalry shattered, they pulled back and even this cost them hundreds and hundreds of men.

When the fighting had ended, the battlefield was a graveyard.

A slaughterhouse.

As far as the eye could see, bodies and parts thereof, men blown up into trees, horses disemboweled by cannonball, soldiers cut in half from musketry. It looked like an image from Bruegel's *The Triumph of Death*—smoke and fire, cadavers and shattered wagons. Pitted earth. Pools of blood. Thousands of flies lighting off the dead and those near to it. Men begged for medical aid, for water, for their mothers and sweethearts, for an ounce of life so they could do just a little more killing.

As Cobb walked through the carnage, his buckskins wet with blood and burned from blazing shrapnel, he saw living men drag themselves out from under corpses. Wild-eyed, blood-drenched things, they brandished empty pistols and gored knives. They bayoneted the already dead and those begging for death. Battle-shocked officers in blackened uniforms stumbled out, cursing and crying and shouting out orders to dead men. They called for corpses to rise and give chase to the enemy, while amongst them soldiers shambled to and fro, looking for fallen comrades, dropped weapons, and lost limbs.

Cobb and his blood-stained, fire-baptized volunteers, moved through the burning fields of corpses, parting seething mists of smoke, and began mutilating the Mexicans. Scalping and dismembering, chopping off fingers and ears and plucking free death-masks and hands. They laughed with a deranged cackling as they arranged Mexican corpses in obscene displays.

And Cobb urged them on to new and more twisted atrocities as the birthmark on his back blazed and steamed and pulsed.

Something in him was very pleased, very satisfied with what it saw.

War is hell.

And for whatever was in Cobb, this was like coming home.

***

Fire and heat and smoke and screaming.

The schoolhouse was burning.

Voices inside cried out in Spanish, bastardized English, Indian tongues…begging, pleading to be released, released for the love of God. And Cobb had every intention of releasing them—right into the hands of their maker.

Cobb watched the fire, fed on it, felt it burning inside him, too. His blood was acid that bubbled and seethed. His heart a red-hot piston hammering and hammering, throwing sparks and oily steam. The birthmark at his back was like an iron brand scorched into his flesh.

The volunteers ringed the schoolhouse, muskets at the ready.

"Any of them chilis get out," Cobb told them. "Drop them bastards."

The volunteers had tracked the Mexican guerrillas here to a little town called Del Barra. This is where they lived, operated out of. Just a shabby collection of shacks and adobes leeched by the sun and blasted by desert wind, all lorded over by an old Spanish church and schoolhouse. In the basement of the church, the volunteers found rifles and ammunition, uniforms and weapons stripped from American dead. Many of these still had bloodstains on them.

The priest had refused to let them see the cellar.

Cobb slit his throat.

So the schoolhouse blazed in that hot, arid country and the wind was that of pyres and crematories, the sun melting like a coin of yellow wax in the cloudless sky above.

Sweat ran down Cobb's face like tears, cutting clean trails through the ground-in dirt. His eyes were wide and unblinking, red-rimmed like the boundaries of hell. A pink worm of a tongue licked salt from his lips. He could hear the sounds of the shouting and shrieking within. Flames had engulfed one side of the schoolhouse now and were greedily licking up another. Inside...old men, women, children. Pounding and screeching to be let out.

There was a sudden wild, roaring sound and the entire schoolhouse was engulfed. It didn't take much. The wood was dry as tinder, caught flame like matchsticks. Smoke twisted in the air, black belching funnels of it. It stank of charred wood, cremated flesh and singed hair.

The screaming and pounding was dying out now.

"Just about all fried up, I reckon," Jones said, scratching at his crotch.

A few flaming forms burst from the inferno now, stick figures swallowed in yellow and orange flame. They stumbled about, arms waving about crazily. If it hadn't been so profane, it might have been comical. Volunteers opened up on them dropping them as danced through the doorway. More followed. Anything, anything to escape the flames. The volunteers fired, primed and loaded, fired again.

A final form came running with a weird, jerking gait, flames licking from it in flickering plumes. It carried something. Cobb figured it was a mother carrying her child.

He held his hand up.

The volunteers did not fire.

She made it maybe ten, fifteen feet, collapsed in a smoldering heap. Cobb watched her until the fire died out and she was just a folded-up, blackened window dummy, her flesh falling away in cinders. She and the child had been melted together in a roasted mass. Their faces were incinerated skulls. The smoke that came from them was hot and stinking.

Within an hour, as the volunteers sat around drinking mescal and chewing on tortillas looted from the adobes, the schoolhouse had fallen into itself in a jackstraw tumble of soot and blackened beams.

There was nothing left.

After a time, the volunteers burned the church and dynamited the adobes until there was nothing left to mark the village of Del Barra but embers and smoke and the stink of death.

And that's how they left it.

***

But, of course, the war had to come to an end.

After Monterrey and Camargo, Buena Vista and Vera Cruz, Cerro Gordo and Palo Alto, the Mexicans, beaten and weary and just simply tired of the carnage, signed the Treaty of Guadalupe Hidalgo and the war ended.

The Americans filtered back into Texas and New Mexico.

Some were grateful that it had come to an end.

Others just went looking for another fight.

James Lee Cobb went looking for something, too…he just wasn't sure what.

5

Long before the Mexican-American War, the Mexican authorities paid private armies to hunt down and kill marauding tribes of Indians—particularly Apaches and Comanche's—that were harassing Mexican towns and villages. The Indians would swarm down from the U.S side of the border, killing men, kidnapping women, stealing livestock and horses…in fact, anything they could lay their hands on.

The Mexican army simply couldn't contend with these raiders, so scalp bounty laws were enacted. The scalps acted as "receipts": each worth roughly a hundred pesos. And for industrious, prolific bounty hunters the rewards could be quite lucrative indeed. One might think the repellent nature of the business would limit the amount of hunters, but this wasn't so. After the Panic of 1837, there were plenty looking for quick cash. And they weren't real particular as to what they had to do to get it.

During the Mexican-American War, Indian depredations diminished somewhat. Mainly because U.S. soldiers spent their free time hunting down renegade bands. When the war ended...the Indian raids picked-up considerably. Comanche's and Apaches killed hundreds of Mexicans, stole thousands of heads of livestock, and kidnapped an untold number of women and children.

The scalp bounties were revived in most Mexican states, but particularly in Chihuahua and Sonora...and with a vengeance.

The price was now $200 American for a single "receipt".

James Lee Cobb, like many other soldiers, found himself suddenly working for the very government he'd done his damnedest to sack during the war. The whole thing became something of a cottage industry complete with regulatory committees and inspectors. Standards were set by the Mexican authorities to prevent fraud—a scalp had to include either the crown or both ears and preferably both. This prevented fresh scalps from being stretched and sliced-up, sold off as a dozen or more.

Cobb worked with a team consisting of himself, two ex-Texas Rangers, and three Shawnee Indians who were expert at removing scalps. They hunted down Apaches, Comanche's, even Seri Indians. They scalped men, women, children...sparing no one.

Since it was easier to work on a freshly-killed body—the living ones protested the practice vehemently—Cobb and his boys usually put their rounds into the chests of their victims. A clear heart-shot simplified the hell out of things. Their prey went down dead and you could get to work on them right away, instead of waiting for them to expire from their wounds. Because scalp-hunting was a business like any other and time was money. Of course, to save time you could slit their throats or stab them in the heart to speed things along. Women and children you could lay in wait for, lasso 'em like stock and gun them down.

Drop 'em and peel 'em, as Cobb liked to put it.

The braves took a little more stealth. Sometimes Cobb and his boys sprang carefully-arranged ambushes to bring down hunting parties and sniping from a distance had its merits. The Shawnees were real good with the wet work. They'd slit around the crown of the head and then, sitting with their feet on the victim's shoulders, yank the scalp free. They could go through a dozen Indians in record time.

Of course, Cobb and the Texans were no slouches either.

After the scalps were yanked, they were salted and tied to poles to preserve them until they could be cashed-in.

One time, in Durango, Cobb's hunters killed a party of thirty braves by sniping them in a dry wash with long rifles. After they'd dropped and peeled 'em, they backtracked to the Indian's camp and slaughtered no less than sixty women and children. Though, truth be told, they spent most of the day beating the brush for those that had run off.

Eventually, the scalp business fanned hateful animosity from the targeted tribes. They began a program of bloody reprisals. This more than anything made Cobb and the boys start hunting peaceful tribes like the Pimas and Yumas in Arizona Territory. In a single raid, they took nearly four-hundred scalps. But the real boom for them came about the time the Indians started actively hunting the hunters.

See, Cobb had come up with a better idea.

Scalps of Mexicans looked the same as scalps of Indians. There was no true way to tell the difference...so why not? Let the Mexicans pay for the murder of their own people. It was a novel idea.

One of the Texans, a fellow named Grendon, wasn't entirely taken with the idea. "I don't know," he said. "I mean, shit, killing injuns is one thing...but Mesicans, they's almost like real people."

"Ye killed 'em during the war, didn't ye?" Cobb put to him. "What's the difference now? They ain't real folk anyhow, they's just injuns what like to act like white men. All the more reason to drop and peel 'em, ye ask me. Fuck, son, we got us a crop ready for the harvesting, one that'll turn into lots of green and folding...if ye follow me on that."

The others agreed most heartily, particularly Coolan, the big ex-ranger who it was said decapitated no less than two dozen Mexican officers during the war...using nothing but a short-bladed hunting knife. But Grendon just couldn't get by his morals and ethics, so they shot him and Coolan scalped him as a joke.

They hit a Mexican village and caught the entire population in church. They charged in on horseback, pulling triggers and throwing knives and hatchets until their arms were sore and pistols smoking and the dead were heaped-up like sheaves of wheat. It took them the better part of four hours to scalp all two-hundred of 'em, but they went at it with the diligence and zeal that marked the professional. They made a broad sweep through central Mexico and harvested so many scalps, they began wiring them together in bails.

In 1850, just before the boom died out, they rolled into Sonora with nearly 8,000 scalps piled high in the bed of a wagon.

Shortly afterwards, the scalping business went belly-up and Cobb rode hell-for-leather out of Mexico with a price on his head for murdering Mexicans.

But as Cobb said later, it was fun while it lasted.

***

The next twenty-odd years of his life passed in the blink of an eye.

Cobb rustled cattle and horses. Worked as range detective for various cattle combines, a hired gun for just about anyone who would pay him. He robbed banks and stages, made something of a name for himself as a road agent. Was arrested no less than three times and escaped the noose each time by breaking out of jail. He served as scout during the Indian Wars, sold guns to renegade Apaches, and managed a brothel in San Francisco. But that came to a crashing halt when it was discovered that he and the ladies under his employ were not only robbing their patrons, but murdering them and burying their remains in the cellar. After that, he ran roughshod through Indian Territory, stealing and killing and forcing Indians and whites alike to pay his gang protection money. He became something of a terror along the Canadian and Arkansas Rivers.

Then in 1873...he lost five-thousand dollars gambling in Deadwood, Dakota Territory. Lost it to a professional gambler named Maynard Ellsworth. Cobb pulled his hatchet and split the crown of Ellsworth's head. After that, he lived his life pretty much on the dodge.

But in 1875, he was arrested for extorting mining camps in the Big Horn Mountains of Wyoming Territory and sentenced to five years in the territorial prison. Of which he served every single day. As the warden was heard to say to a parole board, "James Lee Cobb is completely lacking in anything which might be even remotely considered human. He is, gentlemen, the very epitome of what the territories need to be purged of—creatures that walk like men, but think like animals."

When Cobb got out, evading bounty hunters and numerous warrants out circulating for him under various aliases, he joined three men—Jonah Gleer, Lawrence Barlow, and Butch Noolan—in a peculiar undertaking. Cobb had coerced them into following him up into the Sierra Nevadas to search out a gold mine he had heard of in prison.

Problem was, Cobb didn't really know where it was.

See, a voice in his head told him that up in the high Sierras he would find his destiny. The voice was not vague as usual, but quite absolute and determined that Cobb should listen to it.

So he did.

And this is how the elements of his life—a vile stew at best—finally came full circle.

6

Six weeks then.

Six weeks Cobb had been trapped up in the high country, just waiting and waiting. Gleer, Barlow, and Noolan waited with him...though Barlow had suggested a heroic outbreak through the snows that had sealed off the pass and locked them tight at the foot of the summit. Nobody took him up on it.

At least not yet.

They weren't desperate enough.

But it was coming, God yes, you could see it just as Cobb was seeing it now as he looked into those weathered, rutted faces burned by subzero winds and discolored by frostbite. You could see it there along with the bitterness and unease and animosity that was fermenting in them. For the past week it had been raging inside each of them, a potent and toxic brew bubbling up from the seething pit of each man. A brew that was sheer poison, seeping and simmering and smoking. It was fast becoming a palpable thing in the confines of the cedar-post cabin and its stink was raw and savage.

None of them had spoken in three days now.

They were reaching the point where their choices were being made for them. By nature. By God. By whatever cruel force had imprisoned them up in the mountains with no hope of deliverance. It was fed by hatred of Cobb, of course. For, although none of them had voiced it yet, they all blamed him for their predicament. He was the one that had insisted they stay into the winter, hunting that mine, and by the time January had sealed them up tight...there was nothing to do but wait.

Wait and go mad.

Yeah, they went through a stiff semblance of culture, but culture, like ethics and morals, died a long, hard death in those godless wastelands. Gleer still worked his traplines. Barlow went out hunting each morning with his Hawkens rifle. Cobb and Noolan still cut brush for the fire. But there was no food coming in and a warm fire and plenty of water didn't fill their bellies.

They were slat-thin to a man, like skeletons covered in membranous flesh. Eyes jutting. Cheeks hollowed into cadaverous valleys. Teeth chattering and bony fingers wrestling in narrow laps. They had already eaten the horses. Even boiled the hooves for soup. Barlow had been nibbling on his belt and Gleer was chewing on a deerhide knife sheath.

So, if there was madness here, it was born of hunger.

Of solitude.

Of hopelessness.

No game was coming in and even the few rabbits Gleer had brought in last week were not enough to stave off the hunger pangs for more than a few hours. They needed meat. Real meat.

Their bellies cried out for it, their teeth gnashed for it. Their tongues licked fissured lips, dreaming of venison steaks and beef shanks. Blood. Meat.

Of all of them, only Cobb took it in stride.

Something in him was enjoying the plight of the others. Was enjoying how they'd slowly become living skeletons, ghoulish figures that would've looked perfectly natural...or unnatural...wandering from the gates of a cemetery worrying at their own shrouds. As starvation progressed, social amenities failed one after the other. Their thoughts were of meat. Their dreams were of meat. In that high, wind-blasted netherworld of snow-capped peaks, shrieking winds, and whipping blizzards, there was only one way to *get* meat.

One last, unthinkable way.

Cobb was waiting for it. He already saw it in the dead pools of their eyes. The way they looked at each other and at him. Survival had canceled out any bond they'd once shared. To a man they knew one thing in their fevered, deranged minds...only one of them could come out of this in the spring.

And the hunger was upon them. The taboo lust for flesh of one's own kind. And in the close, confined atmosphere of the cabin, you could smell it...a heavy, sour, vile odor tainting the very air.

And maybe it was starvation that was bringing it on, forcing them into damnable regions of thought, and maybe it was something else.

Maybe it was what they found in the cave.

Or what found them.

***

It was Barlow who located it.

He had been out hunting with Noolan. They both stumbled back to the cabin, winded and worn, with something like fear in their eyes. They stood in the doorway babbling, framed by a field of white and blowing death, rifles in fur-mittened hands, snowshoes on their feet.

"What?" Cobb had put to them. "What in the name of Christ is it? What did ye find?"

And maybe part of him was thinking, *hoping*, they'd found the mine...but he didn't really believe it. For what he saw in their eyes plainly told him it was not good. If a regiment of injun ghosts had descended upon them, they could not have looked more grave.

"You better come," Noolan said. "You just better come."

So, wrapped in buffalo coats and bearskin hats, swaddled up like babies in all their gear, they fought through the drifts and winds that tried to knock them off the narrow trails along the jagged cliffs. The world was white and whipping and immense. The sky seemed to reach down and become mountain and it was hard to say where one began and the other ended.

Noolan led them to a little cave mouth set into the base of a limestone bluff with craggy walls and a jutting overhang which looked as though it might fall and crush them at any moment.

Cobb could see the snowshoe prints leading away. Looked like they'd been in one hell of a hurry to get some distance between themselves and the cave mouth.

"All right, goddammit," Cobb said, his breath frosting in clouds. "What is it? Goddamn mother lode or the Devil his ownself?"

"You better just go in," Barlow said, secretive as a schoolboy.

Cobb went in first, with Gleer at his heels. Both of them were grunting and puffing as they wedged their way in flat on their bellies. The shaft was barely big enough for a man to snake his way through. With the heavy furs and leggings, it took some time to corkscrew themselves into the central chamber. Like forcing a wadded-up rag through the neck of a wine bottle.

Inside it was black as original sin.

Cobb called out to Gleer and his voiced echoed eerily into unknown heights. Gleer had the oil lantern. He struck a match off the cave wall and touched it to the wick, adjusting the flame. The cavern was big enough to shelter two freight wagons side by side. It continued on up a gentle, pebble-littered slope into another darkened chamber. Cobb looked around, seeing lots of granite and gravel, great masses of bedrock that had fallen from the roof in years long past. He saw nothing else noteworthy.

Yet...*yet*, there was something here. Something unusual. He could feel it same way a man can feel his own skin or the balls dangling between his legs. There was something here. Something important. Something secret.

Gleer held out the lantern at arm's length, wild lurching shadows darting about them. Rising and falling, swimming and diving and leaping. He licked his lips. Licked them again. It was warmer inside and ice began to melt on his beard, water dripping onto his shaggy coat.

"What the hell did they find in here?" he wanted to know. "Ain't shit but dirt and rocks. Ain't shit else."

But there was and they both knew it, *felt* it, but did not dare let their lips frame it into words. Instead, they stood side by side, waiting and wondering and maybe even worrying. Way a man will when he knows something is circling his campfire. Something big. Something awful. Something with teeth and attitude.

Cobb did not feel afraid.

He told himself in many a situation that as far as fear went, he inspired it, he did not experience it. And maybe that was true and maybe it was bullshit, but, at that moment, he was not afraid. For a voice in his head was telling him that yes, yes, this is what he had come to find. Somewhere in this cave and it passages was sheer revelation.

"Ain't nothing here," Gleer said, his voice dry. "So let's just—"

"There's something here, all right." Cobb looked over at Gleer, motes of dust drifting around him like moths. "Cain't ye smell it?"

"Yeah...yeah, I guess I can."

Cobb was likening it to decay. Sweet, gassy decay like a bin filled with rotten potatoes or a flyblown corpse washed-up on a riverbed. A moist, rank smell which simply did not belong in this dry, hollow place where even the air was grainy and tasted of dust.

A muscle was jumping in Gleer's throat. "Don't like it none. Let's make to getting the hell out."

"Follow me," was all Cobb said.

He followed the stink like a tasty aroma, led it pull him into the kitchen of this place where the goods were simmering and steaming. He moved up the slope, stepping carefully around razorbacked outcroppings and over flat tumbled stones. Together they moved up into the passage which was tight and twisting, the ceiling brushing their fur caps. And in the next chamber, they found—

They found bones.

Maybe some animal bones, but mostly human.

A great central pit had been carved out of the floor, hacked out as if with picks and shovels to a depth of maybe ten or fifteen feet and it was filled with bones. An ossuary. A charnel pit of ulnas and femurs, vertebrae and ribcages. And skulls...Jesus, what seemed to be hundreds of skulls. Adults and children. And the only thing all those bones had in common was that they were charred...as if they had been *roasted*. Blackened skulls stared up at them, alluding to ghoulish secrets they would not tell.

A scapula shifted and it caused a minor rain of arm and leg bones. A skull tumbled from its perch and grinned at them, its lower jaw missing.

"Moved," Gleer said, his face lined with tension. "Something in there...Mary, Mother of God, *something in there moved...*"

He had his Colt pistols out and he wanted very badly to empty them into something, anything. Because he was a man who handled the unknown with knife and gun, hatchet and bow. And what was eating into him then could not be found nor defined quite so easily.

"Dead," Cobb told him. "All long dead. Just settling is all. If they was just rocks and one fell, ye wouldn't come out of yer skin, would ye?"

Gleer calmed, shook his head. "Suppose not."

"Well, them bones cain't hurt ye no more than rocks can."

But what he wanted to say was that he had a weird, unearthly feeling that whatever was in the cave, whatever was hiding and whispering around them, just might have *caused* those bones to shift. Just like it might cause more trouble. And maybe, hell, maybe it would make them bones stand right up and walk about.

Cobb and Gleer moved around the chamber and came to another just off the first.

And it was the same. Bones. More and more bones. Whoever had owned them had been long dead. There were what looked to be ancient, rusted ringbolts pounded into the high, flat table rock above. From them…ancient lengths of hemp rope hanging like dead snakes. From a few of them were brown, mummified hands. As if, people had been hung there and left, allowed to putrefy and drop, only their hands left to mark the grim occasion.

Cobb touched one of the ropes…it began to flake away in his fingers.

"This place," Gleer said, his eyes fixed with an almost religious ecstasy, "it's goddamn old. I mean *really* old, Jimmy-boy. Lookit at all, will you? This place…ha, ha…I think it was chopped right out of the mountain. People…injuns…worked it like we would a mine shaft."

Cobb studied the rough-hewn walls. You could see they'd been chiseled, hacked from solid rock. None of it, save the original cavern was natural. The tool work on the walls was all-too apparent.

Gleer was making a funny sound in his throat that was somewhere between gagging and laughter. He played the light around some more. There were pictures on those walls. Primitive paintings, etchings. Mostly run-of-the-mill stuff like bear and mountain lion and bison. Things Cobb had seen splashed or carved into many cave walls and rock faces in the Southwest. Even up north in the Montana and Dakota Territories. Herds of animals. Stick figures hunting them. Dancing. Sitting around fires. Just your basic depictions of tribal life.

But Gleer, whose mama was half-Chickasaw, seemed fascinated by them. He studied them, making those gulping/giggling sounds in his throat, whispering things beneath his breath.

"See? See?" he said. "See how down low here, down here you got your oldest images. Most of these are faded, worn by time...shit, hundreds and hundreds of years old if not more. Maybe thousands." He was breathing hard now, licking his lips. He followed the paintings and cuttings up the wall with the lantern. "You get up here, Jimmy Lee, you get up here and, sure, you can make 'em out better. These ain't as old, eh? But still old, old, very old."

Cobb still was not impressed. Just injun-art. What of it?

But Gleer wouldn't let it go.

He explained in some detail what it all meant, what the rock was saying to them, how it reached out across the centuries telling them a tale of life long gone from these hills. Hunting. Fishing. Battling enemies. Birth. Death. Religious ceremony. Marriages. Funerals. If you could read it and it wasn't too hard, Gleer said, it was just like a book.

"Looks like a village there," Cobb said, indicating a cluster of lodges. "Wonder what the hell happened to it?"

"Probably down there in that valley, what's left of it," Gleer said. "Covered in snow." He followed the art across the wall. "See? See this?"

Cobb saw it. Was so impressed he stuck a cigar in his mouth and smoked it, knowing there was more here than just silly injun-art.

"They...they were working this mountain, maybe these caves, tunneling..."

Cobb could see it fine. Stick figures at work. Using what might have been primitive shovels and picks, staffs and baskets to haul out rock. Looked like drawings of ants working their hive. Figures everywhere.

Gleer was getting real excited now. "Right here...Jimmy, right goddamn here, something happened," he said, stabbing the wall with a dirty index finger.

"What?"

Gleer told him it was big, bad medicine, whatever it was. All the symbols and hex signs attested to that. To Cobb it looked as if down in their tunnels they had dug into another chamber. The chamber was represented by a jagged gouge...and out of it, something like smoke misting out.

"A catastrophe," Gleer said. "See? All them figures are laying about now. All dead."

"Gas probably. Hit a pocket of poison gas."

"No...no, I think it's worse than that." He was panting now, rubbing grime and settled dust from the walls, close to something, but he wasn't sure what. "There...not gas...something else...something they dug out of the ground, something real bad..."

Cobb was studying it pretty close himself now.

Another representation of that jagged chasm, more smoke or mist seeping up and out. Only the mist was now shown to have gathered above the dead and the living like some storm cloud. A storm cloud made of skulls and devil-faces. The drawings went on and that cloud appeared to have come up out of the cave and settled over the village.

"It got to 'em," Gleer said, his eyes wide and the lantern trembling in his fist now. He looked afraid. His face was tight and set with wrinkles and taut cords. "It got to 'em, Jimmy? Don't you get it? Don't you?"

The paintings abruptly ended there and there were no more.

Cobb didn't really get it. Something was crawling in his belly like worms and it made him feel giddy. The birthmark on his back was throbbing. Something was happening to him, but he didn't see. Not really. Not just yet. The Indians had been mining or something. They had cut deep into the mountain and uncovered a hidden chamber, dug into it...and something, something had come out. Something that killed a lot of 'em. Something real bad came out of the ground.

Gleer was half out of his mind now.

He was running around, handling bones and skulls, waving femurs and tibias about. He set the lantern at the edge of the pit and dove into all those bones like some insane swimmer into a charnel sea. He paddled and sorted, handled and searched. His fingers traced the craniums of skulls, poked into orbits, tapped at yellowed teeth set in pitted jaws. He stroked the rungs of a ribcage, eyed a blackened pelvic wing like maybe it was his own.

"Get the hell out of there," Cobb told him and meant it. "Yer losing yer mind, damn ye!"

Gleer climbed out, the bones falling away from him with a sound like tumbling kindling. Cobb grabbed him by the scruff of the neck and pitched him to the floor.

"I ain't mad, Jimmy! It's just...hell, it's just that I know! *I know!*" He was cackling now, drool running from the corners of his lips. His entire body was shuddering. "These bones...lookit 'em, will ya? Look close."

Cobb did.

And then he got it...or some of it. The bones—all the bones in fact— were riddled with tiny cuts and gashes and nicks. Somebody had been hacking and cutting on their owners. And maybe worse...because he found what looked to be teeth marks set into them.

"Cannibals," Cobb said in a low voice. "Just like in them Pacific islands I read about when I was a kid. Man-eaters..."

"That's right, yes sir, that's right." Gleer was still laughing, but tears had welled in his eyes now. "But they didn't do it on their own, Jimmy Lee, no sir! What they cut out of the ground...whatever it was...it *turned* 'em that way, took hold of their savage heathen minds and turned them into monsters..."

Cobb took hold of him and got him out of those caverns. Gleer was stark raving by that point. And maybe it was just Cobb's imagination, but that high, hot gassy smell seemed almost stronger. Rancid, even.

As if whatever was dead in there, had begun to decay once again after many long years.

***

Cobb got Gleer outside and with the help of the other two, they wrestled him back to the cabin. But he was in a bad way. They had to shackle him to the wall with chains snapped from beaver traps and nailed into the logs themselves. He was talking crazy, shaking and gibbering, hearing things scratching around outside that none of the others could. Talking with people that weren't there. Going native like his mother's people and asking for protection from the Great Spirit. So they left him shackled for a week like that, pissing himself, drooling and screeching.

"Think I'm crazy, don't you? Think I've lost what mind I did have, don't you?" he rambled on incessantly one afternoon as the wind made the cabin shake. "But I ain't nohow crazy. Because I know what was up there...I could smell it there and I can smell it here now. Maybe you, Cobb, or you, Barlow...maybe you don't know what I'm taking about. But Noolan...I don't know about you. It might have *touched* you the way it touched them injuns. Ain't saying it did...but it got to one of us, 'cause I can smell it! Hear? *I can smell it*. One of you, yes sir, you know what I'm talking about on account you're just waiting for the lights to dim so you can feed on the others. I know it! I know it! Oh...ho, ho, my God, my dear Lord Jesus, them injuns, them injuns. Roasting babies and sucking brains from skulls and chewing on the flesh of their young...eating, eating. Offering up their daughters to that, that *thing* come straight out of hell..."

"Shut the fuck up!" Barlow snapped finally. "You shut up with that talk or I'll kill you! *I swear to God I'll kill you!*"

Gleer was getting to everyone by that point. Maybe even Cobb. But you couldn't tell it from that cool smirk on his face. Noolan calmed Barlow down and took him outside for some fresh air being that it was the one thing they had plenty of.

When they were gone, it was just Cobb and Gleer in the cabin. The logs popped and shifted in the hearth. The air was smoky and thick. It stank of body odor and charred logs. What it didn't stink of these days was food.

"Ye've got to get a hold of yerself, Gleer," Cobb told him. "Ye carry on like this...well, one of them boys is gonna shoot ye dead."

Gleer just played with his chains, running the loops through his fingers. He nodded. "I know, I know...but I'm scared, Jimmy Lee. I'm damn scared. I'm thinking...thinking that one of us just ain't what he appears to be. That something got in him...inside him...and that man, he's a monster now..."

Cobb considered it a moment and shrugged. "Maybe ye right," he said. "Maybe you and me, maybe we better had keep an eye on them other two."

***

Eventually, Gleer came back to his senses.

Barlow managed to shoot a couple wolves. They were rawboned things with hardly any meat on them, but it was something in their bellies. And Noolan made a hearty soup from the blood and fat. It didn't taste all that wonderful, but it stuck to the bones. With some meat and soup in him at last, Gleer came to his senses.

They cut him loose.

But they kept an eye on him.

In fact, everyone kept an eye on each other. It was like everyone was afraid to be alone with anyone else. All four of them went about their daily routines with knives and pistols hanging from their belts. And when one came upon another out in the woods or poking through the ice that covered the stream...well, it was only sensible to give advance warning. For up there in that awful place, only the guilty sneaked around or moved silently.

Things got bad in the week following Gleer's release.

The wind shook and rattled the cabin continually. It picked up sheets of snow and flung them all and everywhere. Visibility outside was down to eight, ten feet at any given time. The air was unnaturally cold. Sometimes the wind carried funny sounds with it, sounds like weeping or screaming. The voices of children chanting in some distant place. There were odd noises in the dead of night...noises like something walking up on the roof or scratching at the shuttered windows. A pounding at the outside walls. Weird distorted tracks found in the snow outside. Tracks that started suddenly and ended just as abruptly...like something had leaped down from the cold stars above and then leaped back up there again.

Noolan and Barlow could be heard whispering prayers at night.

Gleer just hid beneath his elk hides silently.

And Cobb, he just grinned, head always cocked like he was listening for something.

Because he had secrets from the others.

They didn't know about him slipping off that night they'd found the cave. About him crawling in there in the frigid, dark hours. Walking amongst the bones with a lantern in hand. They didn't know how it was for him when the gassy, fetid odor rose up from the trembling marrow of the mountain and fell over him like a shivering, stinking blanket. Or how it held him and made communion with something already hiding deep within him. Something planted there like an obscene seed in the blighted soil of his soul by his father. How it reached out and found this sleeping other and became one with it.

Because Gleer was right—there *was* a monster among them.

And it was getting hungry.

***

It had been three weeks since they found the cave now.

Two weeks since the last of the soup and wolf meat was eaten. Their bellies had been stark empty since and something in each and every man was decaying at an unpleasant rate.

Except for Cobb.

What was in him had already rotted to carrion.

***

Cobb was alone in the cabin...or nearly.

Noolan and Barlow had run off hours ago. Run off when they'd returned early from their hunt and found Cobb dressing out Gleer's corpse, happily sorting through meat and muscle, selecting the finest cuts for steaks and the poorer ones for stews.

"Hungry, gents?" he'd said, gore dripping from his mouth because, well, dammit, it was hard to do that sort of work without a little taste here or there. "Pull yerselves up a seat and see what old Jimmy Lee can do when the proper victuals is available."

Barlow and Noolan just stood there, rifles in hand, mouths sprung like spittoons, staring and staring. One of them—Cobb couldn't be sure which—let out a wailing scream and together they'd run off into the snows. Damn fools left the door open, too. Born in a goddamned barn, the both of 'em.

That had been three, four hours before.

But Cobb knew they'd be back. Unless they decided to winter it out up in the cave; but they wouldn't like that very much. It was one thing to be up there with light and heat...but when the lantern died out and the blackness swam up like some ravenous shark from a primeval, godless sea like it had for him, well that was an entirely different kettle of fish, mind you.

Cobb had long-since finished slaughtering Gleer.

When Cobb had pulled his Arkansas toothpick and walked up to him, speaking in the voices of long-dead injuns, Gleer had just gone to jelly. Slicker than shit, Cobb had slit his throat ear to ear and Gleer just accepted it. Now, there wasn't nothing but a pile of bloody bones to mark his passing. His skin was drying on a rack before the fire, smartly salted for leather. His organs were gently layered in a black pot of brine, seasoning up for a fine stew that would last Cobb for weeks and weeks. The meat had been carved from his buttocks, belly, and breast and packed in snow so it would keep fresh and sweet. His blood had been drained off into buckets for soup and broth. Even his fat was saved. His ligaments and sinew were drying for catgut. And right that moment as Cobb listened to the wind speaking and cackling in the chimney pipe, he was grinding up muscle and organ to be stuffed into bowel casings for sausage.

Gleer's head was sitting across from him.

The eyes were blanched and the tongue protruded blackly from those seamed lips. His bearskin cap was still on his head. A few greasy strands of hair had fallen over the sallow, blood-spattered face.

If Cobb concentrated real hard, he could even make it speak.

When he was done stuffing his sausages, whistling some old Indian deathsong he'd never once heard in his life, he nibbled on a little finger food he'd boiled from the bones below. One of Gleer's legs was spitted and roasting over the fire, carefully seasoned. It was getting nice and brown, gobs of fat dropping from it and sizzling in the flames beneath. The meaty, rich smell filled the cabin and went up the flue.

Cobb knew the meat-smell would bring the others home.

They wouldn't have a choice.

And he would welcome them, surely. He figured two more kills and he'd have more than enough meat to put up until spring, if he practiced a little conservation, that was. Avoided his usual gluttony. But he was no savage. He would invite both Barlow and Noonlan to break bread at his table. He'd give 'em both a good meal before putting them to the knife.

It was the Christian thing to do.

So Cobb nibbled and waited, a curious light flickering in his eyes.

He remembered the night he'd crept back up to the cave, something in him telling him it was the right thing to do. That what was in there, what was hiding in the cracks and crevices and maybe the bones, too, was the very reason he had come. Not gold. But...*it*. Whatever in the hell *it* was. The very thing them injuns had cut from the ground. He could remember it started with that gassy smell. A foul, yellow odor it was, a terrible sweet smell of unburied corpses and miasmic tombs.

It had touched him.

Physically touched him.

In his head—as it held him tightly, nursed him against its breast like an infant—it had told him what to do. How long it had waited for him. How it was he could survive if he could simply overcome certain social taboos, that was.

But Cobb would not listen, would not.

He'd been thinking along those lines, but he wasn't ready just yet.

And the thing had pressed him into itself, squeezed him so that he thought his bones would come busting out of his mouth. It told him there was no other way. If he wanted power...and he did want that, didn't he? Then there was only one way to have mastery over men. Same way you had mastery over animals—by eating them. Devouring the flesh and absorbing all that they were and could be.

This, it said, was the path to invincibility and immortality.

But Cobb just was not sure, so the thing sweetened it a bit for him. It talked to him like an old friend. It didn't try to intimidate or terrify him, it just talked in a natural, easy rhythm.

And, funny thing, it had a deep Southern accent, a hellbilly accent just like his kin from the Missouri Ozarks.

Well, at least it seemed that way...but maybe it was just a breathing gray sibilance forming words in his head.

Now, let me tell ye something, Jimmy Lee. Jus' mind me and listen, hear? Shet up now, this here's important. Once upon a time, there was these injuns what lived up here in these hills. Just yer ordinary savages, I reckon. They was some shirttail kin of the Shoshoni called themselves the Macabro. Well, cousin, these Macabros, they started tunnelin' in the earth like worms into pork...well, sir, weren't long before they dug somethin' up, somethin' mebbe they weren't a-supposed to find at all. It jumped up, said hello and how you be, and rode down hard on them savages like Christ come to preach. Now this thing here, it crawled into their skins. Ran roughshod all over the tribe like Yankees marching through Georgia. I shit you not. Ye remember them bad things what were supposed to live down in them hollers back home in Missourah? Yessum. This thing, it was like that. Now, it weren't exactly neighborly, this critter. It got into them injuns deep. Sure as Christ was hammered to the cross, the Macabro belonged to this thing.

Now, cousin, lemme tell ye how it were fer them.

These injuns, they took to etin' human flesh and what not, sacrificin' their firstborn and all. The shaman would et the little shitters raw and wrigglin'. Yep, their own children, that's what I said. But adults, too. Jus' about anyone. And virgins...heh, that sumbitch what out of the ground, he was real sweet on maidens, see. Now, the Macabro were always fighting one tribe or another. When they caught some, they'd make burnt offerings of their enemies, nail 'em upside down to poles and sometimes put 'em to the flame and sometimes jus' left 'em there to rot to bone.

Now wait, son, keep yer Henry in yer pants...yep, there's more. See, these Macabro...they started digging up their dead and the dead of anyone they could find, yessum. Started worshipping bones and skulls. Made altars of 'em and doin' things with the dead uns ye just don't want to think about. They was jus' real soft in the heads, this bunch.

Now these shaman, priests—whichever ye want to call them baby-rapin' devils—they was quite a bunch. They called all the shots. Sumbitches didn't cotton to bathin' no how. A filthy lot what jumped and hopped about in their cloaks of baby-skins, snakes just a-twisting in their long filthy hair. They sang them profane songs and wore skull masks and chattered their teeth what were filed to points to rend and tear, ye see. These shaman, they controlled everything. Their bodies were tattooed with snakes and symbols and witch-sign, what they called the Skin-Medicine. Some sort of conjurin' and magical formula written right on their skins. It was said that with this Skin-Medicine, them heathen devils could control the spirits of the dead and change themselves into man-eating beasts jus' any old time the need struck 'em. Now on nights of the full moon, the Macabro priests would light big fires and them injuns would dance naked in the snow while the priests read from their own skins. Injuns what had been captured from other tribes would be slaughtered, their flesh eaten, and the snow would just stain red with their blood. And if the Macabro could get some of those injun's young-uns, well, a regular party they'd have chompin' up that fine, fat squib.

Well, cousin, ye get the picture.

These injuns was mad, yessum, but they had it half-right about etin' other peoples to absorb all they had. Now the Macabro, they was all wiped out by the Ute two-hundred year ago, but what ye found in the cave, yes sir, that was their legacy. See, the Ute herded them Macabros what weren't killed outright and all the dead uns up into that cave, burnt 'em up alive, seeded their bones in them pits. Yessum, the cave. It was fitting, I reckon, in that the cave is where a lot of that pagan sacrificin' went on.

And now, Jimmy-boy, ye understand? Do ye? Do ye?

Cobb didn't remember much after that.

Just that he wasn't quite the same. Sometimes he was himself and sometimes part of the thing that had impregnated his mother and sometimes part of that rabid hillbilly out of the cave. Sometimes they were all just one mind. The next day and all the days after, Cobb just waited and plotted the getting of skin and meat and bone.

And that's how it all came about.

Cobb, a chunk of finger meat packed in his cheek, went over and turned Gleer's leg on the spit. He poked it with a fork and the juice ran free and clear, telling him it was done. His belly was rumbling at the nauseating stench.

Just then, he heard movement outside the cabin.

He grinned, his eyes flashing with hellfire. It was Barlow and Noolan being real quiet and stealthy, sneaking about like red savages. They were doing a good job of it, too, but Cobb heard them. The sound of their boots breaking the crust of snow. The roar of the blood in their veins, the throb of their hearts. And mostly, yes mostly, he could smell their fear and to him it was like freshly uncorked brandy.

Cobb went about setting the table.

His back to the door, they came bursting in, the both of them. They held pistols on him and they were both shaking from the cold, their faces pinched and mottled and edged with fear.

"You're crazy, Cobb, you sick sonofabitch," Barlow said. "Now real careful like, I want you to take that pistol out of your belt...with your left hand. Real slow now, let it drop to the floor..."

But Cobb just giggled. "Ye stop with that talk, friend. I'm just a-setting the table here. I want the both of you to sit with me and have a fine meal. Ye know ye want to, so why fight it? We'll have us some eats and discuss this like men."

Barlow and Noolan just stood there, not sure what to do. Cobb was insane, sure, but why was he so damn calm? What was that funny light reflected in his eyes? There was something very wrong about all this and it wasn't just the cannibalism either.

"We better just shoot him," Noolan said.

"That wouldn't be very neighborly, *cousin*," Cobb said.

"See? See? He's crazy! Watch him now, watch him real careful, because James Lee Cobb he's right fast with that Colt," Noolan was saying. "He can pull it so fast you—"

"Drop that gun on the floor," Barlow said.

Cobb sighed, shrugged, went for the gun with his right hand. And actually cleared leather before two bullets ripped through his belly. But all that did was make him laugh as his blood dripped to the floor. He dipped one finger into the hole in his buckskin shirt like a quill into an inkwell. He pulled it back out, licked the tip. His face was narrow and pallid, real tight like a skull wearing skin, his eyes lit like glowworms.

But he had his Colt out and, barking a short laugh, put a slug right between Barlow's eyes, dropping him dead in the doorway.

"Now," he said to Noolan. "Why don't ye join me for supper? What's say?"

The pistol dropped from Noolan's fingers and he started to whimper. Whatever was in Cobb's eyes had him tight. He stumbled over to the table, his own eyes wide and unblinking and filled with tears. He sat down and watched dumbly as Cobb pulled the leg off the spit and began to carve it up.

Then he began to eat.

His fork jabbing and his teeth chewing and his throat swallowing, his mind gone to a formless putty. He ate and ate while Cobb watched him, all the while holding Gleer's head by the hair. And the real bad thing was that Gleer was *speaking*, that white furrowed face was speaking. The eyes were rolling in his head and that black tongue was licking his lips. Cobb asked him questions and he answered in a dry, whistling voice, telling Gleer exactly what it was like down in that black pit of death and how Noolan's kin were all down there burning with him.

Sometime later, Gleer's head screaming and the cabin filled with chanting injun voices, Cobb slit Noolan's throat and dressed him out.

***

In the Spring, Cobb came down from the mountains on foot, his parfleche still packed with dried human jerky. His travels after that were unknown for the most part. What *is* known is that he assembled a crew of blooded killers with similar leanings and tastes as his own. That they accompanied him back to Missouri where there was something he needed to collect. And sometime later he made for the Shoshoni peoples. Knowing he had something in common with them now.

And somewhere along the way, he heard about a Snake medicine man called Spirit Moon.

PART FOUR: THE GOOD, THE DAMNED, AND THE DERANGED

1

Whisper Lake by daylight.

It was afternoon by the time Tyler Cabe rolled out of bed and even later by the time he stepped out onto the streets, his brain still reeling with the sight of the murdered prostitute. He stood before the St. James Hostelry, breathing in the air which, although not cold as the night before, was kissed by a chill blowing down from the mountains.

He hadn't even been in Whisper Lake a full twenty-four hours yet. It was hard to believe. He thought of the crazy hillbilly Orville DuChien. Jackson Dirker. The crazy tales that bartender—Carny—at the Oasis had told him about the local animal attacks. The Texas Ranger, Henry Freeman. Sir Tom English. Virgil Clay laying dead in a pool of his own blood. The jail and Charles Graybrow. And, yes, Mizzy Modine.

It all came together in his brain and made his head ache.

He lit a cigarette and wondered what would come next.

Licking his lips then, he made his way down the muddy, rutted street, taking in the town an inch at a time. It was his first real look at it. Whisper Lake was like other mining camps he had ridden through: a congested, dirty mess of humanity.

High above town, clinging to the rises and mist-cloaked slopes were the looming steel headframes and drum hoists of the mines themselves, the outcroppings of assorted buildings and sheds that rose up around them. There was a constant thundering and booming and clanking from up there, as the earth was gutted of silver. Ore wagons made the run continually from the chutes to the looming refineries down by the lake itself...you could see the gray, toxic smoke that belched from the stacks and fell back to earth, dusting everything in filth.

It looked oddly as if the town itself had once been part of the mine systems above and had slowly slid down the muddy inclines to its present position.

It was laid out with no plan or pattern, just a haphazard collection of log buildings and false-corniced stores, tents and shanties, brush huts and wooden shacks cut through by a maze of intersecting dirt roads that dipped into little hollows and climbed up low hills. There were a few brick buildings and an elaborate system of board sidewalks. Just a crazy-quilt of hotels and boarding houses, assay offices and saloons, brothels and churches, liveries and lumber yards with a Union Pacific railroad spur winding around the northern end.

Everything from privy to meat market was darkened with soot from the mines and refineries.

The roads were filled with horses and wagons, prospectors and business-owners, immigrants pushing carts and dirty children chasing balls with sticks. Cabe saw ladies with parasols clustered in whispering groups and whores in their petticoats emptying chamber pots into the streets. The ground rumbled from the industry of the mines above and voices chattered and people shouted and bodies threaded in every which direction. Unlike other frontier towns, you saw very few people lounging about. Everything was business and money and there was no time for loafing.

Cabe, his boots plastered with mud up to the shafts, stepped up onto the boardwalk, then stepped back down again as a trio of elderly ladies passed. He touched the brim of his hat to them. A freight wagon and team roared past him, nearly running down a group of black-faced miners, and splashed dirty water over his pants. A group of men fought to push a buckboard that was buried to the axle in a muddy hole. The batwings of a saloon flew open and a drunken man stumbled out, leaned over the hitching rail and vomited out coils of foam. Dark-clad foreigners gesticulated and mumbled in a dozen different dialects. Indians in blanket robes stood around, watching the ruin of their land.

Cabe kept walking, weaving through groups of miners and laborers, trying to find a place where he could get away from all the noise and activity. But everywhere he turned, every alleyway and street, was crowded with more people and more wagons and more industry.

Dear Christ, he thought, maybe Dirker was right...there's just too many people here, I'll never find the Strangler in this piss-pot.

But he wasn't about to give up.

He would crawl into every crack and alcove of this seething, pulsing hive if he had to.

But he was going to run the Sin City Strangler to ground.

2

Jackson Dirker, looking decidedly pale, said, "I've seen atrocities, Doc, I've seen true horrors...but this, something like this, I can't begin to even understand it."

Dr. Benjamin West, a Whisper Lake surgeon and the Beaver County coroner, just nodded. He was a tall, reed-thin man in a charcoal suit with a gold watch chain that flashed in the sunlight like a winking eye. He clutched his derby hat to his chest and ran long, delicate fingers through his sparse white hair. A cord jumped in his throat.

"Although I'm a man of science," he finally said. "I would think the Devil rode through here in a black mood."

Dirker did not disagree with that.

They were standing outside the general store that had served as not only the market, but saloon and gambling house in the placer camp of Sunrise. They stood outside the double doors, looking and looking, and seeing and wishing they were blind. Because what they saw in Sunrise was permanently burned into their vision like a sudden, hurting arc of light.

Dirker was studying what was on the door.

A man with an eagle tattooed on his back had been skinned completely, his hide nailed there in one piece. No less than three heads hung over the entrance like ghastly lanterns. Copper wire had been jabbed into their ears and looped to nails above. The faces were splattered with dried blood, blanched eyes staring dumbly. The head on the left looked like it was about to say something.

Doc West waved a few flies from it. Though the wind had a bite to it, the sunshine was heating things up. Bringing the bugs and the ever-present reek of bacterial decay. "I'm guessing that these heads," he said, "were not cut off as with a hatchet or knife, but actually *ripped* from their bodies."

Dirker had already figured that.

At the stump of the necks there was a great deal of tissue and vertebrae hanging out like party confetti. No clean slice was evident. Someone...or something...had the strength to actually *pull* a man's head from his body. Dirker didn't like to jump to fantastic conclusions like that, but what else was he to think? The evidence spoke volumes.

Sighing, as used to the carnage now as he would ever get, he looked over the shacks and weathered buildings that had made up Sunrise in its heyday before the veins of gold had played out. It looked like a cemetery to him...the gray, windowless structures very much like tombstones in some lonesome, windy graveyard. The mountains brooding above looked down silently like mourners.

A miner named Jim Tomlinson had ridden down from the high country to provision at the store and found the massacre. He was so overwrought by the time he made it to Whisper Lake, Doc West had to shoot some morphine *into* him to get anything sensible *out* of him. An hour later, Dirker, West, and two deputies—Henry Wilcox and Pete Slade—made it up to Sunrise.

Henry Wilcox—a man who'd seen his fair share of blood and guts—took one look at what was in the store and promptly ran outside to vomit. The other three were inclined to do the same, but held their own.

Massacre was what Tomlinson had called it and massacre is what it was. Period. There was no way to tell just yet how many had been killed. Corpses and parts thereof where littered about like bison carcasses at a buffalo camp. The bar was heaped with dismembered limbs...legs, arms, hands, feet. Some hands still gripped pistols and some legs still wore their boots. There was blood everywhere, oceans of it dried in sticky pools on the floor and splashed on the walls and spattered up onto the ceiling. Tables had been overturned, chairs shattered to firewood. Sacks of salt and flour had ripped open, their contents powdered over everything like a down of snow. Poker chips and playing cards scattered in every which direction.

Slaughter, plain and simple.

The store had sold everything from picks and shovels to Rochester lamps and sluice boxes. One of the picks had been put to good use—it had been used to impale a man to the wall, his feet a good six inches off the floor. Dirker couldn't even begin to imagine the strength it would take to do something like that.

And if all of that was bad enough down here, upstairs...Jesus, even worse.

Like a slaughterhouse. The corridor was actually painted red like a child's fingerpainting, filled with bodies and limbs and viscera. Dirker didn't do much exploring up there—the sight and smell of all that spilled blood and raw human meat was simply too much for any man—but what he had seen was enough to haunt his dreams forever. Whoever or whatever had been at work up there, had taken their time. Unlike downstairs which was, save a few grisly examples, like a free-for-all just this side of Hell, in the upstairs corridor, the fiends had been in no hurry whatsoever.

Five bodies had been ritually pulled apart—limbs and heads cut from torsos—and then reassembled on the walls where they had been nailed in place. Dirker suppose that was evidence of a sick, grim sense of humor. When he first saw it, he thought he was looking at bloody manikins, but the truth found him soon enough. He hadn't bothered with the other rooms up there. No doubt they hid more horrors, but he simply wasn't up to it.

Downstairs with Doc West, Dirker watched the medical man examine the bodies. He probed punctures and gashes with instruments, measured wounds and abrasions. Dirker was thinking about the others. About the miners that had disappeared up in the hills these past months. And the ones that had been mauled by animals...at least what he had thought were animals.

Now, well, he knew better.

But if it wasn't animals, then what? Lunatics with dogs?

There were bullet holes everywhere—in the walls, the ceiling. Slugs had ripped through barrels of salt pork and jerky, had shattered the liquor bottles behind the bar. Shotgun blasts had blown holes in tabletops and pellets were peppered in the plank flooring.

Doc West sighed. Examined an obvious bite mark in a woman's buttocks. "Some sort of animal did this...but the spacing of the teeth, I just don't know. Like the others before." He stood up slowly, a immense weight bearing down on him. "These people were killed in a number of ways. Some were shot. Others stabbed. Still others had their throats torn out or were eviscerated. But, ultimately, they were all partially eaten. Killed for sport and for food. And as a bonus, most of them were scalped."

That was a new wrinkle, Dirker knew. The other bodies they had found in weeks previous had not been scalped.

Dirker cleared his throat. "So we've got ourselves a pack of animals that carry weapons and scalp folks like Indians?"

"That would be correct, yes."

Dirker licked his lips with a tongue dry as sandpaper. "The scalping...we'd better keep that to ourselves. People hear that and they'll be running Indians again."

Doc West nodded. "We had better keep *most* of this to ourselves."

Dirker walked back outside, to get that abattoir stink out of his face. Outside the wind blew and howled amongst the leaning, ramshackle structures. In his mind, it was the wail of ghosts demanding justice. He thought of the bounty he had put out. The one on the animals he had hoped were responsible. So far, hunters brought in three pathetic black bear, two slat-thin wolves, and a badger of all things.

It would have been mildly humorous, if it weren't so terrible.

Henry Wilcox was leaning against the shack across the road. The door was open and there was another body sprawled in there. This one had taken a load of double-ought at point-blank range. Probably the only truly normal death in Sunrise.

Wilcox and Dirker avoided looking at each other.

Dirker, his belly filled with something like wet sand, followed the muddy, overgrown road up amongst the empty buildings. The killers had impaled a series of heads on waist-high stakes to mark the path. Considerate of them. They had found three other bodies in one of the shacks—an old assay office. They had been hung by the feet and disemboweled. Dirker tried to suck in fresh air, but all he could smell was decomposed, maggoty death.

There was a gray false-fronted building at the very end with boarded-over windows. Dirker hadn't checked that one yet. He supposed he had to, like it or not.

He had to kick the door free of its hinges to get in.

And right away he smelled it—a wet and rancid stink. Feeble sunlight filtered in through gaping rents in the walls where boards had peeled loose. Motes of dust danced in the beams. The building had been something of a hotel once, but the furnishings had long ago been stripped away. Even the staircase leading above had been purloined, probably for firewood. It was dirty in there, shadowy and dank like a crypt. There was a bloody handprint on the faded wallpaper, a single bootprint pressed into the settled dust.

Dirker, sucking in a lungful of stale air, walked over to a door that was open maybe an inch. He could hear the wind whistling through holes in the roof, making the building groan and creak and tremble. There were another noises, too…the buzzing of insects. Meatflies, no doubt.

Dirker grasped the door, yanked it open.

A man stood there before him.

Stood stock still for a split second, then fell straight forward like a post and almost knocked Dirker on his ass. Dirker let out a little strangled cry, but the man was dead. A bubble of hysterical laughter slid up the sheriff's throat, but he would not set it free.

Just another corpse, that's all. The insides hollowed out, the face covered in flies. In the room behind him, there was dried blood everywhere. Bloody bootprints led to a window where planks had been knocked free.

Dirker left the corpse there and made for the door.

He heard the sound of hooves hammering up the road.

He knew it was Pete Slade riding back in, but for moment, one moment he thought that maybe it was—

Outside, Slade was speaking with Wilcox. Dirker made his way over to them.

"Anything?" he said.

Slade just shook his head, stroking his mustache. "I followed the tracks up pretty high. I'm figuring seven horses, but no sign of animal with 'em, dogs or otherwise. About three miles from here, the riders cut into a stream. I followed it for a mile or so...but I saw nothing that made me think they ever cut up the bank." He pulled a cigar butt from the pocket of his leather vest, stuck it in his mouth. He did not light it, just chewed on it. "That stream winds through the mountains for miles and miles. Maybe if we had some dogs, we could cast for scent."

Dirker swallowed. "That's fine. I don't want you to go up against...these *people* on your own. Our time will come, just not yet."

Slade said, "I think these boys...I think they know what they're doing. They been tracked before, I'm guessing, and their smart."

Dirker told him and Wilcox to bury the heads on the poles, what bodies they could find. Then he went back to the general store. He didn't bother trying to drag the bodies out. When Doc West was done, he spilled kerosene around and lit the place on fire.

A cleansing then, of a sort.

3

Although Dirker very much wanted only a sanitized version of events of what had occurred up at Sunrise to circulate through Whisper Lake, the miner who had discovered the slaughter beat him to it. By the time Dirker and the others made it back to town, the story was out. It was out and people were crawling up the sheriff's ass like mites.

Over at the Callister Brother's Mortuary, Caleb Callister and three other men—James Horner, Philip Caslow, and Luke Windows—were gathered in the upstairs rooms, speaking in soft, careful tones. The rooms had once been used by Hiram Callister, but were now a sort of meeting place for Caleb and his friends.

"It's worse than anything thus far," Caleb said to them. "An out and out slaughter and I think we all know who's responsible."

"Scalped, too, you say?" Caslow asked.

"Yes."

Horner looked angry. "I'm not surprised. Them goddamn Mormons think this is their place, that the whole of Utah Territory belongs to them. They'll do anything to push real Christians out."

Windows lit a cigarette. He was a blacksmith and his hands were huge, callused. "See? What they got in mind is for us to blame injuns. That's what they want. But we ain't rising to that bait. We got us a pack of them Danites, them Destroying Angels hiding over in Redemption or maybe Deliverance."

"Exactly," Caslow said. "It's only a matter of deciding which snake pit we root out first."

"Redemption," Caleb said to them.

He knew if he suggested Deliverance, he'd get no takers. No man in his right mind wanted to ride up to Deliverance, not with what was said about that place. Maybe all of it wasn't true, but if some of it was, then it was enough. Besides, even the Mormons shunned the place.

"Tonight then," he said. "Tonight we sack that heathen nest and burn it to the ground."

No one disagreed with that.

4

Sitting atop packing crates in the alley behind the Red Top Saloon, Jack Goode was saying, "I'll tell you something, Charlie Graybrow. Just between you and me and that heap of dogshit over there, this town has the curse all over it. Yes sir, right from its bones to the roofs above, cursed, that's what. Lookit me for instance. Just take a look at me and tell me what you see." Goode paused, pulling from a bottle of whiskey, wiping a few drops from his white beard with the back of his hand. "No comment? That's fair. Sure enough. Well, I'll answer it for you. You're looking at a man what won't see sixty again. Hell, won't see sixty-five, I reckon. A man that's been here and there and everywhere. I fought in the army, I trapped in the mountains. I whipped a mail coach down the Overland trail and I was even a Pony Express rider until some Cheyenne bucks in Wyoming Territory filled me so full of arrows they could've used my ass to water flowerbeds. What I'm saying, my red brother, is that I ain't afraid of shit. Never have been."

Charles Graybrow took the bottle, had a taste. "But now?"

"Now things is surely different, ain't they?"

Charles Graybrow agreed with that silently. He knew bad things were happening and would continue to happen. All those disappearances and killings out in the hills. And now this latest massacre. Bad medicine. That's what it was. Then the vigilantes out tormenting the Mormon squatters and now that prostitute getting slit from kitty to chin.

Not good, not good at all.

Even a fool (or a white man) had to sense the bad aura in and around Whisper Lake these days. It was so thick you could hold it in your hand. Almost as if that particular corner of Beaver County was a gathering point for noxious forces. Made a fellow think. Even made an injun think.

"Things keep up," Graybrow said, "well have the army in here."

Goode pulled from the bottle. "Yes sir, you probably got a point there, my friend. Damned and dandy if you don't. Because I'll admit before God and the Democrats and gladly so that I'm shit-scared over this place and what's happening here. You ask me, there's a poison here and old Whisper Lake is just rotten to the roots. And it's getting worse by the day. This town, my friend, is as surely fucked as a three-dollar whore." He sighed, looked skyward as if he expected the hand of the Lord to smite him from above. "And you know the worse thing of all, Charlie?"

Graybrow shook his head.

"I think I'm to blame," Goode admitted. "Somehow, some way...I brought hell down upon this here burg."

Graybrow took the bottle from him. "How do you figure that?"

Goode sighed. "It's a long story, but I'll make it quick for you, I reckon."

"Yeah, I'm an injun and all, so don't go confusing me. I'm real simple."

"Now, don't be like that, Charlie. That's not what I meant. You know I got nothing but respect for your people."

Graybrow nodded. "Surely. Amongst my tribe we consider you to be something of a holy figure. Many is the day we pray for your guidance."

"No shit? Goddammit...you're tugging my cord again."

"I'm funny like that," Graybrow said. "Maybe it's because I'm an injun."

Goode told him that might be the reason, yes sir. "Anyway, about seven months ago I landed me this job. I was hired by this injun, a Goshute, from the Skull Valley Band. He wanted me to transport this body from up there down here to Whisper Lake. A hundred U.S. Treasury greenbacks he promised me. I jumped on it. Figured I'd come down here, maybe do a little panning up in the hills. Now, this body we were talking about belonged to a fellow name of James Lee Cobb. You hear of him?"

Graybrow washed whiskey around in his mouth. "Some sort of killer, I think. Outlaw. Pistol fighter. Something like that."

Goode clapped him on the shoulder. "And then some. A cold-blooded killer is what we're talking, Charlie. Cobb came out of Missouri and his trail was red and hurting. Fought in the Mex war. Robbed. Killed. Raped. Got trapped up in the high Sierras with a few saddle tramps, ate the sumbitches for breakfast, lunch, and dinner. Well, you get the idea. Old Cobb...why he was just as low as the belly of a squashed rattlesnake in a wagon wheel rut."

"Why'd that Goshute have you bring him here?"

Goode shrugged, shook his head. "Hell if I know really. Said something about it being Cobb's last wish. Had some sort of half-brother living in these parts. About all I could figure is that Cobb was wanted for just everything just about everywhere, so he was on the dodge in injun country."

"So you brought the body here?"

"Yes, damn if I didn't. Me and this little squirt of piss name of Hyden brought the box clear from Skull Valley and right across the San Fran mountains..."

Goode went on to tell him what that had been like. And as he told it, his eyes got wide and staring, his face rubbery and discolored. A tic jumped at the corner of his lips as he told his story, gazing fearfully into the distance as if he saw the Devil riding in on horseback. When he finished...he was shaking and breathing hard.

"Sounds like what?" he finally said. "About thirty pounds of prime manure? Maybe. But I swear it's true. That body in that box...it weren't dead. Least not in the way we understand dead, you and me. It was crawling and scratching and nails were popping free...and Jesus, Charlie, I coulda pissed myself. Whatever was in that box, well, it weren't right at all. Like its spirit had just gone sour like bad milk."

Graybrow listened and kept his sarcasm to himself, because he knew Goode. And Goode was about as superstitious as most atheists. He wasn't above telling a few tall ones, but Graybrow knew this was not one of them.

Goode pulled hard off the bottle. "I never told a living soul about this, Charlie. And I'm telling you only because I trust you and we killed a few bottles together and you're an injun. You people know about shit like this. White folk? Hell, we're black and white from toe to skull. Something don't fit in our worldview, we pave it over with bullshit so's we can sleep at night. But Indians...yeah, you people ain't afraid to look the dark things in the face, ain't afraid of admitting that there's black, evil things that can drive a man mad to look upon."

Graybrow appreciated that, even though he didn't say so. "You think that Cobb wasn't human as such any longer?"

"I don't know what to think," he said, "but what was in that box...well, I'm not above admitting that if it had gotten out, I wouldn't be here right now."

"And you think that Cobb brought hell to this place?"

Goode licked his lips, thought it over real carefully. "Well, I keep my ear to the ground and I hear things. We brought the body to Callister's Mortuary. And that night, they say, Callister was found dead. And it weren't suicide. Rumor has it Cobb's body was nowhere to be found, but the other Callister—Caleb—he shushed it up. Now, I don't think I have to tell you what's happened over in Deliverance since then. Even the Mormons themselves won't go within a mile of that place."

"And you think Cobb went there? That he's the...focus of this?"

But Goode would only shrug. "Those are the facts way I know 'em. First chance I get, Charlie, I'm gonna fill my poke and ride out of this graveyard Hell-for-Leather. The idea that old James Lee Cobb might come knocking at my door one night keeps me awake until the wee hours."

Graybrow thought it over for a long time as they finished the bottle. Either Goode was crazy or maybe he had something. But even if he was right, there wasn't a man in Whisper Lake that would ride out to Deliverance to check it out.

"Well, dammit, enough confessing, Charlie. I ever tell you about the time I sold my wife for a dollar? Truth. She was a mean outfit from back east used to gargle with scrap iron and piss tacks. One time we was in this saloon at a mining camp up in the Big Horn range, Wyome Territory. This big dirt-mean sumbitch named Johnny Houle says to me, 'How much fer ye wife, son?' And, hoo! Me and Thedora, we had been going at it for hours. So I say, a dollar. He pays me, drags her off. She shows later, dress torn and face bruised, just a-ready to skin and scalp me. Next day, old Johnny finds me. He's walking funny like there's a boot and spur up his ass sideways. You know what? He wanted his dollar back..."

But Graybrow was not listening.

He was thinking of Deliverance and James Lee Cobb. Wondering just what it was he could do about it. And right then, he thought of Orville DuChien. His second sight. Orv would probably know if Cobb was up there. And if he did?

Graybrow started thinking about Tyler Cabe then.

5

Tyler Cabe thought about it real hard and decided there was only one way to hunt the Sin City Strangler: He had to make friends with the whores in town. These women would be the Strangler's targets and if he haunted their establishments, well, just maybe, he might catch sight of the bastard. If nothing else, Cabe could put the word out about who he was and what he was doing and that might make the Strangler nervous. And that would either make him bolt...or do something careless.

And if it was the latter, Cabe planned on being there to capitalize on his mistake.

Although Whisper Lake was like any other wild mining town and had its fair share of sin and vice, its red light district was restricted to a seedy run down near the refineries ubiquitously known as Horizontal Hill. Caught between mill and lake, but hidden from the rest of Whisper Lake by a high, juniper-covered bluff—Piney Hill—this run of brothels, sporting houses, tents, and cribs was no less busy than the rest of the town.

And at night, a sight busier.

It was allowed to operate by Jackson Dirker for two reasons. The first being that if he tried to close it down, the miners and railroad men would no doubt jump him and stretch his neck within an hour. And the second...because each and every establishment had to be licensed by the county. And that meant that the senior county official did the licensing—the county sheriff.

Dirker licensed not only whorehouses, but gambling halls and saloons as well. And pocketed an easy 10% of not only the licensing fees, but the taxes themselves.

Anyway, the whores plied their trade and kept it (for the most part) in and around Horizontal Hill and the genteel folk of Whisper Lake didn't have to look upon it, so it kept right on rolling and swelling week after week.

Tyler Cabe strolled right into that den of vipers and fit like a hand in a glove. Just another prospector or gunman or hunter with iron in his pants and cash in hand. He worked the circuit and talked with dozens and dozens of madams, their prostitutes, and assorted freelancers. He made it known to everyone within earshot who and what he was.

His spiel generally went something like this: "Afternoon, ma'am, name's Tyler Cabe and I'm here on business."

The average response was: "Well, I'm in business, Mr. Tyler Cabe, so you surely came to the right place."

At which point, Cabe would have to be a little more specific about what his "business" was. The whores listened to his tales of the Strangler with great interest and considered Cabe to be something of a saint for wanting to protect them. They fed him and gave him drinks, offered him free lodging. Shanghai Marny Loo, the Chinese madam of the Orient Bathhouse, tried to hire him strictly to protect her girls. She was something of a legend in her own right in that she carried no less than six short-bladed knives on her person at any one time and could throw them with frightening accuracy. Cabe told her he'd keep the offer in mind.

It was, all in all, an interesting and enjoyable way to spend the afternoon and evening.

But there were hazards, of course.

More than one whore wished to show her appreciation in a more intimate way, and Cabe found himself in bed twice that day with grateful ladies—one a handsome high yellow girl and the other a flame-haired vixen from Alabama. But every job, of course, had its waters that had to be waded through.

He visited cribs that were no more than wooden shacks to sporting houses where expensive French girls ran the gaming tables and would take you straight to heaven for several hundred greenbacks. There were high dollar joyhouses like the Red August Social Club that featured deep-pile carpeting, cut chandeliers, gold leaf mirrors and tables, and imported European tapestries and Greek sculpture. A man could drop thousands in such a place, enjoying exotic delights beneath stained glass ceilings...but was assured of satisfaction and refined sin. Then there were mid-range bordellos like the San Francisco Common House where the girls were no less attractive, but they were all trained thieves who specialized in picking pockets and rolling drunken men. And if your poke wasn't full enough for those places, there were cheap brothels like the Russian Café where you could get drunk and fucked for the price of a grubsteak...long as you weren't too picky about the cleanliness of your lady.

Cabe hit them all and heard all the stories.

He found that while most of the girls were just your average poke-and-tickle painted ladies, many went the extra mile. One particular high-priced Asian girl named Songbird could do amazing things with oils and hot candle wax. Abilene Sue, a buxom free-living Texan, generally employed a double-cinch saddle and riding crop into her act. And Fannie the Fortune Teller liked to start her sessions by diving your future. A future which always ended the same way—with her riding on top of you, trying to break you like an ornery bronc.

Somewhere along the way, Cabe met Mama Adelade, the proprietor of Mother French's Old Time Theater. What it was, was basically a steakhouse with vaudeville acts and imported French girls—or just girls who could affect a convincing French accent—and a booming business upstairs. Place smelled of fine French perfume and offered Parisian wine and cuisine.

Mama Adelade—a slight black woman who could not have weighed much more than ninety pounds—dressed in a yellow silk dress with embroidered purple roses sprouting at the bosom.

"Honey," she told Cabe after he introduced himself, "I surely appreciate what it is you're doing. My girls are getting more than a little skittish. And I can't have that, no sir. For here we offer only one real thing and we offer it three different ways. And that would be love—the fine, the mighty fine, and the very fine. Now, I'm thinking what you need is the mighty fine. The very fine...no, boy, you ain't up to it."

"What's the 'very fine'?"

"Hee, hee," Mama Adelade tittered. "The very fine is just about dying and going straight on to heaven. It involves two girls and sometimes three, hot oil and busy hands."

Cabe admitted he surely wasn't up to it.

Mama Adelade told him that she had been a slave on a Baton Rouge plantation. When she got her freedom and, Lord, how she'd wanted that, it wasn't as easy as she'd thought it would be. "Boy, the massah, you know, he might of owned us, but least he fed us and put a roof over our heads. I think maybe some of us forgot about that. For when we was freed...hell, we had to fend for ourselves. No easy bit, that."

Mama told him that it wasn't long before she realized that there was only one way a black woman was going to make any money in a white man's world. So she started small and built up her stable year by year.

"Had me a son, too, Mr. Cabe. But as he grew to manhood, he found religion and didn't care much for how his mama made her living. Last I heard of him, he went out to Indian Territory to preach. Hee! You imagine that? A black man slinging the white man's gospel to a bunch of red heathens! Something funny about that, you think?"

It was a long day, but by the time Cabe retired from Horizontal Hill, he was no closer to the Sin City Strangler than he had been before. But something had to give. Sooner or later, it was going to.

While he was at a teahouse, he bumped into Henry Freeman, the Texas Ranger, who claimed he was out "inspecting the stock." And that made Cabe remember he had to wire the Rangers in Texas, see if old Henry was who and what he claimed to be.

Because, honestly, Cabe had his doubts.

6

The riders thundered into Redemption like demons loosed from the lower regions of Hell.

The vigilantes had arrived.

They came pounding up the dirt street on black mounts, seven men wearing long blue army overcoats and white hoods set with eye slits pulled over their heads. They carried repeating rifles and shotguns and Colt pistols. They charged down the streets and down alleyways with an almost military precision.

What they brought to the little Mormon enclave of Redemption was death.

And with it they brought every intolerance and prejudice that had been boiling in the black kettles of their hearts for weeks and months and even years.

Without haste then, they started shooting.

The Mormons knew they would show, but had hoped it would not be for some time for they were ill-prepared to fend off such a bold attack. Men carrying muskets and bolt-action rifles ran out to oppose the riders and were cut down in lethal rains of well-directed gunfire. Women screamed and children cried and shotguns boomed and pistols barked. Lead was flying like hail, peppering doors and shattering windows and killing livestock that had not been carefully stabled.

One of the town elders stomped out onto the porch of his house, his three sons at his heels. A rider passed by, giving the elder both barrels at close range. The buckshot blew a hole the size of a dinner plate in his chest and splattered gore over his sons. And the sons had little more time than to shriek as gunfire from Winchester and Sharps rifles raked them, killing them on the spot. An old woman ran out amongst the vigilantes, waving a prayerbook at them and they rode her down, crushing her beneath the hooves of their horses. The same fate met three young children who'd seen their mother and father put down by pistol fire.

The wise townsfolk stayed behind locked doors or returned fire from gunports cut into shutters. But they were not seasoned fighters, and very few of their rounds came within spitting distance of the vigilantes. Though a single bullet—whether directed or ricocheted—ripped through the throat of a vigilante and he collapsed in his saddle.

But that didn't even slow the killers down.

They reigned and fired, tossing flaming kerosene torches into bales of hay and piles of lumber and very often right through the windows of stores and homes. And in the midst of that, they kept riding and shooting and killing and scattering horses and mules, using cattle and sheep for target practice.

Within twenty minutes of their arrival, Redemption was blazing like the nether regions of Hell. Flames engulfed barns and livery stables. Licked up the walls of houses. Vomited from exploded windows. The town became an inferno of fire and smoke and screaming. Bucket brigades worked to douse the conflagration even as the vigilantes shot them dead.

In the noise and confusion and shouting, a lone figure clutching the Book of Mormon stumbled into the streets, already bleeding from a stray bullet that had creased his temple. He made quite a sight out there on foot, shouting prayers and oaths, trails of blood streaking down his face.

"...the Antichrist will come among the people, commanding his legions...and ye shall know him by his name! Nation shall make war, horrendous and godless war upon nation, man will kill his brothers in a rapture of evil! Evil! And...and...the unclean shall make unclean laws to enslave the righteous and the fornicator will be smitten by the hand of the Almighty..."

He never got much farther than that, for a lasso of horsehair rope swung down and over him, locking his arms tight against his body. The rope was tied off to the saddlehorn of a vigilante's horse and then lastly, finally, the riders rode out of the purgatory they had created.

Rode out, dragging the preacher behind them.

***

They dragged him for maybe a mile.

Over rocks and stones and stumps, through dry ravines and up craggy hillsides. When the vigilantes did finally stop, atop a low flat-topped hill fringed by rabbit brush, the preacher was barely alive. He looked, if anything, like a threadbare scarecrow. His rag and straw stuffing was hanging out and sticks were protruding from his legs and arms...except it wasn't rags and straw and what stuck out weren't sticks. The flesh had been worn from his face and the backs of his hands. He had numerous compound fractures and broken bones. His jaw was dislocated and still he tried to speak, a bloody gurgling sound bubbling forth.

One of the vigilantes pulled off his hood. It was Caleb Callister. Squinting his eyes in the darkness, he watched the glowing, flickering bonfire in the distance. Redemption.

"If your people are smart, preacher-man," he said, slipping a thin cigar between his lips, "they'll heed our warning this time. Because next time, next time—"

"Next time there won't be anybody left when we ride out," another vigilante finished for him.

This got a few chuckles from the others.

The preacher, though broken and peeled, tried to crawl, straining at his leash like a fool dog testing his boundaries. The vigilantes watched him, just expecting him to curl up and expire...but it wasn't happening. He coughed out loops of blood, legs pistoning him forward, arms still fixed to his sides. Slinking and inching along like some human worm. And just as freedom, maybe, seemed to beckon...the rope snapped taut.

"Best accept the fix you're in, preacher," one the vigilantes said to him. "It ain't like rain...it won't go away."

"Much as you might like that," said another.

They sat on their mounts, smoked, passed a bottle of whiskey, and watched Redemption burn like a torch in the distance. Gradually, slowly, the blaze became separate fires that were brought under control one after the other.

Then they drew straws on who got the preacher.

Luke Windows was the lucky man. He decided to drag the preacher around for awhile. And he did. After another twenty minutes or so, he got tired of it and the preacher still wasn't dead, so he emptied his Colt Navy .44 into the man.

Then he joined the others to celebrate.

7

After a somewhat exhausting day spent making the rounds of Horizontal Hill's varied brothels, Tyler Cabe walked back to the St. James Hostelry. His belly was empty and his temples were pounding like jungle drums from all the free liquor he'd swallowed. He walked into the dining room and Jackson Dirker was there, along with his wife and five or six other guests. Dinner consisted of roast chicken and potatoes with an apple crumb for dessert. It was damn good and Cabe's respect for Janice Dirker went up a notch.

Jackson Dirker was surely a lucky man.

Cabe and Dirker made small talk, but mostly just listened. One of the tenants was a medical supply drummer from Wichita named Stewart. He spoke at some length—and in unsavory clinical detail—about his products which ranged from liver pills to trusses, hygienic whiskey to colonics. Particularly the latter…which, of course, didn't do much for the digestion of the apple crumb.

After he excused himself and the other tenants slipped off, it was just Cabe and Dirker together, with Janice flitting back and forth collecting dishes.

"Mr. Cabe tells me that the two of you are acquainted," she said to her husband.

He barely looked up from his newspaper. "In a manner of speaking."

Same old Dirker, Cabe found himself thinking. Cool as ice. If he had any emotions buried in that thick hide, it would have taken twenty men with shovels to unearth them. Maybe if Dirker had simply said, yes, yes, we know each other. We fought against each other…but that was years ago. Maybe had he said something like that, Cabe would have been satisfied to let it go. But now he felt surly.

"Yes," he said, "once upon a time, your husband and I were brothers in arms. We fought on opposite sides, but spiritually we were one. Ain't that so, Jack?"

The newspaper lowered an inch. A set of crystal blue eyes found Cabe, did not blink. The newspaper slid back up. "I wouldn't go that far," was all he would say.

"Nonsense. Maybe your recollections of me are vague, Jack, and rightly so…but mine of you? Hell, sharp as a whip. How I remember you at Pea Ridge! What a fine and striking figure you were!"

"That's enough, Cabe."

Cabe smiled now, fingers brushing the webbing of scars that ran across the bridge of his nose, cut into the cheeks. "Your husband is modest, Madam. I would say that Jackson Dirker was an officer and a gentleman. Fair and sympathetic in all matters."

Dirker was staring holes through him now.

Cabe was staring right back.

Janice, sensing something was terribly amiss here, just cleared her throat and picked at imaginary lint on her velveteen dress. "If I may be so rude and impertinent, Mr. Cabe…did you, did you get those scars in the war?"

But if she was rude or impertinent, it only made Cabe's grin widen. His fingers explored the familiar slash-and burn-geography of those old scars. "Yes, I received them in the war. I carry them with a certain amount of honor. Battle wounds. You remember when I got these, Jack?"

Dirker set the newspaper down. "Yes, I do. But, tell me, Cabe, how did you find our brothels? Word has it you spent most of the day there. Did you find our red light district to your liking?"

Whatever Cabe was going to say evaporated on his tongue. Dirker. That wily sonofabitch. "I...um..."

Janice smiled thinly. "Our Mr. Cabe certainly is a saucy one."

"Isn't he, though?" Dirker said, enjoying himself now.

Cabe swallowed and swallowed again. "It was purely business, Madam. The man I'm hunting preys upon prostitutes, so what choice do I have but to befriend them? To know them and the places they work."

"The things a man must do to make a living," she said, shaking her head. "Tsk. Tsk. And all day you spent among them? How tired you must be...after such an exhausting enterprise."

"Madam—"

Dirker was smiling now. "You are a most determined man, Cabe. If any man can root out this killer it will be you."

Now here Dirker thought he was being funny and it made Cabe smile, too. If the man was more like that on a regular basis and not so damnably stiff and formal...he almost would have liked him. Cabe figured he was being baited, so he did what came natural to him: he rose up and bit down. "Yes, Madam, it was tiring, but I kept at it until most men would have been spent with fatigue."

Janice blushed...blushed, but did not turn away. There was something smoldering behind her eyes and she made sure Cabe saw it.

Dirker raised an eyebrow. "Did you now? Gave them the what-for?"

"Oh yes."

"I'll leave you gentlemen to it," Janice said, leaving the room.

Cabe figured he'd either offended her...or excited her. In his experience, Southern women could be like that. Excited at what they found most offensive. It was the breeding, that's what. Antebellum society said a lady had to repress her basal instincts. That such things as lust and desire had no place in the higher scheme of things...but like any beast, the more you starved it the hungrier it became.

And there was hunger in that girl. A barely-concealed need to cast-off her upbringing and get down and dirty.

Dirker said, "Is it going to be this way every time we meet, Cabe?"

Cabe looked away from him. So many things he wanted to say, but to what end? What true end? He'd already violated two rules of his upbringing—that a man did not bring his business or personal affairs to the dinner table and that he did not hash out problems with another man in the presence of a lady. Maybe now was the time...if he wanted a fight, then it was high time to quit beating around the bush.

But he did not want that, not anymore. "No," he said, surprising even himself, "I would prefer we could put all that aside. I reckon it would be the proper thing to do. At least for the time."

"Agreed. But just so you understand, Cabe. What happened at Pea Ridge is not something I am proud of. A day does not go by that I don't think about it, wish things had been different."

"You willing to admit that all we were doing was scavenging some essentials off them dead boys?"

Dirker nodded. "I know that, yes. Maybe I knew it then, too, but I lost my head. What I did was wrong."

Damn. Now if that didn't suck the wind right out of a man. Dirker admitting he was *wrong*. Cabe felt suddenly very loose, boneless. He almost felt embarrassed that he'd even brought it up. "All right, all right. Fair enough. We were all young and hot-headed, I guess."

"What did you do after the war, Cabe?"

Cabe told him about his years riding steer and nightherding, being a railroad detective and shotgunner on the bullion stages. How it all led to bounty hunting. "Yourself?"

Dirker sighed. "I stayed in the army. Was sent west to fight Indians." His eyes narrowed. "I thought what I had seen in the Civil War was bad. But it didn't prepare me for what I saw out there. The atrocities, the wanton murder of innocents."

Cabe didn't press it. He knew plenty of what had happened out there, the indignities and cruelties pressed upon the tribes. And generally, unwarranted. Treaties were made between whites and Indians. And the ink was barely dry before the whites had again violated them.

"But you left the army?"

Dirker was smiling now. "No, I was relieved of my command. A band of Arapahos had raided a settlement and I was told to hunt them down and massacre them. Well, we couldn't find the perpetrators, so my commander decided that *any* Arapahos would do. There was a village of maybe fifty on Cripple Creek. They had nothing to do with the raid and that fact was well known...yet I was ordered to go in there with my men. And when we came out, I was instructed, there was to be nothing left alive."

"You refused?"

"Yes, I did. And I am proud of that fact. I was a soldier, not a hired killer." Dirker sighed, licked his lips. "I was relieved of my command, court-martialed and discharged. Honorably, much to the dismay of some."

"And after that?"

"I was a lawman. One town after another. Eventually Janice and I bought this hotel. Of course, there was trouble between the miners and the Mormons, the Indians and the settlers...I was approached and given the job of county sheriff on the spot."

Cabe took it all in. His story was no different from that of many a veteran—trained as a soldier, they invariably became either lawmen or outlaws, sometimes both. Cabe rolled a cigarette, lit it up. "Tell me something, Sheriff. This business I've been hearing about a little camp called Sunrise...anything to it?"

Dirker nodded after a time. "Horrible, horrible."

"What are you going to do about it?"

"I'm going to hunt down who's responsible, of course."

"Of course. And while you're at it...there's this fellow named Freeman. Says he's a Texas Ranger. Think you could look into that for me? Maybe wire the Rangers?"

"You think he's lying?"

Cabe told him he wasn't sure what he was thinking. "All I know, Dirker, is that he's giving me a real bad feeling in my guts. And I can't figure out exactly why..."

8

Later, at the Oasis Saloon, a knot of men gathered around Cabe as he tried to drink his beer. Tried to relax a bit and put all this business with Dirker into some sort of perspective. Were they friends now or enemies? And what about his wife? Cabe had been around, he knew very well the way she was looking at him and what such a look entailed. She had gotten down right excited as he joked about the whores and what he'd done with them. He had not imagined it.

"So, this killer, this Sin City Strangler," one of the men said, a miner with a shaggy gray beard and no upper teeth. "They say he slits 'em clean open. That true?"

"It is," Cabe told him.

He had been casually discussing a few particulars of that business with Carny, the bartender, and it had drawn the others like a rope. They wanted to know everything, everything.

Another said, "Why in Christ he rape 'em? Whores? You don't have to rape 'em...they give it up for two bits, some of 'em."

"Yeah, why did he rape 'em?" another wanted to know.

"He never says."

A tall man in a gray wool suit and polished black boots was shaking his head. "Seems to me, sir, that this is no fit conversation in the presence of
ladies."

The miners were looking around, trying to find the ladies. All they saw were a few whores mulling about. They didn't figure that sort counted as being ladies.

"They ain't no ladies here, chief," a miner said. "In case you haven't noticed."

"I find it objectionable all the same."

The miners laughed at that to a man. Looked like maybe they were going to start trouble over it...but then they saw the pistols hanging from the man's belt. Fine and sleek they were, Colt Peacemakers with ivory handles. The weapons of a shootist.

The miners filtered away, figuring today wasn't the day to die.

"And you, sir," the tall man said to Cabe. "If you are a bounty hunter as you claim, if you are indeed hunting this man, then I seriously doubt you will find him in the bottom of a glass of beer."

Cabe looked at Carny, just shook his head. "Listen, mister. I came in for a drink, not to listen you run that silver-plated mouth of yours."

The tall man took a step forward. "All the manners of a rutting hog. How wonderful that is."

"Like I said, I just want to drink my beer. So will you kindly go fuck yourself?"

The tall man's face drained of color. "That, sir, is no way for a gentleman to talk. Profanity is the product of a weak mind."

"Well, that's me—weak-minded Arkansas trash. I claim to be nothing else."

An easterner. A dandy. That's what this fellow was. These days, didn't seem you could spit without hitting one. Cabe generally just left them alone, regardless of how he felt about that sort. Most of 'em didn't bother no one. Then there were this kind.

"No, sir, you are certainly no gentleman, surely. You are rude, coarse, and obnoxious."

"Yes, sir, as you said." Cabe set his glass on the bar, put his hat on. "Now please kindly step out of my sight before the doc has to pull my spurs out of your fine white ass."

But he wasn't moving and Cabe was starting to wonder if he'd have to bury this sumbitch, too.

"If your mother had any sense, bounty hunter, she would've drowned you in a sack before you grew to stink up this country."

Cabe felt the hairs along the back of his neck bristle. No, no, he wasn't going to let this bastard push him into something he would regret. Just wasn't going to happen. He was walking away from this one.

The tall man had positioned himself between Cabe and the door now.

Which meant that Cabe had two choices: go around him or right through. It wasn't much of a decision for Cabe, being that he went around no man. It wasn't his way. It had cost him in blood and bruises through the years, but he backed down from no one.

He thought: I will not pull my pistol, not if there's any other way.

The dandy stood his ground and Cabe came right at him, not slowing, not so much as breaking stride. When he was precious feet away, the tall man pulled his Colts. Pulled 'em pretty fast, too. But not fast enough. By the time he cleared leather, Cabe was close enough to smell. A few quick steps and he had hammered the dandy in the face with two quick, straight jabs that put him to his knees. Cabe kicked him in the belly to keep him down. Somewhere during the process, the tall man lost his pistols. Cabe saw them and kicked them away.

"Now," he said, just plain sick of bullshit like this, "y'all go home to Boston or Charlottesville or where ever in the fuck you came from. You go back home to daddy's money and his title. Because out here, you're gonna get your fool self killed."

Cabe went right past him, left him coughing and gasping, blood bubbling from his dislocated nose. He had almost made the front door when the dandy screamed out obscenities and pulled a little five-shot Remington Elliot .32.

Cabe just stood there, knowing he couldn't move quick enough.

The gun was on him.

The tall man was filled with rage and hate.

Just then two men carrying shotguns burst through the door. They were dressed in dusty trail clothes and plainsman-style hats.

"You there," the first said. "Drop that pistol or I'll cut you in half."

The dandy lowered it, let it slide from his fingers.

The second one turned to Cabe, looked him up and down. "You Cabe? Tyler Cabe? The Arkansas bounty hunter?"

"I would be."

The shotguns came around in his direction now. "Then you better come with us."

9

For some time after Tyler Cabe left, Janice Dirker found herself thinking about him. About how he carried himself, the way he spoke, that unflappable honesty that was the earmark, it seemed, of who and what he was. She found herself thinking about these things and knowing that he excited her. Excited some part of her that had lain long dormant like a volcano just biding its time until it would erupt.

Tyler Cabe was a free-spirit.

He seemed to be entirely unconventional. Had no true respect for money or position, for authority or cultural values. He lived as he chose, said what he pleased to whom he pleased. He was a rogue element. Seemed to have more in common with the red man than the white. Maybe this is what excited her. He was so different than the other men she'd known. Now, her husband Jackson, was completely the opposite. He had bearing, had station, had unshakable confidence. But he was stiff and unyielding and emotions seemed to be a foreign thing to him. Mere malfunctions of character, rather than compliments to it. For though Jackson was a good man who invariably did the right thing at the right time, he was cold. Terribly cold and methodical.

And Tyler Cabe?

Anything but. He was tough and trail-weary, had ridden the backside of society for far too long. He was surely lacking in refinement or social graces, but what he lacked there he surely made up in warmth and humanity. He was warm and friendly and wore his emotions proudly. He had depth and sincerity and compassion. He was everything Jackson wasn't and was not afraid to be so. Her father would have despised him. And although Jackson was a Yankee, he was exactly the sort of man her father would have paired her with—a man of dignity, resolve, and bearing. His idea of what a man should be. And Cabe? Her father would have instantly dismissed him as "hill-trash".

Cabe, however, was not the most outwardly handsome of men.

He was tall and lanky, powerful without being manifestly muscular. His face was weathered from hard-living and hard riding, set with draws and hollows, lined by experience. Then there were those scars across his face. He would have been a menacing character had it not been for those beautifully sad green eyes that offset the rest and gave him a pained, melancholy look.

There was no doubt in Janice's mind that she was attracted to him.

Maybe it was the hotel and the staff and daily drudgery of keeping things running. Jackson was part of that, she supposed. Just another reminder of toil and unhappiness...and perhaps all these things combined is what made Tyler Cabe seem so fresh, so exciting. For he was, if anything, the image of a pirate from her teenage fantasies—a scoundrel, a libertine, a wolf in a world of sheep and dogs.

These were the things Janice mulled over that windy evening when the giant came through the door.

Maybe *giant* wasn't entirely applicable, but there was no getting around the fact that her visitor was closer to seven-feet than six. He was dressed in a shaggy buffalo coat that was just as ragged and worn as the hide of a mangy grizzly. Crossed bandoleers of brass cartridges were belted over his chest. A big Colt Dragoon pistol hung at the crotch of his fringed deerskin pants. His face was hard, his eyes like unblinking iron, a steel gray beard hung down to his chest.

Janice felt her insides go to jelly. She begin to quiver at the sight of him. "May...may I help you?" she managed.

He stepped forward, casting a shadow over her. His belts were set with knives and pistols. He took off his hat and his head was just as bald as wind-polished stone. He tapped the ledger with the barrel of a shotgun.

"Surely," he said. "And evenin' to ye, ma'am. Name's Clay, Elijah Clay. I'm a lookin' fer the squeeze of shit what killed m' boy."

Janice just stared dumbly.

He looked around, nodded. "Ye happen to know the whereabouts of some Arkansas trash name of Tyler Cabe? I'm gunnin' fer this yellow-livered, dog-rapin', greasy squirt of hogfuck and I don't plan on leavin' till I get him."

Janice wanted to lie, but deception was not among her natural rhythms. And this man...well, you didn't dare lie to him. "He's not in, I'm afraid. He...he just left about a half-hour ago. Didn't say when he'd be back."

"Didn't, eh?" Clay sighed and shook his head. "That's probably fer the best, I reckon. Ye got yerself a fine place here, ma'am. Just fine. And with all due respects to ye and yer fine establishment, I wouldn't want to a-dirty it up none with the likes of Tyler Cabe and spill that goatpiss he calls blood here, there, and everywheres. When I git him and I surely will git him, I'll take that drip of shit outside and carve him like a rutting buck. Use his goddamn ball sack fer a tobaccy pouch. Yes, sir."

Janice was speechless.

"Ye figure ye can tell him I stopped by, ma'am?" Clay said, oddly cordial for a monster. "Tell him I been here and I'll be back and have no earthly intention of leaving until his scalp's a-dangling from m' belt." Clay slapped the sodbuster hat back on his head, turned and made for the door. Hand on the brass knob, he paused and touched the brim of his hat. "Ma'am."

And then he was gone.

10

The finest hotel in Whisper Lake was undoubtedly the Stanley Arms which catered to mining officials, rich cattlemen, and wealthy investors from back east. It was owned by a two-fisted Scotch highlander by the name of McConahee who came to this country to fight for the North in the Civil War and later made millions as a cattle broker. The Stanley boasted furnishings from European castles, imported Italian tile, and not one, but three French chefs.

And it was here that the two men with shotguns took Tyler Cabe.

Once outside, the guns were lowered. The men made it clear that he was not their prisoner, but equally clear that he was going to go where they said. Cabe was ushered through the great carved oaken doors, up the marble steps to the third floor where he was deposited in a suite of rooms carpeted in oriental rugs and told to wait.

And he did...drinking it all in.

There was a rosewood étagère set against one wall with a crystal mirror and ornamented shelves. Turkish armchairs, rose-carved side chairs, and a medallion sofa all upholstered in plush red velvet. There was a swan coffee table, high mahogany bookcases, and a gleaming eight-arm brass chandelier above.

A British manservant decked out in spats and tails told Cabe to make himself comfortable. Which wasn't too difficult on a camel-backed loveseat that nearly swallowed him alive in plush comfort. So Cabe sat there, a snifter of Napoleon brandy in his hand, amongst the lush accoutrements, pretending he was some high-born lord.

But all the while he was thinking: Okay, Cabe, you must've really pissed-off somebody important this time. So enjoy your brandy, because it might be your last.

Cabe was smelling his buckskins and armpits when someone entered the room. It was a white-haired man with a hawkish nose, just as thin as a porcupine quill.

"Mr. Cabe, I presume?" he said, sounding more than a little amused.

"You...ah, presume correctly, sir," Cabe said. "And don't get the wrong idea, Mister, I don't go around smelling myself like an ape in the zoo all the time. I was just concerned about stinking up your nice couch."

"Sofa, Mr. Cabe," the man said.

"Sofa?"

"*Sofa*." The man was high and mighty and something about him seemed to demand that. He poured himself some brandy and turned to his visitor, his eyes simply cold as ice chips. He cleared his throat. "I apologize for the somewhat unconventional invitation, but it was important I speak to you immediately."

"And you are?" Cabe said, knowing that to this guy not introducing himself was a grave social error.

"Yes, of course. Excuse me. Forbes, Conniver Forbes. I'm the chairman of the board and controlling stockholder of the Arcadian Mine, which is a merely a holding of the National Mining Cooperative. Perhaps, you've heard of us?"

Cabe had. They had more money than any three countries and more pull than a dozen state senators. "Sure. You people own lots of people. Folks just like me."

Forbes arched his left eyebrow. "I have some business I would like to discuss with you...perhaps over dinner?"

But Cabe shook his head. "I just had me some pickled eggs. Besides, that French food gives me the gas something awful."

"Yes." Forbes sat down. "I'll make it simple then and lay my cards out for you. I'm here as not only a representative of National Mining and the Arcadian, but of the Southview and Horn Silver mines as well. You see, we have a problem. A problem you may be able to help us with."

"Such as?"

"I understand you're hunting this deviant known as the Sin City Strangler?"

"That would be true, yes."

"And the compiled bounty on this individual is...?"

Cabe rolled himself a cigarette, amused as always how rich folk could never say what was on their minds. "About five-thousand, I reckon. Seems to go up every month."

Forbes nodded, stroked his chin. "I would like to hire you, Mr. Cabe. Hire you to address a problem which is much more severe than this Strangler. You see, there has been some problems in this town of late..."

He explained in some detail about the murders and disappearances up in the hills. Those which were originally thought to be the work of some large predators, but after the slaughter at Sunrise...well, other avenues of thought were being considered.

"See, Mr. Cabe, this Strangler business is bad, yes, but our problem here is tad bit worse. The Strangler has killed...what? Seven, eight women? Horrible to be sure, but minor in comparison to dozens and dozens that have disappeared or been slaughtered outside this town. And when you levy on top of that the massacre at Sunrise, well, you can no doubt see the time has come for action."

Cabe lit his cigarette, told Forbes it was not his problem. That such things were being handled by the county sheriff. He had put bounties on the animals thought to be responsible. And if they weren't animals, then just what in hell were they? He was not much of an investigator. Not given to wild leaps of speculation in general. He usually went after a man or an animal that had been identified in some way. But this, this was—

"Out of your realm?" Forbes said. "Maybe, maybe not. The fact is you're a bounty hunter, Mr. Cabe. You hunt for a living, men or beasts. As far as being an investigator goes, I think you're being modest. Your record is impressive. I want you to turn your complete attention over to our problem here."

"Why should I?"

Forbes, not a man used to having to beg, told him that there was a bigger issue at hand here than lives. There was money to be considered. If the killings and disappearances continued, the mines would be in trouble. People were already running scared. More than a few had already left and what they—the mining people—did not need was a mass exodus which would put a stranglehold on profits.

"A mine does not exist without men to work it," Forbes pointed out.

"Well, shit, you're right," Cabe said. "Men dying is one thing, but when all them bodies piling up starts to cut into the profit...well, damn, something had better be done."

Forbes just stared. "Whether you agree with our motives or not, Mr. Cabe, is beside the point. We'll pay you and pay you well to handle this matter."

"Why don't you bring in hunters from outside?"

"The time factor. This has to be moved on and contained immediately."

Cabe thought it over. Decided he did not like this manipulative sumbitch who stank and stank bad of boardrooms and privilege. "Sorry, but I got me other matters to attend to." He butted his cigarette and stood. "Now, if you'll excuse me—"

"We'll pay you fifty-thousand dollars, Mr. Cabe."

Cabe felt light-headed. He sank back down on the loveseat. He cleared his throat. "Course, first thing you need in something like this is facts. So, tell me what you know…"

11

Like vultures gathered around a fresh, meaty kill, the vigilantes (sans hoods) gathered around the body of James Horner. He was laid out on a slab in the mortuary, just as dead as 150 pounds of trail-killed steer. His eyes were glazed over, but wide and staring.

One of the vigilantes, a mine captain named McCrutchen kept pressing them closed, but the lids just popped back open. He crossed himself. "Don't like that," he said. "Don't like that at all."

A few others laughed.

"Nothing supernatural about it," Caleb Callister explained. He took a brown glass bottle of liquid and brushed the inner eyelids, gumming them shut. He held them closed for a moment and when he released them, they didn't open back up.

Horner was covered in dried blood. It had soaked into his blue overcoat and spattered across his face. The side of his throat was a great blackened chasm.

"Slug must've ripped out most of his neck," Luke Windows said.

"And his carotid artery with it," Callister said.

He pulled a sheet up over the body, the dead face making the others uneasy. They were down to six now without Horner— Callister, Windows, Caslow, McCrutchen, Cheevers, and Retting. They had been harassing the Mormons for better than three months now. Mostly they preyed on small groups caught away from the villages. The raid on Redemption tonight had been the first action of its kind. But now with Horner's death, it would not be their last.

Windows said, "I grew up with Horner, I grew up with him."

"He died bravely for the cause," Callister said, although it had a decidedly hollow ring to it. But what else could he say?

McCrutchen had been uneasy since they got Horner's body back to town. "I wonder if this is some sort of omen," he said.

Caslow just shook his head. "Since when is a shot man an omen?"

"I'm just wondering is all."

"Crazy," Retting said. "Crazy talk."

But Cheevers wasn't so sure. "Maybe we offended God with this business and we're being punished."

"Shut the fuck up," Windows told him.

Callister knew he had to get control of them or this infighting would be the end of their little society. "All right," he said, stepping between Windows and Cheevers. "Enough of this horseshit. We're all part of the same thing here, we're brothers. We all took the oath, did we not? As far as Horner goes, his death had nothing to do with God or the saints or the Devil himself. It was an accident. We rode in there shooting and burning. With all that lead flying about, we can count ourselves lucky no one else took a round. Maybe the Mormons hit Horner or...maybe one of us did. Ricochet. It's possible, very possible."

That shut them up, gave them something to chew on for a time.

"So enough of this nonsense," Callister said to them. "Those bastards'll pay for this, just not tonight is all."

"And what about Horner?" Windows wanted to know.

Callister sighed. "We have to get rid of the body."

"Now wait one goddamn minute," Windows said angrily. "He was my friend. I grew up with him, I—"

"We have to get rid of him," Callister cut in. "You mark my words, the Mormons are going to come screaming to Dirker first light. If they saw him get shot, they'll tell Dirker as much. If Dirker gets a look at Horner's wound, well, that wily sonofabitch'll put two and two together. He knows who Horner's friends are, he'll know who to roust."

There was silence after that. A great deal of it. All you could hear was the wind outside and the ticking of a mantle clock inside. Callister told Windows and the others to take the body out into the hills, plant it in a shallow grave where it would never be found.

"Horner will have his day of reckoning...through us," Callister promised them. "Maybe tomorrow night, maybe the night after, but he will certainly have it. The next time we ride on Redemption, we'll be carrying more than guns and kerosene."

"Like what?" Caslow asked.

"I was thinking about all that dynamite up at the mines," Callister said.

The others began to grin.

12

The next morning dawned cool and overcast, a light rain drizzling over the San Francisco mountains and the towns and mining camps that had sprung up around them like weeds.

In Redemption, a group of men dressed entirely in black stood in a large barn. They stood staring down at the bodies laid over an expanse of hay bales. They were the bodies of men, women, and children killed by the vigilantes. They numbered nearly two dozen.

Though the men followed the teachings of Brigham Young and the path of righteousness set forth by the prophet Joseph Smith, they were not like other Mormons. These men carried Colt pistols and Greener shotguns, repeating rifles and army carbines. In a religion that espoused the gentle way of the lamb, these men were wolves, hunters and predators.

They were called Danites, though gentiles knew them as the "Destroying Angels".

They were the ultra-secret, ultra-clannish enforcement wing of the Church of the Latter-Day Saints. Since before the days of the Mountain Meadows Massacre when as many as a 150 California-bound gentiles were slaughtered by Mormon militias and Indians under the direction of the Danites, they had been actively righting wrongs and settling scores for the Mormon populations of Utah Territory. And this under orders of Brigham Young, though he had denied the same again and again.

And now they were in Redemption.

A village elder was pacing before the bodies, openly weeping. "Only through the Holy Scriptures may we know of God's plan, the beauty of God's mind and will," he was saying. "For we are all God's children, are we not? Man, woman, and child? And are we not promised salvation for our toil and trouble and earthly torment?"

There was a chorus of "Amens".

"Yes, brothers and sisters, we have been charged by the Lord Almighty to go amongst the nations and spread His word. We are empowered by Him to baptize the heathen into His Church. And this, oh yes, this is our task, nay, our divine right! Yet, there are those who would visit foul deeds upon us! Foul deeds perpetrated by foul minds and foul hearts! They spurn the word and the teachings of the Lord God of Hosts! Not only do they refuse to be saved, but they refuse the way of salvation and eternal life! They spit in the face of His Son Jesus Christ! And worse, yea, possibly worse, brothers, they would burn and murder us from the very lands promised to us by the Prophet Joseph Smith! And when they molest our children, are we not angered? When they spill the blood of our kin, are we not enraged? And when they murder our brethren, are we not moved to revenge?"

The "Amens" of those gathered in the barn were loud and resounding now. The elder was openly plagiarizing both the Book of Mormon and the works of William Shakespeare, but no one seemed to notice. The elder was known for his fiery sermons and no one was disappointed this morning as they looked upon the burned and bullet-ridden corpses before them.

"The Lord has told us to love Him, to love all His Children...but what of they who do not love us? That do not chose the way of salvation and peace? What then, you may well ask? Well, brothers, I will tell you! For as the Lord has said that vengeance is mine, so is it ours! Our blood-right to avenge the murder of our kin! And, brothers, so shall it be..."

The Danites stood there, neither smiling nor frowning, but knowing that a task had been handed them and that they would accomplish that task even at the cost of their own lives.

So it was.

13

Charles Graybrow tracked Orville DuChien down to a shack on the edge of the lake itself. It sat on a little hill crowded by trees that were all dead from the filth pouring down from the nearby refinery stacks. The air stank sharply of chemicals and industrial waste. The water washed in a slick of black foam. Orv was sitting on a rock, staring over the misty waters, mumbling something.

Graybrow came up behind him, making sure he made a lot of noise so Orv would know he was coming.

"They told me about it, yes sir, all about it," Orv was saying. "Said this injun's gonna come and gonna want to know things. Gonna have questions for you, they say, and when they say...sure, they's always right, ain't they? Well, ain't they?" Orv rubbed his temples. "Sometimes...sometimes I talk crazy on account m' head, it hurts, just plain hurts, what with them voices, blah, blah, blah!"

Graybrow nodded, figured it probably wasn't easy. "Mind if I sit here by you?"

Orv scratched at his beard. "Injun, ain't you? Don't matter you being an injun, just saying it is all. I knew injuns back home, yessum, lots of injuns. Cherokee. Cherokee Nation, sure. Yes, you sit down there, Charlie...see, I remember you from way back."

Graybrow had brought a bottle of whiskey with him. He took a slug and passed it to Orv.

"Right neighborly of you, Charlie. Yessum." Orv took his drink and passed it back. "I try...I try to keep m' head, but it don't always work. I start talkin' in circles and what not. But you...you understand me, don't you? Some don't, but you do..."

"Yes, I think I understand."

Orv was gnashing his teeth. "Deliverance...the town the Devil built. Oh, think about it, Charlie! Them that don't like the light, but the dark places! Them that lives in cellars and attics, them that don't come out by daylight! Them that likes the meat and blood of men! Them with the Skin Medicine...oh, yessum, tattooed on their flesh!"

"Who are they?"

But Orv refused to answer. He just held himself until whatever it was drained out of him. "You...you remember Johnny Hollix?" Orv wanted to know. "He...he was the Indian Agent back home, gave them Cherokees a real bad time. Course, some of m' kin did, too. Like Cousin Stookey...but he weren't never worth a shit to no one. But I recall Johnny Hollix...he used to fish river cats with Grandpappy Jeremiah down on the south fork of the Suck River. Sometimes I went with 'em and sometimes that Cherokee medicine man...you recall his name, Charlie?"

Graybrow just pulled off the bottle. "Afraid it escapes me."

Orv began slapping his hands against his legs, shaking his head. "Yes, yes, yes, I remember! You don't have to shout! Charlie! Tell 'em not to shout!"

Graybrow went up behind him, feeling a great deal of pity for the man. He laid his hands on his shoulders, massaged the bunched muscles there the way his mother had once done for him. Gradually, gradually, Orv stopped trembling.

"You got them hands, good hands," Orv said. His head tipped forward until his chin touched his chest. "Yessum, I hear, I hear. That Cherokee medicine man, Charlie, his name was Spoonfeather or something like that, but everyone called him King Paint. King Paint. Him and Grandpappy Jeremiah had a love of the roots and herbs, power doctors, eh? King Paint's wife—that pretty young one that was all legs and tits and big eyes, yessum, that one—she got herself mixed up with Johnny Hollix. One day, old Johnny just disappeared and that squaw? Hee, hee, hee! The most horrible thing, the most horrible!"

Though Graybrow had come there to learn certain specific things, he knew he would have to let Orv talk in circles. Let him do his bit and, sooner or later, he would get to more pressing matters. So Orv told him about King Paint's squaw and the awful punishment visited upon her for laying with Johnny Hollix on a regular basis. There was a horse that was lying in a ditch, ridden to death. Using ropes, they strung it up six feet in the air between two trees and sewed-up the squaw alive in the hide so only her head was poking out its flanks. The carcass was full of flies and ants and beetles. Pretty soon, it was full of maggots, too. That carcass was all soft and putrid and wormy. Orv said after a week, it was so filled with maggots that it looked like it was dancing up there, rolling and pulsating. And the squaw, of course, sewn up in that putrescence with millions of worms crawling on her, went insane. Laughing and cackling, spitting and screaming. She bit her tongue off, shredded her lips. The crows and vultures were picking at her face and inside that hide...well, you just didn't want to think of what that was like, just boiling away with grave worms.

"Terrible, Charlie, that's what it was," Orv said, shivering now. "And it was two weeks, two weeks before that horse rotted and fell to ground. And the squaw? Dead, eyes picked out and skin stripped clean off her face...oh, and you don't want to mention the rest, do you? No, sir! No, sir!"

Graybrow had to admit that he'd heard of some positively obscene punishments for adultery, but this one surely took the cake. The icing, too. Orv went quiet, alternately giggling and whimpering, whispering to his brothers Roy and Jesse who were apparently both dead.

"Orv?" Graybrow finally said. "Tell me about Deliverance."

Orv actually let out a scream and began to cross himself. "I cain't! I cain't! Oh, that's him, that's that devil James Lee Cobb! He...he...he was born out of darkness, yessum, I know it. Something that crawls and slithers in them dark places where folks ain't got no bodies, that was his father! Oh, oh, oh...his mother! Jesus help her! Help her! And Cobb, Charlie, hee, hee, Cobb he went up into those mountains and found that other one what had been waiting for him all them years! That which waited in them caves for the Macabro...oh, don't ask me no more, no more! Because it was in Cobb and then Cobb came down...he ate 'em, ate them men...came down and wasn't long, wasn't long before he heard tell of Spirit Moon..."

Orv went into hysterics after that. Crying and shrieking. Graybrow had to keep feeding him whiskey until the man was beyond pain and then he brought him into the shack so he could rest.

He wasn't sure what it was all about, but there was no doubt anymore that James Lee Cobb was the catalyst for something. If Orv could be believed, then something sinister had taken control of Cobb up in the mountains, something that had touched him at birth.

And that something had brought him to Spirit Moon, who was a very powerful Snake medicine man.

Things were beginning to come together and Graybrow didn't care for what they hinted at.

14

It was the next morning that Janice Dirker told Tyler Cabe about the giant who had come gunning for him the night before. As she spoke, she practically went white with fear. And Cabe had a pretty good idea that she was no shrinking violet.

"Elijah Clay," was all Cabe could say, shaking his head. His breakfast of cakes and fried taters suddenly forgotten. "Jesus H. Christ, that sumbitch is really hunting me down. I'll be goddamned."

Janice looked more than a little concerned. "Who is he, Mr. Cabe?"

So he told her, told her everything about shooting down Virgil Clay and Charles Graybrow telling him about the animal old Virgil's father was...half-grizzly bear and half-ogre and one-hundred percent ass-kicking, life-taking, intolerant hellbilly. Those dark, wonderful eyes of hers were on him the whole time and there was real concern in them, real fear.

And Cabe thought: I'll be damned, this lady actually cares about me.

"I don't like one bit of this. Mr. Cabe," she said and her voice was deep and sensual and it made the bounty hunter's insides bubble like sweet molasses. "I fully realize this is none of my affair, but I think it would be wise for you to hide out for a time. Let my husband deal with this human pig. He'll know what to do."

Cabe found himself smiling like a little boy.

Smiling, mind you.

Here he had just about the meanest bastard imaginable wanting to make a tobacco pouch out of his privates and he was grinning like a little boy with a peppermint stick all his own. And it was because of Janice Dirker. Though he wasn't much prettier than your average wild boar (and would be the first to admit the same), Cabe had had his fill of women over the years. He had been desired and lusted after. But no one had ever really cared if he lived or died...and now someone did. He felt a lot of things right then: confusion, bewilderment, and, yes, even fear.

But he liked it all, God yes.

"Ma'am, y'all very kind to me. Very caring to some worn-out saddletramp like me and I can't tell you how I appreciate it," he told her, feeling his voice squeak with emotion. "But, really, I can take care of my own affairs. Always have, always will. And Jackson...the Sheriff, that is...well, I think he's got enough problems without worryin' over me."

Janice was breathing hard and Cabe was, too.

What was it all about? Lust? Passion? Yes, surely those things were evident, but something more too. Something that went deeper. Something that he could feel burning deep inside of him like hot coals and blue ice. There was a word for it, but he didn't dare think it.

"Please, Mr. Cabe. You are, without a doubt, a man who can handle his own affairs, but..."

"But what?"

She averted her eyes. Cabe reached out and pressed his hand over hers. It was like an electric shock passed through him. She started as well. She made to pull her hand away as color touched her cheeks, but didn't. And under his rough, callused paw, her hand was petal-soft and fine-boned. It felt so very good.

She licked her lips. "I don't...oh what in God's name am I doing?"

"Say it," he told her.

She sighed. "I don't want anything to happen to you."

"If that's what you want, then I'll make sure nothing will."

They stared into each other's eyes for a time and then Janice pulled away, rushing from the dining room as fast as she could. And Cabe just sat there a time, feeling like a man flattened by some tremendous wave.

It was some time before he could so much as stand.

15

"Well, I see you're still alive," Charles Graybrow greeted Cabe later that morning. "I was planning on buying a nice whiteman's sort of suit for your funeral. Maybe I was rushing things."

Cabe dragged off his cigarette. "Maybe just a bit."

After his talk with Janice Dirker, he finally found his guts again, tucked 'em back in, and took to the streets. Started walking. Checking Whisper Lake out saloon by saloon. And not for drinks, but for Elijah Clay. At the far end, near the Union Pacific railroad depot, he spotted Charles Graybrow having a taste at a lumber yard, chatting it up with another Indian who was cutting barrel staves.

Graybrow stood there, studying the sky which was leaden and turbulent. A chill breeze ruffled his long iron-gray hair which was tucked under a campaign hat. One eye was squinting, the other open in that solemn brown face.

"Hey, Tyler Cabe," he suddenly said. "You figure I wear a fancy whiteman's suit and hang around the depot, folks might think I'm some rich banker from back east?"

"Doubt it."

"Because I'm an injun?"

Cabe shrugged. "That might tip 'em off."

"Damn, it's hell to be an injun some days. Maybe I'll get the suit, though. Way I hear it, Elijah Clay's in town. They say he's looking for you." Graybrow just shook his head. "So I might get some use out of the suit after all."

Cabe just chuckled. He crushed his cigarette in the dirt and pulled off his hat. Not looking up, he fumbled with the rattlesnake band above the brim. "Already got me dead and buried, have you?"

Graybrow nodded. "Me and a bunch of my red brothers are taking bets. I'm saying your dead before tomorrow morning. But maybe I'm just a pessimist. Folks say that about me. Go figure."

Cabe put his hat back on. "You're gonna lose some money, I think."

"Maybe." Graybrow looked over to his Indian friend. "Hey, Raymond? You think you can fix up my amigo here?" Then he turned to Cabe. "I call him Raymond because his name is Raymond Proud."

"No shit?"

Raymond Proud stood up and he was a big man dressed in wool pants, suspenders, and a lumberjack shirt. "Is this the Arkansas bounty hunter?"

"Yes. Calls himself Tyler Cabe."

Proud nodded, scratched at his chin. "Yeah, I'm thinking I could fit him. I got some spare scrap lumber out back."

"Yeah, that would work. He don't want no fancy nameplate. Just the box."

"Well, I'd need a little money up front."

"That could be arranged."

Cabe just stood there, not getting it at all. "What the hell are you two talking about?"

Graybrow patted him on the shoulder. "Just stay out of this, okay?" he said in a whisper. "I'm getting you a good deal."

"On what?"

"A casket. You'll need one soon enough."

Cabe felt his mouth drop open. "Well, you two just got all sorts of faith in me, don't you?"

"Nothing personal, is it, Raymond? We just know Elijah Clay is all."

Cabe let out a sigh and walked away, deciding to take a look around the depot. Somewhere, that hellbilly was hiding out and he planned on getting the draw on the sonofabitch come hell or high water. Because, honestly, for the first time in a long while he felt that he had a damn good reason to go on living.

"Hey, Tyler Cabe," Graybrow said. "Slow down, I need to talk to you."

But Cabe didn't slow down. "If you found me a nice plot of earth, I ain't interested."

Graybrow caught up with him, put a hand on his shoulder to stop him. "No, nothing like that. Just stop now." He was panting. "It's not that I'm old, but I don't want to show off and run you down."

"Course not. Wouldn't be your way."

Graybrow smiled thinly. "You didn't like my little joke back there?"

"Not much."

"It's my injun sense of humor, it's kind of strange, I reckon. White folks never seem to get it." He followed Cabe to a bench by the telegraph office. "All us injuns got it. Take Custer at the Big Horn, for instance. He would've just waited for the punchline, things would have turned out different."

"You're crazy, that's what."

Graybrow offered him a drink. "It'll settle your nerves."

"My nerves are fine. Besides, it's a little early."

"You white folks...boy, I'll never understand you. You bring the whiskey out here, get my people hooked, then you act like it's not good enough for you."

Cabe smiled. "That's our little joke."

Graybrow took a good pull off his bottle. "Since you already know about Clay being in town, I won't warn you about that. But I hear them miners hired you to sort out all these killings. That true?"

"Word travels fast, don't it?" Cabe said. "But, sure, it's true enough."

"Good. Because you're gonna need my help. I know lots about those killings. If you wanna stop them, then you're gonna have to stop James Lee Cobb."

"Who in Christ is that?"

"You don't know?" Graybrow said. "Well, sit back, because I have a story to tell you. And before you ask, yes, it does have to do with coffins and graves and the like. Just not in the way you think..."

16

The day turned progressively colder as Cabe and Graybrow rode out to Deliverance. They followed the dirt road up out of Whisper Lake and past the Southview Mine, taking the road where it forked at the blasted oak.

Cabe found himself studying that oak.

It was tall and craggy and black, looked something like a huge trapdoor spider climbing from the ditch alongside the road. Cabe could not put a finger on it, but that tree bothered him immensely. He was not one given to omens and portents...but somehow, somehow that tree was a signpost warning him off.

He found himself studying the landscape as it swept past him—the exposed vermilion rock bursting from the heavy bracken and scrub, the clumps of saltbush and horsebrush giving away to grassy meadow and dense stands of aspen. Streams flanked by drooping dogwood trees and leafless willows.

He took it all in, making a mental note of the barren cliffs and thick forests, as if he might never see them again.

But as he rode his sleek-muscled strawberry roan up that narrow, winding road that was carpeted in autumn leaves and pine needles, he knew it was just the wild stories getting to him. Superstitious bullshit that had no place in his line of work. All that business about James Lee Cobb. His life and his culinary habits. Then that bit about him being shipped to Whisper Lake in a casket...except maybe he wasn't dead. Seemed likely what with that Callister fellow being killed (for no one really bought the suicide theory) and the body vanishing. But there was more to it than that. Because Goode—the old saddletramp Graybrow said had brought the casket in—was pretty firmly convinced that what was in that box was not exactly human. You added that to the fact that Deliverance had gone bad shortly afterwards, had sold its soul to the Devil (as the locals claimed) and, well, even the sanest of men started thinking things.

Beside him on his calico gelding, Graybrow said, "Ever tell you, Tyler Cabe, about the two fools that rode into the town of devils?"

"Nope. What happened?"

"They got killed. Way I heard it, anyway."

Cabe licked his lips, felt the cool wind at his mouth. "You scared, Charles? Scared of what we might find?"

Graybrow said, "Hell no. I'm an injun, we don't know fear." He rode in silence a moment, navigated a dip. "Still…I was thinking there might be something I'm supposed to be doing right now, somewhere I have to be. I told the Widow Lucas that I'd stop by and fix that barn of hers. It leaks. Maybe I should be doing that."

"When does she need it done?"

"Oh, about two years past," Graybrow admitted. "But still I think of it. Wonder at times like these if I should get over there. Think so?"

"Nope. Not unless you need my help."

"Figured on doing it alone."

They rode higher and the air was fresher, frigid, so crisp it seemed it might snap. A few snow flurries danced in the air. You could hear the crunching of the horses' hooves through the leaves and loam, the jingling of equipment and creak of saddles, but nothing else. The aspen forests gave way to juniper and pinyon pine as the road climbed and snaked. Above were slopes blanketed in Douglas-fir and spruce, ancient bristlecone pines dotting the ragged peaks just below the snowline.

Cabe had ridden through many mountains. Had spent countless days and nights prowling their wastes…but never was he so struck by their absolute silence as he was here. Tree limbs brushed together and wind hissed through the high boughs, but other than that it was silent. Oddly silent. Deathly silent. The sort of heavy, brooding silence one acquainted with burial grounds and crypts.

And Cabe did not like it one bit.

"Should be just around that bend," Graybrow said, sounding like something was lodged in his throat.

Cabe felt himself tensing. There was no real, palpable threat here. No men waiting for them with guns. Yet, his muscles had drawn up tight and his heart was beating fast. Something was crawling up his spine and he had a mad desire to have a pistol in each hand.

The road squeezed between high timbered banks where the wind rattled stands of dead pines and then they saw Deliverance. But, as Cabe learned, you didn't just see the place these days, you *felt* it. And feel it he did. If something had been crawling up his spine before, it was running up it now. The air was much colder, like a blast of wind from an icehouse. Something in him trembled and curled-up. His balls went hard and his chest was wrapped in iron bands.

"Hell and damnation," Graybrow muttered.

The village sat before them in a little hollow, forest pressing in from one side and rolling fields to the other. Tall stones like monuments rose from those fields, leaning and gray. All the trees were stripped and dead. Nothing moved, nothing stirred. Only the wind howled and whistled and from its timbre, Cabe was certain there was nothing alive in Deliverance.

The town gave him an immediate, unpleasant sense of claustrophobia. The buildings and houses were pressed together too tightly, rising up over the streets and overhanging each other. Wherever there was an open courtyard or lot, rows of shacks and tent-roofed log structures were inserted. The roads were impossibly narrow and congested. There was not a vertical line to be found anywhere, everything was a crazy sprawl of leaning walls, sloping roofs, angled doorways, and clustered shanties. Even the streets and alleyways were zigzagging and haphazard. Most towns were built to accentuate sunlight and space, Deliverance was built to accentuate shadow and repression. It looked, if anything, like some decaying slum back east.

There was a wooden sign set at the town's perimeter.

DELIVERANCE, it read in faded block letters.

Someone had etched a pair of simple crosses to either side of the name. They stood out like hex signs. Cabe felt his throat go tight, he could barely pull a breath down into his rasping lungs.

As they rode down and into the sinister heart of the village, it seemed the entire place was decaying, rotting like the carcass of some cursed animal. There were great gaping rents in the walls and the roofs were falling into themselves. Windows were shuttered, planks flapping in the wind. Everything was weathered a uniform gray like graveyard marble. Huge, macabre shadows spilled from warped doorways and collapsing stairwells, laying in the muddy streets in black pools.

Cabe and Graybrow tethered their horses to a hitching post and just stood there, feeling the aura of Deliverance fill them like a seeping poison. Weeds grew up in the streets and sprouted from boardwalks which were contorted and frost-heaved, if not completely rotted right out.

Carefully, then, Cabe slid his Evans .44-40 repeating rifle from the saddle boot, sucked in a blast of frosty air, and said, "Well, Charles, what you say we have a look around?"

Graybrow stood by his horse, his long gray hair whipping in the wind. He had a Whitney 12-gauge in his arms. "If you figure it's the right thing to do, white man."

Cabe didn't suppose it was at all. Just the feel of the place was enough to make a man jump on his horse and ride until there was no trail left. The air was oppressive, physically heavy as if it were not air, but something slimy and moist. The overpowering, almost vaporous sense of malignancy made Cabe want to wretch. He was afraid to go any farther, to touch anything. Like maybe the contagion would find him, make him part of whatever had ripped the guts...and the soul...out of this place.

He stood on the boardwalk before what might have been a saloon once. A splintered sign creaked on its hinges overhead, but was entirely unreadable, the letters erased by winds and weather. Only a vague shape was still visible. Possibly the head of a horse.

"You telling me this place went to shit only since this Cobb fellow showed up?" Cabe wanted to know. "Looks like it's been abandoned for years."

"It has," Graybrow said.

He told Cabe that the town had originally been called Shawkesville, after its founding father, Shawkes Tewbury, a New England Yankee. Tewbury had discovered the lead in the hills and had built the town, probably to resemble some crumbling seaport town out east. He had owned everything. Upwards of five, six-hundred people had been living in the town and working the mines as recently as 1865, but then the ore had played out and the railroad passed it by...and it had died out.

"Tewbury was the last to leave back in '70, so I hear. Whole place here, it sat empty until two years back when Mormon squatters moved in, decided to rebuild it. Don't look like they ever got very far."

Cabe didn't think so either. He looked up and down the angular streets. "We're wasting our time, Charles. Can't be nobody left living here."

"That's what we came to find out, isn't it?"

Damn Indian logic. It was always so blasted black and white. And just when Cabe figured he had a good reason to get them out of here. He walked up to the door on the old saloon. It was water-damaged, warped in its frame. He had to put his shoulder against it to pop it open. And then it nearly fell off its hinges. Inside, dusty tables and a mildewed bar. Leaves had blown in through the cracks.

Cabe stepped in there, over the mummified body of a rat, very aware of the sound of his boots and spurs on that crooked flooring. There were empty bottles and glasses behind the bar. A few dirty paintings of whores festooned with cobwebs and covered in filth. Cabe just stood there, listening, listening. Though he heard nothing, he sensed everything. The town was not empty. Not in the ordinary sense. There was an overpowering sense of...*occupancy*. As if the villagers were hiding, playing out some macabre version of blind man's bluff. Just waiting, waiting to come pouring out from doorways and cellars and shuttered attics, to show the two intruders just what sort of game they were up to.

And this more than anything, chilled Cabe right to the marrow.

He pulled a rolled cigarette from the pocket of his broadcloth coat and lit it with a match. He didn't honestly want to smoke, but he needed to smell something other than the stink of the town. Because in here, in this vacant bar the stink was electric. A deep, pervasive odor of depravity and degeneration that told him that this town was blighted, polluted right to its core.

He could not put his finger on the source, but it was there. A loathsome, invidious atmosphere of charnel pits and violated graves. Cabe was not given to superstition, but right then...he would not have wanted to be caught in Deliverance after dark. He would sooner have slit his own wrists.

"C'mon," he said to Graybrow.

Rifles in their hands, they checked out an old assay office, a boarded-up dance hall, the remains of a hotel. It was the same in each and every place. Lots of dust motes drifting in the air, lots of dirt and rotting furniture, but not a lot else. They found buildings where there were trails broken through the dust, but never the people who made them.

They took their horses with them as they walked the streets because the animals were nervous and skittish. There was no doubt they felt it, too, felt it and wanted out in the worst possible way.

Cabe and Graybrow did not look in every house or building. There were certain places they just couldn't bring themselves to enter. And numerous cul-de-sacs where the roofs overhung to such a degree that they created oceans of shivering shadow so impenetrable, nothing could have forced the two men to investigate. But wherever they went, they could feel that sense of spiritual contamination, that deranged aura of pestilence. In more than one building, they heard footsteps in empty rooms or scratching sounds within the walls. And once, a whispering from a dank, stygian cellar.

But there was never anything to be found when they investigated.

Other than that, the only sounds were the wind moaning and their own boots stepping over groaning timbers. But that did not satisfy Cabe that he was imagining any of it. Because, someone or something was there. Behind them, in front of them, maybe on the rooftops or down in the cellars. More than once he had caught movement out of the corner of his eye. And there was no mistaking one thing: they were being watched. Eyes were peering at them from shadowy tangles, leering from behind shuttered windows and staring from dark, damp places.

At the edge of town, they found a few log houses that showed signs of recent occupancy. Beds were made and tables set, firewood stocked and barns hayed. There was dust over everything, but it made Cabe think that whoever had lived in those places had left in one hell of a hurry. In that part of the country times were always harsh and you didn't abandon your belongings and wares without a real damn good reason.

In one of the houses they found a single yellowed bone.

It was sitting in the center of the floor, a human femur. Both he and Graybrow examined it and came to the same conclusion: the marks punched into it were from teeth.

"What do you make of all this?" Cabe finally asked.

But Graybrow just shook his head, saying, "I think it's much worse than what folks are saying. Whatever happened here...maybe I don't want to know."

Cabe just looked him dead in the eye. "You scared?"

"Damn yes, I am."

And Cabe was, too. He had never experienced such a total sense of terror before. And what made it all the worse, all that much harder to handle was that he did not even know *what* he was afraid of. Only that if it found him, if it reached out and touched him, he feared he'd lose his sanity.

They found a livery in which a dozen horses were stabled. They were very much alive and had plenty of feed and water. There were saddles and rigs, bits and reigns. Even shoes and nails stacked on a bench.

"Somebody's here, all right," Cabe said.

They checked out the old jail and then the only church in town. Its spire was high and leaning, the cross missing. If there was one place the Mormons would have set to right, it would have been the church. It stood at the end of a weedy road, surrounded by a rusty wrought-iron fence with spiked corner posts that rose up five, six feet. It was frightful and uninviting, looked like it might fall right over at any moment. The windows had been planked-over and a weird, gassy smell emanated from it.

Cabe climbed the rickety steps and tried the iron door-puller.

"Locked," he said, sounding relieved.

Graybrow stood just outside the fence with the horses. "You see what's carved into that door?"

Cabe did.

He was not an educated man, but he could read. And had read widely in his lonely occupation to pass the time. What he saw carved in the face of the door were signs and symbols generally associated with witchcraft and black magic—pentagrams and pentacles, stylized inverted crosses.

Regardless, he had seen enough.

They both mounted and rode through those streets one last time, each with their weapons in hand. The shadows were elongating and they heard sounds, murmuring voices, distant movement...as if whatever lived in Deliverance was real anxious for the sun to go down.

When they got outside town, Cabe and Graybrow rode like hell was opening behind them and that wasn't too far from the truth.

17

It was well after dark when Cabe finally tracked Dirker down to a sordid rooming house called Ma Heller's Place just this side of Horizontal Hill, the red-light district. He had been all over town looking for the sheriff ever since returning from Deliverance and this is where he found him, staring up at the house astride his gray mare.

Cabe brought him into a tent-roofed saloon called the Mother Lode and laid it out for him over warm beer.

"Empty?" Dirker said.

Cabe just shrugged. "It is and it isn't. There's something there, but I'm not just sure what."

Dirker just gave him those ice-blue eyes full blast. "Maybe you better explain yourself."

So Cabe did. He took his time, telling the sheriff everything he had learned about Deliverance and James Lee Cobb and how he figured the degeneration of the place was definitely connected with the man. At least, it seemed likely. Because something was wrong there, the place had gone from a God-fearing Mormon enclave to a vile pest-hole and there had to be a reason.

Dirker didn't laugh at him or dismiss it outright. He gave it all pause while he sipped his beer. "I'll grant you that something strange has happened there...but witchcraft? Satanism? Christ, Cabe, I just can't swallow that sort of business."

"Don't blame you, Dirker. Not in the least. I wouldn't have swallowed it myself unless it was rammed down my throat," Cabe said. "I think...I *think* what ought to be done here is a posse organized and taken in there. Hell, maybe the army. But something ought to be done."

"Then why don't you do it? I told Forbes that you were the man for the job."

Cabe just stared at him. "I guess...I guess I appreciate that. But this whole thing is bigger than me. Even all that money he promised me, it ain't enough to get me up to Deliverance by myself. That place has to be torn apart and rooted out."

But Dirker wasn't so sure. "When the time comes, I think that'll be my decision."

Cabe just sighed. "Goddammit, Sheriff...listen now, this ain't a matter of who's in charge. It's a matter of something being real fucking wrong up at that place and something having to be done about it."

But Dirker would only tell him he'd think it over, maybe do a little more intensive research on his own. What you don't understand, Dirker told him, was that there was more than just that crazy town to deal with here. There was the vigilantes and last night they had raided Redemption. And word had it the Mormons had brought in the Danites now and things were about to get seriously ugly.

"Way things stand, Cabe, I can't afford to have all my men sniffing around that deserted village, not with what's going on."

Cabe understood that, said, "Sooner or later, Sheriff, this is going to have to be dealt with. And I hope it's before more people are dead or missing."

Dirker agreed with him on that. "But right now," he said grimly, "how about we discuss why I'm out here instead of at my office? How about that?"

Cabe finished his beer. "Why *are* you out here?"

"It's about your friend Freeman."

And it was more than that. It was also about the Sin City Strangler. Dirker told him that not less than two hours before...just about sunset, in fact...the killer had struck yet again, carving up another prostitute. This one was named Carolyn Reese and she worked at the Old Silver Gin House. But the law had gotten lucky this time, for another whore had seen a man with her shortly before it happened.

Cabe was paying attention now. "And?"

"And the description was of a tall man, narrow face, dead-looking eyes. Worn a Stetson and a canvas duster. He also wore the star of a Texas Ranger."

Cabe felt his head go dizzy, felt a rushing sound in his ears. "Freeman...Jesus H. Christ. I figured there was something wrong there, but, dammit, I didn't want to think this."

Dirker nodded. "Well, it just so happens that I wired the Rangers in Abilene. They had a fellow named Freeman working for them. But he disappeared about six months ago back up in Wyoming. He was a short, rotund fellow with an eye patch."

"So Freeman...or whoever we got here...he just borrowed this man's identity?"

"That's how I'm figuring it," Dirker said. "Just so happens, Freeman has a room over at Ma Heller's."

Cabe stood up. "Well, let's bag that cocksucker."

Dirker smiled thinly. "Figured you'd see it my way."

***

It was Cabe who kicked the door in to Freeman's room.

He kicked it in and Dirker went through low with a sawed-off shotgun. But the theatrics were unnecessary for Freeman was not there. In fact, nothing was there. The closet was cleaned out and the bureau was empty. The sonofabitch had made his run again.

But he left a parting gift to the men he probably knew would hunt him: a human heart in a mason jar of alcohol.

Cabe and Dirker just stared at the thing swimming in that brine. It was pale and bloated, obscenely fleshly. It seemed to move with a gentle, unknown motion.

"I guess there's no doubt that he's the Sin City Strangler," Dirker managed, his throat tight.

Cabe just nodded, knowing there was little else to say.

The bastard had slipped away yet again. The only good thing was that Cabe had seen him, would recognize him if the chance came again. But he still didn't know who he was or where he came from. And things like that, he'd found in his line of work, made hunting someone down far more troublesome.

As it stood, "Freeman" could show up just about anywhere.

And probably would.

18

In Redemption, the bullets were flying.

The vigilantes had rode in again in force, but this time the Mormons were ready for them. Or so they thought. The Danites instructed the townsfolk to stay in their homes and cabins, to lock themselves down tight. To wait it out. The Danites wanted them to adhere to the teachings of Brigham Young which meant to avoid violence at any costs. If there was killing to be done, the Danites would do it.

So the Mormons waited it out.

And outside, it was a shooting gallery.

Within the first ten minutes three vigilantes were dead and a fourth seriously wounded. Likewise, two Danites had been shot from their hiding places by expertly placed bullets.

And it became something of a standoff.

Caleb Callister did everything he could to reign in his forces and mount the attack in a precise military fashion, but his boys would have none of it. They wanted to shoot. To burn. To kill and pillage. They saw in the Mormons everything that had ever gone wrong in their lives. And this is why Caslow, McCrutchen, and Retting were now dead and Cheevers was moaning in the street, his guts shot out.

He wouldn't last and Callister knew it.

It was just him and Windows now.

The bad thing was they were outgunned about twenty to one, if not worse. The good thing was they were still in possession of the dynamite that McCrutchen had gotten from the mine. Callister's idea had been to ride into Redemption and start throwing the stuff immediately, but the others wanted to do some shooting and things had simply gone to hell.

Windows and he were hiding behind a barricade of cordwood with their backs against the outside wall of a livery barn. Escape was not in the cards, at least not yet...but on the other hand, the Danites were in no position to overrun their position.

Stalemate.

But it was night and it was dark and just about anything could happen. A few fires were burning, most of them set by the vigilantes, and the illumination they threw was enough to see and shoot by.

A couple townspeople rushed out with buckets of sand and water to extinguish a blaze that had started in bales of hay and was quickly working its way up the walls of a stable.

Windows brought up his Winchester 1866 carbine. Scarcely aiming, he sighted and fired, levered quickly, and fired again. The bucket brigade—both of them—lay dead in the streets.

"Two more dead nits," Windows said.

A flurry of rifle fire grazed the log embankment they hid behind as the Danites tried to flush them out. Callister and Windows returned the fire which came from no less than four different locations.

Callister had no doubt that the Destroying Angels were trying to flank them. Probably crawling over rooftops in order to draw a bead on them. But it wouldn't be easy in the murk.

More bullets ripped into their rampart, chips of wood flying like shrapnel. At that moment, two Danites charged in on horseback. Windows shot one of them through the throat as bullets whizzed all around him. Callister didn't bother with his gun: He lit a stick of dynamite, let the fuse burn down some and tossed it at the other rider as Windows felled his comrade. It was a perfect throw, for the dynamite landed right in the Danite's lap. He saw what it was, made to toss it aside, but somehow managed to get the burning stick caught between himself and his horse.

Then there was a booming explosion and both he and his horse were sprayed over the streets like bloody mucilage. Blood and smoldering bits of anatomy were everywhere.

The Danites had not expected this.

Callister lit another stick and tossed it onto the steps of a log house across the way from which they'd been receiving gunfire. The entire front of the place went up like kindling and what was left behind, collapsed into itself, burying alive anyone who'd survived the initial explosion. Flaming bits of wood rained over the town. The razed log house began to blaze.

"We got 'em," Windows was saying. "Sure as shit, we got 'em."

"Now they're gonna have to make their move," Callister said.

And they did.

A half-dozen men on horseback charged their position. They were spread out with an almost military efficiency. Callister watched them come on and had to admit, even to himself, that those Danites were a courageous, devil-may-care bunch. Tough as any men he'd ever fought with. In the their flapping black coats and wide-brimmed preacher's hats, they were truly something to see, riding hard with smoking pistols.

But their strategy was all-too apparent.

The riders were trying to force the vigilantes out of their holes. Using themselves as bait, the Danites were riding right into the mouth of hell itself so the others could get a clean shot.

But it didn't work that way.

More sticks of dynamite were tossed over the rampart. Not just two or three, but five or six that landed one after the other and resulted in a chain of resounding explosions that not only atomized horses and riders, but blew out the windows of houses and threw riders from their mounts. The shock waves actually knocked men from rooftops.

Whatever the Danites were planning, they gave it up.

They had lost no less than ten men now and had easily that number injured. There were only four or five left in any sort of fighting shape. For the next hour, there was silence broken only by an occasional gunshot so that both sides would know the other had not slipped away.

But slipping away was exactly what Callister was thinking.

And particularly when a dozen riders came pouring down the street, the lead man waving a white flag tied to the barrel of a rifle. Nobody shot at them. The Mormons called out to them to identify themselves, but the strangers would not. They just kept waving and smiling on those black mounts.

"I don't like this," Windows said.

And Callister didn't either. There was something very wrong about all it all. And what was that high, hot gassy smell in the air like rancid meat? Seven or eight of the riders trotted over to the Mormon positions. The others, led by the man with the white flag galloped over to the vigilantes' fortification.

The man with the white flag dismounted, said, "I am unarmed."

Windows told him to keep his fucking distance, but the man waltzed right over and…funny thing, half way there something started to happen to him and he started to walk funny, a real weird odor coming off him. Callister sucked in a sharp gasp of cool air.

For he could see wan moonlight reflected off bone as if the man had no face on the left side. And what he saw confirmed that: a grotesque, inhuman skull knitted with raw quilts of muscle.

"Evening," the man said and that voice was more animal than human. "Name's Cobb. And I figure I got business with ye…"

19

An hour after the revelation of Freeman and the heart in the jar, Cabe found himself again at the Cider House Saloon in need of a drink. He put back two whiskeys and a like number of beers, thinking it all over. About Dirker, who might just have been his friend now (of all crazy things) and Freeman and, of course, Janice Dirker. That was one thing that kept circulating through his brain.

But in all the furor he'd forgotten a few things.

He'd actually forgotten that it was here that he'd put down Virgil Clay only a few nights before. His brain was simply too full with everything else. So when the door opened and a blast of wet wind blew through the bar, the last thing he was thinking of was Elijah Clay.

He didn't even bother turning.

Maybe if he had, he would've seen men falling out of their way to get out of the path of the behemoth in the buffalo coat and gray beard.

As it was, he leaned up against the wall, lost in himself, and that's when the blade of a knife imbedded itself in said wall scant inches from the tip of his nose.

Cabe dropped his drink and whirled around, his hand going for the Starr double-action at his hip. It almost made it, too, but the man he saw moving through the bar room stopped him dead.

Cabe stood there and stared.

He knew who he was; there could not be two men that matched this description in Utah Territory.

All Cabe could do was think: *Oh Jesus and Mary, lookit the size of him...*

The guy had to be seven feet tall if he was an inch. He was bearded and fierce and built like something that wrestled bears for a living. He carried a double-barrel scattergun in his hand and his chest was crisscrossed with cartridge belts. Lots of them. And that was a necessary thing when you factored in all the pistols hanging from the homemade belts at his waist. He carried more firepower than most cavalry platoons. And that didn't even take into account the hatchets, skinning blades, and bowie knives that hung off him.

As folks in Whisper Lake wisely said, when Elijah Clay comes, even the Devil his ownself wisely crosses the street.

Cabe grabbed the hilt of the knife in the wall—a Buffalo skinner with an eight-inch blade—and tried to pull it from the wall. He had to use both hands.

"Ya'll excuse me please," the giant said, tossing men aside like they were stuffed with feathers. "My apologies, gents, my apologies."

He had an odd sort of gallantry and charm about him. Those that didn't get out of his path, he swatted aside like pesky gnats. And some of them were real big men. Big men who found themselves suddenly airborne.

The giant's right cheek bulged with chew. He spat a stream of it at the faro table, soiling the cards. "Name's Elijah Clay," he announced. "And I'm pleased to know ye, one and all." He came right up to a table about four feet from Cabe, just stood there. "Evenin', gents. I'm a-here lookin' fer some worm-brained, sheep-humpin' slice of Arkansas dogfuck name of Tyler Cabe. Any of ye know this mother-raper?" He looked around, those eyes like boring bits. "Speak up now, hear? Way I'm a-thinkin', gents, yer either fer me or agin me. And if it be the latter, than God help yer poor grievin' mothers after I have m' way with ye."

And it occurred to Cabe that Clay did not know who he was. Not yet. Now, any sane man would have bolted and run at the very least. Tyler Cabe out of Arkansas? No sir, no sir, you must be mistaken. I'm Joe J. Crow out of Gary, Indiana, so if you'll excuse me, I got a sick wife to attend to and I think I just pissed myself and all.

Sure, that's what a sane man would have done.

But Cabe?

ND Nope. Not Tyler Cabe who rode hard through more shit in a year than most men rode through in a lifetime. Not Tyler Cabe who was just as fast and sure with his pistols as any man in the Territory and was no stranger to knife and fists. And not Tyler Cabe who knew an inbred hellbilly when he saw one because he was one himself and was not about to back down no how, no way from trash like that.

But, of course, Cabe had never waded in against something like Elijah Clay. The sort of lifetaker that could and would use his bones to pick his long yellow teeth with.

Regardless, Cabe said, "I'm Tyler Cabe. I'm the one you're looking for, mister."

Clay just nodded, but seemed pleasantly surprised. Maybe he wasn't used to men admitting who they were when he hunted them. And being from a hill-clan, he put a lot of stock in bravery and courage. Even when it was foolishly placed.

"Well, Mr. Cabe, yer the snake what shot down m' boy, so lets we two get straight down to it, what say? You fancy shootin' irons?" Clay considered it, shook his head. "Naw, not yer thing, is it? Too wily. Yer the sort that fancies knives and the like. If'n that's yer game, I surely can oblige." He set his shotgun and assorted gunbelts on the table, pulling two hatchets from his belt and stabbing them into the tabletop where they quivered menacingly. "Well, boy, let's get to it. Got me plans fer yer hide, yessum, figure on making yer life last till well past cockcrow."

Men were murmuring amongst themselves, maybe mentally recording the entire thing for future yarning. Possibly making note of that impressive set of balls old Tyler Cabe had, but more likely wondering if he had enough money in his poke to bury him with proper.

Cabe grabbed the handle of one of the hatchets, yanked the blade from wood. "All right," he said. "If it's gotta be done this way, you big smelly piece of shit, then let's get to it."

Clay laughed, pulled up his own hatchet.

Cabe did not waste any time, he lunged in quick, swinging his ax and nearly taking out Clay's throat, but the big man stepped back, grinning with all those piss-yellow teeth. Here Cabe was, figuring this was a matter of survival, a fight to the death...but to Clay it was just an amusement. Something that beat the shit out of watching the corn grow or violating your own sister.

Clay swung his hatchet and swung it fast, so fast in fact Cabe just barely got out of the way. The blade struck the bar and gouged out a four-inch strip of pine. Cabe swung at the big man and their hatchets met in mid-air in a clanging shower of sparks. The impact threw Cabe back against the bar, his arm thrumming right up to the elbow. He got under Clay's next blow and swung at his face. Clay dodged it, laughed, and brought his own hatchet at Cabe's head. It knocked his hat off and before he could react, Clay brought it around backhanded. Cabe brought his up to block the blow which would have been lethal given that the axe was double-edged.

The hatchets met again and the impact ripped Cabe's from his hand and sent him spinning like a top, putting him easily on his ass.

"That's that, I reckon," Clay said and came in for the kill.

Cabe tried to go for his pistol, but his hand was numb right up to the shoulder and the limb reacted like rubber. Clay took hold of his hair, pulled him six-inches up into the air and brought up the hatchet for the deathblow.

And then a voice just as cool and calm as January river ice said, "Drop that hatchet or I'll shoot you where you stand."

Clay froze, hatchet up over his head.

Dirker was standing there with his sawed-off shotgun in his hands. Both barrels were leveled at the center of Clay's back.

"Drop it," he said.

Clay turned and lowered the hatchet, let it fall from his fingers. Let Cabe fall, too. "Goddammit, Dirker, ye always manage to spoil m' fun."

"You all right?" he said to Cabe.

Cabe, with assistance, found his feet.

Dirker marched Clay out the door at gunpoint, Cabe close at his heels. And all Cabe could think of was Dirker and his whip and now Dirker saving his hash and wasn't it just goddamn funny how things had a way of coming around in the end?

20

After Clay was deposited in a jail cell, Cabe made his way back to the St. James Hostelry where Janice Dirker fawned over him, though nothing was really injured but his pride.

"You're lucky to be alive, Mr. Cabe," she kept saying as she drew him a bath. "Just darn lucky."

"Well, the fact that I am...well, it's your husband's doing."

"Jackson is a very dutiful man," was all she would say on the matter.

Cabe had his bath and when he went back to his room, planning on taking a nice long nap while he had the chance, Janice was waiting for him there. She had changed his sheets and bedclothes, had built a little fire in the corner stove. It felt nice in there, warm and comfortable.

"Earlier this evening," she said, "a man came to see you."

Cabe laid on the bed. "Not another one of the Clays?"

"No. Nothing like that. This one was a very polished gentleman, said his name was Freeman."

Cabe sat up. *"Freeman?"*

"Yes. Is that a problem?"

Cabe wanted to lie, but he couldn't bring himself to. He told her who and what Freeman was, how he and Dirker had almost got him.

Janice looked decidedly pale, but recovered herself nicely as only a Southern lady could. "Well, yes, but I'm no prostitute."

"He could've killed you nonetheless."

And Cabe was figuring that was exactly what he'd had in mind. Freeman knew Cabe was after him and what better way to rub defeat in Cabe's face than to not only slip away, but to slaughter the only woman in town he'd truly befriended.

Janice said, "He told me, told me to tell you..."

But it was getting to her now. Even all that breeding couldn't fight the fear of what could have happened. Of what her death might have become. There was no getting around that. She allowed herself to be held and Cabe held her, liking the feel of her and smelling the wonderful musk of her flesh that no perfume could hope to mask.

"Tell me," he said after a time.

She breathed deeply. "He said to tell you that he's off for parts unknown. That you should not follow him...but, but to watch for signs of his work in other places in the years to come."

"Did he say anywhere particular?"

"London. He said, in the coming years he would be busy in London."

But then none of it seemed to matter and all those months of hunting seemed trivial. Freeman had spared Janice and Cabe didn't know why and could never truly guess, but it was enough.

Enough then as she flowed into his arms and they melted together into a delicious pool of something seething and moist that was made of flesh and limbs and hot, seeking mouths. And then it was done and they lay naked in one another's arms, each speechless in the warm afterglow.

And each wondering, wondering, where it could possibly take them.

21

The morning after his wife made love to Tyler Cabe, Jackson Dirker was rooting through the remains of Redemption. The town was nearly destroyed. Even many, many hours after the initial attack that left no less than thirty dead (including Danites and vigilantes), the place was still smoldering. Though some homes were undamaged, most had been blasted or burned and there was stray livestock everywhere.

An icy rain was falling and Dirker stood amongst the wreckage in his yellow slicker, feeling something coil in his belly.

He was standing with a man named Eustice Harmony. Harmony had a farm well outside Redemption like many other Mormons. His family had taken in survivors from Redemption as had many others. But Harmony was more than just another Mormon squatter, he was a former resident of Deliverance.

And the half brother of James Lee Cobb...more or less.

More or less for nobody really knew who (or what) Cobb's father was. His grandfather, the Minister Hope of Procton village, Connecticut, adopted him, packed him and his lunatic mother off to live with Arlen and Maretta Cobb in Missouri. And he himself left Procton shortly thereafter, for no one wanted anything to do with him or his church. They decided there was an evil taint on both. So the Minster moved to Illinois, remarried and, though he was well into his fifties, sired another family. One night, unable to resist the voices that tormented him, the Minister put a shotgun in his mouth and ended it. Eustice's distraught mother christened all the children then with her family name, which was Harmony.

In 1853, Eustice Harmony joined the Church of Latter Day Saints in Nauvoo, Illinois, and shortly thereafter set off for the promised land along the Mormon Pioneer Trail which began in Nauvoo and ended far west near the Great Salt Lake.

Dirker was disgusted by what he saw. And truth be told, he was disgusted by just about everything in his job these days. For most of his life he'd been either a soldier or a lawman, had carried the respect and derision those offices inspire. But not once had he thought of being anything else.

Until now.

For, much as it pained him, he figured he'd had his fill.

He took Harmony aside out of the rain and into an old millinery that was still standing, had been dusted out and was being used by the volunteers as a dry-out shack. There was no one in there.

Dirker stood there, water dripping from him. "You know me, Eustice, you know the kind of man I am. I bear no prejudice against any. I've been good to you and your people. Have I not?"

Harmony nodded. "Yes, you have been that. We could not have hoped for a finer lawman than you. You have been fair to us." Harmony took his hat off, studied the brim. "I know...we know...you have tried to break up these vigilantes, but sometimes, sometimes there are far worse things."

"Such as?"

"The vigilantes raided Redemption the past two nights running. But last night—"

"Last night the Destroying Angels were waiting for them?"

Harmony would not verbally admit to that, but he nodded silently. "But there was more here than just these two groups. From what I have been told, another group of riders came in...and attacked both parties."

Dirker swallowed. "This would be the same group responsible for what occurred in Sunset?"

"Yes."

"And," Dirker said, "would this group just happen to be riding out of Deliverance?"

"Yes," Harmony sighed.

"Tell me about it, Eustice. I need to know now."

Harmony nodded. "It began with James Lee Cobb. You have, no doubt, heard rumors concerning him. Well, they are true, God help us all, they are true..."

Harmony had never met his half-brother in person, not before he showed in Deliverance. And what brought that about was a letter. While safely confined in the Wyoming Territorial Prison, Cobb somehow, through some outside agency, discovered he had a half-brother in Utah Territory. Cobb wrote to Harmony and they began to exchange letters.

"I believe, as our Lord Jesus Christ taught, that there is good in all men, Sheriff. I believed the same of James Lee Cobb. I wrote to him, telling him he must now turn from his life of vice and iniquity, that through Jesus Christ there could be forgiveness and salvation if he were to walk the path of righteousness and confess to his sins," Harmony explained wearily. "And Cobb wrote back that, yes, he now sought only goodness and purity in his life. I wanted to believe this, Sheriff, but I could not. For there was an undercurrent to this man, something black and vile...but as a soldier of Christ, I could not turn away from him."

"But you wanted to," Dirker suggested.

"Yes, God, yes, I surely did." Harmony was lost in thought for a moment. "Sheriff, although I did not personally know Cobb, I knew *of* him. Even before those letters began to arrive. There were things my father wrote down in a letter before he took his own life...things about his life in Procton, Connecticut and what horrors occurred there. My mother told me of them. Of the taint on our bloodline. Well, it is of no matter, I will not discuss these things. They are skeletons that shall remained locked in the family closet."

After he was released from prison, Cobb did not visit his half-brother in the newly-reclaimed village of Deliverance. Harmony had written to him that he must do this, must be baptized into the Church. The next he heard of Cobb was a telegram from up in Toole County telling Harmony he had died. No details were given. Only that he had died while in the company of the Goshute and that his casket would be shipped to Whisper Lake. It apparently was his last request to be buried near kin.

"Well, I'm sure you know what transpired. The casket indeed arrived and it was that night, while alone with it, that Hiram Callister died. The coroner ruled it suicide. I'm sure you recall this..."

"I was not in town at the time," Dirker told him. "Doc West ruled it suicide, though he was not at all convinced it was so. He did this to spare Caleb Callister the unpleasantries of an investigation. For it was widely-known by that point that his brother...well, that he was not exactly a wholesome sort."

Harmony just shook his head. "I know of Hiram Callister's *peculiarities*. The rumors of which, at any rate. But Hiram's death was not suicide. His throat was crushed and although he did indeed slit his own wrists, there are many who believe he was compelled to do it. Or did so rather than face what was in that casket..."

"What *was* in there, Eustice? Was it Cobb?"

Harmony told him pretty much what Cabe had. What was in there nearly scared the life from the men who'd brought it down from Skull Valley. Whatever was in there...no man could look upon it and retain his sanity.

Harmony walked to the doorway, opened it a crack and stared out into the cold, misting rain which was rapidly turning Redemption into a sea of mud. "It was, perhaps, a week or two later when Cobb showed in Deliverance on a dark night of blowing wind. He wore a black velvet hood, claimed to be horribly scarred. He wore leather gloves on his hands. He came in the company of a group of, well, despicable characters. They were outlaws, soldiers of fortune, blooded killers—Crow and Hood, Greer and Cook, Bascombe and Wise..."

They set up in a ruined hotel, Harmony said. The Mormons, being a charitable sort, did not run them off. Maybe they didn't dare to. There was something very wrong about them all. They were invited to service, but declined. They sequestered themselves up in the old hotel, only coming out by night. They brought something with them in a wagon, something they would let no one look upon. Whatever it was, they locked it in a room in the hotel.

"Did you ask what it was?" Dirker inquired.

But Harmony just shook his head. "I did not. But I am certain it was a living thing...or nearly. For at night it howled and screeched and pounded on the walls. In the dead of night you could hear it up there, making the most depraved and blasphemous sounds. Whatever it was...it's probably still there. I only know that Cobb's men were overheard saying that it had come from Missouri..."

Harmony' face had gone bloodless at the memory of it. It took him a moment or two to gather himself. Then he continued.

"There is a draw, a strange seduction to sin, to evil, Sheriff. It is the Devil's primary tool: people will give themselves to Him in order to experience wicked gluttony." Through the open door, Harmony watched men loading bodies in a wagon for burial. "Before long, women were spending time in that hotel. There was an unhealthy influence that Cobb and the others possessed. The young were drawn. By the time we realized that they were being taken over, body and soul, it was far too late. Our breathern had given themselves to the Evil One. Cobb had become their messiah. Those of us as yet uncorrupted, came here to Redemption to start again."

"And Deliverance?"

"No God-fearing man or woman went there after that day," Harmony explained, his face oddly slack. His lower lip trembled. "And those that did, were never heard from again."

"And what of that...*personage* they had locked away up in the hotel? Was it human? Animal?"

"Neither," was all Harmony would say. "But in my mind, it was the seed of human evil. There were those in Deliverance that said it was the Devil himself that was chained up there."

Dirker thought about it all. Thought about it long and hard. "And Cobb...he disappeared from the mortuary. If he was dead, how could that be?"

"I don't think he was dead," Harmony said. "But surely not alive. His was the living death, Sheriff. No man will ever know what happened to him after he climbed from his casket. Some things are better not known."

Dirker was not about to argue with him. He was surely not convinced about any of this. Something had happened, yes, and Cobb was no doubt involved, but the supernatural? Dirker had heard stories and wild tales like any other, but he was not ready to accept such a thing.

"I can see, by the look on your face, Sheriff, that you are skeptical. But what I tell you is the truth as the Lord is my witness. What happened in Deliverance is unspeakable...pagan rites, Devil worship, human sacrifice. It has been said that the first born, all the first born of Deliverance were given to Cobb as burnt offerings. To him and that demented thing up in the hotel." Harmony looked close to tears now. "If God in His infinite wisdom would only smite that serpent's nest from the land."

Dirker said, "Well, maybe God's gonna need some help this time."

22

Cabe pulled off his cigarette, sent the smoke out through his nostrils. "So, I reckon from what you've been saying that you talked to your Indian friends?"

Charles Graybrow nodded. "Yes, I have."

"And...?"

"Worse than I thought."

They were sitting in Cabe's motel room, on the bed, sorting out those things that a week before would have been unthinkable by any sane man. Now, however, there was no choice but to look the devil, as it were, in the face and give him his due.

"First off, you have to know about a Snake medicine man called Spirit Moon," Graybrow said, his fingers coiling uneasily in his lap, unused to being without a ready bottle. "Now Spirit Moon...oh boy, he's big mumbo-jumbo heap plenty bad injun witch doctor—"

"Would you quit the dumb injun bit already?" Cabe said impatiently. "It's funny at times. But now ain't one of those times."

Graybrow nodded, smiled. "Sure, sure, understood. Okay, now Spirit Moon, you know something about him?"

"I've heard a few things."

"What you heard is true. That's one injun with the power, I tell you," Graybrow said with complete certainty. "I won't go on about things he's done, the sick he's cured and the bad ones he cursed...we'll let it go by saying Spirit Moon is the genuine article. He refused to go to the reservation with the others, claimed that the Snake Nation would bow before no man, white or otherwise. So him and his followers hid out up in Skull Valley on Goshute land. And old Spirit Moon, he knew things that have long been forgotten, things others might want to know..."

"Like who?" Cabe asked.

"Like James Lee Cobb."

Ah, that name again. Cabe was beginning to get this picture of that crazy bastard in his mind and he had horns and a tail. Even the sound of that name was starting to leave him cold.

"So Cobb went to Spirit Moon?"

"That's how the story goes. Cobb and his gang of bad men went to pay Spirit Moon a call." Graybrow broke off, wanting to get it right as he'd heard it. "Now, understand that Spirit Moon didn't make Cobb wicked, he already was. They say he was born of darkness. That he lived a life of depravity and the like. That up in the mountains...up there, well, he didn't eat his friends because he just wanted to, but because something crawled into him. The sort of thing the Ojibwa up north might call a Wendigo. A cannibal devil, a soul-eater..."

Graybrow told him then the story he had heard from an old Goshute named He-Who-Runs-Swift.

Cobb and his boys rode right into Spirit Moon's camp, a thing many others would have been afraid to do. At first, Cobb was friendly. He made up some bullshit story about needed sanctuary for a time being that the whites were hunting him and his men. It was a lie, but essentially true in that just about all his boys were wanted for something, somewhere.

But you could not fool Sprit Moon.

He had the gift to look into minds, to see truths, things that had not yet even come about. He instructed his people to be kind to Cobb and the others, for even at that point he knew what Cobb was, hoped only that he would ride off given time. But it was not to be so. For what lived in Cobb, the seed planted there at birth and nurtured by what Spirit Moon called "the Old One of the Mountain", was not in complete control just then. But it had found fertile ground and was blossoming by the day.

Before long, Cobb admitted that he knew of Spirit Moon, knew of his great knowledge and that he had come to learn from him. By that point, everyone in the tribe was afraid of Cobb. Afraid of what was inside him and the hideous smell emanating from him, the voices heard speaking in his tent by night...even when he was alone. Spirit Moon told Cobb he would indeed teach him, but only him. That he must send his men away. Cobb agreed. Spirit Moon had no intention of teaching him; he planned on killing him. There was no other way. For Cobb was evil and he had to be purified and death was the only way. But Spirit Moon knew he had to be careful...for if it was done wrongly, what lived in Cobb would rise up and kill the entire tribe.

"Well, Tyler Cabe," Graybrow went on, "before Spirit Moon could do what had to be done, a woman disappeared from camp. Her remains were discovered shortly thereafter. Cobb had nearly devoured her..."

"Jesus. They caught him in the act?"

Graybrow shrugged. "Perhaps. I do not know. Only that when he was questioned about the crime by Spirit Moon and the elders, he freely admitted that, yes, he had *eaten* her. He boasted of it. Of the many people he had eaten. That his strength was absorbed directly from the flesh of those he feasted upon.

"Well, it took no less than five or six strong warriors to hold him down so he could be shackled," Graybrow said. "So maybe there was some truth to what he said. And next..."

What happened to Cobb next, was not pleasant.

The Snake called it "the Living Death". It was a sacred, dark ritual reserved only for those who could not die in the normal way and were possessed of something discarnate and malevolent. Spirit Moon decided that it was the only way. For what was in Cobb had to be starved to death. Only this would force it into cold dormancy. So Cobb was cursed with the Living Death. Hung by the wrists, Cobb was bound by the medicine man's sorcery. He was treated with herbs and roots, secret chemicals and wasting prayers. The skin was literally eaten from one side of his body by ants. He was hung in a medicine lodge, dangled from the roof and smoked over a fire of holy balms for three days while Spirit Moon and the other holy men chanted a ceremony of entombment over him. When it was over, Cobb was neither dead nor alive, but somewhere in-between.

"What happened then?" Cabe wanted to know.

"He was nailed shut in a coffin. He was to be buried alive like that. For what was in him had to be slowly starved to death. It was the only way."

Spirit Moon learned that Cobb had a half-brother in Deliverance, so the casket was sent to him via Whisper Lake. But Spirit Moon had underestimated the strength of what was inside Cobb. It should not have woken until it was in the grave, but instead it woke up on the trip to Whisper Lake. And when Hiram Callister opened the box...

"Cobb returned to the land of the living," Graybrow explained. "Returned in probably a foul mood. A week later, maybe, he and his confederates rode on the Snake camp. They killed everyone, including Spirit Moon...Cobb was too strong to fight by then."

But Cobb's gang did more than kill the Indians.

They ritually slaughtered them. Women were raped and skinned, men drawn and quartered, children roasted over fires and eaten. Spirit Moon was encouraged to eat the flesh of his own young...when he refused, he was cooked himself. Cobb and the others ate him and absorbed all that he was.

"They became beasts, Tyler Cabe," Graybrow said, looking very concerned now. "They had tasted that which was taboo. It brought out the beasts within each man. And Cobb, now in possession of Spirit Moon's secrets or those the man's soul could not covet into the afterworld, was far worse than before. He was in possession of what the Snake call the 'Skin Medicine'."

Cabe's mouth was dry by this point. "What...what the hell is that?"

"A system of black magic, I suppose. Very ancient and forbidden. Instead of a formula written in a book or scratched on a rock, it is tattooed into the flesh. The Skin Medicine allows the beast that lives in all of us to come to the surface, to make itself known in blood and flesh..."

"And that's what's killing people? These Skin Mediciners, these beasts?"

Graybrow nodded.

Back home in Yell County there had been another name for men who changed into beasts. Werewolf. Cabe recalled a story he had heard as a youngster about a village of them that were supposed to live high in the Ozarks. Just a story...or was it?

There was a knock on the door and it swung open.

Jackson Dirker was standing there, looking gallant and handsome in his fur-trimmed overcoat and round buffalo hat. His eyes blazed like blue fire. "Charles," he said, "I need to have a word with Mr. Cabe."

The Indian nodded. "Sure, sure. There's things white men can't discuss before injuns. I was just here to see if I could be of service. You know, shining shoes or emptying chamber pots."

If he found himself amusing, it wasn't working on Dirker. He left the room and Dirker closed the door.

And Cabe was thinking: *He looks pissed-off. Looks like he wants to kick the shit outta me. Maybe he knows, maybe—*

Dirker sat next to him.

Close like that, he could see that Dirker wasn't really angry. Something was broiling in him, but it had nothing to do with the man he'd come to see.

"Cabe," he said, staring down at the floor now. "*Tyler.* May I call you that?"

"Of course."

Dirker patted him on the leg. "We've surely had our differences, haven't we? You've spent years hating me and I don't blame you, for I think I've spent years hating myself over that business at Pea Ridge. But it is over. The war is long gone and we are one people again. I like to think since you've come here, things have changed between us. If we are not friends, then surely we are allies now. Would that be a correct assumption?"

Cabe swallowed. "It would be."

"Once we fought on opposite sides and I honestly don't know any longer who was in the right...sometimes, sometimes I can't remember what it was I was fighting *for.*" Dirker smiled, then looked embarrassed. "The time has come when we must fight side-by-side. So I've come to you with an open heart to ask you, to beg you even, to ride with me on Deliverance..."

"You want me at your side?" Cabe said, overwhelmed by emotions he couldn't even begin to guess on.

"Yes. I would trust you at my side more than any man now living. I would like to deputize you, have you lead a posse with me on that hellish place. Am I out of order asking this of you?"

Cabe cleared his throat. "No, you are not." He felt something warm spreading in his chest. He stood and looked out the window at the streets below. He turned back to Dirker. "I would be honored to ride at your side."

And then they shook hands and everything for them, finally, ultimately came full circle.

23

Two hours later, the posse assembled outside of the Sheriff's Office.

The freezing rain had become snow now that drifted through the frigid air like ash blown from some huge funeral pyre. And that seemed pretty fitting given where the men were going and what they were going to do.

There were some fifteen men there when Cabe rode in on his strawberry roan. Most of them were miners that Cabe did not know. But Pete Slade and Henry Wilcox were there, the office left to another deputy. Sir Tom Ian, the English-born pistol fighter was there. As was Charles Graybrow and Raymond Proud, the big Indian carpenter. The one that really surprised Cabe was Elijah Clay astride a chestnut mare.

"Afternoon, Mr. Cabe," he said, quite cordially. "The sheriff here has let me join this huntin' party. He says I have to behave m'self. As far as ye killin' Virgil, well, I knowed he weren't nothin' but trash. So I don't hold no grudge no more."

Cabe relaxed a little at hearing that. He pulled his Stetson with the rattlesnake band off the saddle horn and place it on his head. "I'm ready, then," he said.

"Okay," Dirker said. "You know where we're going and what we're going to do. So let's get it done. And we don't come back until Cobb is put down."

"Yessum, Sheriff," Clay said. "I'll tell ye boys one thing and I'll tell ye just the once. If'n I get that peckerwood devil in m' sights, I'll shoot that trash just deader'n Jesus on the cross. Yes, sir."

And that, it seemed, was a good parting remark.

They rode.

***

It was at the fork in the road, at that old lightening-blasted dead oak, that they found more riders waiting for them. Mormons. Eustice Harmony was there. As were four surviving Danites—Crombley, Fitch, Sellers, and Archambeau. All of whom were anxious to destroy what lived in Deliverance once and for all.

So, then, twenty men rode on that town.

Twenty men who were willing to give their lives to stop the killing and what lived in Deliverance was more than happy to take them.

One by one.

***

By the time they passed through those high banks of withered, dead pines outside of Deliverance, the storm had filled its lungs with ice and had become a full-blown blizzard. Visibility was down to less than thirty feet. But no one suggested turning back. What had to be done would not be easy in any weather.

As they came around the bend, everyone brought up their guns.

They saw what they thought were two men waiting for them on either side of the road. But they were not men, but scarecrows impaled on sticks. As the posse got closer, they saw they were actually corpses and ones long dead by the look of them. Their clothes were shredded rags that flapped in the wind. Hollowed, skullish faces with empty eye sockets appraised the riders as they passed.

Although Cabe had seen countless dead men, he found he could not look upon those frostbitten faces. He was afraid they might smile at him, speak to him in voices of cold dirt.

Well, he found himself thinking, you volunteered for this fucking mess. Got nobody to blame but your ownself. If things get ugly—and they will—y'all just keep that in mind, Tyler Cabe.

"Ye can feel it, cain't ye?" Clay said.

And Cabe could only nod, wordlessly.

For he could feel it. Feel some ancient, unspeakable terror erupting in his belly, licking at his insides with a cold tongue. Something in him knew the smell of this place, the malefic feel of it, and not from yesterday but from days long gone. It could smell those that haunted Deliverance and it frantically warned him away, filling him with an immense, unreasonable fear that made him physically ill. It settled into every cell and fiber in a black, wasting totality.

And then, as they rode in guarded silence, the town began to appear. It swam up out of the blizzard like a decaying ghost ship out of ocean fog: the masts and prows, decks and rigging. Yes, the ruined buildings and sharp-peaked roofs, false-front stores and boarded high houses all described by churning tempests of snow that shrieked through the streets.

Deliverance was laid-open before them like a sprung sarcophagus, daring, just daring them to look upon the secrets its moldering depths concealed.

Cabe saw it, really *saw* it, and felt like a little boy lost in a graveyard full of whispering voices and ghastly screams. And he heard these things, too, but only in his head. For that was the sound of the town—a humming, dead neutrality composed of agony and tormented screeching reduced to a single low and morbid thrum.

It made his mouth go dry and his heart pound like a hammer at a forge. His skin was tight and cold, his internals pulling into themselves. Adrenalin rushed through him, making his hands tremble on the reigns and his eyes go wide and unblinking. For everywhere around them, shadows seemed to dip and scamper in the blowing wall of snow.

In the street then, in the very black heart of the town, they dismounted and tethered there horses to a hitch rail.

Harmony stood there in a flapping black coat, a shotgun in his arms and the Book of Mormon in his hip pocket. "What you will see here will look like people," he said to the posse, the wind turning his voice into a weird, wailing sound. "But they are not people. Not anymore. Not any more than a cadaver in a grave is a person. They may try to talk to you, to get you off alone. But don't let them, by God. Don't let them..."

Maybe not everyone in the posse knew what was in Deliverance. But maybe they'd heard stories, chimney-corner whispers, the sort of crazy tales kids tell late at night and around fires...things, of course, they'd dismissed at the time. But now? They did not dismiss them. They remembered them, locked those tales down deep within themselves where they would not be able to feel the teeth. And maybe that was why they did not question what Harmony said. They just accepted.

"It'll be dark in about three hours," Dirker said to them, his face pale and wind-pinched, but very determined, "and we want this wrapped up by then. So we're gonna break into groups and..."

But Cabe was not listening. Not really.

He was watching those shuttered windows and high, sloping roofs, the narrow spaces cut between buildings. The tenebrous shadows that oozed from them. He was watching and noticing how everything seemed to lean out over the men in the street, wishing to crush them or get them close enough to pull them into dark places where business could be handled in private, away from the light. And what he was feeling was the blood of the town—a toxic, miasmic venom seeping into himself.

"Let's do it," Dirker said.

And they started off.

**

As Dirker led Harmony and the Danites through that howling white death, the church bell began to gong. It echoed out through the storm with a hollow, booming sound.

"The bell," Harmony said, "Dear God..."

Dirker was telling himself that it meant nothing really. That maybe the wind had snagged it, but he knew better. Hands were pulling that rope and he could only imagine why.

The snow was flying thick and fine like powdered glass, dusting the buildings with a sound like blown sand. It whipped and swirled and drifted, lashing at the men in the streets, doing everything it could to drive them back, back. But they refused to be driven. They came on with shotguns in their fists and a ragged, squinting resolve in their eyes.

Suddenly, Fitch stopped dead, his rifle brought to bear. "What...what was that?" he said and the fear was thick in his voice like ice clogging a well-rope. "Over there."

Dirker looked quick, frigid wind blasting him in the face. He saw a suggestion of a form swallowed by the storm. Could have been something. Maybe.

"It had green eyes," Fitch said weakly. "Glowing green eyes..."

But Dirker would hear none of it.

They pushed on past sagging houses and a livery barn with a three-foot drift of snow pushed up against the door like a wave. Next to it was a larger, two-story log building. It had been some kind of community house or saloon at one time.

Dirker tried the door.

It was open.

He kicked it in all the way and the five of them came through with their guns held high and ready to spit rounds. But what they saw stopped them dead. It literally froze them in their tracks.

A couple kerosene lamps were blazing away. Seven or eight people were in there, pushed up to the dusty bar or sprawled in chairs at dirty, cobwebbed tables.

"Afternoon, gents," a fellow behind the bar said. He was a heavy, rotund man with a Quaker-style beard lacking mustache. There were glasses set up on the bar top before him. Using a rag, he was cleaning them out. "Pull up a chair."

Dirker and Harmony looked at each other while the Danites formed a defensive ring, just ready to draw on anything that so much as breathed. Behind them, wind rattled the door, fingers of snow snaking across the floor.

Besides the bartender, there were three men at the bar, a few others at the tables. There was nothing exceptional about any of them. A little boy with flat, empty eyes was in the corner tossing what looked like a ball into the air and catching it. Except it was no ball, but a skull. A human skull.

"Wanna play?" he said, giggling.

Dirker ignored him. "Where's Cobb?" he said. "James Lee Cobb."

The others just looked at each other and started to laugh, as if the sheriff was asking where Jesus was, on account he wanted to buy him a beer. When the laughter died away, Dirker saw a little girl come from the back room. She was no more than seven or eight...and completely naked. She hopped up on the bar in a very childlike, carefree manner. Sat there, her legs swinging. She looked upon Dirker and there was no innocence in those eyes, just a leering, hungry depravity. But what was truly strange was the elaborate tattooing of her belly and chest. Dirker couldn't be sure what he was looking at in the dim light, but it looked like...intertwined serpents and weird figures, configurations and distorted magical symbols.

As he looked on them, the illustrations seemed to move.

He looked away.

A man at one of the tables with a Confederate hat and an officer's coat patched with spreading blotches of mildew, said, "Where's your manners, barkeep? Offer these here fellas a drink..."

"Course," the bartender said.

His other hand came up from behind the bar...except it was elongated, the fingers spidery and narrow. Where the nails should have been there were long black claws curved like potato hooks. Smiling, the bartender used one of the claws to slit his wrist. Then, most casually, he began filling a glass with his blood.

"Blasphemy," Harmony finally said, breaking that bleak silence. "A cancer on the face of God..."

That got them laughing again.

About that time, the sound of gunfire rose up from somewhere in the town and Dirker knew the others had made contact, too. That the party was finally underway.

The man in the Confederate hat began to grin and a spidery tangle of shadows spread over his face. When he spoke his voice was low and grating. *"Now, you boys don't really think you're getting out of here alive, do you?"* he said, his teeth suddenly long and sharp.

And there was a weird electricity in the air, an odd sharp stink of something like ozone and fresh blood. There was subtle motion and a wet, sliding sound.

"Honey," the man said to the little girl, "these men like your pictures, show 'em how the lines meet…"

And as Dirker watched, those weird and diabolic tattoos began to move. Maybe it was the flesh beneath, but suddenly everything was in motion. There was a rending, popping sound as muscles stretched and ligaments relocated to accommodate new and feral anatomies. The girl's chest thrust out in a cage of bones, her limbs going long and rawboned. Thousands of fine gray hairs began to erupt from her skin until you could no longer see the skin. It looked, if anything, like millions of metal filings drawn to some central magnet. Her jaw pushed out into a snout, her nose flattened and her ears did likewise, pressing against that narrow skull of whipping locks and going high and sharp. Her eyes became green and slitted, her brow heavy, the skull beneath grotesquely exaggerated.

She was suddenly more wolf than girl.

Her lips pulled back in a snarl, her teeth sharp as icepicks.

Dirker heard himself mutter, "Shit."

All he could think of was a childhood story of how Circe the witch had changed Odysseus's men into beasts.

And around him…they were all changing.

Flesh became smoke that was blown by secret, cabalistic winds and rivers moved by mystical currents. The girl suddenly leaped into the air, five, six feet until it seemed she would brush the rafters overhead, and then she came right down on Sellers. And this before he could even jerk a trigger or think of doing so. He and the girl-thing went down in a thrashing, writhing heap.

Her mouth was wrapped around his face, those teeth sunk right to the bone. You could hear his screams echoing down the shaft of her throat.

But nobody had time to look at that.

For as the girl made her move, so did the others.

The man in the Confederate hat rose up in a flurry of teeth and claws and growling and was almost on Harmony when his shotgun went off, pitching the man backwards. Suddenly, everyone was shooting. Shooting at shapes and forms and monstrosities from some primal nightmare.

Dirker brought his Greener up and blasted the bartender. The impact blew his shoulder to a bloody mist and threw him against dusty glasses and discarded bottles. There was a crashing and shattering and he came right back up again, his face gone lupine and his teeth bared to bisect human flesh.

Dirker gave him another round that knocked him away and then that little boy was hopping in his direction. Dirker gave him the butt of the Greener in the face, driving him to the floor, broke it open and ejected shells, fed two more in, snapped it close. The bartender was up on the bar by then, his shirt split wide open from the pulsing, bestial muscularity beneath.

As he leapt, Dirker gave him both barrels.

The buckshot blew his snarling head into a spray of bone and blood. He flipped back over the bar and stayed down this time. As Dirker whirled around, the boy hit him hard and put him down, those jaws opening like the mouth of a tiger and coming in for the kill. The Greener still in his hands, he jammed the barrel lengthwise into that mouth, claws tearing great ruts through his coat and shirt and into his chest below. With a scream, he pushed the beast away from him, flipping it off him.

The man in the Confederate hat had Harmony.

His huge, clawed hands were pressed to either side of the Mormon's head...and he was lifted an easy two feet off the floor, rivers of blood running from his ears and eyes as his skull was crushed. Then the teeth darted forward and his face was literally stripped from the bone beneath.

Dirker saw the beast standing there, Harmony's face hanging from its jaws like a bloody scalp.

And then the boy came back at him, but Dirker was on his feet.

As the boy charged in, Dirker unleathered his .45 Peacemaker in one swift, easy motion. He fired once, punching a hole in the boy's sloping forehead and blowing skull out the back of his head. The boy shuddered momentarily on all fours, gore oozing down his face. Then he pitched straight over, trembling on the blood-slicked floor.

Two of the beasts were on Crombley.

Fitch dropped another by following Dirker's lead and shooting it in the head. Dirker put three bullets into the thing that was devouring Harmony. Then the door exploded in with a roaring wall of snow and long, furry arms powdered white took hold of both Fitch and Archambeau and dragged them screaming out into the storm.

Dirker killed one more, reloaded his Greener and ran out into the storm, the world of Deliverance a cacophony of ringing church bells, shooting, and howling.

***

The storm was reaching its peak out in the streets.

The snow rose up into a whipping, shrieking wall of white that cut visibility down even further now. Cabe and his crew of miners had to squint and lean into the wind to press forward. They could hear the screaming and gunfire, but with the gusting blizzard turning sound around and into itself, it was hard to say where any of it was coming from.

And the miners were panicking.

They saw shapes hobbling through the snow and were shooting randomly, even though Cabe shouted at them to stop, because they might be cutting down their own men.

They were ready to bolt and run.

But where to?

To either side they could see the vague, white-shrouded forms of buildings, but it was hard to say where they were in the town now. Paranoia and confusion had turned them back on their own tracks half a dozen times. And each time, their tracks had been erased by the storm.

"Goddammit," Cabe cried out at them, "stop this business, we've got to have some order here."

And that's when he noticed there were only three miners with him, the fourth missing.

"Where's Hychek? Where the fuck did Hychek go?"

"They got him! Something grabbed him...something with green eyes!" one of the miners shouted. "I'm getting out of here, I'm getting out right goddamn now..."

But before he could, a trio of riders came pounding up the street and the miners, thinking the cavalry had arrived, waltzed right out into the streets to meet them. But it was not a rescue party, but a gang of Hide-Hunters. They thundered through the storm, parting the snows like roiling mists. They wore dusters and flat-brimmed hats pulled low over wolfish, snarling faces.

One of the miners let out a strangled screaming sound as a lasso looped over his head and was pulled tight like a noose around his throat. He was yanked from his feet and pulled away into the storm by one of the Hide-Hunters. Another miner was similarly roped.

Cabe ducked under a lasso meant for him and, quickly levering his Evans .44-40, knocked a Hide-Hunter from leather with three well-placed shots. He hit the ground, his horse racing off.

And Cabe got a good look at him.

He had the rough shape of a man, but was hunched-over and moved with a jumping, hopping side-to-side gait. His eyes blazed like wet emeralds and teeth hung over his narrow black lips like those of a jungle crocodile. With a resounding roar, he came at Cabe, the three bullet holes in him seeming to make little difference.

Cabe couldn't believe what he was seeing.

That repulsive, shocking face and gnashing teeth, the loops of drool hanging from the crooked slash of a mouth, the furry hands with the ten-inch fingers and claws just as sharp as scalpels.

He put another round in the beast, mainly just to keep it off him.

But it didn't even slow it down.

It slammed into him, pitching the both of them into a snowdrift. Its claws were at his throat, those fingers encircling his neck. The beast stank of tainted meat and diseased blood, saliva hung from its jaws in vile ropes.

Before it fed on him, it did something that truly sucked the wind from Cabe's lungs: it spoke.

"*Gonna die now, friend,*" it said in a slavering, raw voice that was more akin to the growl of a rabid hound than the speech of a man. "*Gonna die like an animal like in the old, forgotten days...*"

But Cabe had other ideas.

As the beast reared up, letting out a wailing, howling noise that made Cabe's ears explode with rushing noise, Cabe pulled his bowie knife from its sheath at his hip. And when the beast came down to fill its belly, it came right down on the blade of the knife. Nearly a foot of razored steel slid right into its throat and out the other side.

With a mewling, whining sound, it pulled away, the knife erupting out the side of its throat. Its head hung at a sickening angle, most of its neck slit clean through. It spilled blood to the fresh snow, tried to run and fell, tried to rise up and stumbled, its life's blood running out in a torrent.

Cabe saw his chance and jumped on its back, knocking it face-first into the snow.

Before the beast could so much as whimper, Cabe drew its head back by handfgul of that filthy, greasy hair and sank the knife deeper in its throat, sawing and slitting. The creature came alive, twisting and fighting and it was its own misguided strength more than anything else that finally severed its head.

Cabe tossed it into the wind.

The body still tried to crawl, but didn't make it very far.

The head stared up at him with those stark, green eyes and the jaws still worked.

But it was done and Cabe knew it.

Drenched with the reeking blood of the Hide-Hunter, Cabe stumbled out into the storm to find survivors.

***

The only survivor from Cabe's group was Lester Brand.

He was a shift boss at the Silver Horn Mine.

And he was also a dead man.

When the Hide-Hunters attacked, he ran. He fought and blundered through the streets, ducking down when he heard a sound or sensed motion. He slipped into a doorway when two more Hide-Hunters rode by, sporting heads speared on poles. He saw the heads...they were the heads of miners, men he'd worked and drank with.

Brand was trembling badly now, wheezing, pained sounds coming from his throat. Though it was bitterly cold and his face just as stiff as leather, he was sweating profusely. Trails of perspiration ran down his spine. He had lost his shotgun and the Colt Army pistols in his gloved hands felt oily like they might jump from his fists at any moment.

He was moving down a street, but he had no true idea where he was.

The town was not that big. Though he had never been to Deliverance before, he remembered Dirker saying it was cut by a central road and that four or five other roads intersected it. So if he just kept walking, he was bound to make his way out sooner or later.

But he thought: *Oh Jesus, oh Christ, what, what if I'm the last one left alive?*

But he knew that couldn't be, for now and again he could hear gunfire. So he had to keep his head. He moved forward slowly, the snow wild and flying all around him. It sculpted weird shapes and shadows. The buildings rose up like headstones, leaning out at him. He kept seeing forms moving past him, but he didn't dare shoot. Not just yet. For there was death everywhere now, screaming white death and what it hid in that whipping white cloak was far, far worse.

He moved past a row of warehouses, then a barn, a boarded-up dry goods store. Then directly ahead he could hear a low, guttural growling sound. And then many. As if a pack of wild dogs were bearing down on him.

Quickly, he darted down an alley that twisted and turned, spilling him into a little courtyard pressed between the hulks of buildings. There was no way out. He would have to break into one of them and take his chances.

Right then, he froze up.

The wind was making a shrill, howling sound and he wasn't entirely sure that it actually was the wind. He looked up quickly...thought, thought for a moment he saw something up on a roof. Something that faded away into the belly of the storm. He wasn't sure he had even seen it.

There was a rapping noise off to his left.

A door was swinging open and closed in the wind. It thudded hollowly against the weathered gray wall of a feed mill. Pulling up what strength he had left by that point, Brand moved over there, the door banging and banging.

He went to the door.

It had slammed close again. His throat full of cinders, Brand hooked the barrel of one Colt Army around the latch and threw it open. And saw...saw a figure come drifting out of the darkness like a wraith. A woman. A woman in a white soiled dress. Her hair was long and fire-red, blowing around like meadow grasses in a high, angry wind.

"You," Brand managed as she neared the doorway, "you...you gotta help me get out of here...I'm lost...I'm..."

But he saw that she was grinning like something from a dark wood that snatched away wayward children, something that gnawed on bones and sucked blood. Her eyes were huge and wet and lustrous like wet jade. They found him and held him, that mouth set with long needle-like teeth.

Brand screamed and then those long fingers speared him and that slobbering, savage mouth thrust forward. And it ended for him there in the snow, in a red-stained heap. And as he died, he could hear the sound of her chewing on him.

***

In the lobby of the hotel, Graybrow paused.

He listened.

He knew from years spent stalking that he was not alone, but where the others were, he could not say.

Though he had sung his death song before coming on the raid, Graybrow did not want to die. He would never see seventy again, but there was a vitality about him, a spunk, a gleam in his eye that age could not hope to wither.

He did not want to die...yet, he was willing.

It was an honor among the Utes to die in battle. And it would be honor for Graybrow as well. And if he had to die, at least he would die knowing grand secrets, horrible secrets and malign truths, but his soul would be stronger for it. Nourished.

Graybrow had been with Henry Wilcox and Sir Tom Ian, but had abandoned them long ago. He preferred to hunt on his own. And be hunted if that was the case. Because, honestly, he did trust whites with guns. They had a nasty habit of shooting at anything that moved and if he was going to die, it would not be with his guts shot out by some crazy white.

The hotel, he knew, had been called the Shawkesville Arms once upon a time when Deliverance went by its original name and was a lead-mining town.

Since those days, it had been abandoned to the weather, to nature, to whatever chose to call it home. And if what Harmony had said was true, Cobb and his henchmen had called it home for a time.

Slowly then, Graybrow moved towards the old stairway that was covered in filth and curled brown leaves that had drifted in from the innumerable holes in the walls and roof. The handrail was wreathed in cobwebs. The stair carpet was mildewed and black. Though it was dim, it was not dark. Scant illumination—and snow—drifted in.

Outside, the storm was howling like a blood-maddened beast, throwing itself at the ramshackle buildings and making them creak and groan and sway on their rotting foundations.

There was a high, unpleasant stink that had little to do with woodrot or animal droppings. It was a sharp, violent smell that got inside Graybrow's head and made him think of slaughterhouses and mass graves, insane asylums and death wards...places filled with death, with pain and horror and madness.

He started up the steps, feeling now how fully alone he was.

But you are not a white, he kept telling himself. *You are not a white who feels safe in crowds or needs the presence of many. You are an Indian, a Ute, and solitary, lonely places do not frighten you.*

And that was great in theory, but it wasn't working so good in practice today.

For the stink was getting worse and there seemed to be something crackling in the air like some negative charge of potential energy, some static electricity that was building and building. The farther he went up the stairs, the more he felt it. It was all around him, heavy and dark and threatening. He could feel it from the top of his head right down to his balls and it was a foul, reaching hostility like hands poised to strangle him.

Upstairs.

More leaves, more dirt. But you could see now that there had been traffic up here. The hardwood floor of the corridor was thick with collected dust, but a trail had been beaten through it.

Graybrow thought: Okay, old man, okay, just do it.

So he did.

He began going from room to room and finding little more than additional cobwebs and some old crates and moldered furnishings. The covering of dust was disturbed in some of them as if maybe Cobb's men had tossed their bedrolls onto the floor to sleep.

In the corridor, the garish wallpaper was spotted with fungus. It was faded and disintegrating and peppered with wormholes. In the gloom, Graybrow was beginning to see evidence of claw-marks ripped into the paneling and old, browned blood smears.

That smell was still thick around him, but there was another smell, too. A repellent fetor of putrescent meat and spilled blood. The stink was vaporous and gagging, enough to make him—

Suddenly, without a sound, a shape stepped from a darkened doorway. So very quick and so very silent that Graybrow could barely even register surprise before the Whitney

12-gauge was yanked from his hands and tossed down the hallway.

Feeble light choked with dust motes and a powdery rain of snow illuminated the shape. Graybrow saw it, felt his heart give a jolt of pain. He knew what he was looking at was James Lee Cobb. He knew that, but it took him some time to acclimate himself to the horror.

As it was, he felt faint.

Cobb was tall and cadaverously-thin, a mummy from a sideshow. A sombrero with a short, curled brim was pushed back on his head. The crown was scarved in the skins of desert snakes and set with feathers and the talons of raptors and the teeth of wolves. He wore a poncho of pale hide that was stitched together in a crazy quilt from human pelts. Around his corded throat there were a half-dozen necklaces of human fingers, ears, and teeth. At his waist were a brace of ivory-handled pistols and hatchets. There was a sash from shoulder to gunbelt and it was sewn together from...*faces*. Faces tanned to death masks with the scalps intact.

And it was all dreadful enough...but Cobb's own face, it was the very worse thing.

The right side was pale and the skin was tight and seamed, barely covering the skull beneath. A single unblinking green eye with a huge, dilated pupil like a translucent moon stared out at Graybrow. But the left side of his face...just gone. Red tendons and pink muscle were stretched obscenely across an exaggerated skull like starving dogs had eaten the good stuff away. There was no eye there, just a black scarified cavity.

Graybrow managed to start breathing again before he passed dead out. "Suppose...suppose I'm in for it now, eh?" he said.

Cobb nodded that fright mask. Lips pulled back from sharp, yellow teeth. "I reckon ye are, friend," he said in a hissing voice. "I reckon ye are."

"Don't suppose I could—"

"Doubt it," Cobb said. "But since ye came this far, there's something I'd like ye to see."

But Graybrow just shook his head. "Don't think I want to."

And when Cobb made to grab him, he brought out his hunting knife and buried it right into the devil's belly. Not that it did him shit-good. Cobb took hold of him with a strength that was amazing. Those clawed hands—the left one was skeletal and skinless—took him by the shoulders and smashed him against the wall until Graybrow went loose as a rag.

The fight had been pounded out of him.

The knife still hanging from his belly, Cobb took hold of Graybrow's long, white hair and dragged him up the corridor by it. Graybrow swam in and out of consciousness. He could hear the clomp, clomp, clomp of Cobb's Spanish boots and then he was dumped unceremoniously before a door at the end of the hall. A door covered with old, bloody handprints.

Cobb fished out a key and unlocked it.

Graybrow found himself looking into an abattoir. He heard the clink of chains and smelled spoiled meat and festering carcasses.

Cobb kicked him in there. "I'd like you to meet my mother," he said and slammed the door shut behind him.

***

Deputy Pete Slade, Elijah Clay, and a trio of miners were going from house to house, killing anything that moved. They heard the shooting and the dying, but Slade held fast that they had a job to do and the others would have to watch out for themselves.

They learned quick enough that the only way you could put the Hide-Hunters down was by blowing their heads apart. After no less than four run-ins with the beasts now, they didn't aim anywhere else.

But now they were trapped in the streets and things were getting ugly.

The beasts were up on the roofs, watching them and diving down at them when they thought they stood a chance. Green, shining eyes watched from the dark depths of barns and from behind shuttered windows.

"We gotta link up with them others," Clay said, not frightened really, but surely not at ease. "Ye think, Slade? They's just too many of them and too few of us."

Slade knew it was true.

But there was no time for that, not now. For the double-doors of a stable flew open behind them and the townspeople began to flood out en masse. They were a slat-boned, pasty group with sunless faces and gleaming green eyes. But what was probably the most disturbing thing was that they were not dressed in clothing, but hides. Human hides. Hides that included flapping limbs and skinned faces, blowing locks of hair.

It was an appalling thing to see.

To watch them vaulting forward like a vicious pack of wolves, green-eyed and merciless, those spiked jaws snapping and great gouts of drool hanging from those lips. Dressed-out in human skins to boot.

"Kill 'em!" Slade shouted. "Kill 'em all!"

They came on in a flurry of sprouting claw and tooth, making yelping and barking sounds like hunting dogs and Slade and his boys began to unload on them with everything they had.

They dropped half a dozen, scattered a dozen more, but the others went right over the top of them, howling and snapping. Two of the miners went down. A third was just gone. Slade sank beneath a throng of four or five biting, chomping children.

Clay knocked them away from him with the butt of his shotgun, gunned down two others, felt claws open up his face and tear into his back, and fought free through his sheer size and bulk. And as he did so, he watched in amazement as the townsfolk rent the bodies of the posse, children stealing away with limbs in their mouths and going straight up the sides of buildings like spiders.

He got out while the getting was good.

***

One of the miners from Slade's group ran when the attack came. He saw the sheer numbers and knew a fight was out of the question. His name was Rafe Gerard and he was not a coward. The fact that he had come with Dirker to clean this mess up said that he was anything but.

But he had been through both the Mexican War and the War Between the States, and he was surely a man who knew how to stay alive.

And alive he planned on staying.

He kicked through the door of a little house and slid the bolt in place after he was in. A powdering of snow like spilled flour dusted the floor. There was some blood mixed in with it. A set of tracks led right to the hearth and disappeared, as if one of them had escaped up the chimney.

Something Rafe Gerard decided was entirely possible.

He sat with his back against the wall, tried to think this out. Clay was right: They had to link up with the others. So it was pretty much a matter of finding them or waiting for them to find him.

So Gerard sat there, watching the hearth and the front door, the partially-boarded window, the doorway leading into another room. He rolled himself a cigarette and smoked it calmly. Waiting.

That's when he heard the crying.

A pathetic, pitiful whimpering is what he was thinking. The sort of sound that was designed to yank at the heartstrings of anyone with warm blood in their veins. It worked its melancholy magic on Gerard. For once he'd had a boy, a tawny-haired wonderful little boy who'd perished of influenza one long hard winter. And although he knew that Deliverance was filled with monsters, he could not help but be moved by that sound.

He stepped through the kitchen and into a plain little bedroom at the rear of the house. A bureau. A frame bed. A wash basin. There were droplets of blood spattered up one wall. Above was an attic hatch, more blood smeared on it.

From up there, came the sobbing.

Gerard stood there, not wanting to look, but the human being in him demanding it. He dragged the bed over, stood up on it. The sad little voice was calling for its mother, its mother.

Something cold unfolding in his chest, Gerard slid the hatch aside.

What light spilled in showed him a little boy that was dark with blood. And before Gerard could pull the trigger, memories of his own lost son washing through him, the boy was on him, his teeth in his throat.

And Gerard died as he had lived: violently.

***

Beaten, bruised, and blood-soaked, Sir Tom Ian and Henry Wilcox were all that was left of their little group. The others had been slaughtered by the beasts. And Graybrow had just vanished. As it was, Deputy Wilcox had been badly gashed in the belly and ribs and had lost a lot of blood.

But he would not give in.

Not while there was strength left in him.

Ian and he were investigating a freight office, having followed a blood trail through the snow before it was covered over. Inside, it was pretty much empty. All the furnishings and office utilities long gone. But there was blood on the floor. The bloody prints of children and something wet they had dragged along with them.

There was a door at the back of the office.

It was closed.

"You up to this, mate?" Ian said.

"As up as I'm ever gonna be," Wilcox admitted, his large frame seeming to sag now as the blood continued to soak through the makeshift bandages wrapped around his torso.

Ian took hold of the tarnished knob, turned it.

Heard commotion, wet tearing sounds.

He threw the door open and saw a cluster of children kneeling on the floor. Their eyes were green, but their bodies naked and hairless. They grinned up at the two men and their teeth were like icicles jutting from those blackened gums. They were clustered around the body of a Danite...maybe Fitch...though it was really hard to tell, such was the degree of mutilation.

The children were all nude and tattooed-up, their faces smeared with blood.

"Dear Christ," Wilcox said and kept saying it.

The children rose from their kill quite slowly, advancing on the men. Wilcox began to sob...kids, just goddamn kids. He couldn't bring himself to pull the trigger.

But Sir Tom Ian had no such compunction.

He pulled his .44 Bisley and it had barely cleared leather before the first round jacked into a little girl and another erased the face of a little boy. Making a wild, moaning sound, Wilcox finally followed suit.

For they were not children.

They were more beast than human, those eyes filled with a flat, relentless appetite. They would stalk their kill and take it down without remorse.

And that's how he was able to kill the children with Ian.

The guns saved their lives, but they also made a hell of a racket in the enclosed room. Like thunder echoing and echoing until each man's hearing was dulled, numbed.

And that was why they didn't hear the others coming through the doorway at them.

Didn't know it until they felt claws and teeth and smelled rancid, hot breath at their necks.

***

Cabe said, "After you, Sheriff."

Dirker nodded and pushed through the door of the old hotel. Cabe followed in behind him, a Greener shotgun in his arms. His Evans was slung across his back. The stink hit them right away. Thick, hot, nauseating. It had no place in an abandoned hotel on a freezing day where the wind was driving snow into drifts and licking everything down with ice. Yet, the smell was there...like some breathing, consuming, living thing. A malignant sentience. Both men stood, breathless, waiting for whatever inspired that stink to come slinking down the stairs at them.

But there was nothing but silence.

"If what Harmony said is correct," Dirker began, carefully re-loading both his .45 Colt Peacemakers, "then Cobb and his crew were living upstairs here."

"Jesus, that stink," Cabe said.

"Let's go," Dirker said.

There was a pair of oil lamps hanging from a hook near the stairwell. Both were nearly full. Cabe took one, lit it up. A dirty yellow light sprang from it, revealing the ravages of nature—the animal bones and bird's bests tucked into holes in the walls, the leaves and sticks and pine needles.

They went up the stairway side by side and paused at the top.

Paused, noticing that the atmosphere now was positively mephitic and pestilent like that of a malarial jungle death camp. The air was heavy, moist, and viscous with that putrid, flyblown stench of wormy meat. And hot, dear God, hot and wet and oppressive. It trembled thickly like gelatin, laying on their faces in a rank, slimy humidity.

They moved up the corridor towards that door at the end. The door with the furrows cut into it and the abnormal bloody handprints. Or something like handprints.

"Lookit the floor," Cabe said.

Dirker did.

Just outside the door, for maybe four feet down the floor...a weird, creeping fungal mass of decay. As they stepped on it, it squished like wet leaves, some reeking black juice oozing from it.

Dirker prodded something with the tip of his boot. "A shotgun," he said. "Recognize it?"

Cabe nodded slowly, wearily. "A Whitney. That's Charlie Graybrow's."

Outside the door then, Dirker tried the filthy knob and it was locked.

Cabe stood there next to him, a wild and phobic terror threading through him. Whatever was in there...whatever gave off that noxious, eldritch stink...Jesus, it just could not be good, could not be.

Dirker handed his shotgun to Cabe and picked up the Whitney. He placed the barrel against the lock and pulled the trigger. The knob and its housing were blown into the room, leaving a smoking black hole.

Dirker kicked the door open.

And they stepped into hell itself.

As they passed through the doorway, Cabe's lantern casting bobbing, phantasmal shadows, a black wave of fetid heat actually pushed them back a step or two. And the smell...a nauseous effluvium that was more than just organic decay and dissolution, but a noisome, contaminated stench that made their knees weak and sent their stomachs bubbling into their throats. It reminded Cabe instantly of a field hospital he'd been in during the war. A reconverted barn in Tennessee that stank of putrid battle dressings, amputated limbs, and gangrenous flesh. This was like that, a huge and polluted stink of pain, disease, and vomit.

Steeling themselves, they stepped in farther.

There was no furniture. The flowery cream wallpaper was spattered and stained with whorls and dripping patches of old blood. Even the ceiling was splashed with it...like some insane butcher had been casting buckets of the stuff around. The floor was wet and seething with more of that crawling gray fungus, but here it was matted and webby and seeping with black ichor and bloody mucilage. A gelatinous stew of rot and bones and gnawed limbs, several inches deep. There were bodies and parts of them everywhere, all covered with flies and beetles and creeping worms. A few soiled, peeled and jawless skulls stared up at them.

"Dear Christ in Heaven," Dirker managed and his voice would barely come.

Because they saw what brooded here, what Cobb had brought back from Missouri.

It might have been a woman once, but now it was a chained ghoul with wet, leprous flesh, flesh that was pitted with gaping holes and hung from the bones beneath like a windblown shroud. That flesh seemed to move and wriggle with pulsing currents, but that was just the action of parasites and vermin nesting within. The skullish head was capped by long, greasy hair latticed with cobwebs and the deathmask face was shriveled and withered, jellied green eyes bleeding tears of slime.

It made a low, bleating sound, holding out hands that were more skeleton that flesh, the skin hanging from them in strips and loops. The fingers were sticks ending in long, curled nails that seemed to coil and convolute in the air. It began to slither in their direction, sending ripples through that pestilential sea of organic profusion. The skin had long ago melted away from the pulsating face, the nose just a hollow and those mottled gums on full display, gums set with gnarled, discolored teeth.

It came forward with a slinking, creeping motion, mewling now like a drowning kitten, a pustulant, writhing worm.

Cabe and Dirker started shooting.

Shells were flying and the air was suddenly filled with smoke and the bitter smell of gunpowder. They fired and fired, reloaded and fired again. And did not stop until that squirming human jellyfish was blown into fragments.

Then they left the room.

They shut the door.

Down the corridor, both trembling, Cabe tossed the lantern against the wall and it shattered, flames licking up over the walls.

Outside, both men fell in the snow, gasping and gagging.

***

It was ten minutes later when they stood before the church.

The bell had stopped ringing now.

They stood near the high wrought-iron gate that surrounded the church, came right up to the steps. The uprights were rusted and tall and lethally sharp. They rose up like spears.

"Well," Dirker said, " I guess no one else if left, Tyler. Just you and me."

Cabe said, "Let's show these fucks what a pissed-off Yankee and a Johnny Reb lunatic are capable of."

Dirker laughed. Couldn't help himself. It just came rolling out of him and soon enough tears were rolling down his face and Cabe was laughing, too, and how damn good it felt to laugh.

"I didn't even know you *could* laugh," Cabe said.

Dirker's laughing became a coughing and a rasping. He wiped his mouth with the back of his hand. "Sure I can," he managed, "it's just that I'm usually alone and laughing at myself."

That got them going again and they reeled like drunken men, slapping each other on the backs until it finally died out and was replaced by a somber silence. The silence of the wind and snow and eternity.

"Sounds like I missed the party," a voice said. "Next time, ye all invite me, hear?"

Elijah Clay came waltzing out of the storm, a pistol in each hand. "And here I thought I was the last one."

"I never thought I'd be glad to see you, you goddamn hillbilly," Cabe said.

Clay grinned. "Now mind yer manners, boy. I'm a-hear to save yer bacon."

"The others?" Dirker asked.

But Clay just shook his head.

Together then, they went up the steps. The double-doors were locked, but Clay hit them with his massive shoulder and they flew wide open. Then the three of them charged right in, moving low, with shotguns in their hands.

Pews.

They saw the rows of pews, many of which had been busted into kindling. The altar was occupied by an immense scalp rack. There had to be fifty or sixty scalps on display. Scattered around them in carefully arranged piles, skulls and bones. On the cross there was no Jesus, but a mummified body nailed up instead. Dirker recognized it as Caleb Callister...at least he thought so.

But there was no time to find out, for James Lee Cobb and four of his Hide-Hunters stepped out from behind the altar. They carried rifles and wore gray dusters and were caught somewhere between animals and men.

"Looks like a stand-off," Cobb said, laughing then, his laughter boomed and cackled and echoed.

Cabe got a good look at him, at the architect of this nightmare. The skin on the left side of his face was simply missing; muscle and bone exposed. It was as if some surgeon had slit a line of demarcation down the center of his face with a scalpel, leaving the right side relatively unscathed and peeling the left right to the basal anatomy. He was like some anatomical demonstration that was allowed to walk.

Clay said, "Uglier'n a trail-dead squirrel in a fat fryer."

And then the lead started flying.

Cabe and the others dropped their shotguns and pulled their repeating rifles—Cabe's Evans, Dirker's Winchester, and Clay's Henry. Bullets zipped around them like angry wasps, biting into pews and sending wood splinters spraying everywhere.

The trio returned fire.

But the Hide-Hunters were possessed of a deranged, primeval rage. They came running off the altar right into a flurry of bullets. The two leading the charge danced momentarily like marionettes as slugs ripped into them, punching holes through them and scattering blood and meat in every which direction. But Cobb was still shooting and one of his slugs caught Clay in the shoulder and another ripped a gash along the side of his head, taking his earlobe with it.

He went down, bleeding and moaning, but sitting back up and shooting a Hide-Hunter at point-blank range right in the face. The bullet cored his nose and the skull behind it came apart as the round bounced through his head like a drill bit, shredding everything in its path. Another Hide-Hunter, one with no less than a dozen holes in him, almost broached their position but Cabe put one through his throat that spun him around and finished him with a slug in his temple.

Dirker rose up and dropped the third Hide-Hunter in a mist of blood and brains and then clutched his chest, and fell over.

And then the final Hide-Hunter leaped.

Cabe put a round in him, but it didn't even slow him down. He crashed into the bounty hunter and they went rolling in a heap. He was incredibly strong and Cabe fought and cursed and thrashed, trying to keep those teeth away from his throat.

And then Dirker, the entire front of his overcoat wet with blood, was on the beast's back. Another slug ripped through him from Cobb, but he would not relent. His face drawn in a mask of agony, he yanked the creature's head back as it made a lunge for Cabe's throat. Yanked it back and pressed the muzzle of a .45 Peacemaker to its skull. He jerked the trigger of the double-action pistol and blew the beast's head to ribbons.

The beast fell over dead.

And Dirker with it, his hands clutching his chest, dark blood bubbling forth between his fingers.

Clay fired off two more shots at Cobb who took advantage of the confusion and ran along the far wall, firing his pistols and disappearing through a low doorway not twenty feet from the men.

But Cabe was only concerned with Dirker.

He cradled his head in his lap. "Oh, Christ, Jackson, Jesus Christ, look at you..." He felt tears coming down his face and he realized that Dirker had saved his life, but at the price of his own. "Why'd you go and do that, why'd you do that?"

Dirker reached out and found his hand. "Tyler," he said, blood running from the corners of his lips. He coughed and choked and tried to swallow something back down. "Tyler, I'm...I'm done in, just done in—"

"No, you ain't, I ain't lettin' you get away like that—"

"I am," he insisted. "Back in town...you...you take care of my wife, take care...of Janice. Swear to me you will..."

Cabe was sobbing now, overcome with just too many damn emotions. "I will, I swear I will. But Jackson, you can't go and die on me, not now, not now, we're friends, we're goddamn friends finally..."

Dirker found a smile and put it on, but it faded soon enough. He stared up into space, breathing real hard. "Pea Ridge...I can see it, Tyler, it's right before me...the woods...the hills...oh, Tyler, you remember how cold it was...so very cold and snow...in Arkansas yet...in Arkansas yet...you boys, you boys, pull back now, dear God pull back the rebs the rebs is overrunning us...no, no, no...I'm dreaming, Tyler..."

Cabe was holding his hand tight. "I'm gonna get you on a horse and get you back to town. That's what I'm gonna do..."

He felt a hand on his shoulder. It was Clay's.

"He's gone, boy," Clay said softly. "He's gone."

His face wet with tears, Cabe lowered Dirker to the floor. He stroked his cheek and sniffed, tried to get a hold of himself. He saw his shotgun and picked it up. "Where," he said, "where did that fucking prick Cobb go?"

Clay, trying to patch his wounds, said, "Through that door yonder...give 'em hell, boy..."

Cabe, just pumped hard with iron and hate, went through the door like an artillery shell. If Cobb had been waiting there, he would've slit him right in half like a sword through cheese.

But he wasn't there.

Cabe was in a very narrow passage that went straight up to the belfry. A set of cramped, spiral stairs climbed up its throat like a spiral worm. There was blood on them. And blood smeared on the railing.

Cabe thought: *He was hit then, that cocksucker was hit...*

Sucking in a sharp breath, Cabe went up those steps as quiet as quiet could be, the shotgun in his hands. He crept and inched like a stalking cat. At the very top there was a hatchway.

Steeling himself then, Cabe crouched and threw himself up through it.

He rolled across the plank floor.

Eddies of wind-driven snow lashed at the bell. The bell-room was about ten feet square, open on all four sides with a waist high ledge. The floor was drifted with snow, old leaves...and drops of blood.

James Lee Cobb, his face sculpted into that of a human wolf stepped around the bell. The left side of his face was more skull than flesh and that skull was of some ravenous beast.

"I ate all the souls in Deliverance," he said, "and now I'm gonna eat yours..."

A hatchet flipped end over end past Cabe's face and went flying out into the white, whipping streets below.

Cabe let the demon have first one barrel of his Greener right in the belly and then Cobb jumped at him, jumped with an amazing speed and balance for a gut-shot man. In mid-air, Cabe gave him the other barrel which threw him back against the bell. The bell began to swing and gong with a resounding, thundering peal. Cobb left a bloody smear on it and pulled himself up by the ledge, his back to the blizzard.

His torso was blasted clean open in a burning, smoking valley. Flames were licking at his poncho from contact burns and the stink was of cremated flesh and burning hair.

But what froze Cabe up was that Cobb had no internal organs. His body cavity was filled with a chittering and crawling life. Locusts. Thousands upon thousands of locusts. And then Cobb began to laugh with a high, weird cackling that rose up and joined the gonging bell in a hammering wall of noise.

Cabe let out a cry as the locusts fled from Cobb's torso and filled the air in a buzzing, busy swarm, descending on him like he were a field to be stripped. They heaped over him, biting and scratching and droning and Cabe was half out of his mind, clawing madly at the green, piping carpet of insects. They chewed and nipped, got under his clothes, tried to press into his ears and mouth, nostrils.

They would strip him to bone.

Cabe, knowing it was now or never, threw himself at Cobb with everything he had. He struck the grinning, cackling bastard, struck him real hard. So hard Cobb lost his balance. He fell back over the ledge of the belfry with a manic, pained barking sound. His arms bicycled in the freezing, snowy air...and then he fell, spinning end over end into the blizzard.

He let out an enraged, piercing shriek.

The insects curled-up brown like dead leaves and fell from Cabe. He leaned against the ledge, looking down as the snow let up for a moment and he could see Cobb below.

He was impaled on the fence.

Three blood-slicked uprights were jutting from his chest a good fifteen inches if not more and he was stuck sure as a bug on a pin. He contorted and fought, his arms whipping and his mouth howling. But that just forced him farther down on the uprights.

Iron, Cabe found himself thinking, *iron*.

The uprights were iron and he had read that the Devil feared iron for it signified earth. That's why people hung iron horseshoes over their doorways. Iron was a basic element of earth and an enemy of demons and the discarnate.

Cabe felt the entire church shaking beneath him as Cobb screamed in what seemed a dozen different voices...men, women, children.

Cabe half-climbed, half-fell down the stairs. He dragged himself through the door and Clay was still there, still waiting. Together they made it out of the church.

Cobb was no longer moving.

He had withered into something like a brown, emaciated scarecrow that was flaking into motes.

The church began to tremble and shudder, swaying this way and that as if it were trying to pull itself up from its foundation. There was a sudden groaning, crashing noise and it fell into itself in a heap of lumber. The bell came down last with a final etching gong.

Cabe and Clay were out in the streets making for their horses by then.

Cobb's good eye flickered open, the socket filled with maggots. His blackened, blistered face peeled open in a roaring shriek. The evil blew out of him in a yellow, searching mist, erupting from dozens of holes and slits, kicking up tornados of snow and smelling of bone pits, brackish swamps, and human excrement. There was a flash as if of lightening, a rumbling, a moaning, and the ground shook and the sky went suddenly black as something like a million buzzing flies rocketed upwards...and that was it.

Cobb was done.

Cabe and Clay found their horses, cut the others free.

Then they rode out of Deliverance, neither of them speaking for a time. When they were well away and night was coming on dark and fierce, they stopped.

"Place'll have to burned to the ground," Clay said, "come spring. Then the ground'll need to be salted."

"Suspect so," Cabe said.

They rode on.

EPILOGUE

Cabe didn't wake until the next morning.

He woke in Dr. West's surgery. Woke on a couch that was at once comfortable and comfortless. His back was sore and he was stiff and seemed to hurt just about everywhere.

Elijah Clay was sitting in a chair near a cabinet of chemicals. His head was bandaged and his arm was in some sort of sling. He stroked his long gray beard, smiled with all those bad teeth. "Looks like ye'll live," he said. "I suspected as much."

"It...it really happened?" Cabe found himself saying.

"It did. Now, we'd best forget it." He stood and pulled on his smelly old buffalo coat very carefully. "Ye done good, boy. I was proud to be at yer side. Now I gotta go. I got kin in them hills, don't like leavin' 'em alone. Ye'll see me come spring, then we'll burn that hell-town flat."

He left and Dr. West came in, giving him a cursory examination, but asking no questions. From the look on his face, Cabe could tell he already knew. Clay must've told him about it all. And that was fine.

He left and Janice Dirker came in.

She sat by Cabe and held his hand. She was dressed in a black velvet dress, very somber and understated. A dress of mourning. Her lovely brown eyes were puffy from crying.

"I'm glad you lived," was all she could say.

Cabe squeezed her hand, not able to take his eyes off her. He wondered if he could love her and figured he already did. Knew that though he had joined Dirker out of duty and new found friendship, there had been something else that had driven him. And Janice Dirker was that something.

But looking on her, he was seized by a sudden melancholia.

He thought of the people he had met in Whisper Lake, the friends he had made. Jackson Dirker. There was a warmth and a sadness acquainted with his memory now. They had come full circle since the war. Cabe was no longer bitter and angry, always looking for a fight. He felt calm now, easy, accepting. He didn't think he'd be able to hunt men anymore. And Charles Graybrow? Oh, that crazy smart-mouthed Indian. Damn, he was going to miss him.

Janice said, "My husband...was his death...unpleasant?"

"He died in some pain," Cabe admitted. "But it did not last. I was with him...with him at the end."

Janice nodded. "He spoke highly of you. He said...he said you had known each other in the war. He would not tell me anymore. Can you?"

"Yes," Cabe said. "I think so. I think I can do just that. I'm gonna tell you all about Jackson Dirker, ma'am, the finest and bravest man it has ever been my pleasure to know..."

--THE END--

www.severedpress.com

ABOUT THE AUTHOR

Tim Curran lives in Michigan and is the author of the novels Hive and Dead Sea. Upcoming projects include a novella, The Corpse King, from Cemetery Dance and a novel The Devil Next Door from Severed Press. His short stories have appeared in such magazines as City Slab, Flesh and Blood, Book of Dark Wisdom and Inhuman, as well as anthologies such as Horror Beyond, Flesh Feast Shivers IV, Hard Boiled Cthulhu and Dead Bait. Find him on the web at:
www.corpseking.com

LaVergne, TN USA
14 October 2009
160821LV00004B/33/P